The D river

Book I

Decision

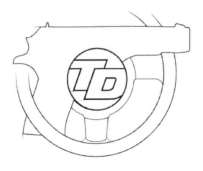

By RL Turner

19, April 2022

To my wonderful family!

Whatever I do, I do it for you

"Racing is life. Anything before or after is just waiting."

Steve McQueen

Chapter 1

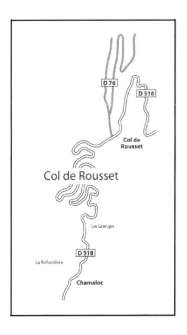

The dark metallic-gray Maserati Quattroporte sliced north along the French A-7 Autoroute toward Lyon. The *Driver* stayed in the passing lane, flashing his high beams. Peugeots and Renaults moved out of his way as if pushed by a shockwave.

Something was bothering him. Most Engagements were trouble-free drives, taking *cargo* from one place to another. A *Driver* seldom knew what his cargo was—it could be things or people or things and people. This *Driver's* cargo, a small box, was secure inside the specially built safe in the Maserati's trunk, surrounded by sheets of soft foam rubber to keep it from sliding around. Rene Dufour had been doing this for a long time and something about this Engagement made him uncomfortable. Usually when he sensed an Engagement was going to be dangerous, possibly life threatening, he knew what was causing that feeling; a sixth sense honed over years of experience. Today he felt nothing specific, only a persistent uneasiness. Glancing in the rearview mirror, once again he reviewed the events that began when he had picked the cargo up in Marseilles, hoping to identify what it was that was bothering him.

He recalled driving into a rundown abandoned warehouse near the wharf, his headlights peering through the shadows and dust, illuminating three men standing next to a silver BMW M5. Rene had pulled to a stop and got out. He remembered scrutinizing each of them. They had French underworld written all over them. Two wore silvery gray tight-fitting suits, buttoned up, the outline of pistols visible in their waistbands. The third, in a very expensive black suit and wraparound sunglasses, his dark hair tipped spiky blond, stepped forward to meet Rene. Tattoo's blossomed up along his neck and up behind his jaw—flames with the tips changing from bright red to yellow just finishing underneath his ears. *Classy!*

Identities verified, Tattoo Man flashed a pearly white smile visible even in the gloom of the warehouse and brought the small case from the trunk of the BMW and gave it to Rene who took it and headed toward the rear of his car. Before he could open the trunk, the trio had turned, got into their car, and disappeared with a shriek of spinning tires and clouds of billowing smoke. Rene cocked his head to listen. The BMW continued accelerating until the roar of the engine faded into the distance. *Strange,* he remembered thinking, *usually they watch me leave.* Not much to go on, but his unease remained. Rene returned his focus to completing the Engagement.

The consummate professional, Rene Dufour never failed to deliver once contracted for an Engagement. His plan was to contact his clients when he reached Lyon and give them an update on his progress and a new ETA for Reims, his final destination. He toggled the switch on the console to his right, activating the rear camera, one of several modifications specially built into the Maserati. He studied the cars following further behind him, looking for any indication that he may have a tail. *So far, so good.* He switched to the front camera. Nothing.

He drove for a few minutes getting his bearings from the GPS in his dash, spotted an Agip nearby on the way to Morieres-les-Avignon and at the last second veered off the road into the service area, just east of Avignon. He pulled up in front of the main building, which housed a restaurant and shop. He sat for a moment to see if anyone followed him into the rest area. Not seeing a suspicious vehicle, he turned the car around and backed it into the parking place. Exiting the car, he pulled his ever-present iPhone from his suit jacket pocket. He used it to lock the car and set the extra security systems before heading inside for a visit to the restroom before grabbing an espresso.

Rene stepped inside the restaurant and paused, looking back. The tinted glass gave him excellent cover to observe the cars passing. For the briefest moment, he stared at his reflection in the glass. Almost 1.7m tall, broad chest, and about 77kg, his brush cut black hair, graying here and there. He could not see his intense blue eyes, covered now, as they frequently were, by sunglasses. His thick lips and thin nose combined with a slight olive complexion let him pass for Italian, Spanish and—with some additional facial hair—Middle Eastern. Vain about his clothes, he wore designer suits, especially Canali and Zegna, but unlike the tattooed man back at the warehouse, Rene preferred loose-fitting jackets that gave him freedom of movement and concealed his shoulder-holster. His easy, self-confidant movements—second nature after a career in law enforcement—announced to anyone paying attention, 'Do not mess with me.'

No cars had followed him into the parking lot. *Good. Makes things simple*, he thought. He went to the restroom to wash up and stopped by the counter. He ordered and paid for a double espresso. When the order arrived, he added several sugars, ritually stirred the espresso until the sugar had completely dissolved, then quickly gulped the hot, sweet liquid down. He looked at the Maserati. It had only been out of his eyesight for a few moments, but he had to check it, he always did. He pulled out his iPhone and ran the security program. The response was quick: no explosives, no bugs, no tampering.

Rene punched another button, remotely starting the car and unlocking the driver's door; it gapped open slightly allowing him to enter the car without having to fumble with the door handle. He walked quickly outside and was in the car, putting it in gear and heading out in less than eight seconds.

Exiting the Agip, moving along the access road onto the A-7, he noticed a staid black Mercedes E55 AMG saloon up ahead idling in the emergency lane. Dark tinted windows, smoke rising softly from the tail pipes, a coincidence this car happened to be sitting precisely at that spot? Not likely. Instantly on full alert, thinking, planning, he quickly pulled into the emergency lane himself, careful to stay about fifty meters back from the Mercedes. Using another modification to the car, Rene used the thumb wheel on the steering wheel accessing the front camera, he zoomed in and snapped a photo of the Mercedes' license plate. Looking up, he noticed what seemed to be an identical Mercedes coming up behind, now slowing to pull in behind him. They had him pinched in between; no doubt they had assumed they could easily take him down. So it was time to change the rules to their game. He slammed the shift lever into reverse and charged the oncoming Mercedes. The startled driver stood on his brakes and started backing rapidly too, only to swerve back into traffic. A blasting air horn from a lorry coming way too fast to stop and unable to move left because of a second lorry running alongside, caused the now totally flummoxed Mercedes driver to lurch forward entirely into the emergency lane again just in time for the lorry to roar past.

Rene was on the throttle, rocketing ahead on the tail of the lorries, zooming past the first Mercedes that had been lying in wait. The rearward Mercedes recovered quickly and came along behind. The left-most lorry had now moved into the right lane and Rene floored it. Rushing forward as the Quattroporte's modified 680 bhp came on tap, Rene quickly accessed the rear camera to zoom in and shoot a photo of the license of the second Mercedes. He touched a button on the dash display and it brought up a list of people he could send the photos to. He scrolled down the list until he saw the name Jean Paul Degas, an old and useful friend who still worked for the *Direction Centrale du Renseignement Intérieur*. He touched another button and transmitted the message as an SMS text with an attached image.

Hopefully Jean Paul is awake at his desk and gets this, Rene thought.

His attention returned to the A7 Autoroute. Now approaching 250 kph, he was no longer flashing his high beams, instead using the other cars as obstacles to keep the two Mercedes several car lengths behind him. Rene knew that if the French Highway Police became involved, there would be unwelcome complications. Better to take secondary roads, where he could use the terrain and curves to his advantage. But which road to use?

Traffic picked up as they sped north from Avignon towards Chateauneuf-du-Pape and Orange. Weaving among the lorries, he did not see the third Mercedes until it was alongside. The back window of the Mercedes rolled down and an automatic assault rifle emerged and started firing. Rene heard dull thunks as bullets hit the embedded Kevlar sheets behind the Quattroporte's doors and body panels and sharper splats as the bullets bounced off the custom-tinted bullet-proof Polymer windows. He smiled, the cost of these mods just went to zero where his life and the safety of the cargo were at stake. He slammed on the brakes and downshifted, now swerving into the right emergency lane until a frantic lorry driver, air horn screaming, almost kissed Rene's rear bumper. The Mercedes driver pulled into the right lane as soon as the lorry passed, just as Rene hit the gas and swung back to the left. Now Rene was on the Mercedes' tail.

The Mercedes slowed, its driver obviously unprepared for this reversal of roles, as two large lorries, horns blasting, rumbled alongside in the passing lane. Rene stomped the accelerator again, matching their speed and, swerving into the space between the two, barely big enough to hold his car, slid past the now thoroughly disoriented Mercedes before swinging back to his right and blasting off down the road. Obligingly, before the Mercedes could react, the second lorry pulled into the right lane in front of it, which now found both lanes momentarily blocked as the Maserati accelerated away.

"*Merde*, I need you to wake up!" Rene shouted to the non-responsive Jean Paul.

As if on command, his iPhone rang. He touched a button on the steering wheel to engage the Bluetooth connection and answered.

"*Allo*," he said aloud.

"Bonjour René, c'est Jean Paul. Ca va bien?"

"It is about time, *mon ami*. Did I wake you?"

"*Mais non*! I have been hard at work since I came back from my two-hour lunch," Jean Paul laughed.

"It is nice to hear you are having a lazy afternoon. Me, I am a bit busy right now with three Mercedes saloons trying to take me out. Did you get those license shots I sent you?"

"Yes, yes. Are you all right? *Merde*!"

"OK for now, but what about those license plates?"

"I ran the numbers. They're registered to a holding company out of Frankfort. I can't trace them further."

"I suspected as much—hold on!"

One of the Mercedes was overtaking rapidly, possibly intending to ram him. Using the Quattroporte's superior power and torque, Rene hit the throttle and began pulling away.

"Rene, do you want me to call the highway police?"

"No! I will take care of these guys by myself. Hold on one

minute …"

Rene had spotted something up ahead, a low guardrail that extended out 25 meters in front of an outcropping of trees. If he could manage to push the front or better yet the side of one of the Mercedes into and over the guardrail, the car would not be able to stop until the trees stopped it.

He glanced at the rear camera's view, showing the Mercedes closing again, presumably thinking he had his prey at a disadvantage because the Quattroporte had come up behind yet another big rumbling lorry. The Mercedes was going to ram him. Slowing to get space between himself and the lorry, Rene accelerated at the last second to minimize the impact. As the Mercedes hit the Maserati, Rene lurched forward against his belts. He swerved the car a little more than necessary to the left, closing the gap with the truck ahead.

"*Allo*! *Allo*! Rene are you still there?"

Rene was silent, concentrating on the task at hand. The Mercedes now shot the gap and went to Rene's right, in the emergency lane. The assault rifle re-emerged. When they were only 50m from the guardrail Rene sawed on the wheel, steering the Maserati to the right, tapping the Mercedes behind the front wheel well. The impact was just enough. The black saloon rode the rail up and over, starting to flip as its driver lost control. The car's speed plus angle of attack had it over the guardrail sliding first on its side and then on its roof as it continued to flip. It closed the gap to the trees and slammed into them at over 130 kph. There was a satisfying crunch as metal and flesh compressed in milliseconds against the trees. The car burst into flames.

The two big lorries started braking and sliding all over the road as other cars slammed on their brakes reacting to the wreck. Rene fishtailed in between the two trucks and continued accelerating up the Autoroute. He knew he was not safe yet. He scanned the road ahead and behind, trying to eyeball the other two cars.

"*Allo*! *Allo*! Rene are you OK?" shouted Jean Paul again.

"You can expect that there will be a call to the police now. There was just a bit of an incident south of Montelimar."

"Are there still three cars?"

"No, just two now." Rene's eyes continued scanning, knowing that the people chasing him would not give up so easily.

"So Jean Paul, I am thinking—why is it that the bad guys always pick the Black Mercedes Saloon. I mean why? Do they go to bad guy school and this bad guy instructor says to them, 'Always make sure to take the Mercedes. It is what bad guys drive.' And you know what? It is always an AMG. They should show some originality. Why not a BMW or maybe a Jaguar? That would be a nice challenge for a change."

"So my friend, do you need my help?"

"I have it from here. I am going to take them on a little trip up to the hills, a very scenic trip."

"Please be careful".

"Of course. *A bien tout.*" Rene disconnected.

He spotted the two remaining Mercedes just behind, trying to catch up. He stayed in the right lane, allowing the lead car to pull up beside him. Both front and back windows slid down. The rear passenger took a shot at him.

They never learn, do they?

He thumbed a different toggle for the built-in side camera and caught a perfect photo of both driver and passengers, just as the front passenger opened up with a large-caliber pistol. *Fortunately*, he thought, *not large enough,* as the bullets slapped the windows, bouncing away.

Rene hit the throttle as the other Mercedes smashed into the rear of the Maserati again, then swerved into the emergency lane and sprinted down the shoulder toward the onrushing exit ramp, the two other cars in hot pursuit.

The D104 was a secondary route running past the small town of Die, past which was a series of mountainous stretches that would take him north and finally back west. The many narrow switchbacks through the mountain passes, would give him opportunities to set each car up and take them out, one at a time. As he got close to Die, the phone rang again. He thumbed the Bluetooth connection.

"*Allo.*"

"Bob, you are late for your check in."

Drivers like Rene had a handle or *nom du guerre* that they used. It would not do to have a client—or anyone else for that matter—know a *Driver's* real name. Years ago Rene had chosen *Bob*. It suited him. Short and to the point.

"It seems I have some company," replied Rene.

"Oh, what kind of company?"

"The black Mercedes saloon kind—three of them. Well actually two now.

"They always pick the black Mercedes," commented his client flatly.

"Hold a minute," said Rene. He thumbed back to the photos he had taken, selecting the best one.

"I'm sending you a photo. Let me know when you get it".

He kept his foot on the accelerator, continuing to cruise along at more than 190 kph, the two Mercedes right behind him. Not knowing the road made overtaking him almost impossible, especially for these *cochons*.

"Got it," said the client.

"Do you recognize anybody?

"Yes, the driver. He's a competitor, goes by the name Benoit." A long pause.

"Bob. Bring him to me alive and I will substantially increase the fee, plus damages of course."

"Deal. And there is a lot of damage. I will call you when I get to Reims." Rene disconnected.

Just before Die, there was an incredible mountain road, its tight sinuous curves challenged even the best drivers. The faster a car went, the higher the degree of difficulty—and danger. He knew the curves like the back of his ex-wife–the narrow passes, the tight bridges, and the vicious switch-backs–the places to take out a tail.

Rene turned up the D518, heading north, the two re-maining Mercedes close behind, neither car able to pull abreast. Instead, they reverted to the old B movie stand-by, shooters leaning out of the window and firing shots towards the Maserati. The bullets harmlessly bounced off the rear deck and window.

Rene's plan was to eliminate one car as soon as possible, but toy with the other car containing Benoit until the time was right. The cars twisted and turned, heading up the switchbacks towards the Col du Rousset. First one car, then the other tried to get alongside the Maserati only to run out of road before another turn, where the chaser was forced to drop back and regroup.

Just before Col du St. Alexis, both cars tried to take him out once again. There was one long stretch, perhaps a kilo-meter in length, that was fairly straight and both tried to pull alongside the Maserati, one on either side. Bullets flew. But Rene shifted down two gears to out accelerate them be-fore the road narrowed again.

They're getting desperate. Maybe they're running low on gas, or out of bullets, he thought.

Taking the D76 towards Vassieux, Rene decided, now or never. A few kilometers ahead running up from Vassieux there was a 180° turn that dove back down a sharp incline to the Col du la Chau. He could hit top speed up to the hairpin curve, slamming on the brakes as he turned so as to pivot on his front wheels, then speed down the incline ahead to spring his trap. As luck would have it, the car with Benoit had dropped back letting the second black Mercedes take over. Even better.

There was an outcropping of rocks just past the Col. Rene knew he could get there ahead of his pursuers and out of sight for a few brief seconds. They would panic—look up the road ahead and not at the rocks.

The Maserati arrived at the point, locking up the brakes activating the ABS. The car came stuttering to a stop, Rene reversed the car between the rocks, shifting to first and holding the brakes and the throttle down.

As the second Mercedes rounded the curve, Rene side-stepped the brakes, hit the throttle and slammed into the car just at the very edge of the rear bumper. It swerved violently and skidded off the road and into the waiting ravine, tumbling until it smashed onto the rocks at the bottom. There was no explosion, only the grind of metal against rock as the black Mercedes disintegrated.

Benoit's Mercedes smashed into the Maserati's rear

quarter panel, but Rene was prepared for this. As his car pirouetted across the roadway, he fought to correct it with opposite lock and return it in the right direction. Benoit's Mercedes fishtailed back and forth before finally correcting and heading up the road, but now the Maserati was behind it. The two passengers leaned out and fired their pistols back at the Maserati, but the bullets bounced harmlessly off.

They were clearly desperate now. The Mercedes swung wildly back and forth from one lane to the other. Taking advantage of his superior horsepower, Rene rocketed around the Mercedes just past the Col des Limousines.

As they approached the next switchback, he slowed just enough to let the Mercedes alongside. He counted on the men's desperation to make them sloppy enough to try to knock his car off the road. As they swerved over to the right and accelerated, he hit the brakes hard. The Mercedes shot ahead and into the switchback, crashed through the low rock wall and hit several large boulders causing it to skid sideways and flip over on its roof before it stopped, spinning like a top.

Finally, Rene thought. He stopped and reversed his battered and beaten car to the hole in the rock wall.

He approached the smoking Mercedes warily. First, he looked in the front passenger compartment. Dead. Apparently the passenger hadn't buckled his seatbelt after leaning out to shoot at the Maserati. The rear passenger was alive but unconscious. Rene left him and went around to the other side. The driver's door swung open as Benoit slowly tried to crawl out of the wreck. The airbags had saved his life.

"You, you bastard! You should be dead by now."

"Not quite my friend," said Rene, drawing his pistol.

Struggling to stand up, Benoit pulled out his own gun and tried to shoot, but Rene using his own pistol calmly took aim and shot him in his right thigh. The force of the bullet dropped the man to the ground.

Benoit grunted as he dropped backward into a sitting position, still trying to aim his gun. Rene walked up and calmly kicked the gun from the man's unsteady right hand then kicked him on his right temple. Benoit fell over, unconscious.

"You are worth a lot to me now—so let's get you nice and comfortable –you shit."

Rene dragged Benoit back to the Maserati, dropped him by the rear passenger door and went to the trunk and removed a very sophisticated first aid kit, a towel and restraints. After treating the wound, he shot the still unconscious man in the neck with a mild sleeping compound out of a one-time syringe, then dragged him into the back seat. He put the towel under the wounded leg (having no intention of staining his beautiful cabernet-colored leather seats), then he used several looped zip-tie restraints on the man's hands and leg. He threaded them into hidden steel loops integrated into the rear seats, essentially keeping the unconscious man tethered.

Stepping back slowly, he took one glance at the damaged Maserati and slowly shook his head—*catastrophe*. Seeing car lights approaching in the distance, he jumped into his car and headed west, rejoining the A7 north of Valance for the final sprint to Lyon and then to Reims, the ultimate destination. Conscious that the formerly new Maserati was now a conspicuous mess, Rene was happy that night had fallen. He drove carefully, just under the speed limit, trying not to attract attention. A short while later, he arrived on the outskirts of Reims. He punched a number on his iPhone and dialed his client.

"It's Bob. Where do we meet?"

"We were getting worried, you're so late." A pause then, "I'll text you the address, third floor of the parking complex, we'll be waiting."

"And the funds?"

"And my competitor?"

"Sleeping nicely in the back."

Rene heard the smile in the client's voice when he said, "We'll be anxiously waiting!"

Twenty minutes later, he piloted the wounded Maserati up into the parking complex, stopping on the third floor. Two cars waited with their lights on: a BMW 7-Series and an Audi S6. Pulling up and switching off the motor, Rene opened the driver's door and slowly got out. As he emerged, the client got out of the Audi's back seat. He walked to Rene, extending his hand.

Rene looked him over; young, but already possessing a vibe of power and confidence. Even in the night, the client wore expensive Prada sunglasses. Sporting several earrings, he wore a white silk shirt opened to reveal several thick gold chains; the cuffs of the shirt were rolled back perfectly exposing a gold and diamond Rolex and several gold and black bracelets. He looked raffish, like a successful rap star or the underworld figure he undoubtedly was. Most important, he was rich enough to pay the fee for such an Engagement. Rene shook hands.

"Please note, Bob, we do not drive the black Mercedes saloons," sweeping his hands back to take in both of his cars.

"I can tell you have taste."

"The cargo?"

Rene walked to the rear of the Maserati. He forced open the damaged trunk and reached inside. Using his personal code and the Fujitsu Palm Reader (which measured, mapped and authenticated the blood running though the palm veins of his hand), he opened the safe, removed the cargo and handed it to one of the client's associates. The client smiled.

Rene then opened the rear passenger side door. He dragged the competitor, Benoit out and onto the ground.

As the client and his associates gathered closer, Rene reached into his pocket and removed some smelling salts which he broke under Benoit's nose. With a gag and cough, the man awoke and tried to focus his eyes.

"Shit" was all he said before the client's closed fist slammed him back into unconsciousness. Two associates carried the once again unconscious man to the waiting BMW. His feet dragging on the ground with a soft scrape, a softer moan coming from his bloodied mouth as they shoved him in the back seat.

Wiping his hand on an expensive silk handkerchief, the client calmly remarked "Bob, as usual you have surpassed all our expectations. This is a very nice way to conclude our Engagement."

"Thank you, I always do my best."

"Here is the payment, plus a little extra" then a laugh, "you'll need it if that's what is left of your car."

Rene weighed the package in his hand before he put the thick envelope into his suit pocket. He smiled and put his hand out for his client, concluding the Engagement.

"It feels like a nice amount." noted Bob.

"You should count it in a quiet place," said the client as he turned to leave.

"Agreed. Until next time," said Rene.

Turning back, the client smirked, "Until next time. Oh,

and Bob? Try not to trash your car quite so much. I hear it really diminishes the resale value."

Rene sighed as his gaze took in the pitiful hulk of his car. He distantly heard the other vehicles pull away. He placed his hand along the car's flank, touching it as he moved from front to back, feeling all the bullet holes and dings and dents. He felt as an old lover who once again feels the body of his first true love, betrayed by age. The Maserati did not deserve this, to age so ungracefully. Turning one last time, his gaze lingered on the disappearing taillights of the two retreating cars.

Rene stood next to what was left of his Maserati Quattroporte. He was exhausted. He thought back to Marseilles and the unease he initially felt. Yes, uneasiness and bullets did not mix, that finely attuned sixth sense had let him down on this engagement. He sighed again.

"Maybe I am getting too old for this game," he said to himself.

Chapter 2

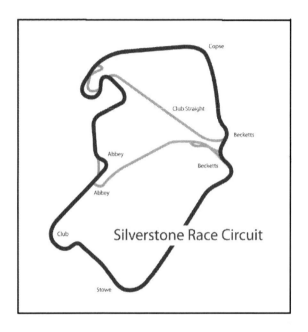

The Red Mist. The fog of battle. Every professional racer experiences it, a penetrating veil of competition blocking out everything else, narrowing the racer's focus down to one thing: beating the car in front or behind. Racers push the throttle too hard and too long before the next fast-approaching corner. First one to lift off the throttle — blinks.

Silverstone Circuit is the most famous racetrack in Great Britain. Its fast corners, like Copse and Becketts, put fear and reverence in a racer's heart. The former WWII airbase has seen it all: classic cars to Formula 1, all the famous racers from Moss to Schumacher to Hamilton.

On this sunny May race weekend, however, Silverstone Circuit was hosting the first race weekend of the GT3 Euro Championship. Serious sports car makes like Aston Martin, BMW, Chevrolet, Ferrari and Porsche take to the hallowed ground.

The rolling start, just past the Start/Finish line, launched twenty-five GT3 race cars all aiming for the same patch of asphalt. At the first corner, they bunched up, some going wide, some pinching the corner, but all the racers easily managed Woodcote's fast and wide turn. Heading towards the second series of corners, a fast series of right–left , right–left turns, mayhem suddenly developed when a two-car collision splattered the track with bits of metal, aluminum and razor-sharp shards of the carbon fiber that most modern race car components are made of.

Yellow flags alerted the twenty-three remaining racers of a full-course caution; track crews came out to clean up the tire-shredding carbon fiber bits and the rest of the debris. The pace car appeared. The drivers reduced speed behind it, continuing in a single line weaving back and forth to keep their tires hot. After five laps, the track stewards, satisfied that the course was sufficiently clean, alerted the pace car to come in, allowing the track to go green. As the twenty-three

GT3 racers turned the last corner, they all accelerated. Seeing the green flag drop, they collectively hit the throttle again aiming for the same patch of asphalt.

After many minutes of furious racing activity, only seventeen of the original twenty-five cars that started the race remained with less than ten laps to go. Four of the fastest cars had broken off from the main pack. This closely bunched group, separated by only 3.8 seconds, kept up a breakneck pace. The Red Mist, alive and well.

First - Martin Fincher, driving the #43 Team RBR Aston

Martin DBRS9.

Second - Luca Marchesotti, driving the #00 Team

Parabolic Ferrari 458 Scuderia.

Third - Marc Lange, driving the #13 Team Technik

Porsche GT3 RS Cup.

Fourth - Luis DeSilva, driving the #22 Team Fortunata

Porsche GT3 RS Cup.

Racing out of Woodcote on their twenty-fifth lap, the four cars were almost nose to tail. Martin Fincher in the Aston Martin took the first corner, Copse, flat out in sixth gear. Slowing for the next series of corners, he shifted down one gear to transition from Maggots to Becketts. A quick stab of the brakes, a fast shift down to fourth, he took the sharp right kink heading into Chapel, before shifting up two gears and rocketing down Hanger Straight.

Just behind, Luca Marchesotti gave his throttle a bit of heel and toe to keep the revs up, then down shifted to third gear for Stowe corner. The long right-hand curve set his Ferrari 458 up to blast down the short straight heading to Vale. Then a sharp, almost ninety-degree left-hand turn transitioned to another even sharper turn taken in second gear, coming out of Club.

Blasting down the International Pits Straight leading to the mid speed right hand Abbey, then the sweeping Farm curve and before the twin 180° switchbacks – Village Corner and The Loop, third place Marc Lange in the yellow, black and white Porsche GT3 RS, kept his focus on the track ahead and on his main rival, Luca Marchesotti, driving the red and green Ferrari just ahead. With seven laps to go, Marc was on Luca's bumper, filling Luca's mirrors turn after turn. Each time Marc tried to feint a pass on one side or another, Luca blocked him. After two more laps, however, Marc had a plan to set up Luca for a pass after the Maggots/Becketts turn complex. He'd have a greater speed advantage down Hanger Straight and be able to take the Ferrari by outbraking his rival.

Marc pulled the Porsche alongside the Ferrari as they swept through Woodcote, racing towards Copse. Marc, on the inside line of the racetrack, needed to get ahead before the turn or he would have to back off as Luca had the better line. Marc kept his foot on the throttle, but so did Luca. 300 m, 200 m, 100 m and still neither driver braked. Finally, Marc slammed on the brakes to take the corner. Marc was slightly ahead of Luca on the track and as he entered the corner, Luca turned the Ferrari, hitting the front left corner of Marc's GT3 along the edge of the front wing, knocking small pieces off the aero package. The GT3 swerved slightly as both cars tracked out. Cursing to himself, Marc fought to straighten GT3; in milliseconds he was back on the Ferrari's bumper. At the next corner, Marc tried his same maneuver and again Luca turned into him, crossing the corner just in front of Marc.

Dirty Bastard. Just like that son of a bitch to pull that shit! Marc thought.

Marc Lange did not just dislike Luca's driving style, he hated the guy, and the feeling was mutual. Luca enjoyed knocking other drivers out of the race, making him the most detested racer in GT3. But the hatred Marc and Luca had for each other went way deeper—down to the granular level.

With only four laps left, Marc knew Luca would pull the same stunt again, so this time Marc feinted right then pitched the car back to the left, down the front straight. Now Marc had Luca right where he wanted him: on the inside going into the first turn at Copse. As they started braking, Marc turned the GT3. He saw the Ferrari pinch the corner, having to take an early apex before it quickly ran out of road unless Luca corrected. Luca tried to nose the Ferrari ahead going into Maggots/Beckett, but it was Marc's turn now and he won the corner, taking it before Luca.

The GT3 accelerated towards Chapel. Marc saw the corner workers waving yellow flags along Hanger Straight indicating trouble up ahead. He lifted his foot off the throttle then saw the debris of a recent collision on the track. Two slower back-marker racers had collided, spinning them off track, littering the course with sharp-edged carbon fiber bits. Marc tried to weave around the debris as best he could, but he heard the tell-tale sound of something rattling around the wheels and through the fender wells. He hoped Luca caught some of the sharp fibers too.

Crap—not now! thought Marc as he thumbed the radio button on his steering wheel.

"Bala! I just ran over some carbon fiber. May have picked up a puncture!"

His crew chief, Bala Masurkar, replied with his thick British accent, "I'll check the telemetry. Watch the handling and keep up the pace, Mark, we're going for second place!"

But not for long, thought Marc. He automatically checked the GT3's back-end stability as he went through Bridge and Priory. The trick now was to determine how bad the puncture was. If a slow leak, he'd nurse the car for the remaining laps and still salvage some points. A fast leak meant heading to his pit to change tires, and no chance to finish in the points for this race.

Slow leak—slow leak, thought Marc as his radio crackled.

"Marc, right rear is losing air pressure. Seems pretty slow at the moment so try to push for three more laps."

Marc took stock of his situation. He lost his second-place spot as Luca's Ferrari quickly swept past him under hard braking going into Abbey.

"Shit! He avoided the debris!" Marc shouted to himself inside his racing helmet.

Next, Marc's best friend, Luis DeSilva in another Porsche, rushed past him as both cars exited Luffield. A quick hand salute from Luis as he entered Woodcote; with just a touch of opposite lock, he disappeared down the front straight. This dropped Marc to fourth. He knew with three laps left, he was in for a fight to hang onto position and points.

Keenly aware that his tire was going flat, Marc pressed harder. His radio crackled in his helmet again.

"Marc, pressure dropped from 35 psi to 26. You're losing air quickly!"

"Got it Bala, thanks. Let me know when it drops below 15—although I'll probably know before you," replied Marc. He was in for a tough fight just to keep his GT3 in the race.

Marc's mirrors suddenly filled with two more cars: the #55 Nissan GT-R of Yoshi Nakamura and close behind Horst Schnellenbach in the #78 Audi R8 LMS.

Two more laps—come on. Give me two more laps! prayed Marc as he pressed down Hanger Straight, dropping down to third gear for Stowe. As he turned in, setting his car up for the apex, he felt the car fractionally slide and had to use more opposite lock to correct. He glanced in the mirrors to see Yoshi and Horst close behind. He knew both drivers watched him and each other. Pressing harder, Marc executed each turn to complete one more lap.

Now into the last lap, Marc accelerated down the straight heading for Copse, his car sliding more. He thumbed the radio button and barked into his mic.

"Bala—pressure?"

Bala, with forced calm, replied, "12 psi and still dropping. Come on Marc, try to keep it up!"

Bala turned off his mic, and moved toward the pit crew, fingers crossed on both hands.

"We need this result boys. Marc's gotta bring the car home." They all grunted or nodded in reply. Bala turned back to the telemetry monitor.

Just after Club, the Nissan GT-R shot past Marc as he overcompensated for his deflating tire. His race car swung wide putting a tire over the curbing, kicking up grass and dirt on the track. Marc controlled the skid and barely managed to stay in front of Horst before the Abbey and Priory turn complex. But R8 was back on Marc's bumper as they went through Brooklands' and Luffield's twin 180° turns.

Horst finally rocketed past the Porsche as they rounded the big right-hand curve in front of the start/finish line near Woodcote.

Marc's wounded Porsche wove back and forth on its own as the tire went completely flat. Heading out of Woodcote, another car went past, dropping Marc to seventh place. He slowed just after crossing the start/finish line, the tire carcass falling apart on the wheel rim.

"Way to go Marc. Brilliant drive!" shouted Bala

Marc pressed his lips together. He had taken Luca's second place. If he had been able to keep that place at race end, it would have been a podium finish. But racing rubber cannot compete with razor sharp carbon fiber bits and if this race had lasted only a couple more turns, his GT3 would have coasted across the line—or worse, stopped on the track with no points for Team Technik. Still, this was the second race of the weekend, the team managed to score points in both, coming in fourth in the earlier one.

At the end of a race, it is the custom for the corner and safety workers to come out on the track and salute and wave to the racers. Without these people, who communicate track conditions to drivers and are the first to arrive if there is an incident, there would be no race weekend. Marc took the Porsche down to second gear. He waved to everyone lining the track while trying to control a car running on only three tires.

While driving the cool-down lap, Marc thought about

the race. Once again, he was in position to score a first, second, or third podium finish, and better yet he had almost
beaten that bastard Luca, but Lady Luck was not smiling
lately.

Flipping open his visor, a fresh blast of hot air hit his face,
stinging his eyes. Yes, Lady Luck was starting to take a dim
view of Team Technik's fortunes. It seemed something was
blocking his way and the team's success. After the first race
of the season, he knew he needed to find a way to push
through. Marc refocused and piloted the car around the remaining turns of Silverstone Circuit, waving and flashing
his lights in salute. Entering the pits, he coasted to a stop in
the team pit box and killed the motor. He took a deep
breath and opened the door as Bala, co-driver Michael
Llewellyn, Director of Operations Stella Beru and the rest
of Team Technik rushed to greet him. Getting out of the
GT3, Marc removed first his gloves, then helmet and balaclava, and tossing them to one of the pit crew, he slapped
Bala on the back. The team was all smiles. Seventh place
paid prize money and sponsors liked it when their car finished in the points.

While Marc's skill in bringing his team into the money
and making a sponsor happy gave Team Technik its edge,
it was Marc himself who pulled everything together. With
innate skill and cheerful self-confidence, he was a born team
leader. Sponsors loved his athletic good looks. It helped to
sell the team package which helped pay most of the bills.
But like all teams with small budgets, Team Technik relied

on the old standby, the "gentleman co-driver" to fund many of its essentials. Michael Llewellyn was their deep-pockets guy. And, as co-driver who drove the first part of many races, he frequently helped set up a good position for Marc to complete the race in the money.

After a round of backslaps, hugs and plenty of fist pumping from the team, Marc turned around and watched the three top finishers mount the steps of the award podium:

First – Martin Fincher

Second – Luis DeSilva

Third – Luca Marchesotti

Waving to the team, Marc walked toward the award podium smiling.

Great, that means Luis passed Luca. Marc's smile got broader. Both he and Luis hated that egotistical Italian bastard. Marc laughed and wondered who Luca would fire for this.

Suddenly a camera and microphone were in his face. He heard the slight breathy, Cockney-tinted voice of the British Racing TV (BRTV) interviewer Elaine Bollard.

"I'm here with Marc Lange, the American Pro driver for the #13 Team Technik Porsche GT3 RS. So Marc, seventh place—not bad since it looked like you had trouble with your car on the closing laps."

"Yeah, after I passed the Ferrari for second, I picked up some debris and a slow puncture with about three laps left."

"It looked like you had the measure of Marchesotti today—you were all over him."

"Yes, I did." Marc paused and sighed a little, enough to convey his feelings.

"I thought I saw his Ferrari turn into you several times, even after you won the corner. In fact, one time it appeared he hit your aero package. Marc, you've raced for a long time. How does he continue to get away with that kind of racing?"

"Ha, ha" replied Marc raising his eyebrows. "That's Luca for you. It seems that he drives with ah … an irrational exuberance. I knew I could take him after Copse, going into Becketts. You know sometimes, when you're racing that close, everything you see is through The Red Mist. You're only focused on that one thing, passing the car in front of you."

"But then you hit some debris and after that, you were all over the road."

"For sure. A tire going flat can make the car difficult to control." said Marc with a wink.

"Still, you managed to bring the car into a points-paying position."

"Fortunately, it was a fairly slow leak, but I gotta tell you Elaine, two more corners and the race would have had a different outcome."

"Well, cheers, Marc. You drove a great race. Better luck

next round."

"Thanks Elaine. Gotta go congratulate a friend. See you later."

Marc turned and continued walking towards the podium. Thinking about what Elaine said made him realize, he had been racing a long time, in fact, almost his whole life.

He seemed born with instinctive car control, as bringing his car home in-the-points today demonstrated. He would probably have been a champion or star by now if he had signed with a top team, but Marc wanted to run a team his way without a helping hand. He remembered how ashamed he had been once, years ago, when his father had to use his considerable personal and political capital to help Marc out of a tough spot. Marc never forgot that; it was what drove him to push himself and his team to success.

A slow smile spread across his face remembering how he had started racing Karts in the U.K. when he was nine. Three years later his father's trans-Atlantic career brought the family back to the U.S., where he continued racing in U.S Junior Karting classes. When the family moved back to Europe, Marc entered the Intercontinental A Karting Series and became U.K. series champ just in time to return to the U.S.A. Marc was seventeen. By then, Marc was driving his father's Porsche. He moved up through the ranks of the Porsche Club of America Drivers Education series, then the Porsche Club Racing series, where he became the youngest ever Club Race Champion at age twenty. Young and talented, he got the call to move to a professional team. But he agreed with his parents, college first, racing later. He studied mechanical engineering at U C Davis.

But he almost did not graduate, a brush with the law, no, more of a huge back handed slap, had come close to ending his dreams. Pushing those painful memories way down deep where they belonged, he focused instead on his first job after graduation, joining a top Grand Am race team as a chassis-development engineer. When he found he could not get the seat-of-the-pants feedback he needed to set up the cars properly from the professional racers on the team, he returned to the cockpit, after the first lap he was hooked. Again. He had to race, and for Marc, Grand Am was not it. Like his dad, his true love remained Porsche, that and racing in Europe.

He moved back to Europe and joined a GT team as a chassis engineer. GT–for Grand Touring–is for automobiles that resemble the design of street-legal production vehicles in principle. GT cars are modified for the track but are instantly recognizable as the production cars they are based on. GT racing, sanctioned by the World Racing Federation or WRF, specifies four classes of GT cars, with GT1 allowing the most modifications and GT4 remaining closest to the production models.

The team Marc joined competed in both GT2 and GT3. Marc chose them because, in addition to his job as their chassis engineer, he got to drive. When the team went up for sale, Marc and a small group of investors bought the GT3 assets and renamed it Team Technik. Initially he and the team were successful. He used most of his winnings to buy the other investors out. He now ran the team with his partner, Bala Masurkur. Michael Llewellyn's infusion of cash helped but managing a business and staying on budget were nothing like driving a winning race car. For one thing, win or lose, once the race is over the racer can focus on the next one up. As the owner-driver, Marc carried the team's needs and concerns on his shoulders all day every day. He and Bala had to deal with everything from transportation to salaries to signing sponsors to race strategy. Lately, Marc thought maybe it was a little more than he'd bargained for and wondered (not for the first time) what it would take to keep the team going–and winning.

Pushing those thoughts away, Marc reached the podium in time to see Luis DeSilva accept the second- place trophy. From his position just off the side of the podium, Marc watched well-wishers congratulate Luis. Luis made eye contact and Marc pointed to Luca across the podium on Luis' right. Laughing, Marc pressed his index finger onto his nose, flattening it to look like a pig snout. He and Luis were still laughing when Luca received his trophy. Everyone glanced at Luis (including Luca), wondering what was so funny.

Classic Marc, Luis thought. *Luca is a pig. Thanks for that!* Turning, he saw Luca and started laughing again.

At that moment, Luca had just noticed Marc standing near the podium. He smirked, winked and looked away.

A*sshole. One day all his bad shit will come due. I just hope I'm around to see it,* thought Marc.

After the awards were presented, the winners wandered off to interviews with the racing press. Marc caught up to Luis and gave him a bear hug.

The contrast between the two friends was striking. Marc, lean and athletic, standing at just under two meters, Luis, shorter and a bit broader at 1.7 meters.

"Great race mate! Loved that wave as you passed."

"Hey, a salute to a wounded warrior."

"How did you take Luca?"

"I watched you," said Luis, laughing, "You had him set up before you picked up the debris and punctured the tire and I simply did the same thing you did to him earlier. He's so thick! You had just done it to him and he still didn't see it coming!"

"So, who do you think he is blaming for being demoted to third? Think anybody will get sacked?"

Both laughed, hugged again and headed their separate ways. Turning his head back, Luis shouted to Marc, "Call me Monday. Jose and I have some new Physio techniques to run through," then he disappeared into the crowd.

Mark and Luis met while racing in karts as teens and had

been best friends ever since. Luis DeSilva came from a wealthy Brazilian family who lived in the interior city of Curitiba. Like Marc, Luis also had uncanny car control. He'd been offered the Formula One route driving racing's Grand Prix thoroughbreds but loved sports cars. Luis thought of Marc as a brother. He knew Marc ran his team on a shoe-string budget, so Luis helped out here and there. Encouraging Marc to work out with himself and Jose was one way he could help without making Marc feel patronized.

Marc returned to the pits, caught up with his team as they broke down their pit area and loaded everything into their team transport truck to head for home base at Milton Keynes, less than an hour's drive. Some of the other teams had return trips to France, Germany, Italy and beyond. The next race at the Circuit Spa Francorchamps in Belgium was over a month off, so Marc and Team Technik had a chance to regroup and get everything dialed in before attacking the next round.

Tom Tambay, the team transport, walked up as Marc was changing out of his racing suit into jeans and a Lacoste polo shirt.

"We'll be loaded up within fifteen minutes and ready to head out Marc."

"Thanks Tom. Do you know if Stella went to collect our prize winnings?"

"Yeah, I think she did. Went with Bala."

"Shit, I hope she doesn't give him the money. He may buy some parts or something before he gets back to the pits!"

"As long as it makes the car go faster, I've got no problem with that Mate."

"Cool, I'll tell him he can buy parts against your pay chit."

"Well, that's pushing it now." Tom was grinning as he walked back to the truck.

Marc watched the rest of the team load the car, raising it on a lift and placing it butt-end first into the top of the team transport. Next, they placed the last of the rolling tool and equipment cases below the car before buttoning everything up. Watching them work, Marc knew they deserved better: better finishes, more points, better money. His thoughts drifted away. When he heard the voices of Bala and Stella approaching, he turned to greet them.

"5000 quid, Marc. The gate receipts were a bit higher than the organizers predicted," said Stella. She gave Marc a pert smile and bumped her hip into him as she handed him the envelope full of money.

Marc smiled back and thanked her. "That's over £12,000 for both races this weekend, not a bad payday for a small team," he replied, thinking that it barely paid for salaries, tires and gas. With other race weekends approaching, Marc knew there would not be enough money to finish the season and without Llewellyn's cash, they would not even be this far.

"Just think if we had won," Bala added, stating the obvious.

Michael Llewellyn appeared, heading toward the group.

"You know more results like this and I'll become an endangered species," he said.

"How's that Michael?" asked Stella.

"You know the paying Gent. The team won't need me anymore." He paused, then frowned.

"I wouldn't hear of it Michael. And besides I was going to ask you for even more money," added Marc.

Laughing, most of the team turned and headed for either the transport truck or their own cars. Marc arrived at his personal road car, a bright orange, highly modified and barely road legal Porsche GT3. He noticed Michael did not head towards his own car. Instead, he walked directly towards Marc with a funny smile on his face.

"About the more money part Marc ...."

Chapter 3

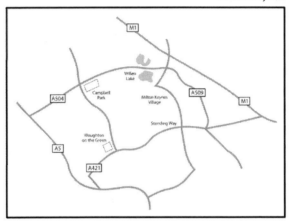

The look on his face said it all. Llewellyn had bad news and could not hide the disappointment from Marc.

"Don't tell me you're going to hold out on me Mate."

"I don't want to."

"Well then, don't."

"Let me finish, Marc. With all the Brexit nonsense, I've had a huge financial set-back and it's hurt my life, my family, not to mention my whole business outlook."

"What does that have to do with Team Technik? You committed the funds to us for the rest of the season."

"You don't understand. I simply don't have the money

for the rest of the season."

When Llewellyn did not continue, Marc finally prompted him, "I'm listening."

"I can pay you through the mid-way part of the season. That way you can begin to look for a new co-driver right away and have them racing by the July race."

"And if I don't find someone?"

"You will! You have to! Everyone loves Team Technik," said Michael clenching his fists. "Who wouldn't want to be a part of this?"

"Like you said, it's a tough economy."

"I'm sorry, Marc, I really am. You have no idea…," his voice cracking before it trailed off.

"I'm sorry too." said Marc trying not to scream. "You know the mid-way point is our most capital intensive part of the season. We have to buy new equipment, there are the upgrades from Porsche and the mid-term bonus for the team—it's like you've punched me right in my stomach."

"I know, I know. I'm letting you down, the team down— I'm truly sorry Marc."

Marc got into his Porsche, shoved the key into the ignition and twisted savagely. The Porsche started in a roar and explosion of spinning parts, trumpeting its anger out the exhaust, matching how Marc felt. After a few seconds, the car seemed to calm down. Taking a couple of deep breaths,

Marc did too. Michael just stood there and watched, not knowing what to do or say. Finally, Marc rolled down the window.

"Llewellyn, thanks for being up front. I understand things are tough for you right now." The two men stared in silence for a long moment before Marc continued, "Did you inform the WRF? They may have something to say."

"I just came from talking to them. They've agreed to let you find another co-driver."

Marc nodded slightly. He felt no need to thank Michael for that. It was the least he could do for the team. Marc turned to look straight ahead and put the car in gear, letting it surge forward. Then he hit the brakes. Sticking his head out the window, he yelled back, "We'll talk later," before accelerating away.

Another setback. One more bomb I've got to drop on Bala and Stella.

It seemed his racing career with Team Technik was full of them since he and Bala bought the team. How much longer could the team survive? He pounded his head against the seat back. Something had to give. He hoped it would not be Team Technik. Marc felt like he had come to a 'T' in a strange landscape of unmarked roads. He was looking for a sign, any sign.

Rene Dufour was also looking for a sign. He had returned to his home, just south of Dijon in the small town of Gevrey-Chambertin. Parking the beaten Quattroporte in his garage, he entered his house and plunked himself down at the small table near his kitchen. He sat still for a few minutes. Getting up, he opened a bottle of red wine, poured himself a glass and took a sip. A day-old baguette and some left-over cheese provided some much-needed carbs.

The envelope from his Engagement lay on the table where he had dropped it. He stared at it as he thought about the day. The Engagement had not seemed right from the beginning, but he really was not expecting the fire storm he had run into. His instincts used to be spot-on, but today had almost been a disaster! Maybe his senses were numbing. Maybe he had taken too many Engagements.

Focusing on the envelope, he tore it open and leafed through the bills. He started counting. The Engagement contract was €100,000, which was not a bad pay day. But, he realized, this was much more. He kept counting: €125K, €150K, €200K, €250K, €300K!

Merde!

The competitor he had delivered to his client obviously had some *serious* worth and that crack about the Maserati didn't sting quite so much now. Rene put the money back into the envelope. He stared at it for a few seconds, then put it away in his home safe. As he got ready to go to bed, he thought, *I have many phone calls to make in the morning, but where do I start?*

All eyes were glued to their video screens, hoping to see beyond the pixilation and distorted voice of Mr. X. But the technology that X employed was as thorough and unyielding as the criminal mastermind, himself. So Mr. X remained an enigma; a dangerous, ruthless enigma. Mr. X wielded control by tapping into human weaknesses—power, greed, ego, sociopathy—X knew how to push mental buttons, stripping down people to their core weakness to get results. Mr. X understood how to keep people loyal: give them what they want and in return they gave what X wanted. Thus, a perfect relationship. Willing to invest in far reaching operations for success and profit, any criminal activity, no matter how crazy, farfetched, brutal or bloody was fair game as long as results were measurable.

Mr. X ran a criminal empire like a successful business. Key Lieutenants had quotas and were expected to provide business plans stating overarching goals, criteria for reaching milestones and KPIs (key performance indicators). They were compensated based on metrics that measured how much each operation cost and what the outcome was. Sometime the outcomes were tangible–guns, drugs, cash from money laundering, stolen art and sometimes intangible–intimidation, leverage, coercion, each operation graded on what it brought to X and X's subordinates.

All of X's Lieutenants were expected to give status updates on all current and pending operations. X had them report in a video conferencing app. All their faces displayed neatly inside rows of tiles. Except for one. Nobody knew who X was or what X looked like, but each was beholden to a pixilated image and a raspy, metallic sounding voice. What kept them in line? X was very generous in splitting the profits from each operation, barring failure. As long as money and power flowed, X's subordinates asked few if any questions.

"Bridgette, what was the total cost of this operation?"

"We lost two good operatives. But we exceeded the anticipated take by fifteen percent to $3.6 Million dollars." The tall lean German blond said as she peered into the camera.

"Besides the two operatives, what was the cost of the logistics and equipment outlay?"

"Because we needed two helicopters, our operational cost was $960,000."

"Too high, the return is 75% profit. You know our target is 80%. Unacceptable. Plus the loss of two good, high value operatives. I rate this operation as a loss and failure."

"I'm sorry Mr. X."

"That is two unsuccessful operations in the past two months. Bridgette, your failures are mounting." Bridgette hung her head low. She knew what another reprimand meant to her health.

"I understand."

"Send me your next operation. I want to fully vet it, minimize screw ups."

"Yes. Mr. X." Thankful that seemed to be the end of it.

Moving on, each lieutenant gave a briefing on each operation under their control. There were a few other reprimands, but mostly the meeting showed that X's criminal enterprise was flourishing. Success counted in money, power, blood and human suffering. All the most brutal, cruel and inhumane results were on display for X's pleasure and profit.

"Now I want to talk about diamonds." Everyone listened raptly to X.

"I was recently supplied with some very useful intelligence about a certain diamond merchant that controls a large swatch of the worldwide diamond trade. Supposedly this person is based in Europe and I have heard that much of the diamond trade this merchant controls flows through Italy. Anyone know of such a person?" Silence.

"No? You are all supposed to have your finger on the pulse of these sorts of things."

"Very well. This person, we do not know the identity, keeps a very secretive profile." A few chuckles, laughing at the irony of what X was asking.

"No laughing! This is not a laughing matter and yes, I do get the dripping irony here. Go out and hit up your usual sources. I want info. I want access to that diamond merchant. Get me something." A murmuring as each Lieutenant knew that whoever brought info and provided a solution of how to gain access to this diamond merchant would be well rewarded.

"That is all." Mr. X ended the call and pixilated screen went blank. X pushed another button on a console.

"Diego, get Petrovski."

Moments later, Uli Petrovski's dark brooding face filled the screen. His close-cropped silver hair, black and gray stubbled beard, thick Slavic lips and hard black soulless eyes accentuated the menace he projected: a war hardened mercenary.

"Yes Mr. X."

"Bridgette."

"Humph, want me to eliminate a problem?"

"No, send a message. No more failures, no more screwups."

"Understood."

"Make sure the message is delivered loud and clear. I leave it to your discretion of how best to communicate my displeasure."

"Got it." The screen went blank.

"Diego, set up a payment for Petrovski. The usual amount should suffice."

Monday dawned cloudy in the city of Milton Keynes, which was the late spring norm in south-central Britain. Marc woke early. It was going to be a rough day, first breaking the bad news about Llewellyn, then figuring out what to do about it. He might as well get out there and deal with things. He was almost ready to head out from his small flat near the city center when his ancient cell phone rang. The Caller ID read *April*. It would be past midnight on the East Coast of the U.S.

"April! Hi Sweetie, it's really late for you."

"When you didn't call, I decided to call you instead. How'd it go this weekend?"

Long pause. "It wasn't the best weekend."

"I saw the results on BRTV.com. You came in the points in both races. That's awesome."

"Yeah, but I was racing for second. I'd passed Marchesotti and just left him. I was so close to a win!"

"Yes, I saw that too. You hit some debris or something."

"It's *always* something lately! Well anyway, after the race, we all felt pretty good, I mean, like you said, we scored points. And we got a payout."

"You don't sound pleased. I can tell something's bothering you."

He let out a big sigh and pressed his lips together, not wanting to tell her the news.

"Marc, you have to tell me what happened!"

"Michael Llewellyn is leaving the team."

"Oh Marc! That's terrible."

"Llewellyn is paying until the midpoint of the season, but from then on we'll be broke. If I can't find some more money, it's good-bye Team Technik."

"What about going to Luis?"

"Luis and his dad would help in a heartbeat, but they'd absorb the entire team. They've offered before, but you know I've always wanted to lead my own team."

"I am sorry Marc…"

"Besides, I don't know if my relationship with Porsche Motorsport would transfer if I went with Luis. For some reason, Dieter Mendelsen at Porsche HQ really likes me. He's let Team Technik buy their developmental prototypes."

"Their what?"

"The cars they use to test their current racers each season. That's saved us tens of thousands of Euros. Those cars are run hard, but they've always sold us race cars in good condition with lots of spare parts too. No matter what happens, we'd have two choices: campaigning with a year older model or ponying up €200,000 for a new one."

She heard the stress in his voice and she ached to give him hope. "Sweetie—chin up! You'll figure something out. You always do. You're amazing when you're up against an obstacle. That's one of the reasons I love you. Your … ahhh, how should I put this delicately, your intense focus on self reliance? And I'll bet you have resources you haven't even thought of yet."

Laughing Marc finally choked out, "Thanks councilor, I've missed you too! You always find a way to put my bullheadedness into such civilized concepts."

"Well soon you'll have *me*. It's only a few more weeks."

They talked about her upcoming business trip to England for her law firm. They told each other how excited they were getting about being together again as the date got closer. By the time they hung up, Marc felt better. She was right. He was not beaten yet. He glanced at the clock. Time to go! Time to join Luis at Team Fortunata.

Driving to Team Fortunata's HQ, he thought, *Why does everything have to be so damned hard? I ought to be able to balance driving and running a team. I'm smart, dedicated, and I know I've got more talent than most of my competitors. So what then? What is the missing ingredient? Just luck? I've got to find some way to change that. But how? Maybe being the nice guy all the time isn't helping either, I need an edge.*

Team Fortunata was also headquartered in Milton Keynes, just a short ten minute drive from Team Technik's HQ and minutes later Marc, in his own personal fog, found himself in front of the team's sleek glass and aluminum facilities. Everywhere he looked as he approached the facility, he saw the backing of Luis' father.

Marc knew the garage area gleamed like a semi-conductor factory's clean room. There were enough lifts and tools to accommodate several race cars simultaneously, along with the latest fabrication equipment for crafting whatever they wanted. The entire facility was designed for long-term growth. As Luis' career progressed, Team Fortunata expected to expand, racing in more than one series, eventually building their own race cars. The team offices in front of the garage looked like a high-end architectural firm. Bright steel and glass desks supported huge LCD monitors. Behind the desks, Aeron chairs. Sleek but inviting leather seating was scattered about. The techno-bling continued on the second level. The nearby kitchen had black-accented stainless steel on every surface. The coordinated professional cooking components paired with huge black and white action photos of GT racers on the walls suggested a hip new restaurant in London's Soho. Directly across from the kitchen was the exercise studio, open to all employees. The latest glittering cardio and weight equipment offered a complete workout.

Both the kitchen and exercise studio were the domain of Jose Carvalho, Luis' personal chef and Physio—a term which, in the racing world, refers to both a personal trainer and the workouts he designs. And because Marc and Luis were best friends, Jose was Marc's Physio as well. This was help that Marc seriously appreciated. He did not have the money to afford his own Physio, let alone a chef and a full gym. He came to work out, eat great meals and listen to life guidance from Jose at least twice a week, more if his schedule allowed.

Jose's intimidating 2m+ height and 86 kg physique was an advertisement for his commitment to fitness. Add to that a clean shaved head, a penetrating stare and a *basso profundo* voice—no surprise that he frequently intimidated people who were meeting him for the first time. But he had no compulsion to strut. Actually, he was reserved and surprisingly gentle. Still, it was a mistake to make him angry.

Marc, Luis and Jose gathered at 6:30 every Monday morning for three hours of intense training that included aerobics and strength training, followed by Jose's own approach to martial arts. He drew on Jing Wu Men and Krav Maga and incorporated a new strategy he had developed for fighting two or more opponents at once. The idea was to bring both opponents in close, then use upper body strength and twisting motions from Krav Maga to break them. For this morning's exercise, all three were equipped with padding and body panels.

Marc (the earlier fog gone, his mind now clear and focused) and Luis both attacked Jose simultaneously. Jose landed a powerful kick that sent Luis to the ground while grabbing Marc's extended right arm, yanking him in unexpectedly close. Using his other hand, he slammed Marc in the shoulder. As Marc struggled to maintain his balance, Jose pinned Marc's wrists against his body, then using the force and leverage of his upper leg and thigh, he spun Marc to the ground, finishing him off with two successive kicks to Marc's (helmeted) head. Luis had gotten up from the floor and was behind him, trying to land a blow on the back of Jose's rapidly bobbing head, but Jose had never lost awareness of exactly where Luis was and now he pivoted, blocked the blow with a raised elbow, deflecting the shot and leaving Luis off balance. A powerful upward jab with his left leg knocked Luis to the ground once again. Jose jumped up and kicking his leg above his head dropped to the mat, slapping it with his arms to break the fall, his upper leg landing on top of Luis with a blow to his chest that, in a real fight, would have broken a couple of ribs.

"Ow!" moaned Marc as he got up.

"Yeah. Times about six," added Luis, breathing hard, as Marc extended a hand to pull him up.

That was it for conversation as their session continued, except for grunts and thumps. They changed roles from time to time, delivering and parrying potentially deadly blows, until all three were exhausted. They cooled down with thirty minutes of Tai Chi, followed by thirty minutes of meditation. These workouts, two to three times per week, kept Luis and Marc in top racing condition—superb physical stamina plus a capacity for sustained, unblinking focus.

At the conclusion of the day's Physio, they drank filtered water to replace the sweat that had drained from every pore. For several minutes, the silence was broken only by deep breathing from all three men.

Marc toweled his thick, short brown hair as dry as possible. Luis untied his long, black hair and wrapped the leather cord around his wrist. Jose sat and watched them, preferring to simply air-dry his shaved ebony head.

Marc broke the silence. "Llewellyn is leaving the team; I have to find a new co-driver and source of funding by mid-season."

"Damn Marc. I'm sorry. That's a huge set-back," said Luis.

"Something good will come of it, I am sure of it," added Jose. "This is one of those times when life seems to be against you, but Marc—your vibe, your aura leads me to believe that something is waiting around the corner—you only have to look, you only have to believe."

Laughing Marc said; "Jose, only you can turn a set-back into a positive—if mystic—experience! And you're the only man in Britain I take seriously when he's talking about my aura."

"No not mystic, the truth. When you believe in yourself the outcome is a *fait accompli*. Believe in yourself, first and foremost!"

"Sorry Jose," said Luis. "I'm not disagreeing, but let's get back to our Marc's earthly predicament for a minute. Marc, how about letting me arrange an anonymous press release for you? A little news leak that says you're taking on a new co-driver and getting additional funding. It will hit all the racing news services, websites and racing shows on TV. You'll get some media interest. And potential co-drivers should leap at the chance to join you."

"Thanks Luis, that sounds like a good plan. And thanks Jose, even if your advice has nothing to do with racing reality!" They all laughed—exactly the kind of cathartic therapy Marc needed.

Rene woke early and made a list. It helped to put every item and duty down in an orderly manner. Near the top of the list, call his auto agent and arrange to get a new car. He also had to call his auto guru, Hector Delacruz. But first, he needed to go to his banker in Dijon, a very discrete man who represented the Swiss Bank of Lucerne et Velneux. That envelope full of money did not belong in a home safe.

Rene drove his very unsubtle "every day" vehicle, a bright yellow Renault Megane Turbo RS, into Dijon. He arrived at the bank at 8:30 and asked for M. Pontet. He was shown into the branch General Manager's office and after a round of strong coffee Rene made the deposit, €300,000, minus the fee for M. Pontet to handle the transaction. There was a round of handshakes and Rene quickly left. He did not mind the five percent handling fee, since the deposit went unreported and never appeared on the tax rolls.

Returning home, he got on the phone to his auto agent, Phillipe Martin. By not going through traditional auto dealers, Rene avoided having any car actually registered to him. Instead, his agent registered the cars to non-traceable offshore companies in places like Saint Maarten or the Caymans.

Phillipe was located in central Paris, but had worldwide tentacles. He could put his hands on any car and could have it delivered anywhere, anytime. There were fees of course, to keep things off the books and away from prying eyes. Phillipe's custom-developed web-based inventory system, allowed him to see what individual dealers had in stock, what was to be delivered from the factory and what the factory was actually building, both sold and open stock. He could even intercept purchased cars from the factory and have them rerouted to his customers. Money changed hands and strange things happened.

"*Bonjour Phillipe, c'est Rene.*"

"*Allo Rene! Ca va bien?*"

"*Oui, ca va!* Listen Phillipe, I need a favor. I had a wreck in the Quattroporte and I need to have it replaced."

"*Mon Dieu*! Are you OK?"

"Of course. That car is a tank, which is why I want another."

"OK, I'll get right on it."

"Phillipe, I really loved that Grigio Granito color. I also liked the cabernet colored leather seats with dark gray piping plus the Carbon Fiber trim kit on the dash, central console and door trim. Try to find me another exactly like it."

"Ahhh. That is the thing Rene, that could cost a bit more."

"Phillipe! That is why I turn to you. Work your magic, but I need it right away and I will pay you an extra €5,000 beyond your normal fee for the effort. "

"For that I may build you one myself. I'll be in touch."

"*Au revoir.*"

"*A bientôt.*" Rene hit the end button. So far so good. Now to break the news to Hector.

Marc entered Team Technik HQ for the Monday-morning staff meeting in his signature jeans, long-sleeved Team Technik Porsche racing tee shirt and driving shoes. The differences between facilities of Team Fortunata and Team Technik were everywhere. This old garage had served at least three generations of racing teams. It had what

Marc thought of as a *British patina*—faded formerly deep red bricks bounded with age-darkened wood trim. The two large garage doors in front were painted the team colors of yellow, black and white with the team crest on each. The inside smelled of old oil, paint, grease and rubber. To some (mostly men) it was an intoxicating perfume. Some ancient tools and machinery alongside new, Porsche-specific equipment gave the interior the look of an old, well-worn but loved home. They had finally relegated the last of the smokers, mechanic Reg Carmichael (and very occasionally Stella) to an old dust bin ten meters away from the building, so at least there was no longer that stale smell of cigarette smoke to deal with. The team operations staff was minimal: his partner and team manager Bala Masurkar, the team director of operations Stella Beru and himself. The office the three of them shared doubled as their conference room. At least it was big enough for three small desks, a small round coffee table and four comfortable if well-worn chairs. The team's one indulgence was a professional espresso machine by Wega for Marc's espresso, Stella's Cappuccino and Bala's steamed tea.

Marc was certain that he had the best people that he and Bala could afford. All his mechanics: Zeca Reis, Tom Tambay, Susmit Singe, Jimmy Oswalt and Reg could easily work anywhere, with any team. But they stayed out of loyalty to him and to one another. Marc made sure they never missed a payday or bonus and, compared to other teams, they actually were paid pretty well. As for the facilities, they may have been old, but all the equipment was good quality. Even the team transport lorry was fairly new and well equipped. Apart from the team's welfare, Marc's life was austere. One of the reasons he appreciated all the dinner invitations from Luis and Jose, it helped keep his food costs down.

Thinking about his team and its future, Marc realized he had to focus on finding a replacement for Michael Llewellyn. Partly out of pride, but mostly because he needed to do things his own way, he could not go to Luis for financial support. Nevertheless, the financial condition of the team was crushing him and he wasn't sure where to turn. His father had warned him it could come to this. He'd said more than once that great racers should just drive; if they were really lucky they could make a career of it. As much as he loved his father, Marc did not want to give him the chance or the satisfaction of saying "I told you so." At least not yet.

Putting a smile on his face, he entered the office and saw Bala and Stella sitting, waiting for him.

Bala was a second-generation Indian. His family immigrated to the U.K. from Bombay, long before that city was renamed Mumbai. His parents had him educated at the best English schools. Naturally, when he told them he wanted a career in racing instead of engineering, his father was horrified. His mother saved the day, somehow convincing his father that Bala would work only for the biggest, best-funded teams. Now years later, his big team had nine people, operating out of a garage that was already old when Margaret Thatcher was Prime Minister. Still, when it came to race-car engineering, engine set-up and telemetry, this kind, gentle man was tops. He had the same fire in his belly to win as Marc did, even if his belly had spread a bit over the years.

Marc winked at Stella as he sat down. She was the one who kept the entire enterprise on track. Her trim, stylish good looks still managed to suggest the tomboy she was at heart. She controlled the purse strings and managed logistics. She liked the work and the responsibility, but she *loved* the excitement and the men who loved racing. Stella was really the rock that anchored the team (or to use anther metaphor, the glue that kept them together).

If Marc and Bala had ever felt the need to protect Stella because she was a woman in a man's world, they had gotten over it long ago. Now they felt that she protected them. As other people adopt cats or dogs, Stella adopted the men of Team Technik. She just needed to housebreak them.

Marc stated the bad news quickly. "We're losing Michael to a combination of Brexit and the downturn in the economy."

"Bollocks! That completely stinks," said Stella. "We don't have enough cash to finish the season without him."

"Oy that hurts. Michael's practically been our bank. Stella's right Marc. What can we do?"

"Michael will pay us through mid-season, so we're okay for now, but we need to find a new paying co-driver and hit our sponsors up for more funding. Or maybe try to add another sponsor."

"Well, Michael helped with our current sponsor package. Maybe he'd give it one more try before he goes."

"Good idea, Bala. We need to leverage his connections."

Stella reached over to Marc and patted his face. "Now don't worry love. I'll work my magic on him. I'll also call the sponsors to see if there's anything left in the tank, so to speak."

"Perfect. If anybody can get those old boys to dig deeper into their pockets, you can. And on another point, Luis agreed earlier to leak Michael's departure to the racing press. That will give us some visibility. Who knows? Stranger things have happened. Maybe we'll find someone else with deep pockets who actually knows how to drive a race car."

Bala was already getting excited. "Stella, we need a really good write up, some kind of advert that gets posted everywhere and we need to do it right away. I'll work on the racing and licensing requirements and complete the forms. You know Marc, Luis is going to save our arses once again. Doesn't it make it hard when you have to pass him on the track?"

"Never. Not for me, not for him. Out there on the track,

we're racing competitors first and foremost. The friendship stuff comes after the checkered flag drops."

Bala brought up merging with Team Fortunata.

Marc stared at the coffee table. "I've thought about that. Maybe as a last resort, but only after we see what the current season has in store for all of us."

There was a long silence. Bala and Stella quietly left the office to give Marc some time to think.

An incoming communication from Diego. Mr. X initiated the secure pixilated video and distorted audio call. Diego reported in: one of the Lieutenants who went by name of Bronzit scored some intel. There was a former diamond broker in Milan Italy that was said to have info on how the diamond shipments were transacted and may have useful information on the identity of the diamond merchant.

"What does Bronzit want for this information if it plays out," Mr. X asked.

Diego replied, "3% of the gross."

Mr. X approved. "All right 3%, but if the info is not accurate or requires additional resources to vet, the rate goes down to 1.5%."

"Now get me Petrovski."

"Yes Mr. X?" Asked Uli when his face appeared on the

screen.

"Tell me about Bridgette."

"Message delivered. Sending you a photo via secure Signal socket now." The photo showed a woman's hand palm up on a table with a large knife protruding from it. There was a pool of blood starting to form on both the entry and exit wounds.

"Ah, yes. Razor sharp knife through the hand pinning it to the table. It's so subtle. Well played."

"Sliced through flesh, muscle, tendons, bone, but no major blood vessel. It hurt like hell. She will not be using that hand for a long time I think. Want to see her face after I did it?"

"Yes." The next photo appeared.

"Excellent. I can see the horror and pain and just underneath, the understanding. Very good Petrovski. Anything else?"

"I took out two of her bodyguards. Killed the third."

"Acceptable. You received the payment?"

"Yes, much appreciated."

"Good, now I have another operation for you. Head to Milan Italy and inquire about the location and identity of this diamond merchant that so interests me. Diego will provide the details."

"Instructions?"

"Get what information you can. Determine if this source will be useful."

"And if this source does not pan out?"

"I'll leave that to you."

"Understood."

When Phillipe called Rene, he reported he had actually located two Quattroportes, one with exactly the same specs as the battered one in Rene's garage.

"The car is in Paris, and I can have it shipped today," Phillipe said.

"What about the second one?" Rene asked.

"It's in Nantes. It has the wrong wheel/caliper combo, but the dealer agreed to swap out the wheels and brakes."

"I'll take them both. I want them delivered tonight."

"I anticipated that. They will arrive as requested, but it will cost extra for the quick turnaround." He named a sum.

"I agree. I will wire you the funds immediately."

Rene hung up, then called M. Pontet and instructed him to wire the funds to Phillipe's bank account. Then he called Phillipe back.

"The money is on its way. You have a covered two-car lorry, no?"

"Yes," replied Phillipe.

"You know the delivery location. Tell the tow truck to pull off the road. My friend and I will be waiting."

Rene and his auto guru, Hector, liked this location because it had easy access to the highway and there were no security cameras nearby that might make a tape of their activities.

Later, Rene and Hector transferred the two cars to Hector's own covered two-car lorry. After approving the paperwork, the delivery driver was encouraged to forget where he had been. They waited until they were comfortable the tow truck was gone then they drove to Hector's facilities where the wrecked Maserati awaited them. Before long, all three cars sat under the lights at Hector's shop.

Hector Delacruz's love of tinkering and coding software was combined with a serious case of automotive lust. He wore thick Coke-bottle, black-rimmed glasses. His unkempt greasy black hair advertised his questionable personal hygiene. But his talents, inventiveness and electronic genius had built his reputation among a certain group of discerning customers who required very high-end automotive security packages.

It was Hector who developed the Kevlar inserts that fit

underneath the Maserati's body panels as well as the 4-corner camera system that tied into both sat-nav displays and cell-phone systems. The explosive and bug-sensing equipment were from top-secret government sources. They fell into the 'Unobtanium' category as he referred to it. He never revealed how he found them. He integrated these systems so that car occupants could survive almost any ordeal.

Hector's services were dear, but no customer ever complained. He hated to see the damage sometimes inflicted on his creations, but he also knew that was why he built them—survivors tended to be very grateful and did not mind opening their checkbooks very wide.

It was now time to dissect the wrecked Quattroporte and see what had worked and what had not. Hector and Rene pulled on gloves, grabbed tools and got to work. They peeled off inside door panels and removed the Kevlar and Polymer windows. Next, they removed the Kevlar mesh screens in front of the radiator. Hector connected a laptop to the Quattroporte's data port and down-loaded data from the car's onboard computers. They cut the Kevlar panels and removed the bullets, measuring ballistics data to see how everything preformed. Next, they measured the dents and cracks in the Polymer window panels, noting the types of bullets the attackers had used. This data made it possible to make new, safer security elements.

"Look here Rene, there are multiple caliber bullets. They didn't use anything in common. There are NATO rounds here along the passenger side doors."

"That would be when they opened fire with an automatic—their version of a greeting."

"Hmmm, these bullets are more like .40 and .45 caliber. And there are some 9 mm mingled with the other rounds. They opened up the entire arms bazaar on you."

"What about the Kevlar panels? Did they stop everything?"

"They stopped most everything pretty well. Wait a minute. These are high velocity .45 caliber rounds they fired into your door. Looks like they wanted to hit the area around the driver with maximum impact."

Hector had picked up the Kevlar panels, which were marked with a yellow grease pencil, and held up the panel from the driver's door. Imbedded in the Kevlar were the hollow-point .45 slugs. They had ripped through most of the Kevlar layers, but not quite all the way. Hector pursed his lips and shook his head.

Several years earlier, he had developed a process to make the normally strong, many-layered Kevlar even stronger. Most Kevlar is a number of layers sewn and pressed together. Hector's process vacuum-formed the layers in the shapes of a specific car model's body panels. He then baked them at a steady high temperature to make them stronger. Hector worked with his source to develop new, sturdier Kevlar panels by providing hard data to fabricate upgrades.

Hector measured how many layers were intact.

"Last week my source sent me some of the upgraded panels. It is time to test them."

"What about the Polymer windows?" asked Rene.

"I have Polymer for the side windows, but I will have to wait a day or two for the front windscreen and rear-window panel to be custom built."

Hector and Rene looked at and measured the Kevlar screen protecting the radiator and front of the engine compartment.

"Two of the three layers failed," Hector mused, "but good news, the third one stopped them or your engine would have failed.

Rene's face was grave. Too close for comfort.

"I need to recalibrate the layer thicknesses. *Should* work."

When Rene looked startled, Hector laughed.

"Little joke, *mon ami*. They will work"

Next, they inspected the safes in the trunk and car interiors. Both were intact, as was the secret panel built into the driver's seat. They decided they would simply swap out the safe and driver's seat to save time and money. The emergency medical kit would be resupplied and fitted into the new car. New bullet-proof tires had already been ordered.

Finally, the electronics package had survived intact and

would be transferred and integrated into the new car too. The front and rear cameras would need to be replaced.

Considering the Quattroporte's condition, it had survived well, doing its job to protect Rene and his cargo.

Rene stood staring at the car, lost in thought, replaying the details of the drive in the mountain passes over and over in his mind. Whatever he was carrying, many men had died trying to kill him to obtain it. Such a waste.

"Rene. Rene! What about the second new Quattroporte? Should I start to integrate the package into it as well?"

"Not just yet Hector, I may have another use for that one."

Returning to his farm after spending almost 24-hours working side-by-side with Hector, Rene went for a walk among the vineyards as the sun set. He grew Pinot Noir grapes on his small farm. He sold most of his harvest to other wine producers, but held onto some of it, turning his grapes into a signature Gevrey-Chambertin Cote de Nuit for his friends and himself. As the sun set, he marveled at the display of orange and purple fingers stretching across the sky. He knelt beside some of the growing vines and gathered a handful of soil, rubbing it together between his fingers. He slowly spilled the dirt back to the ground with a tiny pitter-patter. Cupping part of the vine, he studied the buds that eventually would become a cluster of grapes. His viticulturist had told him the vines were coming along nicely and, God willing and weather permitting, they would have a good year.

When he purchased the farm, it was in complete disarray. Both vineyard and farmhouse were run down. The former owner had died and his family did not care to keep the land, so Rene had scooped up the property for a very low price. He poured money and sweat into the place for months.

Now the large property next to his was available. Although he had almost one hectare, he would increase his current vineyard holding to more than ten hectares if he bought it. With that much land, he could become a proper winemaker. Of course, it still begged more than one question: would he have a good year? Should he retire? His grown children were out of school and on their own. His ex-wife had recently remarried. Money was still important but becoming less so. He needed to decide how he would spend the rest of his life.

But he still needed to decide what to do? He knew that being a *Driver* was a young man's game. The senses dulled, reactions slowed, it required more and more effort to stay sharp and focused. Did he walk away—or, the thought starting to form in his mind, did he find someone to take over his book of business, to keep his loyal clients happy? Looking around at the beauty of the vines and the land, he could think of worse ways to grow old.

It had been a long day for Marc. He had worked with Stella to revise the budget to account for any potential short fall they might incur while searching for a new co-driver. He worked with Bala to make sure that Team Technik could get the best racer possible based on their very short timeframe. They crafted a set of driving, competition and licensing requirements because a potential driver cannot just walk in and start racing. FIA rules and regulations detail who can participate in a particular racing series based on a racer's level of experience. The GT3 series requires a balanced team of two Silver (or semi-Pro) drivers or the preferred combination, Gold (or professional racer) teamed with a Bronze level or amateur. Most teams mandate that the amateur driver basically pay to drive. Teams like Fortunata did not have to rely on the paying driver and could instead focus on getting the best amateur. But teams like Technik had no choice.

Marc worked with the team mechanics identifying what needed to be fixed on the Porsche's aero elements. Then they started their normal post-race tasks of cleaning and detailing the GT3. After a race weekend, a car was usually covered in oil, dirt and rubber and there were always cracks and gouges that occurred from the stress of a race. The yellow, black and white race car had to look showroom new. The sponsors required it! Besides, their main sponsor, BT Phone, had a new advertising scheme and the car's graphics had to be changed to reflect the new marketing message: "*Free means Free—more minutes for less £, or €.*"

Later that evening, sitting at the long dinner table inside Team Fortunata HQ, Jose, Luis, Marc and a few others from the Fortunata team were digging into Jose's latest masterpiece: seafood and pea curry with rice followed by *haricot vert* in a lemon and garlic vinaigrette. They watched BRTV to catch up on all the various racing-series happenings of the past weekend. All of a sudden, a news flash grabbed the headline. The face of Elaine Bollard filled the screen.

"At this past weekend's GT3 race at Silverstone Circuit, I had the pleasure to talk with seventh place finisher Marc Lange, the American owner/driver for Team Technik. He is a cagy one, never letting on the conflict brewing within his team.

"Now I have it on good authority that his co-driver, Welsh businessman Michael Llewellyn, is leaving the team, another casualty of the recent recession.

"To assist his struggling Team Technik, Lange received a special dispensation from WRF to sign a new co-driver. Earlier today, I had the chance to talk with Stella Beru, one of the team's Directors."

A swift cut and Stella appeared on the screen with Elaine. With her short red-brown hair and stylish red and black suit, she looked younger than her 40 years. Elaine looked almost dowdy next to the radiant Stella. Everyone at the table whistled and whooped when they saw her on the telly.

"So Stella, what's the plan?" Elaine asked, moving her mic toward Stella.

"We had a team meeting earlier today and we're working right now to create an advert looking for the right kind of co-driver."

"You mean one that can race as a competitive driver?"

"Well yes, but one who hopefully has pretty deep pockets to boot."

Everyone at the table laughed. Only Stella could say something that brutally frank and make it sound like cheerful innocence.

"What can we expect?"

"We've already started our driver search. We'll announce when we'll hold a track test and audition as soon as we've lined that up. As a matter of fact, Elaine, BRTV can massively help by posting the advert on its web site."

Elaine blinked a couple of times, then said, "We'll see what we can do. That's it for BRTV's On the Spot in Racing."

Everyone at Team Fortunata howled at the way Stella had just backed Elaine and BRTV into a corner.

Music blared and there was a quick cut to a commercial break.

Still laughing Luis took up his glass of Sancerre and raised a toast adding "I suspect that they *will* post the advert on their site. I have some good inside sources there you know."

Chapter 4

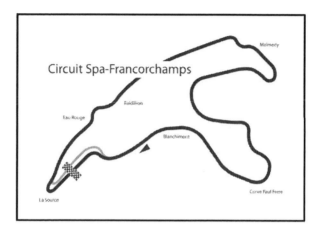

Spa-Francorchamps is one of the world's most fearsome racetracks, fast and brutally demanding. Racers love it. Fittingly located in Belgium's Ardennes forest, site of some of the most savage battles of WWI, it is one of the last of the proper racecourses, originally laid out over existing local roads in the 1920s. The WRF and other racing organizations have tried to tame it over the years, but it can still bite. One of the uniquely demanding things about Spa-Francorchamps is the variable weather of the Ardennes Forest itself—it can be raining at one end of the track and dry at the other. Then there are the white-knuckle corners, with the Eau Rouge/Raidillon combination possibly the most famous and fearsome corner in all of motor racing, followed later in the lap by the flat-out top speed Blanchimont turn.

It promised to be an entertaining weekend of racing. Team Technik had been very busy. Racing prep meant increasingly long days as the race approached: complete brake and transmission rebuild, suspension rebuild, tire remount and rebalance, and a myriad of other processes. To add to all this: the impending auditions for a co-driver to replace Michael.

Stella's advert read:

Driver Auditions for Top GT3 Team:

Team Technik–one of the top teams in the WRF GT3 Euro Championship–is seeking a paying co-driver for the balance of the season. Do you have what it takes to compete with the best? If you think you do and you have the proper racing credentials, Team Technik has an opportunity for you to further your racing career and fulfill your racing dreams.

Location: Rockingham Race Circuit

Date: 25-27 June

Practice: Friday 25 June. You may use your own car for practice sessions or rent one directly from Rockingham Race Circuit.

Test Session #1: Saturday 26 June: 10:00h to 16:00h

Test Session #2: Sunday 27 June: 10:00h to 16:00h. Prior to the audition, each applicant must provide the following:

- ⌐Completed Application (available on the Team Technik website)
- ⌐Recent Physical/Medical record
- ⌐Racing Curriculum Vitae
- ⌐WRF Competition License, Class G, or documentation from WRF indicating that license
- will be granted before 15 July.
- ⌐Audition fee of £2500 (non refundable)

Contact: Stella Beru at Team Technik (info@teamtechnik.co.uk)

Stella had received dozens of emails, faxes and phone call solicitations with interest from (hopefully) well-heeled racers, their agents as well as many others who simply wanted to try their hand at driving a race car. She spent hours every day screening each applicant's qualifications, which included making sure they had the resources for a substantial financial commitment to the team. Michael Llewellyn had put up £100,000 per race. But since the team was in a bind, the three directors knew the amount had to be somewhat flexible. Thinking about this put even more pressure on them to find other ways to fund the team.

While dealing with the co-driver applications, Stella was also responsible for travel plans and logistics, hotel and restaurant reservations. Spa was a drive-away race, so the team had to travel together. As the team transport only held the racing Porsche and its equipment, she rented a small transit bus to transport team members, luggage and other supplies.

And since the race was a big deal, the sponsors would definitely attend. She was responsible for securing their VIP passes and their invitations to the most desirable pre- and post-race functions.

Race day found Marc braced for the onslaught of questions during the Spa race weekend. He knew the sponsors and the racing press would ask about Michael's replacement and how Marc intended to build on the team's in-the-points successes. When they arrived, he tried to stay close to the team pits and close to Bala, who was the buffer between the world outside and the team. But the more Marc thought about it, the more he realized that this weekend was an opportunity. If he could shape every interview into a Team Technik sales pitch, the sponsors and the press would take it from there. It was time to turn this story around, from a setback for Team Technik to an opportunity for a talented, ambitious (and rich) aspiring driver.

Patting Bala on the back, Marc turned and left the pit area and ventured out into the racing world in search of the racing organizers and the press. Minutes later he spotted Elaine Bollard chatting up Pieter Dannenberg, the director of Racing Productions, Inc. (RPI), the company that organized and put on the various GT race series for the WRF. Just the two he wanted to schmooze. He headed straight for them.

"Elaine! Pieter! What racing conspiracy are you up to?"

"Marc, dear! Pieter and I were just talking about Team

Technik. What's your next move?"

"First, thanks for covering our search for a new co-driver. And Pieter, thanks for your help in getting the word out too."

"You know Marc, we have a commitment to the integrity of our teams and frankly everyone loves Team Technik. How would it appear if one of our more popular teams simply faded away? That wouldn't be good for business," he joked

"Not to mention bad for the press," Elaine added.

"Our driver search is getting a great response. I really appreciate the help you've given us"

"Marc, can I cover the live driver testing?"

"I hate to say it, but not this time, Elaine. These guys aren't pros. They'll be under a lot of pressure just trying out in front of me without sticking a mic in front of their faces."

She hesitated for a second still trying to figure out how to turn this around for BRTV and be in the game when it came to covering the latest updates from Team Technik "I see. But maybe you can give BRTV a status update, one that makes the highlight news deadline?"

"Done," finished Marc.

"Done," grinned Elaine.

A black Mercedes E55 sat near the Ticinese neighborhood of Milano, Italy just across the street from Parco Ales-
sandrina Rivizza, its motor running, steam curling from its
quad exhaust. A short heavy-set man emerged from the
park. His long pasty black hair stuck to his head like a wet
mop, his unkept splotchy beard clung to his face and neck
revealing sunken cheeks, a beak-like nose and deep set almost sunken dark eyes. He walked towards Via Vignola. He
looked like he needed both a bath and a shave. He approached the driver's side of the Mercedes and bent down
to peer into the window. The window slid down and the
silver haired, dark bearded man inside nodded his head towards the passenger door. The man walked around the car,
opened the door and sat down heavily with a grunt.

"Brancato?" The fat man nodded.

"Stefan?" The dark bearded man smiled.

Brancato started coughing, the phlegm catching in his
throat, rattling his frame. The dark bearded man, Uli Petrovski using an alias, wished he could spray disinfectant on
his passenger from his head to his feet.

"You OK?"

"Allergies. Always Allergies."

"Sounds worse."

"Hmmm." He sat silently for a moment, then, "How can
I help you Stefan?"

"I am in need of information."

"Everyone is." Brancato smirked, knowing that with information came payment. And information was his currency.

Stefan pulled out a small felt bag, carefully untied it and poured a half dozen perfect diamonds in his hand. He rolled them around for a second and moved his hand closer to Brancato. The other man reached out to pick one up, but Stefan snapped his hand shut.

"May I see?" He pulled a loupe from his pocket. Stefan selected the largest one, placing it between his thumb and forefinger and dropped it into Brancato's open palm. He snatched it up and held it to the loupe examining it closely.

"This is flawless. A perfect diamond. Hmmm, there is a mark. Strange, I am not familiar with it. Oh, it's…" But he did not finish the sentence as another man opened the back passenger door and quickly got in the car. He was a large man with a barrel chest, sporting a coal black beard, short black hair and dark sunglasses. He did not look very friendly.

"Oh, this is my associate. Call him Parker." Parker just sat, boring tiny holes into Brancato's head.

"Oh, I see."

"Please continue."

"You are not supposed to have these. Nobody is. Where did you get them."

"Fell into my hands, so to speak."

"One does not come across Nazi diamonds easily." A tiny thought was forming in the back of Brancato's mind that maybe he should not have taken this meeting.

"Oh this? It's just a bauble. Meant to get your attention. You're paying attention, right?"

"Yes, you have it."

"Good. We are seeking information and we were told you can provide it. Now I will ask this just once. You need to answer correctly, you only have one chance to get the answer right."

"What's in it for me?"

"Ah. WIIFM. A true businessman."

Uli continued, "Answer correctly, you Brancato, get to live."

Brancato swallowed hard. At that second, he knew he should not have taken the meeting.

"There is someone who we only know as The Diamond Merchant. He controls a vast swath of the diamond trade. We want to know how to get to him."

"I, I don't know." He heard the click of a trigger being pulled back and the press of a gun against the back of his head.

"Funny, we heard you did." With that Uli pulled out of his parking spot and threaded his way across the southern part of Milano to the industrial neighborhood of Buccinasco. Inside the car, complete silence. Uli/Stefan glad to let the tension build, Brancato wondering if he was about to die and Parker simply holding a gun to the back of the man's head. The Mercedes entered a warehouse off Via Venato, the garage door closing behind them with a metallic clang.

Brancato was yanked from the car by Parker and placed in a hard metal chair in the middle of an empty warehouse, his hands and feet strapped to the chair with thick industrial grade zip-ties. He could not move. He sat blinking his eyes, tears stream down his face, wondering if he would make it out alive.

"I have decided to give you another chance. I will ask one more time. Answer correctly, you live. Pretty simple. What do you know about the Diamond Merchant?"

"I—I don't know how to reach him. He cut me off a long time ago."

"Ah, now we are getting somewhere. Continue."

"I did some middleman work for him several years back. But I took more cut then agreed. He blackballed me in the diamond trade. I want from being a well-respected diamond trader to penniless."

"That's too bad." Uli raised his gun to Brancato forehead.

"No wait! Please! Give me a chance." Uli did not lower the gun.

"Go on, really your life is hanging in the balance here."

"There is a man. Goes by Horowicz, he has a small, very secure office in central Milano. He does business with the Diamond Merchant. Except we do not call him that. He is simply called 'The Client.'"

"Interesting. The Client. How do the diamond transactions go down?"

"I'm not sure. The Client frequently changes protocols."

"And that's it?"

"Yes, please, that's all I know."

"See, it just takes a little pressure, and you can be persuaded to reveal what you know."

Broncato looked up at and smiled thinking that he was saved. Instead Uli squeezed the trigger putting a hole in the front of Brancato's head and his brains behind on the floor.

"And too bad your precious WIIFM has played out. Call for a cleanup crew." Uli told Parker.

"Right." He made the call.

Rene Dufour was busy also. He spent several days running the newly modified Maserati Quattroporte GT S through its paces after getting it from Hector. He had one client request for a new Engagement. But he had also accepted a "low factor" Engagement from another *Driver* who had somehow managed to double-book himself. The Engagement was a high priority, so Rene agreed to it for a handsome price. He would earn every euro.

The cargo pick up was in Monterosso al Mare, an exquisite coastal enclave in the Italian Cinqueterra region. He pulled into the basement parking area of a grand Palazzo tucked right into the Italian coast. The large steel gate rolled open to let him in, and upon entering he found himself in a sea of four-wheeled, six and seven figure exotica: Bentley Continental R's, Roll Royce Phantoms, Bugatti Veyron's, even a Pagani Zonda. Rene discovered even he could be impressed.

A dark man dressed in a brown suit approached the Maserati and rapped lightly on the glass. Rene opened the window. The man handed Rene a sheet of embossed, expensive paper: the Engagement rules.

*You will not initiate any conversation, eye contact or any other form of communication with your passenger.

*You will not use the rear view mirror to look at the passenger; you may only use it to evaluate the traffic behind you.

*If the passenger communicates with you, you will give very brief/direct responses.

*You will take your passenger to the following address in

Brussels, only stopping once for fuel and a personal/re-stroom break.

*With one exception, that being the time your passenger is in the restroom, you must keep your passenger close by, always within your sight.

*Failure to deliver the passenger to the appointed desti-nation within fourteen hours will forfeit the fee.

These rules are for your protection and sanity. Keep this document if you agree to the terms, or hand it back and depart as the Engagement is then null and void.

"For protection and sanity?" What is up with that? Ah well, I like a puzzle. What is life without a challenge? He put the document into his jacket pocket.

Marc could almost taste the adrenalin as he and the other racers lapped the track, holding their positions behind the pace car in anticipation of the flying start. They had struggled with the balance of the car during qualifying so Team Technik had qualified eighth, which meant that he was starting near the front of the field, right behind the faster cars, such as Luis DeSilva's Porsche GT 3 RS, Paul Matthews' Audi R8 and of course Luca Marchesotti's Fer-rari. Less than a minute later, the pace car pulled into the pit entry and the race began.

Coming into the first corner, the wicked 180 degree hairpin at La Source, Annika Ammensen's Team VGR BMW Alpina B6 sat on Marc's tail, trying to get inside on the turn. Marc fought her off and increased the Porsche's speed, accelerating flat out of the hairpin, approaching Eau Rouge— a corner not just to be negotiated, but conquered. A racer has to trust his car and roar through without lifting the throttle as the car compresses to the suspension stops, lurching left, then right. Next up, Raidillon, also taken flat out as the race cars again compress, going back to the right, the extreme G-forces pulling on a driver's neck muscles, straining them to the limit. The racers rocketed up the long Kemmel straight, never lifting the throttle, always accelerating. Marc checked his mirrors to see Annika fall victim to Aric Vanderpool's #11 BFR Viper. Shifting from sixth gear down to third to take Les Combes and Malmedy, Marc noticed up ahead of him Eddie Kendricks' #08 Reggio-Fina Ferrari, struggling for grip, the car's tires not yet up to optimal race temperature. Going wide through Rivage, Marc swung inside and past him, heading up the short straight before the lefthander Pouhon, leaving Eddie behind to battle with Aric.

After Pouhon the track flowed left-right-left-right through several turns. Then, coming out of Curve Paul Frere (named after the famous racer/journalist), the track straightened out, allowing the drivers to pour it on. The Porsche roared up the straight before the fast Blanchimont, closing on sixth-place, fellow American, Paul Matthews.

Marc took the fast corner flat out; neck muscles rigid, willing the struggling tires to maintain their grip.

Torturing his brakes as he came up on the Bus Stop Chicane (an actual bus stop when there was no race), Marc closed quickly on Matthews' #19 Team Lockner Audi R8. They went through the chicane nose to tail and powered past the start/finish line to complete lap one, heading into La Source to start the battle all over again.

Back and forth, Paul Matthews' Audi and Marc's Porsche battled for position. This was the kind or racing that Marc loved, really mixing it up with racers who knew what they were doing. The TV cameras loved the fight between the two Americans battling for sixth place too; punching and counterpunching, trying to gain track position. Struggling to outrun one another, they soon overtook fifth-place Martin Fincher, who was burdened with a 25 kg penalty-ballast for a post-race infraction at Silverstone earlier in the season. Sweeping past him running down the Kemmel Straight, they continued their duel. Lap after lap they pushed forward, gaining on the leaders. But before they could overtake fourth place Charlie Mashburn in the #37 Team Caldor-Reyes Corvette Z06, it was the half-way mark. Time for the round of pit stops with the required driver change.

Marc and Paul were at the top of their game, professionals who trusted each other, doing what they loved. As he rolled into the pits he thought how different it was from going head-to-head with a racer like Luca, who was, unfortunately, not unique in his willingness to force another racer into a wall. Marc was sorry he had to relinquish the car to Michael for the second half, but those were the rules. He rolled to a stop and Michael opened the door. They moved in a blur, exchanging a few words about how the Porsche was running as they helped one another change places; meanwhile the pit crew cleaned the dirty windshield, intake ducts and changed the tires with a choreographed economy of motion that Bruno Mars would have admired. Thumbs up, the door slammed shut, internal hydraulic jacks dropped the Porsche and its already-spinning new tires onto the track as Michael peeled out, leaving two long, black rubber streaks in his wake.

Marc went to the pit wall and joined Bala keeping watch over the race-car telemetry. They gave each other a thumbs up as Bala handed Marc a headset.

"That was great Marc! I think we may come in fourth or even better."

"Yeah, if Michael keeps his foot in it and doesn't make any mistakes, we should be OK."

"Michael," Bala shouted into the headset, "Keep your foot in it and no mistakes mate!!" As if Michael did not know that already.

In the quiet of the underground parking, Rene heard a large door open and shut. He thought about the large fee he would earn, even with an assured low danger factor, this one paid extremely well, maybe too well. *There must be* some *problem*, he thought. *If not danger, what?* High heels clicked on cement as three new people approached the Quattroporte. He unlocked the doors, got out and opened a rear door. A man and a woman accompanied a small, slender young woman in an expensive black dress and killer Christian Louboutin shoes with four-inch heels. A very smart black hat with a partial veil completed her ensemble.

Prada—or possibly Armani—maybe I'm taking her to a Mafia funeral.

She said something to the man in Italian he didn't catch—dialect, no doubt. It sounded insulting and Rene noticed that the man winced. Her multiple pieces of custom-made Louis Vuitton luggage loaded safely in the trunk, she got into the car and settled in with her tiny Prada purse and a large water bottle. The man reached in and buckled the seat belt for her. Then he quickly stood back, allowing the woman to come close. Rene realized the woman was his passenger's mother.

Strange, it looks like they cannot get away from my passenger fast enough. Pretty little thing, but pouty. Doubtless a handful.

"Do we need to go through this again Mina?"

"I do not see why I have to go, my tan is just getting decent, I hate looking like some pale freak in the summer.

Brussels, *hmmph*, why not send me to my own funeral instead?"

"We have been through this dozens of times, your stepfather wants you to spend time with his family."

Without missing a beat, Mina countered, "And for the hundredth time Mamma, I do not want to! My friends are here and I like to party with them."

"Your friends? Those money sucking shits that drink our liquor, eat all our food, and trash our house? I am finished with those pathetic, money grubbing excuses of too hip, too trendy jackasses you call your friends.!"

With questionable logic, considering her position, Mina shouted, "I'm not going. You can't make me!"

"Phone—give me your phone. NOW!"

Looking afraid and busted, Mina folded her arms and looked straight ahead. "I do not have it."

Her mother stared at her, hand extended, saying nothing. Finally relenting, Mina pulled the phone out of her purse and held it out to her mother, who snatched it.

"You will get it back when you return, you ungrateful little bitch!" The mother slammed the door and put a porcelain smile on her face.

"Bob, your name is Bob, right?"

"Yes Signora."

"Good luck—just get her there. The other *Drivers* we have hired have failed."

"I will Signora."

"Good, because your fee is very generous. We expect nothing less. Now go."

He entered the Brussels address into his trip computer/GPS and with a shrug, departed. It would be a long drive, almost 1000 km. And with only one mandated stop, better not to drink a lot of fluids along the way. Rene glanced in the rear-view mirror at the huge 2+ litre bottle that his passenger held in her lap and hoped she could hold it in too.

From Monterosso, he headed toward Genoa, then northeast for the long segment leading into Milano, which he skirted, passing near Como and into Switzerland. His passenger's mood seemed to have gone from sullen to morose. Now she was sniffling, and he heard her say, very softly, "They never let me do what I want to do—never. They are so cruel, so mean." Then more sobbing.

Rene kept to the rules and said nothing. Finally, outside of Strasbourg, his passenger stopped moaning. She lifted her veil and announced, "Please stop. I have to pee."

"OK."

"Make it soon!"

"OK."

The GPS display showed an *Agip* service station 10 km ahead. A few moments later, he pulled into the gas area, got out and touched the iPhone, locking the doors, keeping her locked safely inside. He opened the gas cap and put several Euros into the fuel pump's payment slot and started pumping high octane gasoline into the Maserati. He also glanced into the trashcan and removing an oil container, turned so that the pump obscured the view and relieved himself into the container. He needed to keep an eye on the girl. Besides, his client was paying more than enough to compensate for his having to use outdoor plumbing. He finished and dropped the container back into the trash. The refueling completed, he got back into the car, heading to the main building. He noticed the girl staring at him.

"Is that how your father taught you?"

"What? How to properly put gas in my car?"

"You know what I mean. You relieved yourself standing in front of me."

"Did you actually see anything?"

"No, but I know what you were doing. That was disgusting."

"Well if you must know, that would be my mother who taught me. And you are no lady to have watched."

"How dare you talk to me like that."

"Based on how you spoke to your mother earlier, you have no room to talk."

"Bastard, what do you know? Nobody talks to me like that."

"Maybe they should …."

He pulled up in front of the main building, got out and touched the iPhone to unlock the rear door. She got out fast and twisted away, but he grabbed her firmly by the arm.

"Do not touch me."

"Then do not try to run away."

She pouted as they walked inside. He guided her to the women's restroom, waited ten seconds, then sprinted to the refrigerated display and purchased two cans of iced espresso, paying with cash as she emerged. She glanced in his direction and made a bolt for the door. Rene had anticipated this and quickly closed the distance. She tried to run, but her dress's tight skirt, not to mention those four-inch heels, kept her from gaining much speed. Rene caught up to her and tried to put his arm around her, but she pushed him away. This was not going to be easy! But then he thought, *Oh yes it is!* Seizing her hand firmly, he pulled her close, then put his arm gently around her waist and marched her outside.

"I command you let me go! Let go you idiot! I will not be treated like this. Let go now!"

She continued yelling and kicking as he approached the car.

Opening the door Rene said "OK you win, I will put you

down now" as he dumped her into the seat with a thud and slammed her door. He quickly retrieved the phone and locked her in. People were staring at him. He smiled very wide, shrugged his shoulders and said, "Teenagers! What can you do? *Mon Dieu*, this one is making me very old!"

He slid behind the wheel and got the Quattroporte moving. He told her to buckle her belt. Instead, she simply slumped down into the seat and cried. He waited until she seemed to be winding down. As he waited, he drank the espressos.

"Are you done yet?"

"I hate you!"

"You have that privilege. Now put on your belt or I will do it for you," he commanded.

She made a face at him in the mirror as she clicked the buckle.

Michael did indeed bring home the car in fourth place, behind Luis DeSilva in first, Marchesotti in second and a well-deserved third going to team owner-driver Anton Lockner. The result had everyone on Team Technik giddy with excitement.

It was a positive sign, Marc thought *if you wanted to be superstitious. Trying something new, the WRF decided to let today's finishing order be the starting grid for the race on Sunday.*

Sunday dawned with a low gray sky and the threat of rain. This meant a different set up and a different strategy. Marc and the rest of Team Technik arrived at Spa about 9:00. The clouds by then had opened up and there was a steady rain. Marc and Bala had already agreed on a wet-race setup. This meant water-shedding tires, of course, and modifying the aero package to force the car down harder onto the track's surface. This greatly improved traction in the wet, but sacrificed straight-line speed. Because most of their fellow racers would follow a similar program, the competition would still be fierce.

At 13:29, with the cars lined up on the grid, there was even more tension than usual. The rain was steady and hard now, reducing vision as well as traction, creating even more opportunities for error. It was Michael Llewellyn's last race with Team Technik and the whole team was rooting for him. Despite his leaving them short of cash and with little notice, he was a very good racer and a great teammate.

At promptly 13:30, under full course caution and behind the Ford Focus RS pace car, the twenty-five GT3 cars stayed bunched in formation. The race stewards wanted to make sure the cars were ready for the conditions before turning them loose in the rain. Finally, after three laps running in formation under caution, the Stewards called the pace car in. The Green Flag dropped and the race was on. Normally a rolling start meant tight-packed fury as the cars scramble for a better track position. But this day, they were treading the track carefully, trying to find traction.

Michael Llewellyn loved racing in the rain. He liked the extra layer of challenge, driving on a different race line, hunting for the less used, less greasy parts of the race circuit. During a normal race, cars lay rubber down on the racing line, but in heavy-rain conditions that racing line works against the driver as it becomes extremely slippery. There are some racers, known as *Rainmiesters*, who excel in these conditions. Many don't. Michael was one of the ones who got it. He drove off-line, only using the turn apex and track-out points when he had to. As the cars struggled for grip, Michael easily moved past both Matthews and DeSilva. Marchesotti had already maneuvered past DeSilva to take the lead and Michael was now right behind him as they completed the first lap under green. Just up ahead, Michael saw the heavier spray of Marchesotti's Ferrari and calculated where he could make his move.

Watching the Ferrari for several laps, Michael noticed Marchesotti slowed his heavier car more at Bus Stop Chicane. Michael smiled. He did not need to slow so much in his lighter Porsche. On the run up after Blanchimont, Michael pressed harder and overtook a surprised Luca Marchesotti just as they had to brake hard for Bus Stop. Michael won the corner, coming out on the left side of the track in order to take the proper turn in. He grinned. He had beaten the Ferrari and the corner was his! He briefly forgot about Luca's nasty habits, suddenly realizing that Luca had released his brakes early as he closed on Michael's left. At the last second, Michael jerked the Porsche to the right, simultaneously hitting the throttle to keep the impact area small. Both cars pirouetted in perfect unison, looking like they had choreographed the slide as they spun around together and slid off track.

The Porsche and Ferrari touched. The Ferrari knocked off the Porsche's carbon-fiber fender blisters extending across the wide tires. It caused mostly cosmetic and only a little airflow damage. The Ferrari fared much worse, losing its front splitter which exploded into pieces as the heavier car spun into the grass. The Porsche came to a stop on a paved tarmac area that was part of the actual bus stop, while the Ferrari stopped just past the tarmac in the wet grass. Michael had used one of the first rules of racing: when spinning and unable to control the car, the racer must put "both feet in"; but with the new semi-automatic transmission instead he briefly put the car in neutral to keep momentum going. Michael's maneuver worked perfectly. Slamming the shifter into first, he threaded back safely onto the track. Brief as it was, in the time it took to spin out, downshift and get back on the track, Michael had dropped from second place to twelfth. Nevertheless, Michael and Team Technik were still in the race.

The same could not be said for Luca Marchesotti. After coming to a stop in the grass and stalling out, Luca restarted the car, slammed the gear lever into first and in a fit of rage dumped the clutch. The engine screamed, hit the rev limiter, and the Ferrari didn't budge. Luca was thoroughly stuck in mud. He raged, pedal flat on the floor, spraying mud and grass all over the red Ferrari and over-revving the engine until it overheated and shut itself down in clouds of steam.

Michael quickly radioed Bala reporting what had happened, assuring him he was OK. Bala and Marc, also concerned about the car, instructed Michael to take it easy the next lap or two. If there was any damage to the car, Michael would notice it quickly. As he came back around to Bus Stop Chicane he noticed Luca standing near the track, being restrained by track-side Marshals. Through the spray of the rain Luca saw the Porsche with Michael in it. Luca took his helmet off and hurled it at the passing Porsche, shaking his fist at Michael. There would be hell to pay somewhere. Luca—of course—would dodge the blame, but not the fine from the track marshals for throwing his helmet onto the racetrack. In fact, Michael thought, Luca's team manager was probably heading to the track stewards already to file a complaint. Michael thumbed the radio and barked into the microphone inside his helmet.

"Luca just threw his helmet at me! And, flipped me off!"

"Did he hit the car?" asked Bala.

"It's Luca; he couldn't hit shit, except maybe one of his poor mechanics! They'll probably file a complaint against us. But it was a clean pass, damn it"

"Don't worry, Michael," he heard Marc say. "If anyone is looking for blame I'll tell them to have Luca look in his rearview mirror. The bastard staring back is the culprit. Just take care of things on the track and Bala and I will take care of that whiney little prick."

Refocusing on the task at hand, namely piloting a race car with more than 450 bhp in a driving rain, Michael finished the last laps of his last stint in the Team Technik Porsche. At the mid-way point he brought the car in for the mandatory pit stop and driver change. Michael and Marc did a quick hug and backslap as they changed places, pleased that they were still in the race and that bad Karma had settled down on Luca Marchesotti like flies on shit.

Marc strapped himself into the racing harnesses and as the car came down off its internal hydraulic jacks, roared off to complete the race.

Michael may have been adept at driving in the rain, but Marc was *der Rainmiester*. He knew that if every race were a wet race, he would be unbeatable. But they were still a long way back in tenth place and the race was starting to wind down. So he pressed on, using his feet, dancing them on the pedals. Moving and guiding the steering wheel, talking directly with the front wheels, telling them exactly where to find the perfect path, he reeled the other cars in. Braking harder and deeper, up to the point right before the tires aquaplaned, he passed Simon Portele driving the #47 Team Siena Ford GT as they went into La Source, gaining ninth place. Next he out-braked Paulo Benetti, driving the #57 Team AGC Audi R8 as the two dove into Rivage and Marc moved into eighth.

And still he was not finished. Nakamura in the Nissan GT-R was next. The Nissans had Super-four-wheel drive, which was supposed to be superb in the rain, but today he was no match for a charging Marc Lange. Now seventh, Marc continued his blistering pace. He distantly heard Bala in his earphone telling him to keep it up!

Kind of an understatement, thought Marc. He asked Bala for the gap between him and the sixth-place car and when Bala told him that it was Portago driving the #17 Ford GT, Marc knew that Felix would be having a handful driving the Ford in the rain. Quickly closing the gap, Marc passed him on the *outside* as they went through Pouhon—the Ford simply could not match Marc's pace in the slippery wet.

Two laps to go, Marc set his sights on coming in fifth. Just up ahead was Matilde Gertner struggling with an ill-handling BMW Alpina B6. Marc kept the gap consistent to give himself a chance to react as they approached the Chicane—turn eighteen—then he made his move, out-braking her into the Chicane and moving into fifth. He swept past the start/finish yelling into the headset and pumping his fist, relishing the sheer joy of his drive in the rain.

"Wow! That was fantastic. What a drive!" yelled Marc.

"Congrats mate, you were unstoppable today." shouted Bala in response.

"Five more laps and I would have had this one!"

"Next time Marc. Next time for sure!"

"OK Bala. Tell Michael he drove a great drive!"

"He knows Marc, he knows."

Continuing on towards Brussels, Rene drove in silence while his passenger alternately sobbed and glowered. As they passed north of Strasbourg and approached Saarbrucken at over 180 kph, she finally spoke up.

"You know, they're horrible people. They are sending me to stay in a hellhole!"

"Well, you should fit right in."

"You bastard, what do you know? They are evil. Monsters! I don't want to stay in fucking Brussels! My stepfather's family is full of idiots. I hate them!"

"Well they should be happy to see you too."

"Shut up!"

"Forgive me if I don't seem sympathetic, but you do not appear to have been deprived. If the place I am taking you to is anything like the place where I picked you up, surely you can find a way to have fun."

She was quiet for all of eleven seconds then, "It is true that they have plenty of money, but you do not understand at all—how could you? They are boring! I will die of boredom."

"I don't know—Brussels is not that bad if you give it half a chance."

"Well I like to have fun and I cannot imagine that fucking Brussels is fun."

She continued to whimper and cry but Rene did not feel the tug. You know how babies have different cries? One is the cry that says, "I'm tired. I'm feeling crabby." You know they just need a nap. And if it will be a few minutes before you can get them into the crib, you can stand it. But then there's the cry when they're really in distress, frightened or in pain. Who can resist that sound? You have to come running, to find what's wrong and fix it, whatever it is. Rene's cargo had perfected the adult female version of that cry, the call of the tender *gamine* who is helpless, abandoned. To a male, that sound can be more alluring than a glimpse of cleavage, transforming him into the heroic knight who will rescue her, slay her dragon, save her young body.

Too bad for her, he thought. *I learned to be immune to that call many long years ago. My God. No wonder her parents want to send her away. They probably need the break from her!*

As if she had heard his thoughts, she went from damsel to dragon before he could take a breath. "Damn you stop this car. Help! Help me! I am being kidnapped! He is a rapist! Call the police! Somebody! Please! Help me!" She had removed one of her €700 shoes and was hammering on the window with the heel.

"Stop that at once you brat or I swear to you I will strap

your arms to your sides with tie wraps and a piece of tape across your mouth!" She was so startled by his tone that she stopped screaming and dropped her shoe.

"Don't you dare talk to me that way. I forbid it."

"Oh? You forbid it?"

"I already told you *nobody* talks to me like that."

"Well, I already said that maybe *someone* should. I think you are a spoiled little brat."

"I'm not listening to you anymore."

"What you need is a good spanking, little girl."

"Who will spank me—you?"

With that he pulled into the emergency lane and slammed on the brakes and came to a stop. He turned to her and said, "Yes. Maybe I will."

With that she started laughing, laughing at Rene, the situation, the fact that no one, *no one* had ever spoken to her like that.

"Okay Mister tough guy, I'll be a good girl. Just drive and get me to Brussels—so I can waste away in that gray shit of a city, with no parties, no sun and a family that only wants to love me."

Rene pulled back out onto the highway.

Several minutes later, she tried again. "You know you already broke all the rules."

"Oh, I do not think so. You started our pleasant conversation off on such a nice note."

Trying a different approach, now to win him over, she continued, "So, do you have any children?"

"Yes, I do. But they are now grown."

"Well how would you feel if your daughter got sent away for the summer to the other side of Europe? What would her mother say? Don't you have a heart?"

"*One*, my daughter does live on the other side of the world. *Two*, my wife and daughter can't stand to be in the same room. They haven't spoken since she graduated from college, by mutual agreement. *Three*, you are a young woman. Act like it."

"So you have no sympathy for me?"

"No, zero. I am paid to drive you from one place to another. My sympathy level may increase a little bit when I put the fee into my jacket pocket and drive off. So …."

"Bastard! Our conversation is over!"

"Suits me fine, my dear. I did not want to begin one anyway."

At last Rene pulled into Brussels and arrived at the address he'd been given earlier in the day. It had taken him just twelve and a half hours to complete the drive and it had been the LONGEST twelve and a half hours of his life that he could remember. He didn't care if he didn't get paid—

well *almost* didn't care. He approached the house, or Chateau rather, it was *énorme*. Past the large double gates, the central drive was surrounded by gardens and steps that swept up to the front entrance; they were positively regal. He wondered who this belonged to, not that it mattered.

There was a man waiting in the lower portico. As Rene pulled up, the man approached the Maserati. He signaled for Rene to lower the car window.

"You are on time. I can only hope you followed all the other rules."

"I tried my best," countered Rene, touching a button that popped open the trunk. "And the payment?"

"Yes—yes," said the man as he started to reach into his jacket pocket.

Just then, Mina shouted out from the rear, "Don't pay him. He's a pig! He broke every rule. And he touched my breast."

The man started to back away and move to the rear door to let the passenger out, but Rene's arm snaked out the open window. He grabbed the man's tie and yanked him forward, bouncing his head off the car door frame. Still holding the tie, Rene kicked open the door, knocking the man's feet out from under him. He got out of the car as the man struggled to regain his footing. Rene grabbed the tie again and wrapped it around the man's neck. He pulled his jacket back revealing a holstered pistol to make a point.

"Now listen here, you *prick*. I have had a VERY long day and I completed my Engagement ON TIME. I followed your stupid rules. I did not talk to her unless she started the conversation, which she did time and time again. I did not look at her while she was in the car. And I ABSOLUTELY did not touch her breast. EITHER of them. But I DID have to drive for over 1000 km with a whiney, spoiled brat. Now I want my fucking money! Where is it?"

"Left inside pocket. Take it and leave"

"With pleasure." He relaxed his grip on the man a bit, Rene opened the rear door and motioned for his passenger to get out.

"It's been a delight, my dear."

"Screw you!"

"Charming," replied Rene.

"My father will hear of this."

"Oh, now it's your father? Well it's your mother and step-father who hired me and she told me not to fail."

She glowered at him, a look of pure hate. He shivered but recovered quickly, he had seen that look of pure hatred once before.

"No you moron, not that rich fool of a stepfather, my real father."

Still holding the flunky that came to fetch Mina, Rene held his ground, meeting her angry hateful stare

"My father, Uli Petrovski."

Rene's blood turned to ice at the mention of that name. His stomach heaved. He felt the danger surrounding him just as if he now faced a hooded cobra. He almost dropped the fee on the ground, but it was half-way in his jacket pocket. As it hit the bottom of the pocket, it suddenly felt very heavy. Her look of pure hate. Yes, he had seen it before and unfortunately it was the same as her father's.

"He will hear about this, I promise." She spat with venom and malice as Rene resisted the temptation to shiver.

Recovering as quickly as he could, Rene shot back, "No doubt, my dear—but as your mother wished, at least you have arrived safe and sound. Remember that!"

Releasing the man, he gestured towards the trunk of the Quattroporte. The man retrieved the luggage, slamming the trunk lid shut and the girl turned and quickly walked away.

Uli Petrovski, anybody but him. As soon as he was clear of the Chateau, Rene pulled the Maserati over on a side road and killed the engine. The memories flooded back and normally cool and calm Rene Dufour found he was sweating. The last time Uli Petrovski and Rene had crossed paths two of Uli's henchmen ended up dead. He knew that Uli blamed him, even though he was blameless. The client who had paid for the Engagement had tracked Rene to the warehouse where he was being held prisoner. The client found Rene bound and gagged, tortured to the point that he had given Uli precious information about the cargo Rene was carrying. While Uli was absent from the warehouse, the client killed the two henchmen, freed Rene and grabbed his cargo.

Rene took a long time to get over that failed Engagement. But when he did, it became the driving force for all future Engagements: no matter what it took, he would complete every Engagement. He would never again fail. And he would never let fear master him.

Now he hoped Uli would not find out about his daughter. Rene hoped but he was also a realist. *I am getting too old for this shit. Now it is decided, I have to find and train a protégé.*

Fingering the fat envelope, Rene felt that he might have actually been underpaid. He placed the envelope in his in-dash safe, put the car in gear and gladly drove out of Brussels. He wanted to put as many miles as possible between the memory of Uli Petrovski and his next Engagement.

"What did you find out?" Asked Mr. X.

"You can tell Bronzit that his source was not very good. Still, I did manage to get another name. Horowicz. This source is said to be in active business with The Client. I am looking for him now."

"The Client?"

"Yes, that is what his middlemen call him."

"Good."

"And Bronzit's source?"

"Played out. All the way."

"Ah, it was your call."

"Find this Horowicz and find a way to leverage him. Make it clear that we do not fuck around."

"Yes Mr. X."

Stella Beru and Marc Lange, his winnings tucked into his pocket, walked close together through the rain. They were both soaked, deep in a discussion of BRTV and one Elaine Bollard. Stella was schooling Marc on how to use the fact that Elaine was obviously attracted to him and how to leverage that attraction to benefit the team.

"It doesn't mean you have to sleep with her, Marc. Just give her the impression that under the right circumstance you might."

"What about April? She'd eventually find out and probably cut off my balls."

"Marc, you're not listening. I'm not saying you should have a shag fest off to the side. Elaine just wants to think she has a chance, maybe in a moment when your guard is down. Pretend to give the girl a chance."

"Geez Stella, I apparently have a lot to learn. I've been a one-woman man my whole life."

"Nothing turns a woman on more than a one-woman man. She's just hoping she's the next."

"I'm serious. You could teach me a lot."

"You have no idea." Stella's smile said it all.

"Lange!" An irate and very hostile Luca Marchesotti walked quickly towards them, along with one of his crew, a bundle of muscles known as Ross Stanton. He had that crazed look of someone on the edge of losing it. His black hair straggled down into his face, little rivulets of water streaming down, his dark eyes entirely rimmed with white.

"I'll have a word with you Lange."

"Why, Luca? Come to apologize for your on-track behavior?"

"Perhaps the woman, she should not listen to what I have to say to you."

"Come off it Marchesotti. Whatever you have to say to Marc you can say in front of me."

Marchesotti shrugged and turned to Marc. "Lange, you know there is a pecking order in racing, and I am personally offended by your *amateur* co-driver's bad behavior."

"Oh really? First, that "amateur" whipped your ass today. And second, for some strange reason I was under the impression we were all racing to win. Am I missing something here?"

"Lange, you should realize the big teams take the top places and the little teams, like yours, finish at the bottom. You and your boys need to learn to stay away from me on the track, because the next time you or your co-driver are crowding me for track position, I guarantee that you will get the message."

"Let me get this straight. You're telling me that my team should just give up track position to you and anyone else that is a top team."

"You have to earn my respect to get those positions."

"Respect, bullshit! I'm a better racer than you will ever be and you will never get my respect just because your team has more backing and more money."

Marc had had enough. He took a step towards Luca and, as he expected, Luca took a step back toward his crew member.

Coward. Maybe on the track you have big balls, but off the track you're a pussy. Marc took another step, his face inches away from Luca's. Puffing out his chest, Stanton glowered at Marc.

"Listen you Fuck. I have the respect of the other teams. Team Technik may not have the budget of Team Parabolic, but we have what you will never have."

Luca swallowed before he answered, trying to summon

up a bit of courage, now that Marc had called his bluster.

"What could you possibly have that I do not already possess?"

"A soul." Laughing, Marc and Stella turned and walked away, leaving a gaping Luca Marchesotti in their wake.

"Good one, love. You left that weaselly bastard speechless. Personally, I'd have put my knee right into his balls. Oh wait, he probably doesn't have any."

Team Technik celebrated that evening in the tiny Hotel Moulin in nearby Malmedy, Belgium. A fourth place and a fantastic fifth place in the rain, after spinning off the track! It had been a successful weekend. Gate receipts were down because of Sunday's rain, so the payout for the weekend was €15,000. But because of the combined race results, the team was presented with three extra sets of tires for the next race, courtesy of Pirelli, the exclusive tire sponsor for the series. The Team Technik brain trust breathed a collective sigh of relief. At last! For once part of the winnings could be used for things besides tires.

This would be the last time they would celebrate with Michael. They wanted to give him a good sendoff and, thanks to the team's performance over the weekend, they were in very good spirits. Besides, one of the sponsors was footing the bill and the beer, wine and Champagne flowed. Still, for Marc, Bala and Stella, concern over team finances kept intruding. The team was close to broke. Marc and Bala had to find a new co-driver who could bring serious funding to the table. The clock was running. Stella agreed to delicately pry more money out of the sponsors.

"The work really starts when we get back," said Bala.

"Yeah, I know. By the way Stella," Marc nodded at one of their sponsors, The Glenkilney Distillery's rep sitting across the room. "Maybe you could start with him."

"Don't worry love, I'm all over it."

Great, thought Marc, *I'm reduced to pimping my people out to get what we need. Shit! I've got to find more funding. I always said to myself that I'd do whatever it takes to win. I guess it's time to man-up and do it.*

He closed his eyes tight allowing the past to surge to the top, *problem is I have—and it cost me the first time. I am not sure I am ready to face that part of Marc Lange again. But I will say one thing—that guy got shit done!*

Horowicz. Just Horowicz, no first name, had a small wholesale diamond operation in central Milano. Access by appointment only. So when the camera showed a stranger standing outside his door, he was not eager to let the stranger enter. Till the man with closely cropped silver hair and dark, closely trimmed beard held up a small bag and emptied the contents into his palm and held it up to the camera. Horowicz looked at the diamonds on the screen. Not fakes, the real thing. Intriguing. He clicked the door open to let the stranger enter.

It had taken time to find Horowicz because he did not want to be found. He had zero online presence, no Facebook, Twitter, nothing. He had scrubbed financials as well. He was for the most part, untraceable. But Uli found one interesting tidbit of information. A lawyer that Horowicz used had not been thorough as Horowicz in erasing every transaction. Uli had discovered a divorce decree that granted custody of Horowicz's only daughter to his now ex-wife. They lived near Toulouse in a small farmhouse with just a bit over a hectare of land. Uli had dispatched an associate that took video of the woman tending her garden, the child arriving at and playing at school and the woman selling her produce at the local farmers' market. Enough to catalog all facets of their carefree and safe livelihood. Except now, it was not safe.

He entered the small inner vestibule. There was a very stout bullet proof window, beyond Horowicz's inner office and sanctum, a small shelf just below with a window that slid up and down. At its base a metal tray covered in velvet. Uli sat at the chair and dropped the diamonds onto the velvet.

"And you are?"

"Stefan."

"They call me Horowicz. Now, what do we have here, what are these?"

"I believe them to be from the Schlisser Diamond shipment that went missing in '46."

"Fssftght." Snorted Horowicz. "Everyone thinks they have some diamonds from the legendary Nazi trove." He reached back and pulled a book that listed diamond trade markings and turned to the appropriate page. Next, he slid open the window and Uli flicked one to the other side of the window. Horowicz picked it up and first looked at it through is eye loupe. His eyes narrowed and there was a sharp intake of breath. He turned and placed the diamond in a much more powerful jeweler's microscope that had a 4K display imbedded in the top. He spent several minutes looking at the tiny gem under extreme magnification, then slowly turned around, looking at this stranger opposite him.

"Where did you get this?"

"I have a source."

"And the others?"

"Check them yourself." Uli said as he swept his hand across the diamonds. The window opened a bit further and Horowicz reached out to pluck the largest one. Exactly as Uli had planned. He reached out and pulled the arm violently through the window, Horowicz pitched forward hitting the window with his head with an audible thwack, stunning him. Next pulled out a knife and slammed it down into the counter just nicking the webbing in between fingers, drawing blood.

"Open the door."

"No," moaned Horowicz.

"The next thrust I slice an artery. You'll bleed out before the police arrived. Now open the door!"

"You'll kill me!"

"Now why would I do that? Co-operate and you live."

"You're just trying to steal my gems."

"Please, I am after something much more subtle. Press the button to unlock the door, do not summons the Police because I will know. Then I will kill you."

The door buzzed. Uli again violently pulled Horowicz again, his head smacking the window. Then he rushed through the unlocked door closing it behind him. Then he went around the vestibule pulling down all the shades. Now–time to deal with Horowicz.

Horowicz came around a few seconds later to find his hands and feet bound to the chair. He could not move. He saw that the Schlisser Diamonds were in a bag sitting on his desk. He turned and focused on the man opposite him. He did not like what he saw, he had been too careless and too greedy. Now a cost of that lapse in judgement would be re-vealed to him.

"I want to know everything you know about someone that is referred to as "The Client".

Horowicz laughed, shaking his head back and forth.

"There is nothing to know, if you did your homework you would know that nobody knows who The Client is or what The Client looks like."

"Fair enough. What we really want to know if how to get to him."

Horowicz shook his head back and forth—no. Uli pulled out his phone and held it before Horowicz and hit play. Horowicz saw his ex-wife and daughter, it was edited like a normal day in their life, except to Horowicz he knew it was to show him that they had them and could get to them in seconds. He could not protect them.

"What do you want?"

"How does a shipment go down?"

Horowicz swallowed hard. He knew what he was about to say would change is life. For the worse.

"I receive an alert via secure fax. The number is untraceable. It usually arrives a day or two before a courier drops a shipment. I pick it up. Sometimes it is here in Milano, sometimes elsewhere. I measure and catalog each diamond in the shipment and send the count to another secure fax number. Then I extract 3% of the total, my fee for transacting the shipment."

"That would be millions. Nice payment for a middleman."

"At least I am smart. Not like that fool Brancato. He got greedy and it cost him his reputation."

"Well actually it cost him his life too." Uli let that statement hang in the air for a second before he continued.

"Do you think that farm in Toulouse was free, or my daughter's private education? I'm careful with my take."

"What happens next."

"The Client never used the same delivery method back to back. But recently he has been using *Drivers* more and more."

"*Drivers*?" Uli's ears perked up. Bob is a *Driver*. He wondered for a second if maybe, just maybe Bob would transact the next Engagement with The Client. If only he were so lucky. Just as quickly he snapped back.

"Well now you work for someone named Mr. X. Play your cards right and you will be far richer than a 3% take. Screw Mr. X and bad things happen. Work with Mr. X and good things happen. Profitable things." He tapped the cell phone to add emphasis. Next, he placed a small cell phone beside Horowicz.

"We'll be in touch. This phone can dial or receive calls from one untraceable number. If something does come up, give us a ring."

Next his knife flicked open. Horowicz drew in a sharp intake of breath as Uli sliced downwards cutting his bonds. Then he turned on his heels and departed, leaving the small sack of diamonds both as payment, a reminder and a warning.

Thankfully, the second Engagement was a simple point-to-point drive, transporting an important passenger from Freiburg, Germany, to Basel, Switzerland for a financial transaction. This one was easy. His passenger used his iPad to watch a movie. Whatever it was, it must have been funny as he chuckled throughout the trip. Rene made a brief attempt to make conversation, but the passenger only held up his index finger and moved it back and forth indicating no talking, only silence. Rene nodded and returned his attention to the road. Actually, after his last Engagement, this suited him perfectly.

He dropped the passenger at the posh Basel Bank Centrale and waited 90 minutes for him to emerge. An SMS text instructed him to take his passenger to a nearby hotel and drop the man at the VIP entrance. As he pulled up, a man approached the Maserati and—at a signal from the passenger—Rene unlocked the passenger-side door. The man held the door open and as the passenger exited, he softly tossed an envelope onto the seat. Just before the door slammed shut, Rene heard the passenger say, "Most enjoyable drive ever. I've arrived completely relaxed." Rene smiled to himself and pulled away.

It was a bit late to return to Dijon, so Rene drove to a nearby luxury hotel. He reached back into the back seat and picked up the thick envelope. He opened it and counted

€6,000; not a bad payday for an easy Engagement. He put
the payment in the inside safe located behind a panel on the
lower dash and exited the Quattroporte, locking it and setting the other security devices as he went inside to get a
room.

It was always best to eat local cuisine, he reflected, so he
dined at a Ratskeller on superb pork Schweinebraten, perfectly crispy layers of skin clothing moist, fork-tender flesh,
accompanied by spaetzle and red cabbage, helped along by
several glasses of the local brew. Following a vigorous walk
around the central city to clear his mind and help with digestion, he returned to his hotel. Not quite ready to fall
asleep, Rene turned on the TV and flipped through the
channels. He stopped on BRTV to get the latest racing
news. Truth was, Rene loved all types of auto racing. He
frequently felt he would have made an excellent racer. He
had the innate car control, skill and patience to become one.
He had even entered many track events in his Renault Megane RS Turbo. But the stars had never aligned for him to
take the leap to full-on racing. Still he enjoyed watching and
critiquing a race. The channel had a report of the GT3 action at Spa the past weekend. A follow-up story about Team
Technik and their search for a paying co-driver came on.
The team needed to replace their current co-driver. A re-
porter named Elaine Bollard told her anchor what a perfect
opportunity this was for a well-heeled or well-connected
racer to drive GT3s and test his or her racing mettle. Marc
Lange's image appeared on-screen talking to Elaine during

one of the week-end's races. Marc had an intensity when he talked about his team and what racing meant to him that intrigued Rene. Not only that, but he appeared to be in excellent physical shape. He certainly gave the impression of being a man who could take care of himself.

I need to find a protégé, but not just anyone. Someone I can trust, someone who won't screw up, who will complete the Engagements and most important, take care of my clients. Hmmm, Marc Lange, racer and team owner—is he desperate enough? Maybe. Maybe that is what I need to do, test my own racing mettle. Maybe Monsieur Lange has what I need too. Could he become a Driver? He has the need. Does he have the balls and the skill to become my protégé? I am going to take a closer look at Team Technik and Monsieur Marc Lange.

Chapter 5

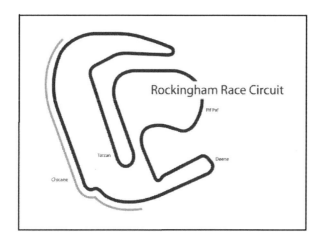

R ene became an expert on WRF GT3 racing. To thoroughly evaluate the talent of this owner/racer, he needed to do his homework. He needed to know *context*. He looked at everything: cars, teams, strategy, schedules, even the rules. After undertaking voluminous research, he now knew that DeSilva came from serious money, Luca Marchesotti was an asshole, Eddie Kendricks hated Yanks and (there were rumors) that the Nissan teams could be bending the rules slightly by running cars with a greater power-to-weight ratio than the rules allowed. However, his principal focus remained on his potential protégé and his team. If Marc was to be the one, Rene needed to know everything about the man.

Marc's background appeared squeaky clean, almost too clean. The guy didn't even have a speeding or parking ticket. He lived alone, paid his bills on time, his longtime girlfriend, whom he rarely saw, was a successful lawyer with a major New York based firm. Rene made a few calls. One of his contacts knew a mechanic who worked for Team Fortunata. Apparently, it was common knowledge that Marc, at DeSilva's invitation, worked out with Team Fortunata's martial arts expert, Jose. And, according to the mechanic, Marc could take care of himself in a fight. Rene tucked that interesting piece of information into his memory for further deliberation. The only thing exceptional about Marc was his racing career. Marc sounded like the perfect candidate for Rene's world.

Rene had more to do before heading to Rockingham racetrack for Team Technik's audition. He got online and downloaded the required forms. He more or less filled them out, leaving big gaps in the personal information area. He realized he needed a Class G WRF license, so he placed a couple of calls to well-connected friends to learn the drill. Easy as popping the cork from a Champagne bottle: send €500 to a specific name and address and a brand-new license came back in the mail.

Now for some fun—back online to do some shopping. He looked at racing suits, boots, gloves and shoes. Rene decided he'd go with all black Sparco driving gear. He bought a black F1-ADV driving suit, black Slalom shoes, black

Profi gloves and finally a complete set of fireproof under-wear and balaclava. A new Bell HP-3 black carbon fiber helmet with black visor completed his look. Rene decided to present himself as a man of mystery to Team Technik: who else but the Man in Black.

He cleared his calendar: no Engagement*s* allowed for au-dition weekend. He called his auto guru and made an ap-pointment for Hector to give the Turbo RS a once over for the trip to the UK. Hector did not stint: lightweight Team Dynamics Pro Race 1.2 wheels, shaved Toyo Proxes RA-1 R-rated tires, a bolt-in roll cage, Sparco Evo seats and a set of Sabelt six-point harnesses. Pro package, all the way. Rene and his Turbo RS were ready to rock and roll.

Team Technik's co-driver test was scheduled for the weekend of June 25-27, with the first day set aside for prac-tice. The next GT3 race was in a few weeks and the team needed to choose the new co-driver ASAP. The team hoped the Friday practice day allowed them to winnow out the worst before the real tests on Saturday and Sunday when each remaining hopeful would take his turn driving with Marc sitting alongside. The team scrapped their first idea, to make the RS Cup car available for the Saturday and Sun-day tests. Team Technik had exactly one race car. A really bad test drive = no race car. Reluctantly, Marc agreed that they would use his personal car, the orange road-rocket Porsche GT3. It had a half roll cage, track-oriented GT2 seats, six-point harness belts, a seriously upgraded race suspension and proper race tires. For the most part, it was a real race car in race condition. It just happened to also be street legal.

Team Technik pulled in a lot of favors to get their favorite test track for the entire weekend, and Friday morning thirty-odd co-driver hopefuls waited at Rockingham to show off their driving skills. Marc and Bala arrived early to watch the practice sessions. Other team members arrived soon after, all of them hoping to find a racer with skills equal to Llewellyn's.

The co-driver hopefuls had each come in his own car and there was quite a variety: older Formula One and Two cars, very expensive vintage cars from the 50s and 60s, expensive "street" cars running with street tires. Whoever these guys were, they could afford an expensive hobby. They would be able to write the checks necessary to keep Team Technik alive. But could they drive?

Stella posted a schedule showing practice sessions' times. Marc, Bala and the other members of Team Technik watched for hours as the drivers took their turns. How had some of them ever gotten their WRF Class G licenses? Or had they?

One gent in a JCW Mini Cooper GP took the entire lap completely offline. He took turns too soon, braked too early or braked too late. Finally, he apexed so early, he ran out of racetrack entirely. Another chap, driving a valuable mid-80's Audi Quattro made the turns correctly, but was so slow that he was passed by the fellow driving the Mini. Another driver in a mid-70s Tyrell P34 six-wheel F1 car impressed them all with his foolhardiness. Not only did he put at risk a car that cost hundreds of thousands of pounds, but he could not drive it straight.

Marc and Bala were appalled at the lack of talent out on the track. Their stress levels rose. The rest of Team Technik passed on their sentiments to the two team leads: *Amateurs! Bloody incompetents! Some of those buggers can barely shift a gear!*

"Oh God, we're totally screwed," moaned Bala.

"Fuck! We're in serious trouble unless we see some talent, any talent," Marc responded.

They watched a few more hopefuls.

"So far, I've seen exactly three of these hopefuls turn in decent times and a couple of others at least have consistent race lines."

Bala nodded.

"But some of those losers are NOT going to drive my GT3."

"I know which ones you mean. I'll start a list."

"Thanks. I'll pre-audition the ones I think can make the grade prior to going out in the GT3. If they're hopeless, they'll at least get a critical review of their driving skills, pointers on how they can improve and my thanks for coming out."

"What if they want their money back?"

"Hey, they're getting advice from a professional racer. That should be enough. And," Marc grinned, "if they pitch a fit, I'll just turn them over to Stella."

Bala laughed out loud. If Stella had anything to say about handing out any refund, and she would, the whiners were in for a rude surprise.

Just then a rare and expensive Morgan AeroMax straight-lined a corner and launched itself onto the grass nearby. It slid along on top of the grass, stopping with a jolting lurch. The front end broke into several chunks, the pieces falling onto the ground.

"Ouch!" Marc blurted. "That hurt. Not to mention the serious money it'll take to fix it."

"THAT guy isn't driving your car tomorrow."

The Morgan's driver got out and stood staring at the wreck. It began to smoke. He continued to stare, perhaps wondering where and when his chances went bye-bye. He walked up to the Morgan and kicked one of the tires, then turned and slowly walked away. Marc and Bala knew he would not be coming back.

Rene waited until Friday afternoon to start his trip to the U.K. He planned to arrive early Saturday morning, park his car nearby and observe the auditions. He wanted to watch how Marc handled different types and styles of drivers and driving and how Team Technik responded to various situations. As he made some notes for the next day's schedule, a memory of his police training as a young man flickered across his consciousness. He could almost hear his old mentor Inspector Deputy: *Never make a major decision without a plan.*

The trip from Dijon to Northamptonshire usually took fourteen hours. Driving toward Calais, Rene tested the Renault: mashing on the throttle to gauge acceleration, even taking the occasional back road to test the new tires' setup and grip. Hector's once-over did not disappoint. The car behaved as beautifully as Rene expected.

He stopped just before the Chunnel. He got a room and enjoyed a good dinner. Rising early on Saturday, he ate a light breakfast, then, tossing his bag into the boot of the Renault, he strapped in for the final leg of the journey. He had decided his audition entrance would be dramatic. He would arrive at the last minute in a mad combination of ripping engine noise, raspy exhaust, skidding tires and brakes. It would make a splendid impression. He would leap from the car, toss his application to the right person and demand to take the test.

After the Chunnel, he cleared customs then continued

his journey. Skirting London to avoid the twenty-four hour traffic madness, he arrived at Rockingham before 10:00. He found a discrete parking spot near the Gracelands' turn which gave him a good view of the entire track. He headed toward the bunch of applicants. Rene's first test for Marc: how he handled people under stress.

Saturday had dawned bright, clear and crisp, with just a few wisps of fog settling close to the ground. The whole team turned out. They hoped for the best. They expected the worst.

As soon as the track was fog free, Jimmy Oswalt and Tom Tambay rolled out Marc's prepped and ready-to-go GT3. It looked like an angry orange wasp, right out of a bad dream. Its glossy black wheels glistened with morning dew, adding to the car's evil look. It either quickened a man's heart or made him quail. When Marc started it up, it sounded the way it looked: LOUD – ANGRY – PISSED OFF! It needed serious driving skill to fulfill its promise: explosive power, sizzling speed. What else is a racecar born for? Saturday's line up of ten co-driver hopefuls, lined the pit area, applications and audition fees in hand. Stella appeared promptly at 9:00 to accept the applications. She posted the day's schedule so each applicant knew his turn. They waited nervously for 10:00 when testing officially began. Most thought about their upcoming ride with Marc, hoping but not really believing, they would be chosen.

The International Super Sport Car Circuit at Rockingham gave a racer a run for his money. Its combination of straights, off-camber curves and fast transitions highlighted the skills and deficiencies of car and driver. Because it was entirely flat, a racer driving his laps was easily visible to everyone.

Those who had arrived early enough were in for a treat as they watched Marc run the Porsche through its paces. The Porsche needed warming up and Marc wanted to make sure the circuit was clean and had at least a little rubber on it before the tests began. He also wanted to let the group of potential co-drivers see what he expected of a racer.

He passed the start/finish line in fifth gear at more than 215 kph, giving it a slight lift before dropping the throttle again. The Porsche scorched the track at 250 kph before he stepped hard on the binders to take Deene curve, heading to Yentwood. He took this in third then accelerated into fourth and fifth as he headed through Chapman before setting the car to take the fast left-hand kink at PifPaf. Next, Short Link and Steel Straight as he dropped one gear to take Gracelands almost flat out. By the time he had to brake for Tarzan, the Porsche kissed 230 kph. Its carbon ceramic brakes glowed orange-red as Marc turned in with just the right amount of slip, perfuming the air with the scent of smoking brakes and tires. Marc tracked out with a flick of opposite lock and sped down the straight towards Brook Chicane, slowing and slicing left-right-left before taking the final turn to complete a lap. The unmistakable snarl of the

Porsche Flat Six was sweet music to most of the drivers waiting their test.

Every eye followed Marc as he lapped the circuit. Intensity flickered in the air around the eleven applicants. Ten wondered if they had the steel to drive the course like the pro Marc Lange was. The newcomer knew he did.

After several more laps of the circuit, Marc pulled into the pit. The overall lap record at Rockingham by a race spec'ed GT2 Aston Martin was 1:22.6. Marc did it in a 1:26.2—in a street car, on a cold race track. Some of the waiting drivers began to sweat.

Marc gave instructions to Jimmy and Tom for some adjustments to the Porsche. Joined by Bala and Stella they turned and faced the applicants. Many moved forward to greet the team, giving Team Technik an opportunity to size some of the potential co-drivers up close and personal. Rene Dufour, dressed in street clothes and a cap pulled low, made his way to the front; it was easy, a gentle shove here, a shoulder there, most did not even realize they were being moved out of the way. But that was Rene's police training, knowing how to move through a crowd without being noticed.

He first shook hands with Marc, his grip firm and formal in the up and down motion, a guy who knew what he wanted and was his own man. The kind of guy that locked eyes with someone and did not avert his eyes. That said a lot; it spoke of confidence and resolve. Good.

Next he shook hands with Bala, whose hands were powerful and calloused from years of wrenching on race cars, yet still there was softness to his grip that could only be accomplished with experience and precision of a seasoned mechanic and engineer. Rene knew that this was a man he could trust. He liked that.

At the end of the small receiving line was Stella. She was a beauty, she had a fire in her, but it was tempered with an easy grace. Her grip was firm, the motion quick; she was already on to the next applicant who happened to have an envelope stuffed with fresh Euros. Ah, someone who knew their priorities, Rene liked that a lot. But as he moved away from her, he stole one more glance. Yes, he liked her for different reasons. Yes, she was that attractive.

Putting a little distance from those in front and stepping up on a box, Marc cleared his throat. Immediately all the talking came to a stop.

"First of all, good morning," Marc shouted.

"Good morning."

"On behalf of everyone from Team Technik, I want to thank you for coming out," smiling to lessen the tension. "Let's go over some ground rules for today's test."

The applicants shuffled around, looking at each other as the instructions were passed out.

"You've been given a number for when you'll be on the track today. Depending on what we saw during yesterday's practice, I may first take some of you out in your car. A few of you are driving old F1 and F2 machines. Since they have single seats, I won't be sitting on a wing or a side pod." A few drivers grinned.

"Some of you will only drive the Porsche. We're looking for a lot of things today. Each and every one of these areas is important. We want to know how you perform in the car, how you approach your driving craft, how you take instructions from me and how you take instructions from Team Technik's race director Bala Masurkar. He'll be instructing via your headset.

"Now, according to your applications, each of you is *supposed* to have some racing experience, so we have great expectations."

He winked at Bala. "This is a great opportunity for someone. If you don't agree with that, I doubt you'd be here."

The men around him nodded.

"We're offering the chance to drive for a top team, in a very fast and competitive racing series. By tomorrow evening we'll make someone an offer to join the team. If you are selected, we'll discuss your financial obligations. Good luck to everyone and God speed. Now, before I turn you over to Bala, are there any questions?"

Several hands raised and the Q&A session began. Most of the questions revolved around how the co-driver would be selected, when payments were due, the possibility of press interviews, would this be a fast track to Formula One, etc. After twenty minutes Bala stepped forward and held up his hand.

"Gentlemen, it's past ten and the clock is ticking. I think your time would be better spent on the track. While these are important questions, they're only important to the one we choose. Let's get cracking."

Having moved to the rear of the assembled group, Rene noticed approvingly how Marc commanded the complete focus of every hopeful. Returning to his parked Renault, Rene prepared to watch how the day's testing played out. He adjusted a setting on his iPhone, allowing him to access the secure digital channel that Marc and Bala would use to talk to each other and the drivers. The technology was a parting gift from Hector. Rene decided it could prove very handy this weekend. He had managed to nick a copy of the day's driving schedule when he mingled with the hopefuls, so he looked at the list of Friday's test drivers. He selected three names randomly to scrutinize their driving. He took out his binoculars.

The first driver Rene chose drove the Audi Quattro. After watching the fellow drive for a few minutes, Rene figured Marc had no intention of letting the guy drive the GT3. He was simply too slow. He decided to listen in on Marc's conversation.

"You can take the corner faster. This car can take it."

"Are you sure? I don't want to over-rev the motor."

"Is there enough oil in the motor?" asked Marc.

"I think so."

"Then PUSH! This car can take it!"

Five laps later.

"Listen. You're very, very smooth, but unfortunately not so fast. You need to work on picking up speed through the corners. Use all of the track to keep up your momentum."

"So I won't be your new co-driver? I mean, I know I can get the proper license."

"I'm sorry, no. Learn to keep your speed up and get some more on-track experience driving a car at high speed. You might consider a high-speed driver's course first. With some more experience under your belt, you might have a chance. Thank you very much."

Rene's second choice to watch was a fiery young Italian. He drove, or tortured, a very rare, expensive Ferrari 250 GT TDF from the late 1950's, worth millions of Euro's. Rene noticed an older, extremely well-dressed man in the group watching the trials. The man resembled the kid and Rene assumed he was the dad. The car must be his, the way he bit his lip every time the car roared by. Turning back to the test drive, he watched Marc do three laps with the kid and then he heard, "Bala, we're coming in to get the Porsche."

As soon as they pulled into the pit, Marc and the kid sprinted to the GT3, belted in and roared off. After two laps he heard Marc say, "Pietro, take it easy. *Calmate*! We want to get through this alive."

"I'm trying my hardest!"

"Yeah, but your HARDEST is scaring the bloody bejesus out of me and you're going to damage my car!"

"Marc, this is Bala. Bring her into the pit now!"

"You heard the man Pietro. Take it easy on the last lap."

Rene saw the GT3 pull into the pits. Then he heard Marc tell the kid the bad news:

"Thank you for trying out. You have talent, but you've got a lot to learn. The key is to be fast, but try not to scare the guy who's testing you—AND THAT WOULD BE ME!!!"

At noon, everyone took lunch, including Rene. He pulled out a baguette, cheese, fruit and bottled water. He listened to Marc and Bala for a minute.

"So, that first batch was a bunch of shit."

"Yeah," Marc said. "God, I hope it gets better after lunch. Can anyone out there drive a race car?"

"For our sake, I certainly hope so. See you in the pits!" The radio went silent.

Using his binoculars again, Rene observed the body language of the various members of Team Technik. They all did their tasks efficiently, but without much enthusiasm.

They seemed discouraged by the first batch of drivers.

He readjusted his binoculars. Watching Stella was very pleasant, a real beauty clearly at ease in a swarm of men. The co-driver applicants drifted towards her, hoping she might give one of them a smile or perhaps a crumb of information. Watching her face and body language, Rene felt he understood Stella. She would be smooth with them. She would offer a few words of encouragement, perhaps a bit more, but the team was her priority. He could tell by the way Marc and his partner interacted that she was a critical member of the team and that they were confidant she could handle her part.

Rene next focused on Bala and Marc. He watched them compare notes. Bala checked his watch, looked over at the next group of drivers and made a few more notes, then turned back to Marc. They both chuckled at something. Marc turned and walked toward Stella and the waiting GT3.

Rene watched the second group of drivers as one-by-one they took to the track. Among them was the third driver he had selected to watch earlier that morning. The fellow proved to be very entertaining to watch, but driving with him looked like hell. Marc took him out straight away in the GT3, as the chap had driven a 6-wheeled Tyrell P34 Formula 1 car to the track and true to his word, Marc was not about to sit on the car's side pod. The driver drove consistent laps for the first few minutes then got cocky. Trying to impress Marc, the guy decided to do his best drifting imitation by sliding through each corner. Clouds of billowing smoke engulfed the car as the tires tried to keep up the grip. It was like watching a car test on TV as the host would torture both car and tires—great fun to watch, but NOT the fastest way around the track.

"Come in NOW!" Rene heard Bala roar.

The GT3 came into the pits to cool off and have its tires changed. Rene knew how much a new set of Michelin Pilot Sport Cup tires cost. This latest session with the Formula 1 wannabe had cost the team a fistful of Euros. Bottom of the list for him.

At the end of the day, the applicants slowly drifted away. Rene watched the team pack up and head out together for an early dinner. Before leaving, they covered the GT3 and rolled it away to rest for the night. Talk about your rough day! He put on a pullover and nondescript cap, then discretely followed them to their restaurant, The Hare at Loddington in nearby Northampton. He took a table close enough to hear their conversations, but not too close. Team Technik paid him no heed.

Rene looked over the menu. Typical British pub food: roast beef with Yorkshire Pudding, fish and chips and *Mon Dieu*! Not *Coq au Vin?* A Frenchman eating *Coq au Vin* in a British pub? He shuddered. Local was (almost) always the better choice. He finally ordered homemade steak-and-kidney pie and a pint of ale. When it came, he tucked in. For

British food, it was quite good. As he ate, he opened his ears to gather information about the day, the team, and most important of all, Marc Lange.

The team mechanics were the most open. They had opinions on every driver, every driving style and the day's final results. Zeca, Tom, Jimmy and Reg all took turns firing off comments about the day's line up.

"We should make a rule right now, if you show up for a trial in an old race car, you're not allowed anywhere near a modern race car, or racetrack or race team," Zeca groused.

Turning to Marc, Stella and Bala at the end of the table, Tom held up his hands at the ten and two positions and mimed trying (and failing) to control an imaginary car. "What I saw was none of them knew how to deal with modern race rubber. I mean it has so much grip, so much more than these guys are used to. They really struggled all day"

"Exactly," Zeca continued. "I saw guys go from oversteer to understeer in the same turn! I mean, you must have been stomping on that imaginary brake pedal on the floor, Marc. Someone needs to check the floorboard tomorrow to make sure it's still solid." Everyone laughed.

"Makes you wonder how they ever got their Class G? I'd check for forgeries," grumbled Jimmy.

Reg placed his hands flat on the table and slowly turned his head left to right to make sure he addressed everyone. He and the other mechanics made eye contact and each nodded in agreement. He then spoke for them all.

"It's like this," he said in his thick Southend accent, "all of us have made an investment in the team. We want the best and what we saw today was mostly bloody awful. We still have tomorrow. We'll have to offer the best of this lot of rubbish a deal to be a part of this team. I know we need the money. It's our job to make sure the chosen driver does his best." He drew in a deep breath and slowly let it out.

"I've spoken to Jimmy, Susmit, Tom and Zeca and although we wanted Michael to stay, we have to move on. If babysitting our new gentleman co-driver is what it takes, we're prepared to learn how to change diapers."

"Hear! Hear!" everyone shouted. They all raised a beer glass in salute.

"Gentlemen," Stella spoke up. "As my Da used to say, *keep the faith!*"

Marc stood, smiled and said, "Stella, Bala, Tom, Jimmy, Zeca, Susmit and Reg. It's funny you know? We bust our arses on a daily basis. We have this goal, this mission to be the most successful racing team in GT3. And you know what? We are. For our budget, for our size, the other teams quake in our presence. Don't just take my word for it; ask Luis and the folks at Fortunata. Or ask Stella. She keeps her—ah—finger on the pulse of what's going on around us." A few chuckles around the table. "Just look at all the press coverage we get."

"It's because Elaine has the hots for you Marc!" shouted Jimmy.

"Well, besides that," Marc grinned. "They give us a lot more coverage than the other teams. And why?" He stopped and counted each point on his fingers: "Because we're fun, because we represent what's good about racing, because we're the little guy trying to slay Goliath. Well, and the fact that we're the best-looking team in all of GT3 doesn't hurt!" he added to applause and laughter. "We're going to find another driver." He paused to let that sink in. "Because Team Technik isn't going anyplace except the winner's podium. We just have to find the right wallet that also knows how to shift gears and hit all the apexes."

Everyone shouted "Hear! Hear!" and raised their glasses again, draining their tall pints of ale dry.

Perfect, thought Rene, who had heard every word.

The team is fired up. They have a great leader in Marc Lange. Bala, Stella, and the rest will follow him anywhere. Marc is desperate to find that winning combination. Could Marc be ready to make the leap to being a Driver? Maybe I can help.

Sunday dawned even brighter than Saturday. The temperature promised to be around 26° C. The drivers queued up for the pre-test drivers talk as they had the previous morning.

Rene sat in his Renault where he'd parked it earlier, near the Gracelands' Turn. He plugged in his earpiece to listen in. He looked at his list of three drivers he wanted to watch today. The first fellow had arrived in a Formula two machine, so he drove the GT3. He drove so slowly, he made the driver of the Audi the previous day look like the Roadrunner. He never revved the engine above 4500 rpm. At the end of his drive, Marc complimented his driving, then added a caution.

"You need to work on smoothness and braking. Find the proper breaking point. It's the key element to setting up a proper turn. Brake too early or late, miss the apex or apex in the wrong spot and you've wasted the turn. Practice that. You'll improve your driving skills. Let's see what you can do in another few months. Thank you for coming."

Next on Rene's list was a young man who looked about twenty. His father, who arrived in a big BMW, beamed proudly at his son. Rene surmised the father would write fat checks to jump start his son's racing career. Rene assumed the boy looked good during Friday's practice session driving his fairly new Formula Renault single-seat racer, or he wouldn't have gotten this far. Rene wondered how the kid would do driving the GT3 out on the track. He got his answer within a few laps. The kid had problems. He tried too hard, thinking raw speed would make up for lack of smoothness. Marc's radio squawked several times.

"You're taking Brook Chicane way offline!

"Watch your apex!

"You're running out of track!"

It took a lot work to keep the Porsche on the track and the kid battled huge slides on successive laps. Rene watched through his binoculars. He heard Marc telling the kid what to do. Finally, the kid pushed the car too hard and it did two complete spins on the track as he tried to regain control. It slid off the racetrack coming to a jerking stop in a cloud of tire smoke, grass and dirt. To add to the pain and embarrassment, the kid stalled the engine.

Rene and everyone in the pits strained to see what happened. The cloud of smoke and debris eventually settled. They saw the Porsche sitting off track. Rene and the pit crew wondered if the car was damaged and if the occupants were okay. After several seconds, the GT3 fired up again and continued its way around the track, very slowly. The young driver killed the engine as soon as he drove into the pits. He tightened his grip on the steering wheel, not wanting to let go of his moment in the car.

"I told you on three consecutive laps that you took the apex too soon and would run out of track."

"But I can do this. I just need more practice. Can we do a few more laps?"

"No. Not today. Not until you learn to listen to instructions. There are a lot of people who can teach you how to drive fast, but you need to LISTEN first and then act on their advice."

"So I won't be your new co-driver?"

"No."

"Shit! My dad will be pissed."

Marc and the kid got out of the car. It was time for lunch and the Team Technik crew had their work cut out for them. Marc's GT3 needed checking out to make sure it was not damaged. They had to change the flat-spotted tires and double check the car for safety before the next driver and Marc got into the car.

Marc went over to talk to the young man's very disappointed father, who was demanding a full refund, arguing heatedly with Stella. As predicted, he did not get one. Rene watched Marc's body language as he dealt with the disappointed father. Rene noted the man was upset, but eventually he walked away, his head down. Rene then observed Bala and Marc comparing notes while they ate their lunch. Their body language showed their disappointment with the morning session. Day two did not look any more promising than day one.

The last driver that Rene selected to watch was so wild that even Rene had to close his eyes more than once, fearing for Marc. The guy was very fast but was also a loose cannon. He did EVERYTHING wrong. He braked too early—then late—in the same corner. He took apexes at seemingly random points, and at track-out, the guy simply ran out of track. Rene knew Marc had to be grateful Loose Cannon was driving his own classic 80's Ford Capri Tickford Turbo and not Marc's GT3.

"You missed that apex back there by five feet," yelled Marc.

"Which turn was that?" screamed the driver.

"All of them."

"Keep your wheels on the pavement! You're way past the track-out point and rumble strips!"

"Where?!" shouted back the driver.

"Everywhere! Take her in to the pits. NOW!"

The hours passed. Rene noticed two potential candidates had good runs driving the GT3 as the afternoon wore on. Just before the second to last driver went out, Rene changed into his racing outfit. His timing had to be perfect. He wanted his arrival to coincide with the last driver getting out of the GT3. He started the Renault to warm it up a bit then drove toward the pit area. It was just past 16:00. Rene knew everyone was tired. This was perfect. He had not formally registered and hoped Stella would be too tired to put up an argument over procedures.

As the last applicant pulled the Porsche GT3 into the pits and killed the motor, he and Marc exited the car, the applicant going one way, Marc walking towards the pits. Suddenly there was a roar and as everyone turned to look, a bright yellow Renault Megane RS Turbo slid around the corner in a perfect 4-wheel drift. Correcting while still in the slide, the car roared up in a cloud of tire and brake smoke. Rene killed the engine and emerged from the car. Dressed in black from head to toe, he tossed the application and a stack of fresh Euros to Stella and walked up to Marc.

"Am I too late?" Rene asked. He deliberately kept his black helmet's visor down.

"Ahhh, no I don't think so. Stella?"

"Marc, if you can do one more, go for it," she replied as she thumbed through the stack of notes.

"Is your car ready?" asked Marc.

Rene decided right then and there that he would drive the Porsche.

"It is, but since this is a driver's audition for a Porsche GT3 RS Cup to be specific, I think we should take your personal GT3, Marc Lange."

"I haven't seen your car out here all weekend. How well do you know the circuit?"

"Not well at all. It should not take me more than one or two laps to figure it out though."

Impressed by the man's cool bravado, Marc motioned for them to move towards the waiting GT3. Everyone gathered together to watch this test.

The GT3 once again roared to life. Marc started to hand the headset to Rene, but Rene waved it off and instead pulled a wire out from his helmet and handed that to Marc. Impressed that this driver seemed ready for anything, Marc gave him the thumbs up and they headed out on circuit.

The first lap was fairly slow as Rene felt his way. The second lap was faster, the third and fourth faster still. Then Rene really started pushing it. Marc was elated and surprised at the same time. This driver was *right* on the edge, on that fine racer's line between mastery of the course or disaster. He took lines that Marc had not tried, finding the apex and track-out points that seemed impossible to hit at any speed.

The Porsche responded with its great heart. It seemed to urge him to push harder, take threshold braking deeper into the corners, apex at the perfect spot, just centimeters away from the curbing. This was the co-driver Marc had been waiting for, someone to step up and *race*. A couple of the earlier test candidates had distinguished themselves, but not like this. This guy was in another class. This driver could compete at any level, with any team, driving any car.

"That was incredible!!!" shouted Marc into the microphone.

"Do we take it to the pits now?"

"Yes, we're almost out of fuel. Take her in. Who are you? Where did you learn to drive like that?"

"Questions Marc, questions. I will answer them in good time."

"Now is a good time."

"No, now is not a good time. We must finish this lap first. We will talk later."

"Okay, so long as we talk," Marc agreed.

Entering the pit straight, the Porsche continued and stopped exactly on its pit marks. Exiting the car, Rene tossed the keys to Marc and started walking the few steps to his waiting Renault.

"Hey, wait. We need to talk. Remember I have some questions!"

"They can wait Marc. Do not worry, I will be in touch."

Rene got into the Renault, started the motor and roared off. The whole team plus all the drivers gathered around the now silent Porsche, watching the Renault drive off.

Bala and Stella hurried up and stood beside Marc.

"Who was that guy?" asked Stella.

"I don't know, but I'd sure like to find out."

And as they all watched, the Renault turned the corner and disappeared.

Chapter 6

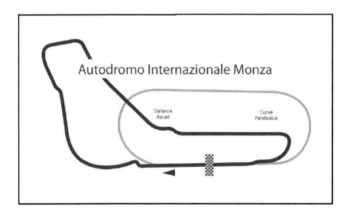

Autodromo Internazionale Monza

Variante Ascari

Curve Parabolica

Physio Monday started as usual at 6:30 am. Marc dragged his tired butt into the workout room where Luis and Jose waited. After a furious weekend of testing seventeen co-drivers, Marc was weary and drained. But he looked forward to the three-plus hours of intense training and conversation. He knew he would be relaxed and energized by the time he left.

Jose had some new Tai Chi positions for them to try. As they went through the motions, Jose kept speeding things up. Each fluid, relaxing move became potentially lethal with added speed and intensity.

They started the first set with their feet pointed straight ahead. Each man flexed his knees deeply, arms akimbo, then, pivoting on one foot, each raised his other leg straight up in the air, foot pointed in line with the leg. Holding the position briefly, each slowly lowered his foot to the floor. When done slowly, the move looked elegant and balletic. When done swiftly, the leg chops down and the heel delivers a massive blow to an opponent. Jose picked up the pace.

They moved fluidly into the next set. Both feet on the floor, they shifted to one foot. Twisting their torsos, they swiveled and did a round-house kick using the side of their foot at the level of an attacker's head. Both moves back-to-back took seconds. Any attacker would be down and out.

They practiced these and other Tai Chi positions for a good hour before switching to upper-body strength training. They used the hard bag, jabbing and punching in practiced patterns, delivering blows to specific areas. When they were through, dripping sweat and breathing heavily, Jose led them in deep breathing exercises to calm their minds and relax their tired muscles. Afterwards, they rehydrated.

"So Marc, tell us what happened with the auditions this weekend," said Luis.

Marc gave them a detailed account of all the potential co-drivers, the too frequent bad ones and the too rare fair-to-good ones. Then he told them of the mystery driver, the one that Team Technik called The Man in Black. Marc and the team knew exactly three things about him: his name was Rene and, based on his accent, he was French. And he could drive. End of story. He arrived, he demanded to take the test after tossing his partially filled application to Stella along with a fresh pile of Euros, he took laps that made Mark sweat, he raced like he was born to it and then he left. Poof! He was an apparition, a really, really fast apparition. When the Man in Black roared away, everyone just stood there next to the pits looking at where his Renault had been parked; as if unsure it had really been there in the first place.

"For a few brief moments, the team thought we'd found the ultimate co-driver, one who was as fast or faster than I am."

"Did you offer any of the others the position?" asked Luis.

"No. After everyone saw what the Man in Black did, they all thought he was the obvious choice and left. To be honest, I thought he would get in touch with me last night. But nothing happened. Now we have to regroup and take a hard look at our options."

Jose was fascinated. "What was his time?"

"You remember, I hold the course record in a GT2 Aston Martin I was testing a couple of years ago with a lap time of 1:22.6. Saturday I threw down a 1:26.2 in my personal road-going GT3."

"Those are fast times. I thought my time in my GT3 Cup of 1:23.5 was incredible," added Luis.

"This guy, this Man in Black, or Rene or whoever the hell he is, did a lap of 1:26.5. Three tenths of a second off my best time in my orange road-going GT3 and that, gentlemen is a bloody blue streak!"

"Shit Marc. And then he just walked away?"

"Luis, he walked away. Disappeared. Just vanished!"

Jose put down his water and looked at Marc. "I assume you have a Plan B?"

Marc's smile was a grimace.

The Team Technik brain trust met a while later to discuss their options and develop their best plan for the team's future in the FIA GT3 European Championship. They had two major criteria: the co-driver had to be a skilled enough racer to keep the team in the points and he had to finance the team.

As they discussed the funding issue, Bala blurted, "Oy, we netted £45,000 this weekend. Maybe we should hold tryouts every weekend!"

"Do you want me to be an old man before I hit thirty-five? If it's such a hot idea, you take those wild-ass so called racers around the circuit. After a few laps, I guarantee you'd think a £45,000 net wasn't worth it."

"You're right, mate. I'd be in the damn gaol for doing something violent to one of those bloody arseholes. Point taken."

Marc, Bala and Stella deliberated for hours. The Man

in Black was mentioned, but there was no point in continuing down that path. He was gone. Finally, they had eliminated all but two candidates. One was marginally faster, but his indifference to the equipment meant lots of wear and tear on the Porsche over a long race season. The second was not as fast, but he did have a decent time, and he was careful with the Porsche.

They decided on the second driver, Raphael St. Germaine. He had recently performed well in the French Porsche Club Spec Boxster Class race series, coming in fourth overall. But his next biggest asset was the nice stack of euros he could provide. As a principal at a large, very successful French ad agency, he could afford to be the co-driver.

They called St. Germaine. The goal was for St. Germaine to pay the same amount of money as Michael had; €100,000 per race. But St. Germaine proved to be a tough negotiator. The team's minimum amount to keep the Porsche on the track and lights on at the team HQ was €85,000. He agreed to pay €90,000 per race.

At the moment, Team Technik's current finances were in the black. Stella had done her part and gone back to all the sponsors: BT Mobile, FIS Financial, The Glenkilney Distilleries and Segurmor and got them to increase their financial sponsorship packages from €350,000 to €382,000. They added this to St. Germaine's per race fee along with the profit from the drivers' audition weekend and they had a €42,000 surplus. The team could breathe a little easier. If

Marc and St. Germaine could continue to rack up the points' paying positions, maybe, just maybe they would be in the black by the end of the season. Of course, one big shunt or mechanical breakdown and they were back in the red. They were that close.

Ultimately, they put together the best package they could. St. Germaine agreed to all the terms and signed the co-driver contract for the rest of the season. The contract essentially allowed each to walk away if the marriage did not work out. There were requirements: the team would provide a competitive car and the proper conditions with which to race, the co-driver had to pay the per-race fee, provided Team Technik competed in each remaining race weekend.

There was a three-week break between the race weekend in Belgium and the next race in Italy. This gave the team precious little time to prepare the car and get St. Germaine ready too. He still had his day job and had to commute back and forth between his office in Paris and the team HQ in Milton Keynes. He was fitted for a new racers's suit in team colors, new helmet with the current SA certification and a HANS Device to protect his head and neck in case there was a crash.

St. Germaine, with Marc along, spent hours on the track in Marc's GT3 and the Team's Porsche RS Cup S.

Stella arranged track time on different tracks throughout Britain. St. Germaine, fresh off a private plane, would meet the team at whatever racetrack Stella had booked. He was a quick learner, but the team asked a lot. He struggled with pit strategy, learning the proper driver's change pit-in/pit-out techniques. He struggled a bit with traffic on the track, as Stella had booked time when other race cars and teams were also testing. He gained confidence and was soon passing other GT3 cars practicing on the track. Things started looking up for Team Technik. They gave regular updates to BRTV which scooped other news outlets regarding changes or updates coming out of Milton Keynes.

Marc and Bala were under pressure too. They chewed over racing strategies, knowing that ultimately they had only two options. Strategy number one: Marc would take the first leg. He would aggressively charge to the front of the pack and stay out in front by keeping his speed as close to his pre-race qualifying speed as possible, lap after lap. He would build up a huge lead before handing the car over to St. Germaine. Strategy number two: St. Germaine would take the first leg. He would probably end up near the middle of the pack (or worse) by midpoint. Marc would take over for the second leg, starting farther back in the pack than he usually did and then use his tactical experience to gain ground coming from behind. They decided to try both methods at Monza and gauge which worked best with St. Germaine.

A familiar number flashed on Uli Petrovski's cell phone. He smiled as he took the call.

"Papa!"

"Mina, my dear sweet girl. Tell your Papa what you are up to."

"I'm in Brussels."

"What? Brussels? How is this possible?" A sudden edge to his voice.

"My idiotic Step-Father has banished me here, visiting his family."

"I was not informed of this."

"Mamma had some man take me. I think he is called a *Driver*."

"A *Driver*, really? Did this *Driver* have a name?"

"It was Bob. I mean how stupid. He only has one name."

"Bob, yes these *Driver's* only go by one name." Trying to remain calm.

"Well he was rude to me and talked down to me the entire time." Uli felt the anger rising with each passing word.

"And listen to this, he touched my breasts."

"He did WHAT?"

"Yes, he touched them and later tried to deny it."

"Mina, dear, let me make some calls, get to the bottom

of this. I'll call you later, OK?"

"You'll take care of this, this Bob?"

"Oh yes. I will." His blood almost to a boil.

Like Team Technik, Rene was busy too. He had taken a couple of engagements to bolster his bottom line. The first took him from Spain to Switzerland. His cargo was a pair of high-profile celebrities who wanted to keep their tryst under the radar. He piloted them serenely from one sensuous rendezvous to another. The two sat in back drinking several bottles of Veuve Clicquot La Grande Dame Rosé Champagne, toasting and nuzzling each other. It made for a pleasant trip and Rene was thankful they kept most of their clothing on.

While still in Spain, a couple of very amateur paparazzi tried to follow them. The very famous and voluptuous diva screamed that it was simply not acceptable for their photos to be taken. Rene tried to explain to her that it was—besides unacceptable—not possible. She and her lover were sitting behind dark-tinted and bullet-proof windows, making them invisible and untouchable. But then he realized her temper tantrum was all part of the drama.

The paparazzi stayed on his tail for several miles and he played with them, allowing them to get tantalizingly close. Then just as the windows opened and cameras emerged,

Rene hit the throttle and pulled slightly away. He tired of playing that game after 50 km and decided to ditch them. Warning his occupants to hold on, he dropped the Maserati down two gears and shot off the Spanish Autovia and onto an exit that had a sharp turn onto a secondary road.

The first car carrying the paparazzi tried desperately to negotiate the turn but slid heavily into and along the guard-rail. The paparazzi were not hurt, but their car was down and out. The other car managed—just barely—to negotiate the turn and chase after the Maserati. The driver was really pushing to catch up, apparently angry at his friends' come-uppance. But Rene knew how to deal with him too.

At the next traffic circle, Rene went around the circle several times making his passengers shift hard to the right in their seats. They whooped and hollered telling him to keep it up, as they slid around in the rear seats, holding aloft their champagne glasses. Rene positioned the Maserati towards the outside edge of the circle to allow the other paparazzi car to take the inside line and pull up alongside and then he simply turned at the last second and took a different road. By the time the car full of furious paparazzi completed one lap of the traffic circle, Rene and his passengers were out of sight.

Rene's passengers applauded and shouted their approval, telling him this was the best driving performance they had witnessed ever. But then magically, as if they had just discovered each other anew, they returned to the nuzzling and toasting. Satisfied there were no more tails, Rene continued the drive, eventually depositing the happy couple in Switzerland.

The celebs' handler gave a very fat envelope containing the fee and, as was tradition, reminded him to count it in a quiet place. Rene thanked him and with a brief wave, he sped off to his next engagement in the U.K. When he stopped to fuel up, Rene thumbed through the payment; the handler had paid in dollars and he counted $30,000. The agreement was for $25K. Apparently the handler heard how smoothly Rene got rid of the pesky Spanish paparazzi, hence the bonus.

The engagement in Britain was an entirely different kind. He was to take a well-known Footballer to a meeting with the general manager of a competing team. This had to stay off the radar. When Rene picked the two men at the agreed-upon location for the delicate set of negotiations, fans of the Footballer's team recognized both parties and a riot broke out. Both men dived into the back of the Maserati.

"Bob, get us out of here before they tear us apart!"

"*Merde!* What is wrong with these people? I thought your fans loved you."

"Maybe too much!"

Rene sped away as the fans tossed cans of ale and beer,

apples, loaves of bread, anything they could put their hands on, at the speeding Maserati.

Big problem. Rene knew the word would soon be out. His Engagement was becoming a hassle. He hated hassles. Engagements were supposed to be invisible. He had a reputation to uphold. *Merde*.

There were two issues: two famous Football personalities from different teams inside his car and the unusual color of the Maserati itself. It would be easy to spot in car-crazy London. Once spotted, fans were sure to pull out their cell phones and text their chums, no doubt emailing photos of the departing Quattroporte to keep track of the car's progress. And, if they were caught, it could get physical once the Footballers emerged. Rene was not happy.

He asked the men if they were okay. Each had the wide-eyed deer-in-the-headlights look of someone who was in over his head.

"Oy! I just got a text message from my fan base. They're pissed. They want to know if I'm deserting the team."

Rene looked at the Footballer in the rear-view mirror. The young man returned Rene's gaze.

"We have a problem mate. My fans are crazy enough to hurt me. What's next?"

"The B-Plan!" Rene hoped he sounded confident as he searched the side street they were on for a solution. He found it. A public garage. It had automated entry and exit, perfect for his needs. He parked the Maserati in a far corner and searched for something that would not be obvious to the uninitiated eye: layers of dust on an older Jaguar XJ. The car had been parked at this facility for a long time. Rene approached it. He used his iPhone to pull up Hector's bug-and-explosion detection system to locate any alarm on the car. Clean. Using a set of lock picks, Rene easily picked both the Jag's door and ignition locks. Finding the parking ticket in the front sunshade, he motioned for the Footballer and GM to join him in the Jag.

"Bob, if we depart this parking facility, we'll be doing it in a stolen car."

"No, not stolen, just borrowed. I intend to return it intact, and since I'm going to pay their ticket to exit, and will replace the petrol we use, they're coming out ahead."

"Makes sense to me mate."

"I have a responsibility to deliver both of you intact and unharmed and that, Gentlemen, is what I intend to do."

After leaving the garage, Rene continued to drive as the two men began their negotiations in the Jag's back seat, hammering out details that would change the fate of the next Football season, break the hearts of many fans while thrilling others. Euros talked. Traditions walked. Rene could relate, as he contemplated a similar situation in his own life.

After agreeing on the Savoy Hotel as a safe place for a

drop, Rene ordered them to duck down in the back seat as they went into the hotel's underground VIP entrance. He left them there. Using his laptop, the GM transferred the funding for the engagement into Rene's account, all €25,000 of it.

Departing the Jag, the GM turned, smiled and said, "I'm supposed to tell you to count it in a quiet place, but this works for me. How about you, Bob?"

Rene opened the application on his iPhone that allowed him to view his bank balance and replied, "Most agreeable, *mon ami*. Thank you."

A little while later, no longer in Bob mode, Rene returned a spotlessly clean Jag to the garage with a full tank. On the passenger seat was an envelope with £200 in it and a note that said, 'Thank you.' Smiling, Rene returned to the Maserati and exited the garage.

Making money on the recent engagement was fine, but the real reason Rene came to the UK was to test Marc. To do so, he needed to find the right people for the job. He drove to the vicinity of Milton Keynes and found a run-down looking pub, The Slanted Rail. His plan was to set Marc up for an 'arse kicking' just to see how he would handle himself in a difficult situation.

After parking the Maserati in a safe place, Rene walked into the pub, took a quick look around at the clientele and decided this was the right location. Uneducated, unemployed and angry, these pub patrons were just looking for a scrap. He found two incredibly surly types sitting apart from everyone else at the bar; so tough that even in this place, nobody sat near them. They looked like clones of each other: huge, shaved heads with flat foreheads and tiny, beady black eyes separated by huge, misshapen noses that had seen several fights. Their garish tats and many scars completed the look. Between the two of them, they had maybe a quarter of a brain. They were also dangerous, the kind that liked to fight because they had nothing else better to do.

Rene pulled up a bar stool next to them. The pub got very quiet.

"Wha' the fuck. Who invited you to sit here?" demanded the more eloquent of the two.

"I am interest in talking to you," said Rene hamming it up with a very thick French accent.

"Fuck me, he's a Frenchy. Let's kick his arse now!"

"If you do *Salop*, there's no, what you call, a payday for you two."

"Wha' the fuck you mean? What payday?"

"Just that my fren. A payday for you and your mate if you do somethin' for me."

"How about we take you outside and pound the shit out of you!"

"*Peut-etre*, but then I take my business somewhere else

once you recover, just listen to what I propose. If you do not like, we can go outside."

They narrowed their eyes and stared, obviously calling on all their combined brain power trying to grasp his subtle insult along with what he was proposing. They were utterly clueless. Rene told them about the job using small words and short sentences.

"Someone owe me a lot of money. Many gambling debt from bad Football bets."

"Better not be Arsenal he bet against," said pug-ugly One."

"Yeah, we like fuckin' Arsenal," said Two.

"Bad news for him then. He always bet against Arsenal."

"Fuck me. He bet against Arsenal? Tha' fuck needs to get pounded into shit!"

"There is more. He is American. He always make joke about UK."

Rene could barely keep the two thugs at the bar. They wanted to find this guy NOW! He knew he had them.

"How much to do him?"

"300 quid each."

"Give it to us now."

Rene knew they would forget the job if they could shake him down for the payment now. He promised them £50 each now and £250 each when the job was done.

"Do not kill him. I need him healthy to pay his debt."

"You just want us to kick his arse real good?"

"Yes, real good. Give me your cell number. When he is alone, I call you with time and location for the job. "

Satisfied with this plan, Rene hoped they would remember. £50 in their pockets was a lot of beer money and they could forget. Just to make sure, he added as he left the pub:

"You know this fellow, he has been to this pub before. "He tell me there is nobody in The Slanted Rail but poofters and turd burglars. I look around here. No poofters here. No turd burglars. He must be crazy!"

Rene walked out shaking his head and laughing as the two thugs and others in the pub exploded with rage. He worried that maybe he had put too much fuel on the fire. Those two might really hurt Marc. But he had to find out how Marc handled himself. If worse came to worse, he would be Marc's ultimate backup.

"Uli, you are not listening! For a change…"

"You sent her on some exile to Brussels to stay with that effete fool's family without informing me?"

"For the hundredth time, you do not have custody of Mina. I do."

"You should still tell me what you plan to do with our daughter."

"And for the thousandth time, you were a terrible husband and father. That conniving little bitch has you wrapped around her finger."

"You cannot say that, calling my precious girl a bitch. How dare you!"

"You do not live with her, I do. And your stupid fucking attempts at being a good father only make matter worse. She knows who you are, what you do and everyone is scared shitless that she will provoke you. She reigns by terror. She is uncontrollable."

"That is a lie! She has enough sense to make her own decisions."

"Good lord, she is fifteen. Not thirty."

"What do you know of this *Driver* Bob? Did he touch her, was he abusive of her?"

"What did she tell you?"

"He was rude to her, he demeaned her, he touched her breasts."

"Uli, she knows how to wrap you around her finger to get what she wants. Think about if for one second versus flying off the handle. She got under your skin for a change. I cannot imagine that poor man did anything other than wanting to get the damn Engagement over as quickly as possible."

"We're done here!" He shouted as he thumbed to end the call. If only he could face Bob and beat it out him. Then he would know exactly what he did to poor little Mina—and pay for it.

Autodromo Nazionale Monza is another storied racetrack. It has turns like Curva Grande, the Lesmos and Curva Parabolica which are among the most famous in all of racing. But Monza is not just a racing circuit. In racing season, it almost becomes a sentient being. Alive with a sea of Ferrari Red, the Tifosi or Ferrari loyalists line the track, wearing only one color—Scuderia Red. They sit everywhere: on the ground, in stadium-style seats, even in home-built scaffolding of pipes and lumber, lining the parameter of the track. Racing fans foolhardy enough to climb up on them, jump up and down on them with excitement, the structures teetering on the brink of tragedy. This was the first time the GT3 circus had hit town and a great show awaited those brave enough to climb up the scaffolding, well-heeled enough to seat in the reserved seats or devious enough to find a scam to bluff their way into the pits.

Auto racing in Italy is almost a religion. All the teams and especially Team Technik felt the pressure. This was the racing season's midpoint. From here on, every race was more important than the preceding one. Every point a racer won was counted toward the championship.

Paparazzi, the media and well-meaning fans swarmed around the teams like ants on a cookie. The teams, however, had been nibbled by these ants before. Tools, parts, cars, anything not packed up by the time the race was over, disappeared as if by magic. Any team without a fool-proof exit strategy, one that had them moving out, gear stowed and loaded, within minutes of the checkered flag descending, seldom forgot to put one into place the next time.

Marc and Raphael stood in a circle with some of the other drivers, looking around at all the pre-race pandemonium. It was a sign of Raphael's acceptance by the team that he was now frequently known as Rafi, which is what he said his friends called him. For Rafi and some of the others, this was their first taste of what real stardom was like.

"Is this what Formula One feel like?" asked Rafi in his thick French accent.

"Not sure. I've never been in the pits of the F1 race," replied Philippe Agronment.

There was a staccato roar as a race car started its motor and the crowd cheered its approval. The racers looked back and forth between the pits and stands amazed at the level of excitement.

"Can you imagine it? Those F1 boys experience this every weekend!" said an amazed Aric Vanderpool.

"Ahhh, it's overrated if you ask me," said Marc. "I think you get real tired of all the glamour, models wearing next to nothing, the celebrities wanting YOUR autograph, the media crush and that constant attention from your team and sponsors."

Just that moment, as they stood around laughing, an Italian beauty walked directly in front of them wearing a very tight, very short Ferrari tee shirt that exposed an unnerving amount of midriff above the shortest shorts and the highest heels at the end of seemingly endless legs. Marc collected himself first.

"As I was saying, all those models wearing next to nothing …."

She turned and winked at Marc and tossing her hips, continued on her way. They all collectively sighed and watched her slowly saunter away.

"Yeah Marc, overrated. I could get very used to overrated!" Phillipe said, pretending to mop his brow.

Marc walked back towards the pits. He saw a media throng pressing in on Luca Marchesotti. Luca caught Marc's glance and glowered back in obvious contempt. *I love you too,* thought Marc laughing as he returned to the Team Technik pit.

Finally, it was show time. Marc strapped himself in the Porsche GT3 RS and drove out of the pits on his reconnaissance laps. Afterwards, he took his grid position, switched off the car and waited for the team to come out and make their final adjustments. One of the pit crew had to get inside the Porsche, so Marc got out and walked back over to the pits to wait. According to his and Bala's pre-race strategy, Marc would start the race and turn it over to Rafi just past the halfway mark. He would have to drive some incredible laps, but based on their overall qualifying time that morning, he and Rafi sat seventh on the grid. Marc recalled his qualifying run earlier. As he had never driven Monza before, it took him a couple of laps to get into the flow. Rafael had not driven Monza before either but proved to be a quick study. Marc was happy with his new co-driver.

Monza is all about straight line speed. It has five long straights and only a handful of corners, so it is critical to get the turns exactly right. The idea is to maximize exit speeds out of each turn so there is enough momentum to propel the race car into the next straight. Monza also stresses car engines, as the racers keep the throttle buried over 75% of the time. It is a very fast, low downforce track where speeds can approach 300 kph. Race car set-up is critical at Monza as every part of the car takes a pounding every lap.

Marc and Bala huddled by the side of the pit discussing last minute strategy. A wall of humanity hovered around each race car, as if trying to absorb a tiny bit of magic by just standing near it. The sheer number of people made it difficult to see the cars.

"We have to do well here, we can't afford any mistakes"

"Yeah Bala, I know, I know."

"You have to really hand Rafi a huge lead, as big as you can manage. It's his first race for us."

"Really Bala? You think I don't know that?"

"Sorry. So many of the sponsors are here and we just soaked them for more money."

"You mean Stella soaked them for more money," Marc said as Stella strode up to them.

"Hey, are you louts talking about me?"

"Always!" stated Marc. "Bala and I were just talking about the sponsors and how you got more funding from them."

"Marc, they're only men!" She flashed her killer smile. "It was easy. I just give them what they want." She turned and waved to several nearby people.

"Which is?"

"You don't know?"

"No. Enlighten us."

"They just want stock tips. Oh—and to stare at my tits."

"Wow! I'd have never guessed that!" said Marc laughing as he walked towards the Porsche.

"Stella. You're something else!" chuckled Bala. "You may be the only person who can make Marc laugh before a race. What a talent."

"Bala, you have no idea." Laughing together, they returned to the pits.

Soon all racers were strapped in, engines idling, waiting for the standing yellow flag to drop so they could take their formation laps behind the pace car. The yellow dropped. They did two laps, keeping in tight formation behind the pace car. They quickly wove back and forth on the track to heat up their tires, jabbing at their throttles and brakes to get the feel for the track. They barely avoided ramming each other, like fighters trying to take punches at their opponents, only to pull back before the blow struck home. De-Silva, Portago and Agronment were just ahead of Marc, with Schwartz, Bofante (Marchesotti's co-driver) and Farik-Mansur further up the grid. They were all carefully bunched up, but once the green flag dropped, the mad dash to move ahead began.

Marc felt his front brakes grab a bit more than normal, so he turned the brake bias knob to rebalance the rear brakes. He also adjusted the fuel mixture for maximum rich; he wanted to grab as much power as possible once he began the race. The circuit of race cars slowly rounded Parabolica and made its way down the front straight. The racers were tense, focused, adrenalin flooding their bodies. The green flag hovered for an impossibly long time for them, barely a second for the fans watching. For every driver, in that briefest of instants, time slowed almost to a stop. Then the green flag dropped.

The track shimmered in the heat of the cars and tarmac.
Car shapes stretched out looking thin and hazy. Suddenly
WOOSH! The drivers in every car mashed the throttle to
the floor, unleashing over 11,000 hp. The noise was deafening. Engine and exhaust notes slammed the air. It took the
breath right out of the spectators. In a frenzy they collectively rose to their feet and cheered as if they had never witnessed anything like this before.

Marc's Porsche shot forward. He feathered the throttle
for just a split second so as not to hit Portago driving the
#17 Ford GT. Marc swerved towards the white line at the
edge of the track and sliding in front of the Ford, he slotted
in front before the first chicane. He was now sixth. The
snake that was the roiling line of race cars slowly gapped
themselves over the course of the rest of the first lap. As they
crossed the start/finish line, the running order stayed the
same.

The Porsche approached 290 kph at this fastest part of
the racetrack. At the very last moment Marc slammed on
the brakes, shifting quickly down from sixth gear to second
to take the Rettifilo Chicane. Many drivers entered the chicane either too fast or too slow, then had to correct mid-
course, making this a prime place to pass another car on the
track.

A fast right, followed by more than a 90° left had the
Porsche hit the curb, upsetting its balance. Marc quickly
righted the GT3 and rocketed past the chicane, accelerating

quickly toward Curva Grande. In sixth gear, the Porsche approached 280 kph before Marc shifted back down to second again for the Roggia Chicane, then hammered throttle and gear box to bring the car back up to speed.

The two Lesmo curves loomed up ahead. These high-speed corners had claimed many victims over a race weekend. Getting them right rewards a racer with an incredibly fast exit speed. Getting them wrong means the gravel and sand traps await (and a probable tow back to the garage). On the short straight from Roggia, cars enter the first Lesmo flat out, then braking and downshifting hard to make the second Lesmo.

After successfully navigating the two Lesmo curves, Marc pushed the GT3 savagely, rocketing up the straight, taking the left-hand kink at the Curva Del Serraglio flat out before downshifting to second to shoot the last chicane on the lap, the Variante Ascari.

All the hard work of setting up the race car came into play now. It was critical to take Ascari perfectly. With the proper balance dialed in, the momentum of the Porsche carried it down the fast back straight, approaching 285 kph. Just one incredibly long, wide turn remaining—Parabolica. Marc tapped the brakes moderately and shifted from sixth to fifth as he entered the decreasing radius corner. Then, mid-turn, he dropped down to fourth to take the set and begin the long, glorious run back to top speed, past the start/finish line to start another lap.

Lap three had him still sitting sixth, now right behind Agronment and DeSilva. Agronment, driving the #67 Corvette Z06, was a bit slower than Marc, holding him up, allowing Luis DeSilva, driving his #22 Porsche RS to pull out a larger lead. Marc was all over Phillipe, but the driving was clean as these two professionals went toe to toe. Marc was faster through the Lesmos, but Phillipe would pull him on the following straight due to his higher hp/torque ratio. Still Marc was sure he had Phillipe's measure. He could wait for the right moment, just not too long. Luis was really starting to pull away. The three cars had gained a large enough lead that the cars in seventh and beyond were no longer a threat. The three were really playing their own game.

Lap after lap, the running order stayed the same, DeSilva in fourth, Agronment in fifth and Marc right on his bumper in sixth. They were running fast enough to keep the leading cars in sight and were slowly reeling them in. The Corvette was marginally faster on the straights, but sandwiched between the two Porsches, could not match their pace under-braking or in turns. Something had to give. Racers like Marchesotti liked to intimidate the driver in front of them, but Marc found that constant and consistent pressure usually yielded the results he wanted, so he bided his time.

By lap ten, Marc looked for the chink in Phillipe's armor to give him the chance to get past. Phillipe bobbled the exit to the Roggia Chicane, putting his wheels higher on the curbing, just slightly unbalancing the car. Marc was on him in an eye-blink and out-braked Phillipe, heading into the first Lesmo. It was a risky move, one that could result in both drivers having an off, but the pass was clean and Phillipe knew he had to let Marc through. The Porsche squeezed by with inches to spare before the second Lesmo turn.

Finally, past Agronment, Marc now focused on reeling in Luis. The Team Fortunata Porsche was closing on the tight pack of leaders. Luis was in fourth and had Horst Schnellenbach in the #78 Audi R8 in third, Duraine in the #43 Aston Martin DBRS9 in second and Renato Bofante in the #00 Ferrari in first place.

Luis saw Marc catching up to him quickly and tried to set up Horst for a pass before Marc caught up. It would be difficult to execute, but the scheduled pit stops began after the next five to six laps, so Luis needed to take the pass at Horst while he had the pace and position to make the pass stick. As he began to make his move, Horst bobbled a turn and had to lift just a bit, forcing Luis to back off to keep from smashing into the Audi. This played right into Marc's hands as he caught Luis up.

Luis took a crazy line as the three cars started to brake heavily before the Rettifilo Chicane. This took Horst by surprise and he backed off for just a split second, but it was enough for Luis to put the nose of his car into the chicane first. He slammed over the curbing, but caught it with massive opposite lock, kept the car on the track, and was able to make the pass stick. Marc could only watch and smile as Luis got through. He knew Horst would not let that happen twice. Marc would have to find another way to get by.

Just before the window for the pit stops opened, Marc's Porsche was still behind the #78 Audi. Horst had not made a mistake and Marc realized that he would have to pass him by out driving him. The Audi had great balance and power, but the Porsche had better brakes; it was time to use them. At Variante Ascari, Marc kept his foot on the throttle longer than he normally would. He diced right then quickly left, while under braking, hoping to get the Audi to commit one way or the other to defend its position leading into the turn. The Audi cut back to the right too much as Marc cranked the wheel left one more time. He was faster than Horst and managed to take the position into the curve first. Marc figured Horst would attempt an up-and-under with the Audi, trying to take the position back, but Marc was able to hold him off. They entered the long back straight wheel-to-wheel, with Marc on the outside, Horst on the inside. They were equal along the whole straight, each car straining to gain a precious foot on the other race car.

Parabolica loomed ahead. Marc had the better position to enter the corner and take the apex, but Horst was not about to give up. The Red Mist loomed. The battle went to the last possible second, the last possible centimeter. Horst had to back off or both cars would spin out. Begrudgingly, he backed off.

Marc smiled as he entered the pits two laps later. He hit the Pit Speed Limit button on his steering wheel and crawled along at 100 kph. Roaring up to the bit blocks, he killed the engine and exited the Porsche.

Grabbing Rafi by the racing suit, he yelled, "I've got it set up for you. Just drive the damn car like I know you can and we'll get in the points!"

Without seeing Rafi's face behind his helmet, Marc felt the man's anxiety. He knew that the next ten seconds could be the difference between him piloting the car like a race-car driver or simply doing laps.

"Rafi, this is your dream! You can drive this damn car. Just drive this bitch like you stole it!"

Grinning ear to ear, Raphael St. Germaine nodded his head emphatically and got into the Porsche RS for the first time in an actual GT3 race and drove the damn car. He did not make up any places, but he did not lose any either. His heart rate and blood pressure up, sweating profusely, he managed to bring the car home fourth, keeping intact Team Technik's string of finishes in-the-points and in-the-money. At the end of the race, he collapsed in a heap in the team garage, hardly moving, just breathing deeply, sweating pools and smiling like a kid just turned loose in a candy store. It was the stuff that dreams are made of.

The team celebrated that evening. They joined Team Fortunata at a *trattoria* just outside of Monza in the small town of Lissone. For the first time, Rafi felt he was really a part of the team. He loved that feeling.

Marc sat with Eric De Vries and Luis, the co-owners of Team Fortunata. As the wine and beer flowed, Marc found himself hoping that Eric would pick up the tab. He felt a tiny twinge of guilt for that, but it soon passed. They discussed the day's action and looked towards Sunday with round two of the race weekend. Both cars had moved up several spots: Luis and his co-driver, Karl Schwartz finishing third, Marc and Rafi finishing fourth. Marchesotti had come in first and the media treated him like he was some sort of Italian racing royalty. Both Marc and Luis spent the better part of the evening coming up with a plan to put that egotistical Italian bastard back in the pack where he belonged. Marchesotti would be in pole position for Sunday's race, but Marc and Luis were close behind.

After dinner, the team returned to their small *pensione* located close to the track. Bala, Stella and Marc argued about team strategy for Sunday, each trying to convince the other his or her plan was best.

"Marc, we need the points! Let's be safe and keep to the plan with Rafi starting and you finishing," said Bala.

"Don't forget, we have sponsors attending too. We have a lot riding on this next round," added Stella.

"Listen, Luis and I know Luca's tricks. We can exploit them to push him down the grid!"

"But you'll still have to get around Luis and Mashburn

and that won't be so easy" said Stella, turning to Bala for support.

"Yeah, it will, I'll take him in the same place I took Agronment today."

"Marc, that assumes he makes Horst's same mistake in the same place," said Bala flatly.

"I've got this covered, I'll hand the car over to Rafi with a good cushion. Bala, you just make sure he's ready to push and push hard"

"I just hope Rafi's ready, he was a mass of runny treacle after the race," said Stella.

"He'd damned well better be," said Marc, turning to head into his room.

After he left, Bala and Stella stood staring at the spot where Marc had been standing.

"What got his pants all in a knot?"

"I wish I knew, love. I think it's the bloody pressure of running this team, being the lead driver and worrying about ten thousand details."

Stella heard the hint of worry in his voice. She felt it too. "God, I hope we do well tomorrow."

"I do too love, I do too."

Sunday. Another hot but glorious day in the huge bowl

that contained Milano and Monza. Surrounded by mountains, there was usually a haze of pollution that put a brown sheen on everything out towards the horizon. But today there was just enough breeze to blow the haze away. Already there was activity in the pits as the teams prepared the cars for the race that afternoon.

Over at Team Technik, Bala and Marc told Rafi and the rest of the team about the change in plans. The crew was not happy. They had prepped the car for Marc as the second driver for Sunday's GT3 race. This new plan upset their rhythm. Rafi seemed to take the news with a sense of professionalism that belied his short racing career in GT3. He had hoped to start the race and show them what he could do when given a competitive car and a good grid position, but he understood Marc's reasoning.

In the blink of an eye it was 13:30 and the cars were taking the green flag. Marc and Luis immediately executed their plans to get past Marchesotti. Luis timed the green flag exactly right. By under-braking before entering the first chicane, he surprised Mashburn in the #37 Corvette Z06S. Then, coming out of the chicane, Mark got past Mashburn too and for the first time in many races they had Marchesotti right where they wanted him, just ahead of them on a completely clear track. Luis' Porsche hounded Marchesotti's Ferrari lap after lap. Luis feinted passing on every straight and Luca cut him off, driving in his expected aggressive manner. However, by lap eight, they had already caught up to some of the slower backmarkers. Luis had plans to use them to get past the Ferrari.

Luis knew that Luca was so aggressive and impatient that he would not wait for any of the backmarker cars to move aside and would try to pass going through a turn. Matilde Gertner, nursing #29 BMW Alpina B6 was one such backmarker. The car had sustained some minor rear-body damage in an earlier off-track incident but was still drivable, and she was soldiering on until the mandatory round of pit stops. Approaching the Rettifilo Chicane, as Luis expected, Marchesotti's Ferrari tried to take Gertner's BMW on the outside. Had he waited until they were through it, Gertner would have let them both through, but that wasn't Luca's style. He squeezed her BMW down onto the apron of the turn. This put his Ferrari on the outside edge of the entry of the chicane forcing him to brake more to turn back to the left. Pinned by the angle of the second part of the chicane, Marchesotti had to scrub off even more speed putting the Ferrari on the wrong side of the track at the point of track out. In a flash, Luis shot past Gertner (who had basically parked her car in the turn to let Luis by), did an up-and-under, taking the Ferrari on the outside. Luis mashed the throttle and was gone.

Marc squeezed past the BMW too and as Luca's Ferrari fought for grip on the wrong side of the track, Marc was on his bumper. Marc flicked his car left, Marchesotti countered blocking the Porsche, but in a brilliant move, Marc feinted back to the right. When Marchesotti countered with an aggressive chop and veered to the right to block, Marc darted

back to the left and passed the very surprised and furious
Luca Marchesotti to take second. By the time they went
through the Lesmos, the Team Fortunata and Team Technik Porches were one and two.

The teams in the pits went crazy. The crowds in the
stands not so much. Their darling had just been relegated
from first to third in the space of seconds. Out front, Luis
and Marc danced around the track as if they were attached
by a rope. They flowed past backmarkers and lapped most
of the cars up to tenth place. They had built up a command-
ing lead heading into the pit-stop window when the pit
crews had to make the quick changes from lead drivers to
co-drivers. Then, hardest part of all, the co-drivers had to
keep the pace up for the rest of the race.

Bala pressed his microphone switch and shouted to Marc
over the roar of cars already entering and exiting the pit
area.

"Marc, in two laps, bring the car in. Box in two laps!
Push it. We need two Quali laps to make sure Rafi's out
ahead of traffic."

"Understood. Two Quali laps it is. Just make sure Rafi's
ready!!!

With Luis having pitted the lap before, Marc was now in
first place. He knew it would take his crew the full 90-second
mandatory pit stop to change drivers and make adjustments
to the Porsche. Bala would be there with a stopwatch mak-

ing sure the pit stop was exactly ninety seconds, not one second more. With two fast Quali laps and a fast pit stop, they would get Rafi out in front before Karl Schwartz in the Team Fortunata Porsche got on the track to grab first place again.

Marc pulled up to the pit blocks, hit the button to unlatch his harness, turned off the motor and opened the door all in one sweeping motion. Rafi helped pull Marc out to make the driver swap happen faster. Jimmy Oswalt threw Marc the seat padding Rafi needed to compensate for his being several centimeters shorter than Marc. After fastening the padding to the seat, Marc helped Rafi get buckled in while Zeca and Reg were changing all four tires. The team had used the same tires for the qualifying laps on Friday. They were especially sticky and held the track better giving more grip. At exactly ninety seconds, Rafi hit the start button and the Porsche roared to life. Coming down off the hydraulic jacks, he put it in first gear, dumped the clutch and in a cloud of tire smoke roared out of the pits. Waiting until the end of the pit straight, Rafi let off the pit limit button and the Porsche rocketed forward.

Rafi exited the pits in first place. He could not believe his good luck. First place in only his second professional race! The traffic ahead of him was a bunch of lapped cars. No problem. However, just behind him he saw Karl Schwartz in Team Fortunata's #22 Porsche and Renato Bofante in the #00 Ferrari. By now they had already done a couple of laps, their tires were race hot and both cars were closing quickly.

Rafi managed to keep them behind him for several laps, but he bobbled his braking as he headed into the Lesmos and struggled for traction at track out allowing Karl to slide past. Now Renato's Ferrari filled Rafi's mirrors, so Raffi pushed harder, trying to reel the Porsche back in to stay in front of the charging Ferrari.

They came up to two backmarkers that were racing for position: Anton Lockner in his #19 Audi R8 and Toni Pagliari in the #08 Reggio-Fina Ferrari. Trying to get around these two, Rafi's luck suddenly ran out. He moved inside to get through the first Lesmo turn, not realizing he was in Pagliari's blind spot. As the Ferrari turned into the fast corner, it punted the Porsche in the right rear quarter panel, sending both cars off the track into the gravel traps between the two Lesmo turns. In the meantime, Renato did some quick maneuvering in his #00 Ferrari, got by Lockner and shot ahead.

Rafi and the Porsche spun in a full 360° arc, slamming into the tire barriers with a sickening crunch. He was shaken but the Porsche was the main victim. Rafi's race was over.

Pagliari's #08 Ferrari also hit the tire barriers but not with the same force. His Ferrari was able to limp back to the pits after a few minutes with assistance from the track marshal's. Waving their arms, they shouted at him to get his car moving and back into the race. They hated seeing a Ferrari down and out.

Back in the pits, the team knew something was horribly wrong. When the Porsche's telemetry went from green to red, they knew the engine had stopped.

Bala punched the microphone button. "Rafi, is everything okay?" Silence. "Rafi, is everything okay?" Marc and Bala looked at each other. Their faces mirrored their concern.

Then, finally, "I crashed the car. I'm okay. The Porsche isn't. I'm sorry."

"Switch off all the electronics and wait for the track marshals to remove the car," Bala told Raphael. He turned toward Marc. He had tears in his eyes.

"I know Bala. I know." Marc could hardly control his disappointment. If only he had stayed with the original strategy as Bala and Stella urged him to do. Goddammit!

The track had gone full-course caution as the tow truck was dispatched to the stricken Porsche.

As Marc and Bala turned back toward the team, they heard Zeca explode, "Shit! This sucks!"

"We were this close," Jimmy moaned, his thumb and forefinger spread an inch apart.

"Come on gents, we have to put everything away before the end of the race. We know what happens if ANYTHING is left out, it'll get nicked in a second" said Tom, turning to start picking up parts, using the activity to hide his disappointment.

"Cheer up mates! We had a good finish yesterday and we can take pride in that." said Bala with a convincing show of bravado. His early display of emotion was reserved for Marc. In front of the team, Bala went back to his positive role of cheerleader.

"Raphael is going to feel like shit, like he let us down. Hide your disappointment and welcome him back, glad he's safe."

As requested, the team struggled to hide its disappointment when the tow truck delivered the wrecked Porsche along with its hangdog co-driver. They stared at their car. The right rear corner had some carbon fiber damage around the wheel flares and the undertray/diffuser where the Ferrari first punted it. The left front corner was a total write off as the front fender collapsed inwards and the left tire was twisted under the car. The suspension was completely ruined and would need replacing along with the whole front aero package. Looking at it, they hoped the tub would not need rebuilding or replacing.

Jimmy and Reg thought the damage needed a completely new front end, but Tom and Zeca thought it was repairable. Marc and Stella were already calculating the costs while Bala not only added up the cost but thought about the additional upgrades that Porsche Motorsports in Germany would shortly be sending to them. Raphael St. Germaine wished fervently that he was anywhere else, just so it was very far away.

During the long return trip back to the UK, members of Team Technik were subdued by the enormity of their predicament. Each wondered what the team was going to do. They stopped for the evening near Reims, staying in the well-lit, safe Holiday Inn Express near the Reims Cathedral right off the A4 Autoroute. The next morning, Marc, Stella and Raphael had a quick breakfast of *café au'lait* and *croissants* and discussed what came next.

"Marc, Stella, I can only imagine how disappointed you must be. We were so close."

"Hey, that's racing. It happens."

"I pushed too much, tried too hard."

"Rafi, listen love, you have to move past the mistakes. If you don't and you dwell on them, they'll eat you up inside. Just ask Marc. He screws up on the track ALL the time. Isn't that right?"

"Yeah Stella, all the time! Remember that time in Germany at Hockenheimring?"

"Oh, yes I remember that one. We were leading the GT3 Touring race when Marc stopped in the wrong pit box, got out of the car and looked around wondering where everybody was. The team yelled and waved, trying to get his attention. He stalled the car trying to move it to our pit. Right?"

Chucking he recalled that moment. "Ouch. Yeah I stalled it for sure and couldn't get the car out of third gear for some reason. I think the clutch had packed it in at just that moment. I got it running and revved the motor to the red line and dumped what was left of the clutch. The car went about two meters and just died right there. Not one of my better moments."

"There have been lots of other too, like the time ...."

"OK Stella, I think Raphael gets it!"

"Thanks Marc. Thanks Stella for trying to cheer me up." Raphael's face was bleak. "I have a lot to think about over the next day or so. *Au revoir.*" He got up and turned to leave. Saluting them, he walked towards the hotel exit. He was headed home to Paris.

"Great. Here we go again."

"Don't worry love, something will come up. It always does!"

Thoughts of Marc Lange and Team Technik were foremost in Rene's mind as he sat in his London hotel room. He witnessed the whole painful weekend watching the Monza WRF Race on his cable service at his farm. He paid special attention to Sunday's race. Team Technik's spectacular run into first place, then Raphael's disastrous mistake: a result of pushing too soon and too hard. Rene replayed the crash over and over. He felt bad for Marc and the team, but it also served his plans. As the team left Monza and headed for the UK, Rene boarded a train for London. It was time to test Marc's mettle. Rene's experiences in the army, the police and hundreds of Engagements taught him a thing or two about human nature. He was banking on Marc's disappointment and frustration exploding into white, hot anger when provoked. Rene looked forward to the test.

Monday evening the team arrived back at the Team HQ and started unloading tools, parts, and their battered car. Putting it up on the lift, they had the first chance to really inspect it. The damage to the right rear was just cosmetic, easily repaired. The front, as suspected, was another story. Although the frame was not bent, the oil, power steering and water radiators, the front left suspension, spindle and brake assembly were all write-offs. There was also extensive body damage requiring a complete rebuild of the front aero package. With all that to fix, they also had to think about the mid-season updates from Porsche Motorsport which were due in a few days. It looked like a very expensive and busy week just to rebuild the car. Bala hoped they had time to integrate the updated package when it came. After getting everything settled in, everyone drifted off towards their homes leaving only Tom and Marc, drinking beer and reflecting on the weekend.

Having arrived in Milton Keynes before the team, Rene phoned one of the two thugs to give him Marc's location. The conversation was short.

"Money now or we ain't doin' it."

"We have our agreement. 50 quid up front and 250 after you finish the job."

"Money now."

"I am not liking your attitude. Maybe somebody else want to make this easy 225 quid."

"Wait, you said it was 250."

"That was before you try to strong arm me. I go get two others to do this easy job. Maybe you are turd burglars like the guy said."

"We ain't no turd burglars. All right. We'll do it for 225. Cash. That guy's gonna be sorry. Where is he?"

Rene had every intention of paying the two thugs, whatever the outcome. He suspected they would earn their money tonight.

To make sure Marc was the last to leave the Team HQ, Rene arranged for a potential sponsor to call Marc late. At 9:00 PM, the phone rang in the team break room and Marc picked it up. A friendly voice asked to talk to Marc about a potential sponsorship package. Tom signaled Marc asking if he should stay, but Marc waved him off and Tom left for home.

And now everything was set. Brainless thugs in place, check. Rene strategically hidden ready to help Marc if necessary, check. An unsuspecting Marc Lange about to be tested in a life or death situation, check and check.

After a few minutes on the phone, the potential sponsor said he would call back the next day to get more details. Marc hung up the phone, wondering what that was all about, got up and headed to the door. Locking it behind him, he turned to walk around the corner to his parked Porsche. But he noticed that the shadows on his street did not look normal. He saw two very large men approaching him from different directions.

This isn't good, he thought.

"Hey gents what's up?"

"You arse-hole! So, you think we're a bunch of poofters eh?" said the guy on the left.

"Sorry, I don't know what you're talking about!"

"Yeah and you really think we're fuckin' turd burglars too?" the guy continued

"Hey, I think you have the wrong guy."

"Not likely—you fuggin' Yank," said the second guy as he started to close in.

The second guy circled behind Marc and the other continued to approach him from the left.

Marc could smell their stale beer breaths and saw the

malice in their eyes. There was enough light from the over-head lamp to see their tats and scars. These guys wanted trouble. No, they *were* trouble. Marc went into extreme alert mode. Jose's lessons took hold. Marc's senses flowed outward to feel what the two thugs would try to do. He guessed their tactics incorporated brute strength. He would use this against them.

They moved surprisingly fast for such large men. The one behind grabbed Marc, wrapping his arms around his torso, but Marc managed to get his right arm free before the guy completed his hold. The other telegraphed his intentions and slowly swung his meaty right fist towards the left side of Marc's head. Marc partially blocked the punch. The smell of stale beer hit his nostrils like a hammer as the goon behind him tightened his crushing body squeeze. The one in front now landed a smashing blow on Marc's ribs, knocking the breath out of him. Marc was dazed for a moment, his vision blurring slightly from the sharp pain. The brute in front grunted as he pulled his fist back, aiming for one more mighty blow, the goon behind laughed as he knew what was about to happen. This puny little Yank was about to learn a lesson in pain, as delivered by his mate.

"His gonna smash your fuggin' head you git" He breathed into Marc's ear.

Marc's mind came into sharp focus, the hours and hours of Jose's training drills took over. Before the goon in front could deliver the knockout blow, Marc quickly bent his knees and pushed backwards. Using his own weight as leverage to lower his body, Marc forced the thug holding him to drop low, too. Now thrusting upwards, Marc pushed both of his legs straight up and back, forcing the man holding him to back up. As the other thug closed again, Marc kicked his right heel into the middle of his attacker's face. Using his leverage, he then pushed back and to the right. This made the thug holding him lose his balance and fall backwards with Marc on top of him. Marc heard the man grunt as his weight hit full force into the thug's diaphragm. One down, at least for now.

The front attacker recovered quickly, dazed but now madder than ever. He tried to crash into Marc with a steamroller move, his sledge-hammer sized fists aimed at Marc's head. Marc rolled off the thug on the ground. He somersaulted up, the first attacker was right on top of him. Marc thrust out his hands slapping the attacker's face to move him to the side. But the attacker landed a glancing blow to Marc's face with enough force to make him stagger backwards.

"I'm not a fuckin' poofter! Now I'm gonna crush you."

He charged Marc once again. But all Marc's training had readied him for this moment. Positioning his body, he flexed his knees deeply, arms akimbo. He pivoted on his left foot and kicked his right foot up, snapping his toes back, slamming the heel of his foot against the attacker's temple. The man staggered. Now, with both his feet on the ground,

Marc spun around with his right foot, finishing the attacker off with a round-house style kick to the side of his head. The thug sank to his knees swaying to keep his balance. Most people would have been down and out cold, but not this brute, so Marc finished him off with a Krav Mega open palm slap to his windpipe. As he gasped for air, Marc landed two open handed blows to the thug's ears. The thug toppled to the ground face first, unconscious. Two down, at least for the moment.

Marc turned and saw the thug who had grabbed him from behind trying to get up. Marc delivered several more open-handed Krav Maga style blows to the front and side of the thug's face, knocking him backwards, whacking his head on the pavement, joining his pal in oblivion. Both men moaned softly from the pain. Two down and out, and this time for sure.

Marc surveyed the situation for a moment before turning and sprinting around the corner to his car. He opened the door, fired it up and immediately peeled out closing the door as he accelerated away.

Mon Dieu, tres bon. Rene smiled and nodded his satisfaction from his hiding place. Marc Lange was the man Rene had been looking for. He had the stuff to be a *Driver*.

Satisfied, Rene walked towards the two groaning men. They were both in obvious pain and would not be going anywhere soon. He tossed the final payment on the chest of the closer of the two me and spoke to them both.

"This is what you get when you hire the amateur. You get two stupid brute with too much tattoo, too much muscle and not enough of the brain. I wanted you to hurt him, but he turn the table on you."

He poked one with his foot and said before he walked off.

"Go back to your pub with your poofters and turd burglars. I think it is safer for you there."

Diego Garza, Mr. X's second in command, watched the hacker's demo with interest. The man had found a way to hack a transit system that utilized RFID chips to track vehicular movement. It could be used on national highways, the hacker told Garza, so that when tracking a vehicle, you knew the second it passed a toll reader.

"Hmm, interesting." Garza told the hacker. "But I do not see the benefit."

Disappointed the hacker continued, "Yes, that is one of the — I would say lessor capabilities of the hack and subroutine software I installed. But what about in a city?"

"What do you mean?" Garza's interest piqued

"Several city parking systems in Europe have just deployed an RFID tracking system for all parked cars. If you were tracking someone, you could track along the highway, when the vehicle exited and then once inside the city track to the exact position where the car is parked. Then with powerful handheld readers I have procured, you can track between 50 and 100 meters depending on RFID placement of your target."

"Ah, this is making more and more sense."

"Once a vehicle is stationary your team can track the last 50+ meters to a target."

"OK, what are you asking for this system?"

"1.5 million euros and a 2% cut of the take."

"Let me run it by management. I'll get back to you." The call ended.

Mr. X had also watched the demo and understood the tool immediately. X figured they needed to trace a diamond shipment and once it was close to the ultimate destination, they needed a tool to track the shipment the last few feet. This could work.

"What do you think of the price?"

"An obvious opening gambit. If we decide to utilize this hacker's tools, offer three million euros with the extra gift of staying alive. Should be convincing enough."

"I'd be convinced." Both Garza and X chuckled.

"Can I change subjects, tangentially speaking?"

"Of course you can Diego."

"It's Petrovski. Do you think he the best point person for

this operation?"

"Why do you ask?"

"It's pretty technical and he is better suited for wet ops."

"He will have a team in place to support him that is better suited to technical. You must understand what I like about Uli. He is the consummate professional, he never screws up or makes a mistake. For this level of money, I need the best. He's the best."

"Understood."

Chapter 7

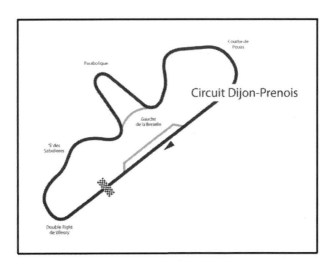

Monday's Physio was postponed till Tuesday. Nevertheless, 6:30 found Luis and Jose waiting for Marc to arrive. Looking for his phone to give Marc a call, Luis heard the familiar sound of Marc's GT3 arrive outside. Seconds later Marc walked in and four eyebrows jumped. Luis and Jose glanced at one another, and then stared at the large red welt across the left side of Marc's face.

"Geez Mate, you look like shit, like you've been in a fight."

"Funny you should say that," Marc said. "Two thugs came to me out of nowhere and tried to take me down."

"It doesn't look like anything's broken—which is good. But you have no idea who these guys are or why they came after you?"

"None. I think it was a case of mistaken identity. They didn't try to rob me. They just got the wrong guy."

"Talk about the wrong place and the wrong time!"

"At least it's consistent with the rest of my weekend."

"So how did you take care of them?"

Marc reenacted the fight to Jose's obvious approval. When Marc got to the point of the thugs' defeat, Jose beamed and announced, "And that, my friends, is why I teach you these fighting techniques, not just to discipline you mentally and physically, but so you can protect yourself when reality surprises you. Now, for today's lesson, we concentrate some more on self-defense, just in case…."

Later, cooling off at the large kitchen table, Marc noticed the lack of activity at the Team Fortunata HQ.

"We gave everyone the day off, except of course for me and Jose."

"Congrats on the Sunday win Luis, you guys really deserved it. I would categorize that as a successful racing weekend."

"Thanks. But too bad about your car. Karl saw the whole thing—St. Germaine got careless. He was pushing,

202   *RL Turner*

trying to get the position back, not realizing Pagliari suddenly had nowhere to go. He braked at the last second, so he saved you some damage I think. So what are you going to do with this guy?"

Marc rolled his eyes. He noticed Luis looking down at the floor, and realized his friend was embarrassed at winning the same race that had ended so badly for Marc

"I don't know. I'm sure he feels bad. I'm not sure he even wants to come back. We'll talk about his future later this week."

"And the funding?"

"Crap! After what happened last night, I haven't even thought about funding."

Later, as Marc headed to Team Technik, he drove on auto pilot. Most of his brain focused on worrying, obsessing really, about what to do next. He had a lot of material to sort through.

There were the damages to the car, the team's flimsy finances, the limits of Rafael St. Germaine's racing skills and reliability, the very future of Team Technik. And then there was April. He bounced between delight that she was coming and concern that he could not give her the attention, show her the affection she deserved. My God she had been patient and generous. It could not last without more from him in return.

He realized his stress level spiked. He took several deep

breaths and began prioritizing, feeling the turmoil subsiding. It took several seconds to realize the distant ringing sound was his five-year-old (practically antique) cell phone. Very few people had the number: his teammates, Luis, Jose, April, a very few professional friends. He answered without taking his eyes off the road.

"Marc Lange."

"Allo Marc. Do you know who this is?"

"Sorry, no clue."

"This is Rene—Rene Dufour, we met very briefly a couple of weeks back."

"Sorry Rene I really don't remember." *What's this guy selling? I'm already tired of this game.*

"Well you should. I think you were very impressed by the laps we did together. But I had to leave very quickly so we were never officially introduced."

"Oh my God! Rene. The Man in Black!"

"Ha, Ha, so that is what you call me. I rather like that. Marc, I think it is time we meet."

"I'm good with that!"

"We each have something the other needs. I think I can really help with the situation of your team."

"Yes, we could use some help right now."

"Marc, if I do this thing for you and co-drive and help to

finance your team, you have to do something for me in return."

"Sure. Name it."

"OK?"

"Yes. OK, but what is this thing?"

"You will find out soon enough my friend. All in good time."

Rene named a time and place to meet in Paris that Friday and Marc agreed. Then, just as Marc was about to hang up, Rene slipped in one more thing: "And Marc, bring your racer's equipment with you." Rene terminated the call.

That was weird. Still, the promise to resolve his anxieties made him euphoric. He coasted into his parking space at Team Technik and literally ran to tell Bala and Stella the news.

"Sweet Jesus, Marc, what happened to you?"

"A bad case of mistaken identity. Two thugs who reeked of stale beer tried to jump me. I might look like I came out on the short end of the fight, but trust me, they got the worst of it."

Bala turned around, saw Marc and his jaw dropped. "Are you okay Mate? Sit down!"

Marc sat in his chair and retold the story of how he routed the two thugs. He thoroughly enjoyed the admiration on their faces.

"Okay, that's the bad news. Now here's some good news. No not good news—great news! On the way over here, I heard from Rene Dufour."

"Who's Rene?" asked Bala.

"The Man in Black!" screamed Stella, who remembered seeing Rene's name on his application on the co-driver test day.

Bala's jaw dropped again. "The Man in Black called you? How did he get your cell-phone number?"

Marc looked startled for a moment, then said, "You know, I haven't the foggiest idea. But I'm not going to worry about that now. He wants to be our co-driver and help fund us. I'm going to meet him in Paris Friday and talk. That's good enough for me right now."

Bala and Stella agreed, now goofy with excitement over their eleventh-hour rescue. The rest of Team Technik was called into the office and told the good news. After many minutes of celebration, they calmed down. There was work to be done. Before Marc could leave for Paris, Team Technik had several decisions to make.

What to do about Raphael, who had called to say he was coming in that afternoon.

Who would notify the FIA about another driver change?

Would they purchase or build the parts needed to fix their maimed Porsche? If they purchased the parts, where would they find them?

When would they receive the delivery of the mid-season updates from Porsche Motorsports?

And finally, BRTV had called wanting an interview with the team. Elaine Bollard seemed to have sensed something big was about to happen at Team Technik and she wanted a slice of it for BRTV.

It was going to be a very busy week for everyone.

It got even busier for Marc. He was looking at the damaged Porsche, waiting for Rafael St. Germaine, when his cell phone rang again. Twice in one week!

"Hi Sweetie! Guess who!"

"April, wow, I can't believe you're calling!" mentally shifting gears from getting ready for the doubtless awkward meeting with St. Germaine.

"Can't I call you any time I want to?"

"Of course you can, I just figured you'd be at your office at this time of day."

"And I am, but I am just finalizing my plans for my trip there."

"What! I mean that's—that's great! When do you get in?"

"You sound busy. Everything is still set for my visit, right?"

"Yes, of course it is. Sorry it's already a hectic week."

"Yes, I heard about the wreck. I'm sorry. That's why I pressed the partners to let me fly in earlier. I think I can find some ways to cheer you up."

"That sounds fantastic!" he said, without much feeling.

"Don't worry. I know you've got a lot to do right now. I won't be in until late Sunday night or early Monday. I have meetings in London with some agents to look at possible locations for a U.K. branch of the law firm."

"April at last! You've been working on getting the U.K. branch here forever."

"I know. I've finally convinced the partners to let me fully scope the project. No promises yet."

He looked up to see St. Germaine walking in looking glum. Marc nodded hello and waved him into the office where Bala and Stella waited.

"If anyone can talk them into expanding into the U.K. it's you, Love. I'm really looking forward to seeing you."

"Good. Me too. I'm sending Stella my flight info because, Sweetie, *you* never check your email account."

"I have an email account?" Laughing he thumbed the button on the phone to end the call. Smiling and shaking his head, he was glad that April could make him laugh, he needed it.

Happy and stressed at the same time, Marc turned his attention to St. Germaine.

Three impassive faces turned to him as he walked in. Marc was not sure if it was really bad news or they were just wearing their game faces. He and St. Germaine shook hands cordially then they all sat down at the tiny round table in their shared office/conference room. Marc expected to hear St. Germaine say he wanted to stay and continue with the team. But instead St. Germaine let everyone off the hook.

"Marc, I'm sorry I've let you down. But the truth is, I've lost my confidence. I'm just not the racer I thought I was and I know I'm not what Team Technik needs. It's better for you if I leave now. You still have time to find someone else and I owe it to you not to cause any more problems. And of course, I'm good for the repairs."

Marc, Bala and Stella saw their own surprised relief mirrored on one another's faces. They would not have to ask St. Germaine to leave. They awkwardly assured him he would be missed. They agreed when he said he was putting racing on the shelf for a while in order to rethink the direction he wanted his life to take.

After they said their farewells to St. Germaine and he departed, they all hugged one other taking just a brief moment to celebrate before going back to work. Bala focused on upgrading the Porsche and putting it back together. Stella focused on working with Raphael's accountants to pay for the damages to the car and registering the new driver change with FIA. Marc focused on everything else.

Bala already had an idea of the parts they needed to fabricate. Some of the more complex ones could be farmed out to Team Fortunata and their fabrication shop. Zeca had permission to watch and supervise the actual creation of the parts themselves. Marc was in the garage with the team mechanics when a delivery lorry arrived, backing up to the shop. The delivery man got out and announced he was looking for Mr. Mar-kur-sir.

"That would be Bala Masurkar, Mate. He's just thorough the door there," said Tom pointing in Bala's general direction.

Marc looked at the invoice. At last, the boxes from Porsche Motorsports. Perfect timing for once.

Every team in the FIA European GT3 Championship got an update from the factory at the mid-point of the season. Maranello sent one to the Ferrari teams, Ingolstadt to the Audi teams, Pratt and Miller to the Corvette and Viper teams and so on. Inside were the magical updated parts that each hoped would carry his team to outright victory for the rest of the season. Unlike F1, where new aero and suspension packages arrived weekly, this GT3 update was critical.

Bala grabbed the packing list. He announced each new subsystem as the crates were deposited on the garage floor. Each was opened to a mixed chorus of "Ooh! Ahh! Cool! Oh, hell yes!"

In the crate marked *Brakes*, were new carbon-composite rotors, said to wear more evenly over the course of a race weekend and supposedly dissipate heat better too. There were front and rear revised brake-cooling ducts. These pumped more cool air onto the rotors while reducing drag.

In the crate marked *Suspension* there were new, harder front and rear bushings made of Delrin, offering more control, less deflection and tolerance over a wider range of adjustments than the previous version, plus revised toe links and upper control arms for the rear. And for the front, new camber plates and toe control arms. With these, the team could revise the suspension settings to accommodate the new front splitter and aero package.

In the crate marked *Transmission* was a new carbon fiber clutch and flywheel that countered earlier imbalances in some motors. There were also new shift forks that gave more positive shifts when using the sequential shifter installed on most GT3s.

In the crate marked *Motor* was new software for the Motor's racing ECU that allowed the motor to rev to 8700 rpm vs. the previous 8500 rpm. There was also a more efficient header and exhaust system that boosted power by helping the engine breath better.

The largest crate was marked *Aero*. Inside were a new front splitter and a front aero package, allowing the team to run the car a bit lower with a bit more downforce. These parts had the additional advantage of better cooling by forcing more air through the front water and oil radiators.

"Oy mates," said Reg. "These replace the parts damaged in the crash! Bloody marvelous!"

Finally, there were new end plates for the rear wing, allowing more adjustability and rear wheel downforce.

The upgrades were not major changes, but were subtle, authorized upgrades available to every Porsche team that chose to use them. Porsche Motorsport management had worked closely with both FIA and ACO to authorize the upgrades availability while not giving any one team an advantage over another. The mid-season upgrades were usually included in the price of the car, but the new aero package added €30,000 to the price tag, a huge amount for Team Technik. Still, considering the payment St. Germaine promised, the team came out about even, if not a couple of hundred quid ahead! Team Technik was jubilant.

On this note, Marc headed for home. It had been a long day. It wasn't until later that evening he wondered, *how* did *Rene get my cell-phone number?*

Mr. X instructed Uli to lean on Horowicz. They needed to know The Client's home base or a location that The Client used frequently. Mr. X suspected it may take a few tries to narrow down the scope of locations, but was willing to take the chance. Garza had communicated Mr. X's counteroffer and the hacker readily accepted the new agreement, thankful for more money up front and the ability to continue breathing.

Horowicz walked into the bustling Milano Galleria and entered one of the trattorias that ringed the inside of the famous Milanese meeting place. He spotted Stefan seated on the patio behind one of the large planters that ringed the outside and slid into the proffered seat. Stefan had a huge plate of pasta with sausage that he was savagely attacking with fork and spoon. Something that the Italian never did. They left the spoon part to tourists.

"Want something to eat? The food here is really amazing."

"If you are a tourist." Horowicz scoffed.

Stefan smiled and piled another bite into his mouth. Wiping his mouth with a napkin, he took a large sip of red wine and put it back on the table. A waiter appeared and offered Horowicz a menu. He pushed the menu away and sat still staring past Stefan.

"Stefan, if that is really your name."

"It is my name for the business you and I conduct." Horowicz nodded.

"What do you want Stefan?"

"Sure you don't want something? I'm buying." Horowicz declined.

"OK then, time to earn your pay." He bounced his head

up and down a couple of times, catching his mistake, there was no "pay" here. He took another sip of wine.

"We need to know more about the diamond shipments: how they arrive and the security protocols in place. And most important of all, where does The Client operate out of?"

Horowicz said nothing, he just stared at the throngs strolling past.

"Maybe you need more convincing." He took out his phone and showed Horowicz the photo of Brancato, his brains spilling out behind them. Horowicz wanted to wretch at the sight of the dead man. Up close, death like that was terrifying.

"And if that is not enough. Be sure to pay attention to the time stamp." The video showed his daughter entering and exiting a dance academy. Her mother picking her up and dropping her off, before she went shopping. Then the next shot showed them back at home using a powerful lens that captured them having dinner together.

"Stefan, this is very difficult. I've been trusted to transact these shipments for years and now you have me in a vice, I have to betray The Client. At least give me a minute to process this."

"Take all the time you need. Just so long as you answer the questions." Stefan continued to folk mouthfuls in between sips of wine. When the plate was empty, it disappeared, quickly replaced with a veal chop alla Milanese.

"You sure?" He pointed at the breaded veal chop. Horowicz wanted to throw up but suppressed the urge. He shook his head no and took a gulp of water.

"The shipments always come in an expensive leather satchel. After I catalog the shipment, I put clusters of diamonds back inside titanium cylinders and then place those inside sapphire glass sleeves. On top rests a device that sprays Carborane Superacid if the locking mechanism on the case is not unlocked correctly. It does not destroy the diamonds but makes them hard to sell as the real deal, essentially making them worthless."

"So far this if very interesting, go on. But I need details on the satchel, brand, exterior color, interior material and color, dimensions, everything about it."

"Once I hand them off to the appropriate courier, my job is done. Until the next shipment."

"How is the lock made safe?"

"I don't know, the locks are provided by The Client. He remotely safes them upon arrival and they are active once the diamonds are back inside the satchel. My only job is to validate and verify and for that I am paid very well."

Uli picked up his wine glass and said "Cheers, Horowicz. Indeed, you are." He cut on his veal for several minutes forking mouthfuls along with a salad of rocket lettuce. Finished he placed his fork and knife down and the plate was whisked away.

"Grappa?" He asked Horowicz who shook his head.

"Suit yourself." He signaled for one.

"Your assignment. We want to know where The Client is based."

"You mentioned that already."

"Horowicz. You have to realize you have no leverage here. We hold it. I do not want to place a call to my associate, telling him to eliminate your ex-wife and daughter. But let me be very clear here. I will." Horowicz hung his head low, his eyes transfixed on the dinner placemat.

"I'll see what I can find out," he almost whispered.

Marc decided to go to Paris Thursday afternoon, rather than very early Friday morning. This allowed him to relax, have a decent dinner and be rested for his meeting with Rene.

Before leaving London, Jose gave him the names of a fantastic hotel and restaurant in the Rue Cler area of Paris. The hotel, Relais Bosquet on Champs du Mars, was not only comfortable, but Jose's friendship with the General Manager resulted in Marc's getting a deep discount. He had an enjoyable dinner at the nearby Le Café du March. Jose told Marc to try the duck confit with pommes frites; it was sublime. And for dessert, Marc walked over to a nearby gelateria. As usual when it came to food, Jose was spot on. One thing was for certain, the guy knew food.

It was a glorious late spring evening. Paris a sparkling gem. Strolling around the lovely Rue Cler neighborhood soon had him thinking about April and his love for her. On cue he noticed a couple across the street kissing and wished April could join him here for a few days. He was surprised at how much his concerns about the team had crowded her out of his thoughts these last few days. He worried about their relationship. Was a deeper relationship even possible? They spent so much time apart, when they were together, it was a really big deal. What would it be like if they were together every day?

He smiled to himself as he ranked what was most important in his life: racing, Team Technik and April. He thought if Stella heard him give his list in that order, she would never let him hear the end of it. He decided he needed to revise the order of what was important. He just needed the weekend to figure it out.

Friday dawned a little cooler than normal. Marc woke early and went for a long run along the River Seine. He stopped by a small park, found a flat spot to help with his balance and went through a demanding set of Tai Chi forms and personal defense sets. Oblivious to passersby, he worked himself into a sweat. Exorcising the demons that had been his constant companion lately, he cleared his mind, readying himself for his meeting with Rene.

At promptly 10:00 he arrived at L'Apparrement Café on the Rue des Coutures Saint-Gervais in the third Arrondissement. This place was very chic and quiet. It had many small rooms furnished with large comfortable couches and club chairs, a perfect place to conduct discrete business. He still had no idea what Rene looked like, but Rene assured Marc he'd be easy to find.

Marc looked. He did not see anyone so he went up to the counter, ordered a *café au'lait* and waited. Using the mirrors attached to the bar, Marc continued scanning and saw no one. He resisted the urge to look at his watch. Instead he started drinking his café. After several minutes, the bartender asked him in English if he was meeting anyone.

Marc said, "*Oui. Monsieur Rene Dufour.*"

"Ah, M. Dufour; he is waiting for you."

"Where?"

"Just there." The bartender pointed to a darkened corner.

Adjusting his eyes, Marc saw a figure seated in shadows. Rising a bit, the man saluted Marc casually. Marc nodded back, thanked the bartender, rose and walked across the cafe.

Finally, he thought, *I get to know something about this guy.*

"Allo Marc, I have been waiting for you."

"Not long I hope."

"No, not too long, just a few minutes."

Rene rose and extended his hand. He was just a bit shorter and broader than Marc had remembered, power-fully built, very fit. More important, he projected a casual, physical self-confidence that suggested, *I prefer to be a nice guy; don't make me hurt you.* Marc was impressed and, at the same time, slightly unsettled.

"At last, M. Dufour, we have a chance to talk."

Rene indicated a chair across from him, then sat down in his own. He took a large sip of his *café* and looked for several seconds at Marc before replying, "Please, call me Rene." Then, "Marc, I think you have had the tough time lately."

"I'll tell you, Rene, it has been one challenging season."

"I can only imagine. New teammate, damage to the car, money problems."

Sitting very straight, ignoring his café, Marc said, "Yes. How did you know?"

"Marc that is an easy guess. Many of the teams in GT3 are not too rich, except for maybe your friend Luis DeSilva and maybe Marchesotti and a few others, so everyone has to struggle a bit. You add to that the driver change, the crash, yes? So, I guess you are having money problems."

"You seem to know a lot about me, but I know nothing about you," Marc pointed out.

"All in good time Marc."

"Funny. You say that a lot."

Rene smiled, "So I do." He paused for a fraction of a moment looking inward. "So, I do. But tell me, Marc ...."

For the next thirty minutes, they punched and counter-punched, testing each other's automotive and racing knowledge.

 Rene had a soft spot for Alain Prost, Niki Lauda and Aryton Senna while Marc thought Michael Schumacher, Sebastian Vettel and Lewis Hamilton were the top racers since he had been racing professionally. Rene loved the classic sports cars duels of the late 60's and early 70's with the Ford GT40s going head to head with Ferraris and the all-conquering Porsche 917s, defeating everything in sight until the racing authorities made the car illegal. Fact was, they were both car geeks and both had careers that depended on their cars not letting them down. In some strange way, it was the common bond of four wheels that brought them together.

As they spoke at length about cars and racing, Marc relaxed. Still, they danced around the subject of the co-driving and funding arrangements. Marc kept probing looking for an opening to start down that path, Rene kept blocking until he was ready. Marc felt that Rene was hiding something, maybe something big, but the things he did say seemed sincere. That perceived frankness put Marc at ease; it made him want to believe Rene was trustworthy.

They took a break and ordered a refill of the *café au'lait* and added some croissants and butter to help quell their appetites. When they returned from a bio break, Rene leaned forward and placed his hands on the table. Marc folded his hands together in his lap and cocked his head slightly.

"So Marc, I have a business proposition for you."

"And I thought I had one for you—driving for Team Technik for the rest of the season."

"Yes of course. That is part of my business plan."

"Your plan? There's more?"

"Of course, there is always more. If I do this thing for you, driving for the team; you must do something for me in return."

"And what would that be?"

"We will discuss that over the course of the weekend." Rene shifted back in his seat and crossed his arms.

"The rest of the weekend? Rene, I have to get back to Milton Keynes. My girlfriend is coming in later this weekend."

"Really? Well, she may have to wait a bit. But love will always wait, right Marc?"

Unsettled and unsure, Marc could only offer, "God I hope so." Pausing for a second to gather his thought about the direction this meeting was going. "What are the plans?"

"You did bring your driver's equipment right?"

"Yes, as requested."

"Very well then. We will spend the weekend driving and getting to know each other. Besides, we need to discuss the fee I will pay the team. And based on how well we work together; that will help me decide on the fee."

Great, thought Marc, *so there* are *strings attached.*

Rene pushed back from the table and stood up. "I have taken the liberty of booking us rooms at a small hotel near the track where we will be driving. As you are not carrying any luggage, can I assume you spent last night here in Paris?

"Yes, I'm booked at the hotel, Relais Bosquet on Champs du Mars."

"A good choice. Not too many Yanks know about it, I think. Let me take you there so you can collect your gear and check out." They walked out of the café and Rene indicated his car, the bright yellow Renault Megane RS Turbo.

An hour later they left Paris. Driving along the Autoroute, Rene expanded on the incompetence of most motorists.

"So Marc—you know—there are some things that drive

me crazy. I see people drive bad all the time. I realize that I can tell a lot about people by how they drive.

Marc was intrigued. "Like what?"

"Number One: Driving only in the left lane! Can you believe that? I mean we have so many lanes on the highway and they are going so slow, they should never use the left lane, only the other lanes! It is like this, you come up on them fast, you flash the light and they do not move over. *Incroyable*! So, you get up close behind, saying out loud *'Allo—I am back here—move your slow ass over.'* And still they do not! *Alors,* you have to pass on the inside, which can be dangerous—for the normal driver, not like us eh? So Marc, what kind of person is he, huh?

"I haven't a clue."

"Come on, think about it." He waited for Marc to answer. Three seconds later, Rene resumed his rant.

"This means they are one of two kinds of people. Either they want to control the world; they are going the 'right' speed so everybody else has to do the same. Or they are stubborn. Since they pay the road tax or pay the toll, they can drive in any damn lane they wish.

By this point Marc was laughing out loud. *And all too true,* he thought. He wondered what else bothered Rene about motorists on the road. He did not have to wait long.

"Number two: Tailgating! *Mon Dieu!* It is not like you can make the cars in front go any faster, so why stay on my bumper eh? And you just think, My God I hope there is no emergency braking or that idiot will have his engine in my back seat. Tell me Marc, what is the cause of this driving characteristic?"

"I am guessing being rude?"

"Yes!! Rudeness! Inappropriately aggressive. And most important, they show no respect."

"No respect?"

"Yes! Yes! Because they think that who they are and where they are going right now is more important than you, me or anyone else on the road!"

Rene sliced the air as he made every point and his voice rose and fell as he became more excited with each driver type. Although Rene was clearly on a rant, Marc thought the ideas he was expressing made a lot of sense. What was next?

"Number three—I really hate this one—passing on the inside! Now sometimes it is understandable because of the traffic flow and the situation. But I hate the drivers that think they can pass when there is not enough room. They start too late to take the pass and discover the right lane is narrowing or they are running out of space. These are people with no understanding—or even awareness—of the relative flow of traffic, the gaps and intervals, how fast their own cars are, how much space there is and when you should execute such a maneuver. So, do you know the mental trait here?"

"You've got me on this one."

"Come on—this one is easy. Do I have to spell it out for you? It is poor judgment."

Wow, he thought, *Rene's really on a roll, but if he carries on like this all weekend it, could be exhausting.*

They stopped for a break to put gas in the Renault and grab some water and snacks before resuming their journey, this time with Marc driving, and as he settled into the flow of traffic, he wondered how much longer it would be until they arrived at the track. He tried to remember a track in the direction they were heading, but his brain was not co-operating.

"Number four," Rene suddenly announced. "The merge! This is for both those merging onto the highway and those already on it. So, picture this. You are entering the Autoroute and you are in the entrance lane and you see the gap coming up to you, but instead of speeding up to merge, you *slow down*! You brake and wait! Wait for what? The special engraved invitation, waiting for me to actually stop on the road and motion for you to enter the highway when you think it is safe to come out? Can you believe that? I have seen it. I am sure you have seen it. They have the space and they just stop! And then, they finally put on the signal too! Who are they? People who should not be allowed to drive, that is who!

"I guess I never thought of that as reflecting a personality trait. What is this trait?"

"Marc, you should be able to guess. They are just too passive! They need to be more decisive, more assertive, not just in driving, but in life."

Traffic was tightening up. A clump of lorries chugged along up ahead. Several of them had moved out to pass the slower ones, slowing traffic down a little. Rene paused to take in the situation and Marc took the opportunity to ask how much longer until their destination.

"We will continue along the A38 Autoroute until just outside Dijon, at which point, we exit at the town of Fleurey-sur-Ouche and head north on small secondary roads to the town of Pasques, before turning east to arrive at our destination, the small village of Prenois and the Race Circuit Dijon-Prenois. We have about another hour before we arrive."

"Dijon? I've never raced there before. Why didn't you tell me earlier?"

"Well I wanted to keep the surprise intact until we were at least close."

Marc could only sit and wonder what they were going to do at Dijon, but at least it was quiet for a bit. *Finally, no more traffic rules,* thought Marc. *They could finish the drive in silence.* He began to speculate on what the track weekend had in store for them.

"Number five!"

Oh crap, not more!

"Rene, can we leave the rest for later—much later—
please?"

"Oh, sorry Marc, I just get so passionate about what I
see when I am driving."

"I do too Rene, except I am more passionate about the
racetrack."

Arriving at the Circuit Dijon-Prenois, Marc found himself wondering what the plan for the weekend was. He noticed that the event scheduled for the Dijon-Prenois today
appeared to be a professional race series. This could create
problems. For one, he was not sure he had the proper licensing or credentials, and for two, the event might conflict
with the FIA GT3 series he participated in. He noticed a lot
of Renaults, mostly, Clios and Magenes. There were a few
other hot hatches, but almost all were Renaults. There was
also a lot of corporate signage with Renault Sport signs and
people dressed in Renault uniforms (both racers and corporate types). *Must be some kind of Renault event,* he thought. *Makes
sense, Rene does drive a Renault.*

They parked the car in the space reserved for race teams
and walked toward the main building. As they covered the
distance between the car and entrance to the 'Registered
Race Team Only' door, Marc slowed and finally stopped.
He stood and stared at the entrance.

What have I got myself into? I need a co-driver who can co-fund the team, but this is getting really strange, he thought. *Besides, I'm in France, when I should be home getting ready for April's visit. Now it looks like I'm going to be racing all weekend. Which, on second thought, could be fun—and I don't really have much preparation to do. Still, this whole thing with Rene is, well, weird.* -

He realized that Rene had stopped and was staring at him. "Rene, what is the event running here this weekend?"

"Oh, I did not tell you?"

"No, you managed to leave that out when you were giving me the dissertation on driving personalities"

Rene let that jab slip by. "It is the Dijon-Prenois round of the Renault Clio Cup Championship."

"Championship? I cannot drive in another Championship!"

"Then don't."

"You mean just leave?"

"No, I mean Marc Lange should not drive in this race, but perhaps your alter-ego can."

"My alter-ego? Rene you just lost me."

"Let me explain."

Oh great—here we go again.

"You know me as Rene Dufour, a grower of grapes in Gevrey-Chambertin, who sells some of the grapes but keeps enough to make excellent wine, if I do not say so myself. I am also known for being a successful businessman, have a keen business mind as well as very handsome, cultured ...."

"I get the point; you have a well-known public persona."

"Ah! Exactly! But Marc, I also have some business dealings that are quite private and sensitive. So, I have another name for this other kind of business."

"And what is that name?"

"Bob."

"Bob? Just Bob? No last name?"

"No, just Bob. It is my *nom du circuit*. This weekend, I am not racing as Rene Dufour, but as Bob."

"Don't people find that strange?"

"Not all that strange. There are many figures in sports and entertainment with a single name: Pele, Ronaldinho or Kaka not to mention Madonna, Bono and Cher. People get used to them, that one name becomes that person's persona."

"OK, so you're Bob. Who am I?"

"Hmmm, I must think for a moment." Rene circled around Marc, looking him up and down—shoes to hair—then, after a moment's hesitation, "Billy!"

"Billy?"

"Yes, Billy. It goes well, I think, and after this weekend

we will be known as *Team Billy Bob*."

Marc blurted out "No Fucking Way! That sounds like a country-western parody! Something out of *Talladega Nights*."

"Country? Western?"

"Yeah, you know: pickin' and grinin', twangy guitars, cowboy boots and the Texas Two Step?"

"Marc I have absolutely no idea what you are talking about. And I am completely uninterested in American popular music, except for American jazz, of course. And some of your serious composers like Philip Glass and Judith Zaimont."

"And I supposed you love Jerry Lewis too?" chided Marc knowing the reverence the French felt for the American comedian.

"I do not see what Jerry Lewis has to do with this, unless *he* is 'country-western.' But it is true the man is a genius! Pure comedic genius. If he were French, we would consider him a national treasure. We are always surprised that you Americans do not hold him in the same esteem."

"Yeah, we wonder about that too—the French part I mean."

"Okay, so no *Team Billy Bob*. How about *Team GT3*?" Rene snickered.

"Oh, that's subtle."

As it turned out, everything was all set. Since this particular series rarely filled the grid every round, there were some teams for hire. Rene had rented Team DeltaMax for this race weekend, to give Marc and himself a chance to see how they worked and competed together.

The weekend's racing program was all 'hot hatch' class, compact family-type, usually hatch back, with very high-end performance capabilities. Some had corporate sponsors, like their Clio Club RS painted in the team color of Green, Black and White, reflecting the team's principal sponsor, DeltaMax Batteries.

The team was very well turned out and had a professional level of race prep. Marc was impressed. This was a very cost-effective way of evaluating driving talent. The more he thought about it, the more he realized Rene's plan for the weekend was brilliant. It would not put any wear on the Team Technik GT3 and would give the two of them a long weekend of seat time to get to know each other's style and racing technique. Why had he not thought of this earlier? It would have saved him a lot grief with Raphael for instance.

He was actually starting to relax just a little bit and to get excited, anticipating the racing, when he realized that he wasn't going to get back home before April arrived. *Damn! This was going to be difficult after all. Nevertheless, I'm here now, and it looks like the future of Team Technik depends on everything working out between me and Rene. Besides, April is so damned understanding.*

He was imagining *exactly* how he was going to make it up to April for his not being there to meet her plane when he noticed Rene supervising the painting of their names on the roof of the car: 'Bob' and a French flag for Rene and 'Billy' and an American flag for Marc.

"Ren…*Bob*, do you think it is safe to have an American flag? There aren't that many American racers on this circuit. I thought the idea was to remain anonymous?"

"*Merde*! You are right. We need a B Plan!"

"Actually, it's called "Plan B.""

"So Billy, how is your language skill, besides English I mean?"

"I speak decent German and Italian and pretty good French."

"Hmmm, you cannot pass for French and you don't look very Italian. However, you are just handsome enough—like me—heh! So you are German for this weekend. *Sprechst du Deutsch*, Billy?"

"Ja, ich spreche Deutsch."

"*Sehr gut*! For this weekend, you are Billy the German race driver!"

"Wow, the dream of a lifetime fulfilled."

Under Billy's name, a German flag was painted on the Clio's roof.

Marc unpacked his racing gear. He placed his racer's suit and helmet on the Clio's hood. The suit was in the official GT3 Porsche team colors: white with two deep blue stripes running down the right side, with the words 'Porsche and 'GT3' on the back. Worse, his helmet was encircled by a ring of Red, White and Blue resembling the American Flag. Marc Lange was boldly printed under the ring. Holding up his racer's suit, he turned to Rene and said, "Bob, what do think of this?"

"I am sorry, Billy. Blame the language barrier. I intended for you to bring only your gloves, shoes and flame-retardant underwear and HANS device."

"I suppose you have the Plan B for this too."

"*Certainment.*" Rene pulled some racing travel bags from the trunk of the nearby Megane, laying out a black racer's suit, shoes, gloves and helmet. He then opened a second bag and pull out similar items.

"I do not remember how to tell these apart. Give me a minute. Ah, the fatter one is for you, with the bigger shoes, gloves and helmet. The smaller, trimmer one, that would be for me," he chuckled.

"Rene, you're a riot."

For the Clio Cup event, Rene had arranged for licenses for Bob and Billy through an acquaintance. Once the car was prepped and the paint with the drivers' names had dried, Rene and Marc took the Clio out for the free practice session. Marc had never driven this course before, but he soon found the rhythm of the circuit. And he was surprised by the Clio; it was a very tight race car with decent performance. However, used to over 450hp, he found the meager 200 bhp of the two liter, four-cylinder engine underwhelming.

He also had to get used to its front-wheel, front-engine drive and its tendency to push in corners. Still, he started picking up the pace more and more with each lap, until he had to hand it over to Rene, so that he could put in his practice laps.

This was Rene's home track, and he knew it very well. Although he had never raced *per se*, he had done many High-Speed Driving Events (or Track Days), which gave him a great deal of confidence. He was an Advanced Level driver, having graduated through the ranks of the Track Day events when students raced against one another. However, in these events only gentleman passing was allowed, which meant not racing for corners.

Rene focused on driving 'the line,' the fastest and most efficient path around the track. Other cars on the track did not hinder him. Having driven in many life-or-death high-speed car chases, Rene really knew how to control a car in a tight situation. Blocking other cars, passing them on a turn or on a crowded roadway were second nature. For the next two days, he would string together all his knowledge while driving in a competitive environment—far less dangerous than his frequent *Driver* Engagements.

As he ran the track, Rene imagined threading through a crowded field while fending off pursuers. He worked on passing and blocking, using other Clios that practiced on the track along with him. They did not realize they were part of his learning process. Chuckling to himself, he thought, *this is far easier than when I am driving for my life. I should have started this sport years ago.*

That evening Rene and Marc went to a nearby local restaurant, Auberge de la Charme. Over dinner, they discussed race strategy. Each would complete one race, Rene on Saturday and Marc for the finale on Sunday.

They started to discuss the financial package for Team Technik, but Rene deferred his commitment until after the final Clio Cup race Sunday. "But," he added, "I think you will be happy with the results of my financial proposal." Frustrated, but still hopeful, Marc could only resign himself to wait.

Saturday morning Rene and Marc arrived at the racetrack. Circuit Dijon-Prenois had hosted several Formula 1 races over the years but was now a track exclusively for local and regional events. The 3.8 km course had eight turns. A map of the course resembled a small cowboy hat. It had a long straight where a Renault Clio RS could reach over 210 kph.

Rene began his practice/reconnaissance laps. He went down the long front straight, shifting from sixth gear down to third to take the first corner, the double right *Droit de Villeroy*. This double apex turn loosens up the pack of cars a little, leading to the 'S's at Sabeliers. From there Rene kept the car in fourth gear, taking the long left-hand curve leading to the Gauche de la Bretelle. He took the Clio up into the crown of the hat and into the tight second-gear corner of Parabolique. Diving back down the hat, he accelerated towards Double Left at La Bretelle, He took that double apex corner in third. Next, a short straight to the kink at Courbe des Gorgeolies. He took the small kink flat out in fourth gear. Staying in fourth, Rene powered the Renault into the right-hand turn at Virage de la Combe, then with a fast shift to fifth, he accelerated hard through another short straight leading to the final corner at Courbe de Pouas. He took the corner flat out into the long front straight. Shifting into sixth gear, Rene shot across the start/finish line to complete the lap.

Marc and Rene realized they could have easily put their Green, Black and White Team DeltaMax Clio Sport on the pole. However, they decided to hang back a bit and not tip their hands before the race started. They spoke at length to the team about the car, how it would perform over the course of the race, what to expect from the other drivers at the start and how they tended to drive throughout the race.

"It can get crazy," said Marcel, one of the team members.

"Crazy? How?" asked Rene.

"Maybe sometimes your car loses some of its paint when everyone is trying to gain track position," replied Marcel.

"Zounds kindt of aggresiff," said Marc in his best German accent. "Danke for zeh tipp."

Later, as Rene sat in the Clio on the forth row, in eigth position, he was hyper-aware of the cars around him, thanks to Marcel's warning.

It was a standing start, with all the cars accelerating from zero once the light turned green. As the lights cycled from red to yellow, he brought the revs up to 6,000 rpm and dumped the clutch as soon as he saw the hint of green. He swerved slightly left toward the Armco Rail and squeezed by the car in front of him. He drifted back to the right, took the next car before he entered the first corner. sixth place by the first corner was not bad for a first time out.

The race was limited to forty minutes and by the mid-point, Rene had maneuver past the fifth-place car, and was battling with the fourth and third-place racers Marta Kendez and Paul Jacquard. They were noticeably better than the rest and put up a fierce battle. Each took turns testing the other, diving into corners, entering others side-by-side. The spectators in the stands were on their feet.

I have to find a way past, Rene thought. *How do I set them up for the pass? This is harder than I thought. They act like they don't want me to pass them for some reason!*

Marc watched Rene's progress from the pits. *Rene's really*

an outstanding racer, but he needs to learn how to pass someone who's as talented and determined as he is or who has a slightly faster car.

Marc was as tense as if he were the one behind the wheel, willing Rene to plot a better line through every turn, carry more momentum out of the corner. *These Clios are momentum cars,* he thought. *Since you can't rely on acceleration to blast out of a corner, you simply cannot brake going in until you absolutely have to. I have to remember that tomorrow. But once they take a set, they really haul through the corners. I just hope Rene figures that out.*

Rene was doing just that in the Team DeltaMax Clio. He barely missed his initial brake point and had to take a quicker stab at the brake pedal to set up for The Double Gauche de la Bretelle and noticed that he carried more speed through the turn and caught up quickly to Kendez driving her Team Total Clio RS directly in front of him. He tried this same thing at the next corner, Virage de la Combe, and instead of catching up massively to Marta, he passed her. Next, he set his sights on Paul Jacquard just up ahead. As he passed the start/finish line, he saw a pit sign telling him had been racing for thirty-five minutes.

Thirty-five minutes already? Unbelievable! I thought it was fifteen. Ha! It is true as they say; the time is flying when you are having the fun!

Charging on after Jacquard, he pushed the motor past 7,000 rpm. He knew he had maybe two laps to take the pass. They entered Villeroy nose to tail, separated by centimeters. Rene feinted to the left as if to pass. Paul Jacquard moved to block. He moved back to the right and Jacquard followed suit. They entered the first Bretelle turn side by side, with Rene on the inside. As they approached Parabolique, Rene knew he had to have his nose ahead to win the turn. If Jacquard got ahead, Rene would be forced to back off or they would both spin out together.

The Red Mist took over: 300 m, 200 m, 100 m neither driver backed off. At 50 m, the last possible moment, Rene downshifted and braked. It was just a fraction of a second later than Jacquard, but it gave him the edge in the corner and he managed to make the pass stick. Paul tried the old up-and-under, but Rene closed the door and accelerated away.

They finished the race with two-tenths of a second separating them with Bob finishing third, a podium in his first race. Crossing the line, they both pumped their fists punctuating the fair duel! It had been a good clean race. They pulled alongside each other and gave each other a thumbs up. Then, waving to the fans and track workers, they took their slow down lap. As they pulled in the pits, the other teams waved at them too. It had been one of the closest races anyone in the series could remember. Jumping out of the car Rene was thrilled, hugging Marc, slapping him on the back before turning to find Paul Jacquard holding out his hand. Their handshake segued into a hug, telling each other that that was one of the best races ever.

Great! thought Marc, as Jacquard walked back toward his

team, *Now he will be asking me for money to drive for the team*

Dropping the German accent since they stood away from the others, Marc congratulated Rene. "Bob! That was fantastic! You were incredible out there. And the best part, I watched you figure out how to push the car faster. That was some serious driving today!"

"You know Billy, that race was forty minutes, but it seemed barely fifteen."

"Good. Now just remember that feeling when we talk money on Sunday."

Laughing, they turned together and headed for the podium where Bob accepted his trophy. Everyone wanted to know their real names, but "Bob" and "Billy" played their parts and stayed in character, not even removing their helmets. Mysterious Bob, the fast outsider who had taught the Renault Clio Cup a thing or two about racing, although there were some teams and fans who were not pleased by the outcome.

When Rene and Marc returned to the garage, they found the crew exuberant. Team DeltaMax had never had a podium finish in this series before. Team members crowded around, yelling and laughing when their team manager asked them if they could race with the team every race.

Marc and Renee watched the team complete post-race inspections on the Clio to get it ready for Sunday's race.

Marc was impressed when the team manager used a grease pencil on various areas of the car to indicate the exact change or component swap he wanted the team to make.

Good idea, Marc thought. *I'll tell Bala.*

Rene and Marc were among the last to leave the team area. As they approached Rene's Megane they saw a group of six men waiting. Their clothing indicated they were mechanics from two different Clio teams. They did not look happy. Rene sensed trouble and put a hand on Marc's arm, telling him *sotto voce* to let him handle it. As they each went to a side of the Renault the six men moved in, three per side.

"*Bon Soir, mes Amis*. I hope all is well."

"No, all is not well," said the obvious ring-leader, a stocky young man with laser-point blue eyes and a neatly trimmed goatee. His body-builder chest and arms announced a fellow who liked to pump iron. His body language said, 'I'm a tough guy.'

"I am sorry, I hope that, after a good meal, you will feel better," countered Rene.

"No. What will make me feel better is knowing who you two assholes are and why you came out this weekend to show us all up. You are both bullshit."

"I am sorry if you feel that way. The race just seemed to come our way today."

"Quit saying you're sorry. It's pissing me off." The other five were now closing on Rene and Marc. Rene looked over to Marc, who slowly nodded, signaling he knew where this was going.

They checked out the other guys. Rene had the big guy, plus two others who looked just as tough as Muscles. The three approaching Marc were young and fit. He watched as their eyes kept shifting between him and their leader. Marc needed to be ready to react. He felt confident Rene could handle himself in a tight spot.

"What would you have us do?"

"Easy. Leave, and don't look back."

"See that is a problem, Monsieur. We paid for the whole weekend and we have no intention of leaving. You will have to tell your drivers to do better."

Muscles moved closer to Rene. "No, *you* have a problem asshole. It will be tough to drive when you have busted teeth and black eyes swollen shut."

Rene and Marc both knew the first punch was imminent. Marc turned inward to calm his pumping heart and quick breathing. He used Jose's relaxing technique to clear his mind: slowly taking a deep breath, holding it for several seconds, then slowly exhaling. He uncrossed his arms and lowered his hands to his sides, moving forward slightly for better balance.

"You are a fool!" Rene said, "If you do anything to us, there will be very severe penalties for your team. Can you afford that risk?"

"Fuck the risk." Muscles reared back and thrust his fist towards Rene, who saw it coming before Muscles knew he was going to throw it. Using the open palm of his hand, Rene easily slapped the fist aside.

This pissed Muscles off even more, so he tried to hit Rene with his other fist, with the same outcome. He became infuriated. He tried to body slam Rene against the parked Renault by grabbing Rene's shirt. But once again, Muscles telegraphed his intension. Before Muscles could complete his action, Rene suddenly slapped the sides of the bully's ears hard with his open palms, popping both eardrums. This all happened so quickly the others—no doubt confident that Muscles would make short work of the mouthy old guy— had no time to react.

When someone is in sharp, serious pain, they tend to show it, but everyone shows it differently. Some shut their eyes tight and recoil, others simply stand there in shock, trying to process the pain. And some scream like a little girl whose bare foot has come down on a sharp rock—first amazement, then a high-pitched wail. This was Muscles' style.

Rene then finished him off with two quick jabs to the diaphragm. The howling ceased. Another blow just below the ear pitched Muscles forward, smacking his head on the side of the Renault. He hit the ground with a satisfactory thump, coiled himself into a ball and began sobbing.

His two backups were momentarily shocked at how

quickly Rene had dispatched their leader. Then all at once they rushed in. As one tried to grab him from behind, the other hit Rene with a glancing blow to his shoulder. Rene snapped his head back hitting the one behind him squarely in the nose, breaking it. Rene slapped aside two blows from the man in front before hitting him, first a solid shot to his chin then one more to the top of the solar plexus. Rene then turned to see the man behind, doubled over holding his now freely bleeding nose. Both opponents backed away as quickly as they could leaving Muscles writhing on the ground.

The fight on the other side of the car went even faster. Marc slapped away several body shots. Then, as one attacker moved in, in a half-hearted attempt to kidney-punch him, Marc blocked the punch, pinning the man's arm while punching into the middle of his face. Sensing the other two were close behind, Marc jerked back with his elbow, catching another attacker in the temple, stunning him. Releasing the first attacker, Marc grabbed both men by the hair and slammed their heads together. They dropped like rocks. The last attacker, who hung back looking for an opening, rushed Marc, but a foot to his chest quickly followed by another one to his groin put him down before he landed a blow.

Marc took a deep breath and blew it out. These guys were tough, but obviously not trained. *Too bad for them*, he thought, smiling. Slowly the soft chorus of moaning grew louder, each man dealing with his injuries as best he could.

Marc surveyed the scene. Muscles, still lying on the ground sobbing freely, his mates long gone to tend to their own injuries. And the three he had easily dispatched were trying to figure out if they should stay down or get up and run away. Marc shook his head. What just happened was surreal! Snapping quickly back to the present he heard Rene say:

"I think it is time that we leave."

"Shit, I'm getting in way too many fights lately."

"Well, Marc, maybe you need to control your temper better."

"Very funny. But it really does seem strange. I've been in two fights in less than a week. Last time I ever had to defend myself was after a Grand Am race five years ago."

"I would love to hear more about your exploits. Let us leave here and go have some dinner. I have worked up a huge appetite."

"Works for me. But what about them?" Marc poked his thumb over his shoulder.

"I am not buying them dinner tonight—they do not deserve it."

"Rene, sometimes you're a riot."

"Again, I am the riot? What is this riot you are always calling me? Do I seem as if I am a group of people making trouble in the street? This is an Americanism, no?"

"It means you're a very funny guy." *In more ways than one*, Marc thought.

Rene had booked them at the nearby Abbaye de la Bussiere, a twelfth century Cistercian Abbey converted into a four-star hotel. Only twenty minutes from the circuit, it had a soothing environment, very comfortable rooms and superb cuisine courtesy of their classically trained chef. Rene's theory was that relaxing over good food and wine, some stimulating bench racing and ultimately getting a good night's sleep would make the racers more relaxed and focused.

"The last thing a racer wants is that edgy feeling you get when you fail to get sufficient sleep. Surely that slows a driver's reaction time. It even affects one's decision making. Do you not agree?"

In fact, this was a new concept for Marc. Team Technik usually booked a (to put it charitably) budget hotel, stayed up late the night before the race, working on the car, eating late-night fast-food or making a quick stop at a cheap restaurant. He had to admit, this was better.

Reliving the fight over glasses of wine, each expressed surprise at the incompetence of their opponents.

"Well, Marc, the thing is, these are small-town guys, what I think Americans call *hicks*, no? They are just not used to getting beaten by outsiders."

"Oh well, you can't live life without taking risks."

Rene betrayed a smile at that. It was exactly what he hoped Mr. Lange would say. As the evening progressed, Rene excitedly recounted the race (several times) lap by lap. It was the first time he had raced on a track full of competitors on an aggressive track day, instead of a drive where he was fighting for his life.

Marc generously praised Rene for taking a well-deserved 3rd place in his first actual race ever, racing against seasoned drivers. He gave Rene some pointers and talked about the difference between racing in a Renault Clio Club RS event and the GT3 world he was about to enter.

After a couple of snifters of Cognac, Marc bid his host good night. Later, he tossed and turned in a very comfortable feather bed as he tried to get a handle on a remarkably busy day. First it was strange to be in Dijon, France, racing a Renault Clio Club RS with this guy Rene Dufour, who was obviously a major character as well as an amazingly accomplished amateur racer. Then there was the fight with the pissed-off Frenchmen.

But Marc had to admit, he was having a great time. The fight had been a little unnerving but winning so decisively was exhilarating. And he loved the racing without pressure. Suddenly, guilt hit him. He was having fun when he needed to secure the funding for the team. But wasn't that what he was doing here with Rene? And what was the deal Rene kept hinting at? The uncertainty, the thought of keeping everyone employed, introducing yet another co-driver to the team, made him toss and turn again. He sat up and hit his pillows to form a hollow for his head. Pulling them close around him, he closed his eyes and imagined April—beautiful, generous April. He just hoped to get back to Milton Keynes in time to see her.

Sunday, Marc was up early and went for a run within the Abbey's lush surrounding property. The sky was still pink with the rising sun, and the combination of the Abbey's beautiful grounds and the morning hush gave him time to focus. He still had a race to drive and now he was ready. Heading back to shower and breakfast, he saw Rene sitting by himself, enjoying his morning *café au lait*.

"Good morning Bob!"

"*Bon jour, Billy, ca va bien?* Ready for the race today? What is your plan?"

"Bob," Marc smiled, "the plan is to win—always."

Arriving at the track by late morning, they went into the team garage and emerged a short time later dressed in their black racer suits and helmets.

Rene took Michel, the team manager, aside and told him of the previous evening's events. After hearing descriptions of the attackers, Michel knew exactly who they were and said he was not surprised by their tactics and that he would deal with their teams following the race. But just to be certain, Michel ordered the Clio to be checked thoroughly in case it had somehow been tampered with. Finding nothing,

Team DeltaMax continued their car-prep procedure and got ready for the last race of the weekend. As it got closer to race time, Marc went out to the pit wall with the team manager to get track and ambient air temperatures so they could set the air pressure of the tires. With his helmet off, the red trim around the eyes and mouth of his Oakley CarbonX double-eye balaclava, Marc looked like a driver from Mordor.

Heading back towards the pit area, another racer intercepted him.

"We heard about what happened last night."

"Was ist das?" Marc asked in his worst fake German accent.

"Do not pretend ignorance!"

"Szorry, I don't know vat chou mean."

"Do not insult me and play stupid. Who are you?"

"Zwei mench havink sehr gut race veekend."

"Bullshit, you guys are pros. We will unmask who you really are. Better watch out for yourself on the track today."

"Is that a threat?" Marc asked, forgetting his German accent.

"No, just a warning. You should be careful."

Marc put his balaclava-masked face very close to the

other driver's face and said very deliberately in his best accented French, "Listen very carefully. If you pull any shit out there, I will put you into a wall or the Armco so fast your asshole will have to run to catch up. So, you be very careful out there. Are we clear?"

Marc saw the other man swallow hard and say that, yes, he was clear. Marc stared at him until the other racer turned and walked away. Marc slowly made his way back to the pit. He approached Michel and saw him raise his eyebrows.

"Billy, these guys are very intimidated by you and Bob. Nobody just shows up and wins against the best drivers in the series. They are, as you Americans say, a bit freaked out."

Somehow Michel realized Marc wasn't German. Marc shrugged, then grinned. "So what? They send their toughest racer to try to intimidate me? They tried that last night too. That kind of back-fired on them, don't you think?"

"Yes, so it appears." Michel paused to say something to his mechanics but glanced back over his shoulder. "So, some advice my friend. I say go out there and kick their arses!"

"That has been the plan all along." Michel could just make out Marc's grin behind the balaclava.

During the recon laps, Marc watched very closely for any sign of problems. Not that there would be any before the race started. He figured that some of the drivers probably agreed among themselves to make it hard on him, maybe block or hold him up or even try to put him into a dangerous spot.

Well, he thought, forewarned is forearmed. *Trite, perhaps, but only because it was true.*

He sat on the grid in sixth place. Now he was entering the zone, feeling the excitement, anticipating, revving the motor, pressing in the clutch and testing the weight and effort to move the sequential shifter, trying to get that perfect feel of exactly how much pressure was needed to shift gears quickly and efficiently, not too hard to grind or force a gear, but not too soft either, coaxing the car into accepting him, making itself an extension of himself. Around him the other racers performed their pre-race rituals.

The sound was a symphony or a cacophony, depending on how you felt about racing. It built to a crescendo as the lights cycled from red to yellow to green and the race roared to life.

Marc was immediately under attack. The driver who threatened him earlier drove the orange and black Clio on his right, beside him. It swerved to block him as the car behind tried to keep him from dropping back, effectively pinning Marc from moving. He left-foot braked, giving the appearance of slowing and the car behind backed off a little. Marc immediately mashed the throttle and flicked his Clio a tiny bit to the right, making the Orange car think that he intended to hit him. Obviously remembering what Marc had told him earlier, the Orange Clio veered back to his right giving Marc just enough room to shoot the gap and pull alongside the fourth-place car as they started into Villeroy. Side by side they entered the turn, but Marc's better inside line allowed him to pull out a slight lead by the time they reached the track-out point. The turn was his. He started calculating how quickly he could close the gap to the cars in front.

Lying third after five laps, he was on the tail of the second-place black and red car sponsored by Petros Tyre. After the Sabeliers esses, Marc feinted toward the outside. The car in front bought it and—as Marc intended—moved to block. Marc immediately moved back to the right but again the car in front blocked. He followed the two front-runners the rest of the lap, not matching their race line through the turns, but there he was, filling their mirrors.

Midway through the eighth lap, Marc sensed his adversaries were losing it. The racer in front paid more attention to Marc than the track and started to take bad lines through turns. The Petros Tyre Clio went wide at Parabolic and in a flash, Marc was inside and past. The other driver tried to cut him off, but too late.

Only one more to go, Marc thought and turning up the wick, he pushed his car just that much harder. After four more laps, he reeled in the first-place car of Henri Buisson, driving the green and blue Clio Cup car sponsored by ACG, the large French trucking company. It was not even a fair fight.

Marc had Henri set up at the left double apex Gauche de la Bretelle, shooting past him before the kink at Gorgeolies, closing the door as they entered the Virage de la Combe.

The Red Mist took over. Marc pressed throughout the rest of the race. He started lapping the slower cars. As he approached them, the corner workers frantically waved the blue and yellow flags, indicating to the slower drivers to move over and let Marc through.

If a slower car tried to get in the way of a car having a large lead in the closing laps of a race, the racer would be shamed by his contemptible bad sportsmanship. The corner workers would not allow any hint of bad sportsmanship in this race

Seeing the 'last lap' white flag, Marc stormed around the track more furiously, setting the fastest lap of the race. Crossing the start/finish for the final time, he punched his fist and whooped and hollered inside his helmet. It had been a long time since he won a race. So many close calls in GT3, it seemed that he had forgotten how damn good it felt to win! He waved to all the corner workers, giving them the thumbs up. He especially waved at those who had thrown so many blue flags to allow him to pass. Finally turning into the pits, he pulled the car into the team garage and killed the motor. As he exited the car, he let out a whoop of jubilation as Rene and the rest of Team DeltaMax/Team GT3 surrounded him, slapping him on the back and jumping up and down in excitement too.

They were soon mobbed with fans and the French motoring press, trying to get close to ask this mysterious team some questions. Marc turned to Rene and asked, "What do I do if someone tries to interview me in German."

"Just use fake German-accented English. Nobody will notice. Remember, for the most part the French hate the Germans. They cannot tell a good accent from a bad one."

"Ja, zat's sehr comfortink."

Marc and Rene looked a bit out of place when they went to the podium to collect their trophies, visors removed but with their black helmets and CarbonX balaclavas still on. Perhaps they had taken this whole Mystery Men thing too far. But, Marc thought, *In for a penny, in for a pound*. They had gone this far. Why spoil the fun now? Everyone knew they were hiding their identities, so in the end everyone had no choice but to play along too. Most seemed to be enjoying the theater.

After the last interview was given (fake accent and all), the crowds thinned out and Team DeltaMax completed packing up the car and tools, it was time to head back to Paris and from there, home to Milton Keynes. Marc Lange and Rene Dufour emerged from their racing holiday to return to their normal lives. Back behind the wheel of his Megane, Rene promised to get Marc back to Paris as quickly as possible so that he could catch the Eurostar home. Rene knew he had stretched things to the limit this weekend, but he wanted to be sure he had the right guy, the right person to bring on as his protégé. Through luck and good fortune, he had found his man.

"Marc, that was a good weekend, no?"

"Yeah, it was fun. We make a good team Rene!"

"Yes. Yes indeed, I believe that we do."

Rene actually changed the subject to Team Technik, surprising and pleasing Marc, who was about to do the same. "So, I believe that I will co-drive for you."

"You will, huh?"

"Yes. I agree. This weekend proved that we make a very formidable team."

"Oh yes, I think we do. Look out GT3, Team Technik is back!"

Rene had a habit when driving that he never looked at his passenger, he felt that it was best to keep the eyes on the road. But now he turned to Marc. "And Marc, I think that we will prove very formidable in more ways than meets the eyes."

The talk turned to money. Marc felt a little awkward. He felt comfortable driving a car on edge at 300 kph. He hated negotiating deals. But he also knew this was part of the business, part of the job description for Team Technik CEO. After the set-back with Rafi, Bala and Stella had agreed with him that the team needed at least €100,000 per race weekend. Raphael had put them in a bind, even though he agreed to compensate them for the damages. They were still behind getting the car ready for the second half of the season.

"I need €110,000 per race weekend."

"I was thinking more in the area of €87,000," countered Rene.

Silence for several minutes.

"Rene, at this point of the season, I can't put a competitive car on the track for less than €105,000 per race."

Rene waited for some time to answer and finally said, "All right Marc, I will give you €105,000 per race. But next week, after you get back, after you see your girlfriend and get everything settled, you have to do something for me."

"What's that?"

"Do not worry. I will fill you in on the details when we meet again."

Smiling, Marc let the last comment slide. He was elated that he had been able to get funding for the team. With Rene, they could win. He reached across the seat and slapped Rene on the shoulder and said.

"Step on it Rene, I better get back while I still have a girlfriend to go back to."

"Gerry, it's Horowicz. I'm worried about our customer The Client. Things seem off," Horowicz said. He decided to call Gerry, a *Driver* who had done several Engagements for The Client. He liked working with Gerry, pleasant fellow, but he was also not the sharpest tack.

"How exactly?"

"Shipment dates missed, protocols not followed. It seems as if he's distracted."

"I don't know Horowicz. I just deliver cargo via a negotiated Engagement. Not my place to divulge info."

"Understood, but what if The Client is somehow compromised? It means you and I no longer eat. That's what it means."

"That's troubling. The Client pays very well, for what is essentially a gravy run, low factor, but huge fee. What do you need to know?"

"The location, or city where you make your drops. I'm worried that changes in patterns might mean he's being controlled."

"The location is never the same. Hmmm, but now that I think of it, the past few have been in Potsdam. But even there the drop off is never the same."

"Ah, yes. That makes sense." Horowicz sounded convincing, covering his lies.

"What makes sense?"

"The locations over the past many shipments."

"What do you mean 'many' shipments? It sounds like I have been missing out."

"Exactly! That's what I'll discover. Why have you been missing out. Let me get back to you."

He hung up quickly, but dreaded the next call.

Arriving home, he unlocked the door and glanced at his watch. Just past midnight, Marc wondered where April was at that moment, when she would arrive. He stepped inside his apartment and was surprised to see her sitting on the couch smiling, waiting for him. Still smiling, she rose to greet him. She still took his breath away every time he saw her. Tall, with long, long perfect legs, he was sure just looking at her made lots of guys weak in the knees. It certainly did him, especially when he had not seen her in a long while. She wore her blond hair just below her shoulders, and its softness complemented her angular features. Her green eyes peering into his made his heart feel gooey. Marc wondered (more than once) why she had fallen for him. She was a very successful lawyer in a very successful law firm. She was on track to be partner. She could have chosen from among a horde of no less attractive, far more successful men. And yet she had made it clear that she wanted him. He dropped his bags, grabbed her up and whirled her around before standing her back on her feet and covered her giggle with his mouth. He hugged her tightly, took a step back and cocked his head, slowly checking her out from top to bottom and back to top, then kissed her again, slowly and tenderly. She gently pressed against him as she kissed him back.

Hugging one more time, he finally caught his breath enough to ask, "When did you get in?" fearing she might be upset about his absence when she arrived.

"I've been waiting hours. I tried calling your cell phone"

"Oh, crap. The battery died and I never recharged it."

"And what's with the bags Marc? Where have you been?"

"I've ah—ah—been in France for the weekend, Dijon. Well actually it started and ended in Paris, but for the most part I was near Dijon."

"France! Paris! Why didn't you tell me? I would have changed my plans to join you." She dropped her arms and stepped back a step, hands on her hips, staring.

"I thought you had meetings in London to look for office space," he babbled.

"And miss a chance to spend a weekend in France with you! Don't you think I could have changed my plans?"

"Look, I really thought I would be back by Friday night at the latest."

"So, who were you with?"

"Ah, I was with Rene, Rene Dufour. This is the …."

'Oh my god, you spent the weekend in France with another woman? Oh, Marc."

"No! That's not it at all. Rene is a guy."

"Oh great! You spent the weekend in France with a guy! Don't tell me …."

"Oh geez April! I'm not going gay on you either. Rene Dufour is the guy who'll be the team's new co-driver. We were racing at Dijon."

"Why didn't you say so?" The corners of her mouth suggested she was suppressing a smile.

OK, that was good. She had only been busting his balls about that last part. "I was trying to, but when I saw you, I forgot everything else." He heard himself say that without knowing where it came from, but he was impressed. *That was a good parry. She's can't argue with that. Besides, it's true.* And he jumped into the story of the race, the theatricality of their appearance, and their double wins. He also fairly gushed about the Abbaye de la Bussiere. "My love, I promise I'll take you there for a romantic weekend in the very near future."

"Believe me, I'll have no problem holding you to that. But tell me more about Rene."

He began, but April kept interrupting, asking precise questions about Rene's background, character and where he came up with the kind of money Marc needed for the team. Marc could imagine her in a deposition or cross-examining a witness on the stand. She was one tough lawyer.

"So this Rene Dufour grows grapes on a small farm and makes only a small amount of wine, which for the most part he gives to friends as gifts. Where does he get the kind of cash it takes to be a gentleman co-driver for a race team, your race team?"

Marc decided not to tell her just yet of Rene's alter ego 'Bob', preferring to leave a few of the details out, fearing that he would set off alarms.

"April, I think I know a thing or two about reading people. Rene might have a couple of mysterious things about him, but I trust him."

She put her arms around his neck and looked into his eyes for several long seconds, then said, "Marc Lange, you know a shit load about driving race cars, race car engineering, race car set up and a bunch of other things that all have to do with driving race cars very fast. But Sweetie, you do not know squat about reading and judging people."

"Ouch! I think I do a pretty good job of reading you, for instance."

"Oh really?" The hint of a smile was haunting the corners of her mouth again. "So how do you read me? What kind of vibes am I giving off right now?"

Moving towards her, he took her in his arms and slid his hands down inside her skirt and pulled her into him.

"Well if I really had to read the vibes you are giving off right now, if I had to guess, I'd say you want me to slowly take off your clothes and make love to you for hours." He bent over and gave her a long, slow, teasing, passionate kiss. He actually felt her go slightly weak in the knees for half a second before catching herself.

He leaned back as she took a gulp of air and said, "Well, I guess you *can* read people. You can certainly read me," and she reached behind his head and pulled his mouth back down to hers.

The call went through on the second ring.

"It's Horowicz."

"I know. Have something for me?"

"Yes, the likely location of The Client's operations."

"Where is it Horowicz? Don't make me come to Milano and beat it out of you."

Horowicz hesitated a moment, yet another betrayal added to the growing list. "Potsdam Germany."

"Are you sure?"

"As sure as I can be. My sources are certain that lately, this is where most of the transactions take place. So yes, I am sure."

"What else Horowicz? Understand that you can never hold back on me." His leverage over Horowicz complete.

"I think another shipment will arrive soon. They usually come within a window of time and that window is open."

"Good. We'll stand by then. But the second you know something, let me know."

Chapter 8

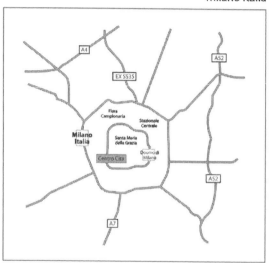

Luis and Jose waited for Marc to show up for their regular Monday morning Physio. But Marc slept in, having enjoyed a different kind of Physio. He even ignored Luis' phone call, preferring to snuggle in bed with April. Finally, around noon, Marc arrived at Team Fortunata HQ, after April urged him to go. She knew this Monday ritual started his week on the right note.

"Sorry, guys. I had an exhausting weekend with the Frenchman, didn't get in last night until really late, and when I walked in, there was April waiting for me. I wasn't expecting her till today. So naturally I stayed up talking. There was no way I could get in earlier."

"Apology accepted. But tell us all about your meeting with *the Man in Black* and what you did for the rest of the weekend that left you so beat," Luis demanded.

Marc grabbed a large cup of coffee instead of the usual filtered water and dumped several spoons of sugar in it. Luis and Jose exchanged knowing glances; their friend must be really tired—wink, wink.

"The guy is a trip, I gotta tell you." Marc grabbed a chair and sat down across from his friends.

"We're waiting!" probed Jose.

Marc went through all the details of the initial meeting, the trip to Dijon (including the life-according-to-Rene driving traits), driving in the Renault Clio Cup Championship and how he'd become a Man in Black, too. His friends laughed when he told them how he got his race name, Billy. He concluded with the good news: Rene agreed to drive for Team Technik.

"That's fantastic Marc, or should I say, Billy!" Jose said jubilantly. Luis gave Marc a thumbs up. They talked some more, then did an abbreviated workout. Jose had mercy on Marc.

Later, as Marc was heading for the door, Luis called out, "You haven't told us everything that happened this weekend. You left out the part about getting home and finding

April waiting for you."

"You guys don't want to hear about that!"

"Yes we do!" Luis and Jose said together, rolling their eyes.

"Geez you guys. Get a life!"

Shaking his head, he fairly sprinted through the door and down the steps. They heard his car door slam and he was gone.

It was mid-afternoon when Marc walked into Team Technik HQ. The place looked deserted. Everyone had taken a late lunch except Bala and Stella, who were at their computers in their shared office.

"Thought you could sneak in?" inquired Stella

"Something like that."

"Welcome back and thanks for calling us to give us a BLOODY update on what the HELL you've been up to this long weekend." Bala had obviously been waiting to un-load on Marc for some time.

"Sorry, my pitiful excuse for a cell phone doesn't work outside the UK."

"Well you could write," said Bala and he wiggled his fin-gers in the air simulating typing.

"Yeah, about that email stuff. I don't really do that."

"We know" they both said in unison.

"Soooo?" inquired Stella.

Marc looked at them for a long time. He saw the anxiety and excitement build in their faces.

"We have a new co-driver! AND, he agreed to pay us €105,000 per race."

"€105,000 per race! Woo-hoo! Yes!" yelled Stella, jumping up and pumping her arms.

Bala was already up and over beside Marc, clapping him on the shoulder. "Way to get it done, Mate! All is forgiven."

"Thank God," from both of them.

"Yes, thank God," echoed Marc.

He filled them in on the rest of the details but left out the bits regarding Rene and his private and sensitive business ventures as Bob. (Marc had misgivings about this stuff himself.) As he related his weekend adventures, including lap-by-lap accounts of both races, he saw the relief spread over their faces, then growing excitement about Team Technik's prospects. Now they could run the team with a full head of steam. No money worries for a change!

"Oh, Marc. What was it like when you saw April?" Stella asked, her eyes wide with innocence.

"Stella, do you tell us about your exciting, uh, dates with the man friends?"

"I would love to if you asked," she purred.

"Some things are just better left unsaid," grumbled an obviously uncomfortable Bala.

"Not to worry Bala, I don't kiss and tell."

"Pity love, I'm all about the details," smirked Stella as she returned to her computer.

Mr. X's technical resources used the tools provided by the hacker and were easily able to penetrate into the German highway toll system. They sent cars out on the road and flagged each one. It was so easy. Then they had cars randomly circle and park in Potsdam. They could descend on them within minutes. They were ready. Now they just needed Horowicz to affix a special RFID chip to the bag. They would be able to monitor it the whole way.

Stefan travelled to Milano and met with Horowicz, giving him the special RFID. It had a larger internal antenna so was easier to track. It was covered in the same satchel material as The Client used. Horowicz' instructions were to remove the adhesive and place it near the top edge of the bag, along the flap.

Stefan assured him that if this went down as planned, Horowicz's ex-wife and daughter would be safe. But he left the threat hanging letting him know that they still had him by the balls. He also promised that if this played out, he would be well rewarded by Mr. X, far richer than anything

The Client paid out. Horowicz was not assured.

Rene decided it was time to put the screws to Marc. If he was going to take Marc on an Engagement and show him the lucrative, if occasionally dangerous, career of being a *Driver*, Rene wanted to insure a successful introduction. Rene's agreement to pay Team Technik for his seat as a co-driver meant Marc owed Rene big time. Knowing the team's finances all too well, Rene decided to make sure Marc was desperate enough to accept his fate and begin training as a *Driver*. He placed a call to Raphael St. Germaine.

A secure fax arrived in Horowicz's email inbox. It simply stated a time that a courier would drop off the satchel and the time he needed to hand it off to a *Driver* — early the next morning. He would receive a one-way text stating the time and location for the drop. He was also responsible for negotiating the fee. His max budget - €160,000.

No time to dawdle. He would be burning the midnight oil cataloging all the diamonds in the shipment. His window to turn this shipment was tight.

He called Stefan to let him know the shipment of diamonds was imminent.

At Team Technik smiles were everywhere. The pleasant chirp of the phone seemed to fit right in. Stella answered its call while Marc and Bala continued congratulating themselves on what a great week Team Technik was having. All the mid-season updates from Porsche had been integrated, parts fabricated or ordered to replace the ones damaged in the wreck. Time had been reserved at Rockingham for Marc to run some test laps as soon as repairs were completed. They would be ready for the next race in plenty of time.

"Damn it to bloody hell!"

Four eyes opened wide as both men jerked their attention to Stella, who was staring at the handset in disbelief. "I don't bloody believe that bastard. That pig! That son of a bitch!"

"Stella, what are you talking about?"

"That bastard Raphael St. Germaine. He's refusing to pay what he agreed to!"

Marc was dumbstruck. Bala was in denial, staring at Stella. "Are you sure?"

"Do I look like I'm not sure? He said that he was sorry, that something had come up that he couldn't ignore and that it would take every penny he had to deal with it. Oh, and he wished us all the best. That backstabbing hypocrite!"

Shit! We've got all those invoices coming due. Bloody hell. I thought St. Germaine was a man of his word. What did that thug call me? Oh yeah. Fuckin' git. St. Germaine's a fuckin' git!

At home that evening Marc told April about the latest turn of events. "Bala and Stella worked all afternoon crunching numbers, playing 'what if' and looking at scenarios from every different angle. They found some solutions for specifics, but the bottom line is that we'll soon be in the red."

April stroked his short dark chestnut hair and kissed him gently on the cheek.

"Hang tough Sweetie, somehow things will work out."

He sat there, saying nothing. April's heart was breaking. His dream might very well be unraveling before her eyes.

His cell phone rang, startling them out of their gloom. Surprised, they stared at one another for a moment. It was late. *Hardly anyone has this number, Marc thought,* He glanced down at the phone. Rene! Smiling, he pushed the Talk button.

"Allo Marc, *mon ami*"

"Hi Rene, how's it going?"

"From the sound of your voice, better for me than for you!"

"Yeah it's been a tough day."

"Perhaps it can get better." Marc did not answer, so

Rene continued.

"Remember your part of our co-driver deal is to do something for me?"

"Yes, I remember …."

"It is time."

"This won't interfere with getting ready for the next race will it?"

"*Non, mon ami.* At the most, two and a half day."

"Okay, Rene. Shoot."

"You will fly to Milano's Linate Airport tomorrow morning. I booked your ticket already. Collect it at the British Air ticket counter at London Gatwick by 9:00. Your flight leave at 11:30. When you arrive at Linate, I will pick you up. We will have a chance to talk, then a nice dinner together and the next day we begin our Engagement."

"What do you mean?"

"You will see, Marc."

Marc hung up the phone. He and April looked at each other.

"What was that all about?"

"I really don't know. It was Rene Dufour. I've got to meet him tomorrow. Like the man said, I guess we'll see."

"Sweetie, I don't know. I don't have a good feeling about this."

"We've already been through a lot together. If he wanted to play any games or do anything strange, he's had plenty of opportunities. Besides, at the moment he's my only hope of salvaging this season, not to mention the team."

She kissed him and told him to be very careful. He kissed her back and said he would, as he pulled her towards him in a deep embrace.

The box from the courier arrived early. Howowicz signed for it, then tore open the large international shipping container removing the satchel. He sent a one-time text that the shipment had arrived. A Moment later, he heard tiny audible clicks as the locks were remotely deactivated.

He knew the sequence as he opened each container, extracted the diamonds, weighed and cataloged each for weight, size, brilliance, carets, color – in other words the standard reporting a gemologist would conduct for each diamond. He would enter all the data into a report and declare an overall value for the shipment. Indeed, this would take him all night long. Last, he would deduct 3% of the total weight of diamonds and keep those for himself. He was never one gram over or under, it was, as it had always been 3%. He felt a tinge of regret and remorse as he plucked the first diamond and started the process.

The next morning, on his way to Gatwick, Marc went by the team's HQ and left a note for Bala and Stella telling them he had to meet Rene to discuss some details of their business arrangements. And yes, he would try to find a way to call.

He continued on to Gatwick in a funk. He hated flying. He felt uncomfortable leaving someone else in charge of his life. Pilots were no exception. Trains were all right, at least you were on the ground; but he preferred driving. He liked being in control of his destiny, trusting his instincts and reactions to deal with any situation.

Collecting his ticket was the easy part. Not so much going through security. He silently cursed the terrorists again for making airport security checks ever more onerous. After what seemed like hours, he got to his gate and waited for his flight.

As soon as the plane was airborne, Marc remembered the other reason why he hated to fly—fellow passengers. He had to sit in a middle seat between a large Italian woman returning home to visit her family and a Middle-Eastern man who smelled faintly of garlic and body odor. Between her incessant talking about her wayward family and the man next to him, leaning against the window, passed out and snoring with his mouth hanging open, Marc tried not to grind his teeth into powder.

The woman's voice droned on and on. Marc saw her mouth moving, but nothing she said registered in his brain.

He looked around him. He saw people connected to laptops, iPods, smart phones and every other type of personal electronics. They were in another world. They were tuned into one they held in their hands.

Marc did not understand this. His world was visceral, defined by what he did with his hands, feet, eyes and brain. For the most part, he shunned TV, movies (except for the classics) and video games in favor of a world that he could feel, touch, hear and smell. His life was action, movement, all senses fully engaged. A race-car driver and a team owner did not need a joy stick.

Yeah, and I'm also in debt up to my eyeballs. If I can't find a way to manage the team's finances, there'll be no more racing, no championships, no moving up in the racing world. So why am I here? What am I willing to do to get ahead? What's pushing me? My past? Hmmph! Such as it was. I'm sure that one brief fuck up is not going to define me. Besides I've pushed it so far down, so deep—but what about this guy Rene? He makes me think there may be another way, another path.

He thought about Rene and wondered what he had meant by *Engagement.* Maybe Rene was taking him some place he did not want to go. Someplace he did not know yet. His mind drifted. The woman's voice droned on. Marc dozed off.

Suddenly the plane slammed into the tarmac and lurched upon landing. Marc woke up with a jolt. The woman on his left was still talking. The man on his right was waking up and rubbing his eyes. Marc waited for his turn to deplane. As he entered the terminal at Aeroporto Linate, his mind was still unsettled.

Marc collected his bag and waited by the curb. Scanning the area, looking for Rene or the yellow Renault, he suddenly heard tires screeching in protest. Focusing his attention, he saw a sleek gray shape heading straight towards him. Marc stood his ground. He knew who it was and knew the display was meant to attract his attention. At the last possible second, the car stopped, centimeters from the curb and Marc's knees. The passenger window slid down and a familiar face turned towards him.

"Need a ride, *mon ami?*"

"No thanks. I think a crazy Italian taxi is preferable."

Laughing, Rene pointed his thumb towards the trunk as it softly clicked open. Marc was unaware that the Maserati Quattroporte GT S was Rene's work car, but Marc was very aware of the Grigio Granito paint job. It was superb, he thought, a deep three-dimensional slate gray that seemed to have both depth and layers. Sliding into the passenger seat, his senses luxuriated in the Bordeaux-colored leather seats piped in dark gray. The carbon fiber trim kit on the dash, central console and door trim might be a bit over the top, he thought. He preferred dark woods in luxury cars like Mahogany or Rosewood. More elegant, in his opinion. He had driven or ridden in more exotic cars than he could remember, but this combination of classic styling, high-tech functionality and sumptuous comfort was going to be his benchmark for a luxury car for a very long time.

"Where did you steal this?" Marc asked as he closed the door with a vault-like thunk and buckled his seatbelt.

"It was sitting by the side of the road, with a sign that said 'please take me, but be gentle.'"

Rene pulled the lever just in front of the steering wheel towards him to engage first, planted his foot on the floor and took off from the airport curb in a cloud of tire smoke and an explosion of sound from the motor, exhaust and tires.

"It's nice to know you can read *and* follow instructions," commented Marc dryly.

"It is good to see you too Marc. We're staying at the Hotel Principe Di Savoia Milano. I chose it because it puts us right in the middle of the city and because it's my favorite five-star hotel."

The trip from Linate to the city center took only a few minutes. They entered Milano from the east and rolled past several of the *Circonvallazioni,* the ring roads that circled the city. Checking in, Rene tossed the car keys to the valet. As he surrendered the car, he pulled out his iPhone, touched a few buttons and dropped it back in his pocket. Marc wondered what that was about.

As they entered the lobby, Marc decided that Rene had consistently great taste in lodging and restaurants. Everywhere they stayed or dined had been first class, certainly way beyond Marc's means. Maybe not his taste, but for sure his bank account. As he and Rene approached the VIP registration area, the general manager greeted Rene by his first name. Marc was impressed.

"I love this city. I have been here dozens of times on business. There is not much to look at for tourists, but it has great restaurants, great shopping and some of the most beautiful and fashionable women in Italy."

Marc smiled inwardly. *Perhaps Rene wasn't just all business.*

"Let us drop off our luggage, then we take a walk towards Centro Citta and I will show you what I mean."

They met back at the lobby and headed out for Rene's tour of Milano. Rene had not lied about the beautiful and fashionable *signore* of Milano, and some of the young *signorine* were spectacular. *April*, he thought, *I love you and only you, but I'm still a guy and I still love to look at great-looking gals.*

Later, Rene took Marc to a famous bakery where they were rewarded with what Rene assured Marc was the most delicious panzarotti in Italy: small pastries made of deep fried pizza dough filled with tomato sauce and cheese, perfect crunchy bliss. They ate three each. Afterwards, Rene took him on a walking tour of Milano that Marc found captivating and charming. Rene was as knowledgeable about Milano as if it were his hometown. He elaborated on the history of the city and its structures, art and politics, including an account of an array of characters that included dukes, popes, whores, beggars, artists, criminals and politicians.

Some individuals inhabited more than one of these categories. His stories ranged from ancient times to yesterday afternoon and were told with wit, insight and a knowledge of scandals that was encyclopedic. By the time they made it back to Principe Di Savoia, Marc's head was full of interesting, funny, gossipy stories.

The panzarotti were a faint memory by the time they dined at the Antica Trattoria della Pesa.

"This is one of my very favorites in Milano!"

Well that's promising. Marc thought. As much as he wanted to jump right into the conversation and discover what his end of the bargain was, he nevertheless restrained himself. Rene had agreed to co-drive and fund Team Technik if Marc in turn did something for him. While Marc could not imagine what this *thing* might be, he had agreed to the bargain. He was still not sure why. Perhaps because Rene made it sound right. Perhaps because he wanted to test himself beyond racing a fast car, to know what he was made of. Who was Marc Lange anyway? He felt he was going to find out with Rene's help. He picked at his food, absorbed in his inner thoughts.

"So Marc, I think that you are wondering."

"Wondering what?" Marc replied trying to sound casual, but he dropped his fork in his plate of Costoletta alla Milanese.

"To begin, I told you I would do something for you if

you in turn did something for me."

"Yeah, I remember you saying that."

"So tomorrow we begin our journey. I mean this both literally and figuratively."

"Literally and figuratively?"

"Perhaps a bit dramatic, no?"

"Well Rene you do seem to have a certain flair."

"That is funny. Normally I am very stoic."

Rene stopped and poured another glass of Barolo and after swirling the wine, took a sip and then took a couple of bites of his osso bucco. "*Parfait,*" he said, very softly, as if unaware he was speaking aloud. "Next time, you must try the *Os buc*. The veal here is without equal and their inter-pretation of classic Milanese dishes is always authentic, but with a contemporary, unexpected twist that one must ad-mire. I really think the cuisine of Milano is superior to that of every other region of Italy." He put down his silverware, picked up his napkin and wiped his lips, then stared directly at Marc.

"Now we talk seriously." His tone had changed, direct and serious, as if another Rene Dufour had appeared out of nowhere. Marc was unprepared, but not surprised. He had suspected that there was this side to Rene and that he would soon see it. "This is very important, *mon ami*. Tomorrow you must follow my instructions to the letter for a successful meeting." Marc sat at attention. This was not what he expected. "We will meet a man. I will introduce you as my protégé. You do not speak unless the other man asks you a direct question and then you keep your answer as short as possible."

Marc stared.

"I will begin negotiations and if things go well, a contract will be struck. You are there to observe, to learn and above all, to keep an open mind. Now, do you agree?"

Marc nodded. What the hell was going on? But he had agreed. Now it was time to see where the agreement would take him.

"Oh, and one more thing Marc. Tomorrow you are going to be Billy again."

"But …."

"No more tonight. You know everything you need to know for now. Tomorrow, watch and learn. Now, I believe a bite of dessert would be pleasant. Will you join me?"

The envelope with the **RFID** sat next to him on the work bench, like a sharp needle, jabbing him, a constant reminder of the job he had to do to keep his ex-wife and daughter alive. Problem was he loved them both deeply. He still did not understand why she just up and left him. It made him sad to know that now he was compromised. They would be dead if he did not do this next thing. Horowicz peeled back the adhesive and placed the RFID along the top edge of the flap. It perfectly matched the color of the interior. It was hard to see it once it was in place. He sent the report to a secure fax number, the placed the report in an envelope, Horowicz put it inside the satchel along with all the diamonds. As he closed the satchel, he heard the same set of clicks, the locks arming themselves. His work done he looked at the clock beside his desk. It was nearly 6:00 AM, he had worked through the night. He felt like shit, he was exhausted and had that pit in the bottom of his gut, the one that said he was guilty as hell.

Before he closed his eyes for a few minutes, he called Stefan to let him know, everything was in play. The next call would be to let him know when the transaction would go down. Then the rest was up to Stefan, Horowicz completed his part of the betrayal.

Ding! A secure one-way text. 10:00 AM, Café Ponte Vecchio near Stazione Centrale in the center of Milano. The text also said he would be handing off the satchel to The *Driver* known as Bob.

Horowicz placed another call to Stefan to fill him in on what he hoped would be the last of the details for this shipment of diamonds.

"The text said I am to hand over the shipment at 10:00AM at a café near Stazione Centrale."

"Anything else?"

"Oh, yes. The text said I am to hand off the shipment to a *Driver* known as Bob."

"Bob? Really, it said Bob?"

"Yes. I said that."

There was a pause, Uli Petrovski's dreams of revenge were about to come true.

"Thank you Horowicz. Just deliver the satchel, then we'll take it from there. Don't worry, we'll be in touch." The call quickly ended.

Horowicz had dealt with Bob before. He remembered he was a very solid, thorough *Driver*. He would try to warn him. Maybe he could let him know telling him it would be a very high factor. Yes, that was it. A high factor would alert him. But how high a factor?

Uli Petrovski thumbed the cell phone to end the call. He could not believe what he just heard. The *Driver* who was going to take the diamonds from Milano to The Client, was none other than Bob. Bob. His dream of killing the one man who had thwarted him twice. Who had killed two of his best operatives. Bob. Who had touched his baby girl and been rude remarks to her, showing her no respect. Bob. The *Driver* who always came through, no matter what. Bob. Only this time he would take the diamonds, take The Client and finally put a bullet into Bob's head. Fuck that, he put several bullets into his head, chest, stomach, he would empty a full magazine of flesh piercing bullets into that little shit. There would be no escape for Bob this time. Only death. But before he fired that one shot, he would make sure Bob knew that he had completely and utterly failed. And in that brief moment, he would know that Uli Petrovski had won.

Vitaly Zerov, Uli's second in command of this operation looked at this boss. He'd seen that look before. He knew that when he saw that look, there was nothing between Uli and his target.

"Uli, what did you just find out from Horowicz."

"Mind your own business."

"This is my business. Mr. X will want to know."

Uli breathed in and out several times, calming himself. He knew he had to report in to Mr. X. He picked up another secure cell phone and sent a message via Signal. A moment later the cell phone lit up with an incoming video bridge. Uli accepted the call and placed the phone on a table.

"Status?"

"The shipment will be handed off to a *Driver* at 10:00 Local."

"Identity of The *Driver*?" Uli hesitated and Mr. X immediately knew there was an issue.

"Petrovski, I sense tension where there should only be

keen preparation, what is it?"

"The *Driver* is someone I have dealt with in the past, his name is Bob."

"And you have a debt to settle with this Bob?

"Yes."

"Let me very clear. Do not let your feelings or some petty vendetta get in the way of our operation. Am I clear?"

"Yes, Mr. X."

"Very well. Based on this new intel, I will have a team follow this Bob."

"Mr. X, please I know how to run this. The RFID system we are using, Vitaly here has it up and running and he assures me that it will allow us to track Bob and the shipment of diamonds. If the final destination is Potsdam, we will successfully complete the operations. But at this point, bringing in another element only increased the likelihood that we run into issues."

"I will not hear of it. I have made my decision. Call me when this operation is completed, when you have the diamonds and The Client. I trust you will deal with this Bob, but, and I cannot stress this enough—the operation comes first."

"Understood." He pressed the button to end the call. He looked over at Vitaly who had his arms crossed, he did not look happy.

"You heard the man Uli, the operation comes first."

"I know how to do my job Vitaly. You do not need to remind me." Petrovski snapped.

Vitaly started laying out the high-powered RFID readers on the table, checking each one to make sure it was correctly calibrated. Next, he went to each laptop that the team would use and made sure the RFID tracking program was up and running. The door opened to their small command base and four other men entered the room, one went to Uli and slapped him on the shoulder.

"Everything is ready, we are good to go if our target shows up."

"Very good. We have a few hours. I suggest we get some good food and good rest."

The next morning they arrived at a small, rundown café not too far from the *Stazione Centrale*—Milan's main train terminal. The café was the kind of place where busy workers make their way to the cashier, pay for their espresso, slide up to the espresso bar and gave the barista their ticket. It was an automatic ritual that they did without thinking, taking the small, well-used cup of hot, bitter, intensely-caffeinated, charcoal black espresso, adding enough sugar to raise the level of the coffee to the cup's rim, then drinking it down in one long sip. They would comment to the barista on the current football, auto race, political scandal, *sciopero*, state of the economy, and leave. Marc was sure that everyone in the place had been starting his workday here in just this way for years. There were only three tiny tables. The regulars swarmed at the bar. Visitors were not encouraged to stay.

Rene and Marc sat at one of the tables. A thin, balding man walked into the café. His squinting, furtive eyes took in the café in one glance. He had that drab look of a bookkeeper or civil servant or bureaucrat who worked only for a paycheck and thought about little in the world beyond his work. Unremarkable in every way, Marc thought, except that he looked nervous. He held a small black satchel a little too tightly. He made eye contact with Rene, who simply nodded towards the empty chair at their table. He sat down, clutching the satchel in his lap.

"Espresso?"

"No, nothing for me."

"I will take another. Billy?" Marc shook his head as Rene motioned to the *barista* holding up one finger indicating one more espresso, but he then turned his hand sideways holding two fingers indicating a double.

"So how are you Horowicz?"

"Fine Bob, it's been a long time. But now, I think we have a problem." He spoke haltingly, like he was trying to think of the words as he spoke them.

"Yes?"

"Who is he?"

"Ah, that is Billy, my protégé."

"This is most irregular. Normally I would protest, but I do not have time to find another *Driver*."

Driver!? What the hell is this guy talking about? It's like we're sitting here negotiating something illegal.

Marc shifted slightly in his seat. Both men shot him stern glances. The barista brought the double espresso to Rene with a look of total disdain.

Clearing his throat Rene continued. "I understand your reticence. It is a departure from past procedure. But I assure you anything we say here is strictly confidential and any agreement we reach will be held in total confidence. Besides, he is sworn to secrecy under penalty of death."

Startled, Marc jumped in his seat just a tiny bit as both men shot him another glance. Then Horowicz turned his focus completely towards Rene, who calmly resumed the thread of the negotiation.

"Destination?"

"Potsdam."

"Known address?"

"You will receive a text en route."

"When?"

"15:30 with the address, so you should plan to be within

40 km of the city."

"Expected delivery date?"

"Tomorrow between 16:00 and 17:00."

"Cargo?"

"Single item."

"Size?"

Horowicz patted the satchel.

Neither man shifted his gaze or moved in his seat. As if this were some type of pre-set, rehearsed scene. Marc sat there amazed, fearful and curious all at the same time.

"And the factor?" Horowicz squirmed in his seat, he was clearly uncomfortable.

"Umm. Could be high." He started sweating.

"How high?"

"Uhhh. Maybe a five." Horowicz panicked for a second. What if he was setting the factor too low.

"Maybe higher?"

"Ummm, could be a six, maybe as high as a seven."

"Hmmm. Of course that increases the fee considerably."

"How considerably?"

"Normally the fee for this type of Engagement would be 85. But with the higher factor, the potential for damage, the fee is 135."

"135! That's impossible! It's robbery!" Horowicz fairly shouted, making even the uninterested *barista* glance in their direction.

"Horowicz, you should really calm yourself. If you can find another *Driver* to make your delivery schedule, please make the call."

Rene rose and signaled to Marc to do the same. Without pausing, he placed some Euros on the espresso bar and they started to the door.

"I'll give you 125."

Rene began speaking with his back to Horowicz to emphasize the point.

"You insult my integrity and embarrass me in front of my protégé. The fee is now 160."

"Ahhh. My God, you are a bandit."

"Suit yourself." He continued towards the exit.

"Okay! I can do 150, but really, absolutely no more," His voice had dropped almost to a whisper.

Slowly Rene turned around and walked towards Horowicz who drew back in obvious fear.

"Horowicz, what are you not telling me?"

Horowicz shook his head that he did knew nothing else. "No there is nothing, just the cargo is very, very valuable."

Bob was not persuaded. He bent close to Horowiz's ear.

"I am not the bandit. I am not one you should fear. But whoever the people are who want what is in that satchel are the ones you should fear. And that, *Signore*, is why you pay me my price."

The three men left the café and stood outside. Rene nodded to Horowicz indicating that he should leave. Rene and Marc watched him walk towards Stazione Centrale and disappear into the crowd before they turned to walk to the Maserati parked out of sight safely around the corner. Tightly clutching the case, Rene popped the trunk and put the satchel into the safe before gently closing the lid and nodding towards Marc to get into the Quattroporte. Marc complied, but in a semi-trance. He entered the car, shut the door and slowly put on his seat belt.

Sitting in the Maserati as it serenely slipped through the traffic, it seemed a perfect antithesis to the mental storm raging in Marc's head. What had he just witnessed? What the hell were Rene's private business affairs and what had he gotten himself into? Where to begin?

"What the hell was that Rene? What the fuck did I just witness; a drug deal, something criminal, something illegal?"

"Marc, we have a long drive ahead of us. I think we'll have more than enough time to discuss things."

"Wait a minute. We're driving to Potsdam Germany? Shit, that's hundreds of kilometers away for God's sake. For what? For €150?"

"Add a thousand to the end of that Marc."

Marc just stared at Rene. He had no comeback. It took him several seconds to realize his mouth was still open.

A very long red light allowed Rene to enter their destination into the Sat-Nav system of the Maserati, check the sync of his iPhone with the car's special sub-systems, and to quickly test the uplink for the off-the-books intelligence feeds from the appropriate police and security agencies. (He did not care that Hector said this feature was still in beta mode.)

Before the light turned green Rene put the Maserati in gear. Using the steering wheel mounted thumb wheel, Rene scrolled through the many options available to him glancing at each sub-system on the video display. He really wanted to check the newest toy that Hector had installed: a military-spec night-vision system, integrated into the exterior cameras. It should give him a very deep field of vision at night, but he needed darkness to play with that. Another option that Hector included in the latest upgrade was the new stealth mode that killed all interior and exterior lights, even while braking. In his own way, Rene was excited about this journey. His danger antennae were attuned for anything that was out of the ordinary, but here in the dense traffic in Milano, it was hard to pick out a tail. Out on the open road, that would be different.

Marc sat very still, his head tilted away from Rene, looking at the view out the window, but without seeing anything.

Rene knew the questions were forming and would come tumbling out. He waited patiently for Marc to sort out the conflict and confusion in his mind and begin what would be the most important question and answer session in either of their lives.

When they left Milano and headed north towards the A9 Autostrada, they began to pick up speed as the traffic started to thin out. Entering the highway, Rene's AutoPass allowed them to speed past the toll station. Reaching into the back-seat floorboard, Marc grabbed one of the bottles of water he noticed on the floor when he got in the car. He took a big swig and slowly put the cap back on the bottle. Finally, he turned to Rene. He was apparently ready to talk.

"I am sure you have many questions Marc. Are you finally ready to talk? Are you ready to listen?"

"€150,000 for one drive? That's just, I mean that's just staggering. Sorry Rene or Bob or whatever the hell you call yourself, but you do not just grow grapes and make a little wine. What are you really!? What do you really do?"

"I will tell you, but you need to listen carefully—with the big ears and with an open mind."

The Maserati increased speed as it moved into the left lane. Rene began the game of flashing his high beams at the slower cars. Automatically, as traffic thinned, Rene started to scan the surrounding traffic, looking for patterns in the groups of following cars. Something so subtle, that only he would notice. His demeanor softened slightly, but his laser focus on the surrounding traffic did not.

"So, Marc, where do I start?"

"You could start at the beginning and tell me who you really are."

"Ah ha, exactly, that *is* the beginning. So, we will start there."

Rene paused for a moment to gather his thoughts. He was so sure he was ready to tell Marc everything, but now that the moment had arrived, it was more difficult than he had imagined. Not only would he have to open up, reveal the real Rene Dufour, but reveal "Bob" as well, the man he frequently became. He had lived this double life for so long that the two had merged. Explaining all this to Marc and keeping the two persons distinct suddenly seemed far more difficult than he expected.

A door in his mind opened briefly. Second thoughts drifted out but he forced that door shut. He had come this far. He would not renege. Rene would tell his story and give Marc the opportunity to decide for himself: live a second, secret life. Or pass.

"Rene Dufour is my real name. And I really am a farmer, a grower of splendid grapes and a maker of wine. But long before that, I was a junior officer in the paratroopers. Later I joined the regional police near Dijon and moved to the *Renseignements Generaux*, now called the DCRI, the French equivalent of your American FBI. I was very good at my job, which was to infiltrate organized crime and expose illegal business activities. In the process, I completed my studies in criminal psychology. Thanks to my military background, I could take care of myself physically. I enjoyed the excitement. And my understanding of criminal personalities let me anticipate them more often than not. I loved my work."

"Then why did you leave that life, if you were good at it and loved it."

"Indeed I was, sort of like you Marc. You love to drive, to race but would you be willing to leave it?"

"Doubtful, but I guess it depends on the situation."

"*Exactement*! It was all about the situation. And for me, how do you say in English? Life hit me right in the face very, very hard."

"I'm sorry."

"Don't be! You make a choice in life and you live with the consequences. It really is as simple as that. My marriage, it finally ended with a bang. I had two children, very smart, each attending an expensive *université*, one studying to be a doctor, the other a lawyer, but my ex-wife poisoned them against me; sadly, they are spoiled, useless, entitled brats. So now I find myself with two house payments, one expensive ex-wife and the bills from the *université*; I was drowning in debt up to my eyeballs. Is that an American expression?"

"Something like that," commented Marc, thinking about

his own debts.

"I made a very good salary for a policeman, but the debt was very bad and for sure, there was no way out. One day I went to a friend—no, more of a professional acquaintance—who, let us say, straddled the line between what is legal and what is not. I do not know why I went to him, but something drove me. Perhaps it was instinct. It was one of those times when you start to open your mouth, the words start to come out and then you realize it is too late. We have let the horses out of the barn, so to speak."

Rene stopped and let the point seep in as he scanned the traffic behind them. Still nothing. He swiveled his head and glanced to see if Marc was listening. Marc was entranced.

"My acquaintance said, 'I may have a something for you. You might not like it, but it could solve your problems.'

"Of course, I asked him what it was. My internal danger detector was going off. He told me he would be in contact if and when something could be arranged. I did not have to wait long. He called the next day and suggested we meet for a glass of wine to discuss this opportunity." Rene took a deep breath before he continued. He had finally come to the moment of truth. He was about to reveal what he did and why Bob existed.

"He was very direct. There was no idle chit-chat. He said, 'So Rene, you need money and I have business associates that have the need of certain services.'

"As you can imagine, the hairs on the back of my neck stood up."

Marc caught himself starting to nod.

"My friend continued. 'My associates have the need to secure your services in what we shall call Engagements. Each Engagement is a trip you make for a client. These are under the radar. A client will ask you to take people or things or people and things from one destination to another, perhaps to several destinations.'

"I stopped him right there and asked if this involved drugs or guns or something completely illegal. 'No, no. Nothing like that.' He acted like I had just slapped his face and insulted him. 'Don't think like a bureaucrat. No, these are very sophisticated clients. It is just that their cargo is very, very important.'"

Rene paused to make sure his words were sinking in. He scanned the traffic again. It had picked up a bit as they drove north. They were in the industrial belts that ringed Milano and large lorries began entering the highway. This gave another car trailing the Maserati good cover, so Rene started scanning for that as well.

Rene gestured and Marc handed him a bottle of water from the back. After several long gulps, he gathered his thoughts before continuing. Marc was transfixed, waiting for Rene to return to the story.

"So, he had my attention at this point. Then he laid out

the details. 'The service, the Engagement, is very discreet and needs to be handled in a professional manner. These people usually demand anonymity. Every Engagement involves precious cargo that cannot be delivered by normal commercial lines because such services can be compromised. Both for the anonymity and for the assurance of delivery, these clients are willing to pay a great sum of money.'

"I asked him how great was this sum. 'Well, that depends,' he said. 'Each Engagement is different, each cargo is different. Sometimes there are complications.'"

"Such as?" Rene cleared his throat, then continued, "He replied, 'Oh the usual. Someone else wants what you carry or you have to deliver the cargo to a dangerous location or sometimes the cargo itself is very dangerous. So, the fee is adjusted accordingly.'"

"If I'm going to consider this secondary occupation you're describing to me, what exactly are we talking here?" Again Rene glanced at Marc and turned back to the road. "And he told me, the fee can go from thousands to tens of thousands to hundreds of thousands of Euros. That's how precious and important the cargo can be."

Marc's mind was reeling. He started to grasp exactly what Rene meant when he said, 'I will do something for you, if you will do something for me.' This was *way* beyond the normal course of racing much less normal business arrangements. This was totally out of Marc's comfort zone and most likely his abilities as well. He felt the interior of the car closing in around him. He took several deep breaths before asking the next question. "Rene. What do you expect of me?"

"I expect nothing of you Marc. I am only showing you a way to make some serious big cash. Perhaps you will like it. Perhaps you will not. Only you will have to decide."

"But why me? And why now?"

"A good question. It deserves an answer. I have participated in this secret career for a long time. I need to slow down. Soon, I hope, to retire. But I have to look after my clients. I have a big book of business that I would like to pass on. I am willing to give it to you, Marc, but you have to be willing to take it. So let me ask you a question Marc: have you strayed too close to the flame?" He waited, but Marc volunteered nothing, Rene continued, "I did. One time, I got too close, I thought about going over to the other side. The money, the power…." He sighed before continuing.

Marc just stared. Rene went on, "It was very intoxicating. In my under-cover work, I had infiltrated a money-laundering organization. Not the kind where someone got hurt, they just moved around a lot of money, but of course illegally. One morning, I took a long soul-searching look in the mirror and did not like what stared back." Silence.

"I took them down hard. I had to, I had to get my soul back."

He stopped for some time before he spoke again, searching for the right words. "So, when this opportunity to become a *Driver* appeared out of nowhere, I knew, having stared into the abyss once before, it was not too hard to take the Engagement. I found that being a *Driver* means that sometimes you have to straddle the gray line. But I think that somehow my fate was sealed, I was staggering beneath the burden of my debts."

Marc shifted uncomfortably in the seat, looking straight ahead.

"Soooo, what about you, ever strayed too close to the flame Marc?"

Marc said nothing; he just sat there, pretending to be someplace else.

"I am waiting…."

"Yeah…" he choked out, that deep place opening a crack.

"In college, I wasn't racing, but I still loved the speed, I really missed going fast. I started running with some of my buddies, it turned into a bit of a street racing gang. It got a little crazy and some people got hurt. I ended up getting arrested."

"Really! I checked your record, there was nothing! It was perfectly clean."

"I know." Marc whispered. "It cost my dad a lot, more than money, it cost a lot of favors. I screwed up and it has been with me ever since. I don't want to talk about it any-more."

"Maybe Marc when you are ready and trust me a little more, you will tell me the whole story. I'd like to hear it."

Rene waited through the silence for Marc to sort things out.

"You still haven't answered *Why me?*"

"Marc, I know where you are in your life. I have been there too. I needed money and this gave me the chance to get my life back. Or in your case, get it back on track. Pun intended!"

They both needed the laugh to break the tension. But Rene continued. "I had no hope. The pressure for me was almost unbearable. I could not fail my family, even if my family, or at least my wife, failed me. You have the same pressure I think. Your team depends on you. They have bills, they must eat, must pay the rent. You must win to get prize money from racing and to keep Team Technik's spon-sors. And I know that you have to buy a new car from Por-sche next year to keep up."

Rene glanced at Marc. Time stood still as the Maserati hurtled down the Autostrada at 190 kph. "So, where are you going to get that kind of money?"

"I don't know where."

"You can get it now by taking this Engagement with me while I teach you how to be a *Driver.*"

Still not convinced, Marc shifted in his seat and gazed out the window for a moment. Finally, he spoke up again. "Rene, that's asking a lot."

"You are right! It is not just a lot, it is a *shit* load!" They both chuckled.

"Look. I am only showing you a path, an option. Right now I am opening a door for you. After you look around, you can choose to become a *Driver*. On the other hand, once we finish this Engagement you can close the door and walk away forever. I hope you like what you see. If you decide to close the door, however, I will not help you beyond what we agreed to for the rest of the racing season. And if you decide right now that you do not want to complete this Engagement with me, I will drop you in the nearest city. Make your decision wisely. There is no turning back," Rene said.

Marc shook his head as if to clear it.

"One last thing. When you complete an Engagement, you are handed an envelope with the fee and Marc, sometimes the envelope is very, very fat."

Marc remained silent. *I've taken the team as far as I can. We've got the talent and drive to win and move up the racing series ladder. But we've had lousy luck and not enough cash. I promised myself I'd do everything I could to make sure the team succeeds, if only I got the chance. Now, this man I hardly know is offering me that chance—but at what cost? And what about April? Could I keep it a secret from her? Not even if I wanted to. I know her. Besides, would I want to?*

Rene drove, guessing what Marc was going through. Hadn't he done it himself? After some time, Marc spoke. His voice was quiet, but firm. No doubts. "OK Rene, let's do this. Let's see how it plays out."

"*Bon! Mon ami.* You will not regret your decision."

It was early afternoon as the Maserati crossed the frontier from Italy into Switzerland. When they passed Como, they moved from the A9 Autostrada to a smaller secondary highway, the E35. Although a four-lane highway, the pace slowed considerably due to the large number of lorries trying to pass each other. Using this down time to his advantage, Rene checked through Hector's latest modifications that turned the Maserati into a driving fortress. He described the structural changes to Marc.

"This car can reach top speed of 305 kph if necessary."

Marc whistled his appreciation. "The windows are bullet-proof Polymer. The body panels are Kevlar lined and there is a Kevlar mesh protecting the radiator. Tires are also bullet-proof. The safe in the trunk is carbon fiber Kevlar and another smaller one is integrated into your side of the dash. There is a full medical kit in the trunk with a defibrillator and oxygen tank. Electronic modifications include a camera package that covers 360°. I can upload and download anything from my iPhone including police and security agency surveillance data. There is also a new night-vision system which needs testing."

Marc had admired the rare beauty of their transportation, but now he was beginning to appreciate its uniqueness. He realized that—having now committed himself—he was excited. And his respect for Rene grew exponentially.

Meanwhile, some odd movement in the traffic behind them caught Rene's attention. He changed lanes to the inside to avoid a larger group of slower moving cars clustered together in the left lane. He decided to stay to the right for a few kilometers, continuing to pass other cars on the inside just to change the pace and possibly flush any shadows out. About five vehicles back, he noticed the nose of a black Vauxhall VXR8 peek out to the left of the last lorry in the line. As soon as the car had a sight line to the Maserati, it tucked back in behind the lumbering truck even though it had a clear opportunity to pass. Rene slowed the Quattroporte slightly as he approached a lorry in the inside lane and let several cars overtake him. Rene wanted to see what the Vauxhall was up to. As if on cue, the Vauxhall dropped back too. And then, Rene saw the second car tailing the Maserati, its driver's inattention to the traffic patterns exposed it to Rene's all-seeing eyes. Rene smiled. Two identical black VXR8s crossing from Northern Italy into Switzerland at the same time, on the same highway? Not in this version of reality.

Interesting choice, Rene thought. *Not something you see every day. More power than the current Mercedes. Except they still like their 'bad guys' black cars.* Like every other car nut, he had read about the Vauxhalls—over 500 bhp under the hood, a top speed of over 282 kph. Two possibilities came to Rene. Either he and Marc were being shadowed or the Vauxhalls were the initial chase team. It was too early for them to make a move. For one thing, too much traffic. For another, they were too close to the Italian and Swiss frontiers. He assumed they had follow at a discreet distance and report on the Maserati's progress.

With the modifications made to the Maserati, including an oversized Kevlar-wrapped gas tank, they had more than an 800 km range, so he was not worried about that. Still, in his profession paranoia was a virtue. He called up the main Sat-Nav screen and ran the bug/tracking device detection app. Satisfied that the Maserati was clean, he drove on.

Marc noticed a subtle difference in Rene's driving. He was much more focused and intense. Several screens popped up on the Sat-Nav and Marc realized Rene was running an application. After a few moments Rene seemed satisfied with what he saw but he did not relax. "We are being followed. Two black VXR8s."

"Great." Marc said with a touch of nervousness in his voice. "Are we in danger?"

"I do not know yet. It is too early to tell for sure. We need a better look at our shadows. They are either just tailing us or perhaps they have in mind something else."

Marc shifted uncomfortably in his seat, although the Maserati seats were sublime. Something was bothering him.

"Back during your negotiation with Horowicz you mentioned the word 'factor' and then when you mentioned additional damage he really seemed to get very upset. What is this factor?"

"An astute question. Part of a negotiation involves determining how dangerous the Engagement might be. That part is called the factor and it is rated from one to ten. A one is a drive in the park with stops to take a piss and perhaps have *an espresso* or two, maybe even have a nice lunch or dinner at a good restaurant."

"And a ten?"

"As you might guess, a ten means you had better be well-armed, have plenty of bullets and the full tank of gas. It will be a very interesting ride, one that you may not survive, but if you do and you negotiated well, the pay is fantastic."

Marc closed his eyes and shook his head back and forth. Of course being a *Driver* was not going to be easy. "Tell me Rene. Have you ever been on an Engagement with a ten factor?"

"Well a factor nine on a couple of Engagements. But a Ten? They are almost mythical, but there's always a first time for everything." Rene chucked at his little joke.

Marc jumped a bit at Rene's joke, trying to decide if he was serious or not.

"Are you armed now?"

"But Marc, of course. Always." Rene opened the left side

of his jacket.

Marc saw the handle of a semi-automatic pistol peeking out of a shoulder holster. He berated himself for not noticing the bulge in Rene's jacket earlier.

Rene then patted the base of his seat. "There is a hidden compartment under here with another pistol, extra magazines and a military-spec fighting knife. It helps to be prepared. Is that not an American motto?"

Now well inside Switzerland, Rene focused on the two cars following them. He decided his earlier move to drop back in traffic had probably not raised the suspicions of the two tails. They apparently did not realize he had flushed them out. He altered his speed slightly to see what the tailing cars would do. They kept their distance. Rene adjusted Marc's side mirror so he could keep track as well. Better to have two sets of eyes on possible opponents. Two lumbering trucks were about to be passed by several cars. *It is the time to play with the shadows again.*

"What do you think this one will be? I mean Horowicz said it could be a five. That sounds pretty high!" said an uneasy Marc. "And Horowicz doesn't seem the type to be an alarmist."

Rene nailed the throttle and the Maserati shot the gap before the approaching group of cars. He had open road up ahead and kept his foot in it.

"Ah, you are correct. Horowicz is just the intermediary

for someone I refer to as "The Client" who has hired me for previous Engagements. Although sometimes people imagine that an Engagement will be more dangerous than it really is, I find it is always best to take the higher factor fee anyway."

"Right," Marc said. He watched Rene touch the Sat-Nav screen to pull up the next segment on the map display. "And the additional damage part?"

Rene accelerated from 200 to 250 kph and held this speed for a moment before he backed off and slotted the car in front of an oversized lorry. He then moved the car over to the extreme right lane of the highway, hugging the line that separated the lane from the shoulder. "It is the, how does one say, it has the self-explanation…?"

"Self-explanatory."

"Yes, *merci*. So, if the car is damaged beyond the factor fee that was negotiated, the client will compensate the *Driver*. Everyone just wants to be happy. The client wants the cargo delivered safely and efficiently. The *Driver* who accepts the job is entitled to understand what is at risk. If the risk is too high, a *Driver* may not accept an Engagement."

"There are others?"

"Other what?

"Drivers."

"*Certainment*! I know many of them. Some are very good people, very dedicated and loyal. Others who would stab you in the back in one second to steal your clients and Engagements." Rene had the best line-of-sight view and could see the two Vauxhall VRX8's come storming up the highway. They thought they had lost their prey and were trying to recover. Too late they saw the Maserati in front of the lorry. Panicking, they both hit the brakes at the same time, one almost rear ending the other. They hesitated for a moment and one accelerated past, while the other dropped back.

"See Marc, they know now that we have seen them. We made them expose themselves. Now one will stay slightly ahead and the other behind. They will stay in constant contact with each other to try and keep us under the microscope."

"Why did you do that, you could have kept going and outrun them. They'd have never caught up."

"That is true, but then I would not know where they are. And unless you really want to lose them, it is important to know where they are at all times. It gives you better options. Besides, if they lose us now they may do something stupid later. And based on what I have seen so far, I believe them to be rank amateurs."

"Why send amateurs?"

"I have been thinking about that too. Amateurs mean that they are only the surveillance team, and not a very good one, since I have already discovered them. What I am worried about is what is waiting up the road."

"There'll be others?" Marc asked. His voice cracked.

"I am not sure, but maybe. I also think the factor of five or six or even seven may have been low."

Rene had been doing this so long, he knew all the signs and this Engagement was now eroding into very, very tricky territory. The drivers of the Vauxhalls seemed new to the business. Rene for the time being, but Marc did not.

To ease the tension, Rene encouraged Marc to talk about driving theory, both on and off the track. On the track, that was all about the race line and how to set up other race cars for the pass in different situations and different kinds of turns. But off the track was an entirely different discussion. The talk turned to how to use racing experience to avoid pursuers and stay alive.

Rene gave Marc the benefit of his experience. "One difference from racing: always you must be alert for the unexpected. And you have to relax and conserve energy—your energy and that of your car. This sounds impossible, but with experience, you learn. You must think like both the pursued and the pursuer. As a *Driver*, you must know when you have the advantage, and when you do not, if you have lost it, how to get it back. You have to react differently to situations."

"Like what?"

"What will you do if the pursuing car is in front of you or next to you or behind you?"

"I don't know."

"Use your racing knowledge. Think about it."

"I am. What else?"

"You must be able to use every possible resource: other cars on the road, the road itself, natural surroundings. Your job is to complete the Engagement. You do what you have to."

"What about now?"

"It's a long drive to Potsdam. Our pursuers are gambling on fatigue setting in—rest stops, gas fill-ups. We do not know how many teams might be involved besides the one we spotted. Our job is to confuse them, make them adjust their own plans to our random acts. In the Engagement everything is fluid. There are many options and choices to be made along the way. You must be prepared for any eventuality."

"Having a car like this helps."

"That is why I've turned this Maserati into a veritable rolling tank. Okay, a very beautiful, very fast rolling tank, but a very safe place to be." Rene recounted the history of how he had come up with the various modifications. His first real Engagement was a disaster. He had run out of gas and ended up running from his pursuers on foot, jumping on a train, then a bus, then sprinting the final blocks to deliver the cargo. Naturally, the first mod expanded the size of the car's gas tank. The mod after that put a safe in the car to protect the cargo in case he was stopped. As he got more experience, he added more mods, until he got to the current state of the Maserati Quattroporte. "This is my fourth Maserati Quattroporte. The previous three are in Maserati heaven."

"You make every Engagement sound like there's a gun to your head or a chase involving multiple bad guys all driving expensive black cars."

"Not at all. Maybe six in ten are like the drive in the park. Two in ten have some danger but are actually pretty tame. The other two in ten? They are the problem ones."

They drove on for several hours. Marc, at Rene's urging, began learning how to use the camera package. He practiced zooming, panning and tilting the four separate cameras as he kept tabs on their shadows. The Maserati left Switzerland and entered Germany. "Both Vauxhalls are still in position," Marc announced.

"Take pictures of the license plates and perhaps the occupants. I will walk you through sending them off for identification." After a few minutes, Marc uploaded the data to Jean Paul Degas. While they waited to hear from Jean Paul, Rene monitored the police bands. There was nothing other than the usual chatter about speeding cars and overloaded trucks. Jean Paul sent Rene a text with predictable results: the Vauxhalls' license data came back untraceable.

"You're not surprised?"

"*Mais non*, I would be very surprised if any of the cars chasing us *were* traceable. But it was worth looking into. Somebody in their organization might be stupid."

Near the city of Ulm, halfway between Munich and Stuttgart, Rene decided to stop for a break.

"We'll stop for gas outside Ulm and get a quick bite to eat."

"What about our shadows?"

"They will stop too and watch from a safe distance. They will probably take turns taking a break, with one car always on the alert. If they are the spotting team, as I suspect, they will want to know if we change our route so that they can inform the others."

"What's our plan?"

"The service place I have in mind has a good restaurant. After getting gas, we will go inside. With luck, the Vauxhall boys will think we have stopped for a good three-course meal and they will let down their guard a little and we will make our break."

"Then what?"

"After we get away, we will lose them. I am thinking there are others waiting to intercept us. But where? That is the big question."

"How many cars do you think are involved in this?"

"I am not sure, but I believe there may be several teams.

They could hit us along either A7 or A9 Autobahn routes—lots of long stretches to cross and little traffic."

Marc pulled up the routes on the Nav-Sat. "Both look like direct routes into Potsdam."

"They are, although A9 is longer. I don't like A9."

"Then it's A7?"

"Bring up A8/A5."

Marc did so. He looked at the map. "It's 300 km longer, Rene. Why this route?"

"It is unexpected. It is longer, therefore the least likely choice."

Normally Rene would take the most direct route and find out exactly what his opponents planned, then deal with it. But this time, he had three problems.

Problem One: Marc Lange. Although this was intended to be a test run to see how he well he held up under pressure, Rene was now confident that the factor was higher than a five, possibly higher than a seven. It was certainly going to be a bit more than Marc had bargained for. He contemplated leaving Marc behind and letting him make his way home. The safest option no doubt (at least for Marc).

Problem Two: Time. They had too much of it. If they got around the chase teams, they would arrive in Potsdam in the morning, so they'd have to lay low for at least five or six hours, depending on where and when the cargo could be delivered.

Problem Three: Potsdam. Just south and west of Berlin, it was a small city. No easy places to lie low, especially since a Maserati with French plates was easy to spot.

"Marc, this Engagement could get interesting and maybe a bit dangerous. If you want, I can drop you at the service station and you can walk away. Just grab a bus and get back to Milano."

Marc considered Rene's options for some moments before replying. He thought it through quickly, but thoroughly. "Thanks for the offer, but I said I was along for this ride. Maybe baptism by fire is the best way for me to see what this is all about."

"OK. You're call," replied an impressed Rene.

They stopped at a rest stop just off the A7 and filled the car with gas, then backed the Maserati into a parking place just outside the attached restaurant. Inside, Rene locked the car and activated its security systems. After a bio break, the two men sat down for an early dinner, at least one of them always having the Maserati in sight.

Marc scanned the parking lot. "I don't see either of our shadows yet."

"If they refuel, we will spot them soon enough. Right now, let us see the menu. Believe it or not, I have eaten here before, although no three-courses today. Too bad. The food here is quite good."

They ordered local fare: hearty soups, bread and simple salads. Their beverage of choice today: bottled water. While they waited for the food to arrive, Marc grabbed some high energy protein snacks for the long drive ahead. They ate quickly. As they were finishing, Marc pointed out that one of the Vauxhalls had arrived and was gassing up.

Rene nodded to the waiter, dropped some bills on the table, remotely started the car and opened the doors. "Let us see how well prepared they are." The two men jumped into the Maserati, simultaneously clicking their seat belts as Rene pulled the paddle shifter towards him, engaging first gear, and they roared off. Rene had made up his mind. He decided on the A8/A5. Better to leave the opponents guessing, especially if he could split the two shadows up and lose them outright.

They peeled out of the service station. The driver and his partner of one Vauxhall were in the parking lot, unprepared for their quarry's fast exit. Relaxed, seat belts released, they were stuffing food in their mouths. Dropping a fat sandwich in his lap, the driver started his car and tried to drive off quickly. Sliding sideways and skidding, the driver—seat belt still released—hung on to his steering wheel to keep from sliding around in his seat. Finally straightening out his car, he slammed the accelerator down, trying to close the widening gap between him and the fast-disappearing Maserati.

The other Vauxhall driver was completely flummoxed.

The fuel nozzle was still in the car when he realized the Maserati was gone. He hit the throttle and lurched off, ripping the hose out of the pump, spraying gas as the car tore out, hose trailing behind, swinging back and forth like a snake. The gas station attendant ran after the car trying in vain to catch it. The Vauxhall managed to go 400 m before the car stopped completely. The engine computer had cut the car's power due to lack of gas pressure! The car rolled to a stop. The driver, clueless, was still frantically trying to re-start when, two minutes later, the local *polizei* pulled up behind, lights flashing, doors flying open, men with pistols drawn running to the car. One car down.

Rene took the local St2023 road towards the Regional 10 highway toward the A8. As soon as he entered the Autobahn, he moved over into the left lane and nailed the throttle to the floor. In the gathering dusk, the car flew along at 300 kph. Now a fast-moving dark gray ghost, the Maserati wove in and out of traffic trying to put distance between itself and the far- off Vauxhall. Rene drove this speed for 25 km before settling into a fast but steady pace of 220 kph, Vauxhall two, left very far behind. Marc remained silent, focusing on how Rene performed in every facet of their dash to safety. He saw the calm under pressure, how his jaw was set, how his eyes scanned and focused, taking in every detail, every nuance of the road and traffic in front and especially behind.

"We have lost the surveillance team. They will know we have taken a new route, but of course I may modify it along the way to keep them guessing."

"Are we out of trouble then?"

Rene was silent for several minutes. He frowned then shook his head. "Something is bothering me. Maybe they want us to get to Potsdam before they make their move. It is possible they do not care which way we go. Almost as if they just want to know where we are."

"Why do you think that?"

"That sloppy, amateurish surveillance team. The more I think about it, they were too easy to spot and dump." He turned to look at Marc. He wondered if his face looked as puzzled as Marc's did.

"Do you ever check the cargo?"

"No. That is not allowed." But Marc had a point. Rene looked in his rearview mirror, visualizing the safe in the trunk. He scanned the road ahead, setting the Sat-Nav display to find a place to stop. He pulled off the road in the tiny hamlet of Aicelberg and pulled in behind a farm and feed-supply store. It was closed. More to the point, it completely obscured the Maserati from the road. Shutting off the engine, he motioned to Marc to follow him as he exited the car and moved to the slowly opening trunk. "I have an idea."

He opened the panel concealing the safe, pressed a combination then used his Fujitsu Palm reader, took the faded black leather satchel and placed it on top of an oil drum a few feet from the car. Using his iPhone, he pressed several buttons on the display to launch the Maserati's bug and explosive system. The scan came back negative, but as he passed the iPhone back and forth across the satchel, a small red light blinked on the readout. Rene had never seen this before. He walked back to the Maserati and pulled up the detection routine on another sub-menu of the display so he could actually read the Help files. Nothing. Nothing at all. The red light however kept blinking with the letters "pd" below the dot. What was *that*? What did it mean? Frustrated, he dialed Hector. On the sixth ring, Hector answered.

"*Alors*, you're calling me to tell me how much you love the new night vision system, eh?"

"I have not tried it. It is not completely dark yet."

"Rene you are so funny. You've been gone three days. Surely you've come across a little night time in your travels?

"I have not needed to use it yet, but I plan to! Maybe this very night!"

"Rene, you could at least TRY IT. You could at least tell me you love it."

"Hector. I love it!" Rene rolled his eyes.

"Oh please. At least when you lie to me, say it with feeling."

"OK, Hector. I REALLY LOVE IT! Happy?"

"Rene, sometimes you really are a complete bastard."

"Hector. I only play that part for you. Everyone else thinks I am some sort of Saint. The Saint of night-vision systems installed by ego maniacs."

"Ha. I think I'll hang up now. Goodbye."

"No, Hector, wait! Do not hang up!"

The phone was silent for several seconds. Hector liked to keep people waiting, but the fact was, people did wait, since he was the best at equipping a car to withstand almost any attack.

"Allo? Allo? Shit, he hung up!"

Silence.

"Ha, you really do need me this time?"

"Yes, Hector, I really do need you this time, you shit!"

"Ha, Ha. Zo vat ist ze prahblem?" asked Hector in his terrible sounding German accent.

"A new Engagement from Milano. Everything went fine until the fee for the factor came up. I began negotiating, of course. The price we settled on was a bit high and the client agreed to it a little too quickly in retrospect. He pretended to be insulted and he still went for the higher fee."

"Then what happened?"

"We left Milano and drove for several hours. Once inside Switzerland, I picked up a couple of low-level amateurs. I was pretty sure they were just an advance team and a more professional interception team was going to eventually pounce."

"Rene—I just know that somewhere there is a question in all this."

"Yes. Yes. *Merde*! I was just giving you the background and if you'd LET ME FINISH, I will eventually get around to it."

"Okay. I'll be quiet. Tell me."

"The sloppiness of the chasers has made me nervous. I now believe the cargo itself is a problem. I decided to stop and examine it."

"Isn't that forbidden?"

"Normally, yes. So far I have not opened the case yet. But this Engagement smells and I need more information before I continue."

"Go on."

"I examined the satchel with your bug-and-explosive app. A strange blinking light displayed on my iPhone. What do the letters "pd" mean? I can't find anything in the Help files."

"*Mon Dieu*! You *actually read the Help files*? I always assumed you wouldn't even know how to open them, let alone knew they existed. Do you know how many times I have spent hours writing up Help files knowing, just knowing, that NOBODY would ever look at them?"

Rene mouthed the word 'unbelievable' and rolled his eyes again, to Marc's bemusement.

"Interesting, Hector, but …."

"Okay, okay. Hmmm. I hadn't expected that just yet. I added that type of detection just recently, but haven't updated the Help files."

"Hector. Why do you think I am calling you?"

"Rene. Relax. We're on the bleeding edge."

"What does "pd" mean?"

"It means Passive Detection. And that, my friend, means there's an RFID tag imbedded somewhere in that satchel. Once a radio wave scanned the tag, a reader recorded the tag number and all its information. Whenever you passed through an automated toll station, you were spotted by a very sophisticated reader. I am quite sure whoever wants to track you has somehow tapped into the highway toll tag system. And what that boils down to, my friend, is the bad guys know exactly where you and your cargo are. Provided you stay on the Autobahn that is…"

"Wait Hector, I have to think."

Rene turned toward Marc and repeated what Hector had told him.

"There's an RFID tag in the satchel and the chasers know where we are?" asked Marc.

"Yes."

"Now what?"

Returning to the phone, "Hector. What you have told me explains many things. Of course they do not give half a shit which way we go. They just want to see that we did not leave the highway."

"What if we turn the tables on them?" asked Marc.

"Rene, what is your destination city?"

"Potsdam."

"I just read something about Potsdam. Give me a second. Oh, right! There was a big press release in a technology Reddit feed I subscribe to. Potsdam launched a new high-tech parking system with RFID tags in all the cars. Even visitors can purchase a temporary tag. It can monitor where and how long any car parks on any street and they send you the bill or deduct the amount from your checking account. But problem is, they'll know your exact location once you enter the city."

"*Merde! Merde! Merde!* This is even more complicated than I thought. The cargo is not the target. It is The Client! Now I am certain."

"I think they will use hand-held readers once your car is stationary. They can use that reader to travel the last few meters to the satchel itself. How is your client to contact you?" asked Hector.

"I will receive a text. But we have to be within 40 km of Potsdam's city center by 15:30 tomorrow for an expected delivery between 16:00 and 17:00."

"Hmmm. That doesn't leave you much time once you arrive."

"Looks like we'll have to put a plan in motion before we ever arrive in the city," said Marc.

"You are right, Marc. See you are already starting to think like a *Driver*."

Chapter 9

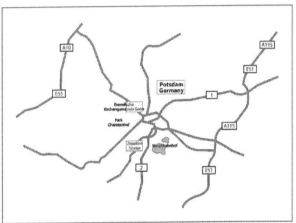

Potsdam Germany

As Hector tried to absorb all the information he had just consumed, something clicked in his brain.

"Rene, you keep saying 'we'. Who are you talking to?"

"*Merde*, I forgot. My protégé Marc Lange."

"You have a protégé? Since when?"

"Since now, Hector. I told you about Marc. Remember?"

"I didn't think you were serious."

"I was. I am. Marc is my protégé. Let us get back to our problem, okay?

Silence. Rene waited patiently for Hector to absorb this information.

"You know I don't like to work with lots of people."

"Hector, this is no time to pull a tantrum. Our lives are on the line. Are you going to help or not?"

Longer silence. "You are my friend, Rene. I'll help. But what if I don't like this Marc?"

"*Mon Dieu*, Hector. He is like me, only American."

"American? Why didn't you say so? I love Americans. John Wayne. Pizza. Amy Adams. Nachos. Les Big Macs. Okay. Let me think."

Muting his phone, Rene turned to Marc. "Hector is having one of his moments. I told him about you, but he chose not to believe I was serious."

"Now what? Is he going to help?"

"Yes. Just be patient."

Rene unmuted the phone then pressed Speaker.

"Hector, I have got the phone on Speaker, so Marc can hear."

"Okay. Allo Marc."

"*Bon jour*, Hector. *Enchantez.*"

Rene smiled. Marc's little courtesy was just right. They waited for several more minutes.

"Okay," Hector said." I guarantee somebody has hacked Potsdam's RFID system so they can keep tabs on you. I think I can fix this problem. I can clone the RFID tag in the satchel so you can use it on an iPhone. In effect your iPhone will look just that RFID tag. You'll need another car. Once you enter Potsdam, tag readers will pick up two signals with the same RFID signature. The one in the satchel and the one on the iPhone. Marc can create a diversion while you deliver the cargo."

"That has possibilities, Hector. You figure out how to clone the tag. Marc and I will come up with the diversion."

"Call me when you have a plan."

While Hector worked on his routine to clone the RFID tag's numeric signature, Rene and Marc discussed the diversion.

"We will need two new iPhones plus mine," said Rene.

"Why three?"

"With two phones loaded with the RFID clone app and the tag in the satchel, we will have three RFID tags emitting the same signal.

"That means two cars, not one. How are we going to do that with just you and me?"

"Good man. Again, you are thinking like a *Driver*."

Marc's smile was fleeting. *'Thinking like a Driver' seems to mean 'think fast, stay alive.'*

"Easy, we will hire a courier service to take one of the iPhones with the RFID tag to a set location. Hector said Potsdam's parking system reads RFID tags on every car parked on every street in Potsdam," Rene continued. "As soon as we enter Potsdam and separate, readers will start reading the three tags. Wherever we drive in Potsdam, the RFID tag readers will track the same signal."

"Three signals in potentially three different locations. Sounds good."

Rene called Hector and told him the plan. Then he and Marc returned to the Maserati. While Hector worked, Rene kept off the toll highways, sticking to back roads and secondary highways. He and Marc passed close to Frankfurt before turning east on roads that took them in the same general direction as the A4 Autobahn. Finally, settling in for what was left of the night, they slept a few hours in the car outside of Braunschweig.

Promptly at 9:00, Rene's phone rang. It was Hector: "I've written an app that clones the original RFID tag."

"Where do I get the additional iPhones?"

"Where are you?"

"Off the A2 near Braunschweig." There was a pause while Hector factored in their location.

"Good. I have an old acquaintance in town. He is the type who can procure things for me with very short notice. He will have the phones. Text me when you get to his place, so I can activate them."

Rene took down the friend's address and entered it into the Sat-Nav before they headed out. It was close by. Once there, Rene paid for the phones plus a Bluetooth headset for Marc. They found a nearby café that Hector's acquaintance had suggested and went inside to fuel up with some breakfast. While in the café, Rene showed Marc how to use one of the new phones. Marc's eyes were wide trying to absorb as much current communications technology as he could. Rene downloaded several applications from his own iPhone onto Marc's, including a GPS application and synced it to the headset. Finally, he showed Marc how to operate the Quattroporte's security system apps that were now downloaded to Marc's phone. If anything happened to Rene, Marc would have access to the car.

They left the café and drove until Rene found a secluded road outside the town. He drove the Maserati several meters down the road and parked. He got out and called Hector as he headed towards the back of the Maserati. He removed the satchel from the safe in the trunk as he spoke to Hector: "We are ready to download the RFID app."

"Good. You also need to download an RFID analyzer as soon as you've downloaded the app. With the high powered reader I am uploading to the phones, the tag should be readable within 40 to 50 m."

Rene and Marc followed Hector's instructions. Using

Hector's ingenious app and the analyzer, Rene held his iPhone over the satchel and cloned the satchel's RFID tag. Marc added the tag to his phone from Rene's. Rene tested the two phones to make certain they read the satchel's original tag from 50 m. Then he called Hector back.

"Cloning complete. Did you find a courier to take the first phone into Potsdam?"

"Of course. Magnusson Couriers has a branch in central Braunschweig. They are waiting for you to sign the contract and give them your package to deliver in Potsdam. It won't be cheap."

"It will be if we save the Client's life as well as our own," replied Rene tartly.

"You have a point, *mon ami*. Goodbye."

"Wait, Hector."

"What? Another favor?"

"No, a most emphatic *Thank you!* I do not know what I would do without your genius."

"Oh. You are welcome. This is not free you know."

"I did not think it was." Rene waited.

"What? Oh. Well, good luck." Hector hung up.

Marc considered the plan as Rene and Hector talked. *It's daring. Rene seems to think these guys are real bad-asses. We'll need a lot of luck, skill and perfect timing—a piece of cake, but am I remotely ready for whatever comes next? Shit! I hope so.*

Next, to the courier agency, where Rene signed the contract and gave the clerk one of the iPhone boxes with instructions to deliver it to Evangelische Kirchengemeinde Golm, Potsdam, between 16:30 and 16:40. Rene had deferred to Hector, who had picked the location because it was away from the City Center and would take longer to reach than other parts of the city. He had turned the iPhone on inside the box, so it broadcast the RFID tag number. Next stop was an auto rental agency where they hired a car for the day. Rene used an app to handle the rental transaction, they never had to see or speak with anyone. Maybe "Bob" had his own credit card too. They selected a black VW Golf equipped with a GPS system. It was inconspicuous and Marc knew it was quick and cornered well.

Finally, they went to an early lunch at a nearby Italian *trattoria*, knowing they might not get to eat for many hours to come. They discussed their plans over Pasta Bolognese and assorted meats and cheeses. Rene brought out his map of Potsdam. Marc familiarized himself with the city's principal streets.

The Magnusson Courier, Marc in the VW Golf and Rene in the Maserati would enter Potsdam at the same time, following closely behind each other. As soon as the three iPhones pinged, it would signal that an RFID reader had activated the tags, reading them as one. All three vehicles would immediately drive off in different directions. Whoever was in charge of the interception team suddenly had three cars to follow, not one.

The courier had the easiest job. Deliver the box containing the iPhone to the church between 16:30 and 16:40, then head back home. It was a tight delivery schedule, but they had paid a steep fee to ensure the box arrived precisely within that tiny window. The church closed up tight at 16:45. Rene counted on their pursuers assuming that the church was a perfect place for a drop off. Some of them would go there to check it out and deal with a tag located in a closed and locked church. Marc's mission was to drive slowly around Potsdam in large looping circles, thereby pulling some of the interception team to follow him. Rene's job was to deliver the cargo and warn The Client.

When they had finalized their plan and finished lunch, Rene sat back in his chair and looked intently at Marc. "Marc, you have been gone from Team Technik since Wednesday. You need to check in. Listen to me. You have a real life with real friends, family and associates. You must make sure this new career does not take over. No matter what happens and what path you take, remember that Marc Lange is the reason Billy exists, not the other way around."

Marc nodded. He could not believe it was already Friday, and he had not called his friends after promising to. After they left the trattoria, he used his new cell phone and called Team Technik's HQ. Bala and Stella were steaming.

"Where the hell have you been, Mate?"

"Sorry, but you know my crappy old cell phone barely

works at home and doesn't work at all on the continent, so I got a new phone. Put this on Speaker, okay?"

"A pissy excuse Marc."

"I know, I know, Stella. Rene said much the same thing and convinced me to buy this new one I'm using now. He's persuaded me to buy an iPhone and it's unbelievable. Why didn't I buy one before now?"

Bala and Stella laughed.

"We've been telling you for ages, Love. Get with the program."

"Yeah. It even has this 'text' feature that lets me send a message straight to another phone. It's really awesome. Stella, as soon as I figure it out, I'll send you a text."

"Marc, my dear, your understanding of any technology that doesn't make Porsches go faster is below that of the average five-year-old." They talked for a few minutes more. Marc promised to call before he came home then ended the call.

"You see, you are already learning how to balance Marc Lange's life and that of Billy the *Driver*."

"Great. That just means I'm starting to become a better liar. Ha! The ultimate test will be with April. Oh my God, April. I'd better call her now."

Rene hid his smile as he watched Marc punch in his girl's number.

"Hey, April, Sweetie."

"Don't you *Hey Sweetie* me, Marc Lange. I've been worried sick. Where have you been? I've been back in New York for two days. You were supposed to call me when I got in!"

"I know, I know. Rene said the same thing, but you know my old phone. It doesn't work outside the UK and …."

"Marc, try that BS on someone else."

"And it doesn't work well on the continent either. Anyway, I bought a new one this morning."

"Hmmph. We'll see. Now, what have you been doing and where are you?"

"Still in Milano. Rene introduced me to some of his business associates. Hopefully, I'll be heading home later this evening or tomorrow morning at the latest."

"Still in Milano? Where are you staying?"

"Where am I staying?" Alarmed, Marc looked towards Rene for the answer. Rene was holding up the hotel key from their hotel in Milano.

"We're at the Hotel Princepe de Savoia. You know, Rene only goes first class. Why?"

Rene gave Marc a thumbs up. Their rooms were booked through Saturday to cover the Engagement time.

"Something happened here in New York last night and

I tried to get a hold of you and couldn't."

"What happened?"

"Oh, maybe nothing. Just one of the usual hassles of living in New York."

"Tell me."

"A couple of young gang bangers tried to grab my purse and some of my luggage as I got out of my cab."

"What! Are you all right?"

Rene sat up, alerted to the alarm in Marc's voice.

"Yes, I'm fine. The cab driver got out of the cab and started yelling at them while I hit the one trying to grab my purse in the face with my elbow. They both ran off down the street."

"Did you call the police?"

"No. What was the point? It was dark outside, they were wearing hoodies and I couldn't see their faces well. I couldn't have given a decent description even if I'd wanted to. But it was just unnerving. I wanted to tell you but couldn't get you."

"April, I am so sorry." *Bloody hell! She needed me, she was upset, and I wasn't there. Dammit!*

"It's okay. Talking to you now makes me feel better. I think this makes me want to move to London even more. By the way, what was the thing you had to do for Rene?

What was the *quid pro quo?*"

Oh SHIT! Marc had a rough idea of what he'd say to her. The trick was going to be convincing her. He would have to sound sincerely concerned and yet nonchalant at the same time.

"Yeah. Well, it turns out that he has another set of sponsors he wants to bring in, maybe as soon as this year."

"Marc, you can't let him dictate those kinds of things to you. You owe the sponsors that have stuck with you. Hell, they even kicked in more money when Stella begged them."

"You're right. It's just that the team always needs money and Rene's suggestion sounded good. Maybe I could bring them on as junior sponsors. We'll see."

"Marc, just do the right thing. I know you will."

Marc breathed a sigh of relief. April seemed mollified. However, now he had a new worry. April's safety. She was thousands of miles away in New York. He wanted her safe and sound in one of London's best neighborhoods where she'd be close by.

"Listen Sweetie, call me when you're heading home. I still don't trust this Rene. I just knew he had his own agenda."

If you only knew. "April, I love you. I'll call when I'm through here and on my way home." He thumbed the phone ending the call.

"You were very convincing Mr. Marc Lange. But your girlfriend—I get the impression she does not approve of me."

"You know, you could be right about that. She knows me better than anybody else. Sometimes I think even better than I know myself. Oh, and you owe me a couple of new sponsors next year."

"That reminds me, I have something for you now." Rene's tone became serious. As they walked to the Maserati, Rene theorized about their pursuers' mental state. "As we have not gone through an Autobahn toll booth since last night, we have fallen off the grid. I imagine our pursuers are a bit nervous and maybe trigger-happy. So, I want you to have this." He reached into the compartment below his seat and pulled a pistol from its hiding place. Checking to see if there was a round in the chamber (there was), he de-cocked the hammer and handed the pistol to Marc. "Have you ever shot a pistol before?"

"It's been years. Not sure what I need to do."

"It is like riding a bicycle. You never forget. Just pull the trigger. There is no safety on this weapon and there is a round already in the chamber. Just point and shoot. There are twelve bullets in the magazine, plus one in the chamber. Hopefully, you will hit something if you need to use it."

"And put these on too." He handed Marc a pair of tight-fitting silk and nylon gloves. Marc robotically did as he was told and slid the gloves on, flexing his fist to adjust the fit.

Reality hit Marc like he'd been slugged. *I might have to actually shoot somebody! God! This Engagement is getting more serious by the second. Maybe I should have taken Rene up on his offer to leave, but I can't back out now.* Still, he thought about it for a second as he looked at the pistol and thought back to when he used to shoot targets at the range. *Just squeeze the trigger. Exhale. Use your fingertip, one smooth motion. Don't jerk.* He felt the weight of the pistol in his hand. The idea that someone might try to shoot him had never entered his head before. Now it was lodged there like a barbed splinter.

They drove to the courier's office and waited. At 14:30, the courier van left for Potsdam. Marc followed in the Golf, Rene right behind in the Maserati.

About 90 minutes away was Potsdam's city center. There, in an old building, was the Pensione Sanssouci. In one of its rooms, a team of grim men watched an array of blank computer displays. Still no sign of the RFID they had been tracking since it left Milano the day before—or rather *not* tracking. Uli Petrovski, was worried. The team Mr. X had dispatched to keep in contact with the target had disappeared. He assumed they had been duped by the *Driver* Bob and eliminated as a threat. Uli threw his cigarette on the floor and ground it out. If those fools ever showed themselves to him again, they were dead men.

Part of his fury was that he had advised Mr. X not to use

new, untried assets, but Mr. X had overruled him. He wanted to keep the interception teams, men he had worked with before, in Potsdam close to their ultimate prey. An additional source of fury was aimed at the *Driver,* Bob. In *Driverland*, the man was a legend. Regardless of the stakes, regardless of the risk, Bob always completed his Engagement. Twice Uli had tried to intercept and defeat him and both times he regretted it. The last time he had been *so close* to grinding that little shit into dust! He rubbed his close-cropped silver hair, remembering.

All of a sudden Uli was back in the moment. That day, Bob's client was not at the meeting point, but Uli and his men were. Uli, posing as the client, lured Bob out of his car and got the drop on him. Uli's gang held onto Bob while he grabbed the cargo. He was able to open the safe in the trunk, but the cargo had a new kind of lock that Uli was unable to break. An unexpected problem. Uli knew that if the lock was not opened exactly right, the cargo was destroyed. He and his men drove to a warehouse where they beat Bob to learn how to open the lock. Finally, Bob revealed that forcing the lock would release sulphuric acid, drenching the cargo and rendering it worthless. After some more persuasion, he revealed, the *immediate* application of a sodium hydroxide would defeat the self-destruct process.

Uli left Bob with two of his most capable men while he went to get the chemicals and tools needed to neutralize the sulfuric acid. He was gone only thirty minutes. When Uli returned, Bob, his car and the cargo were gone and his two men were dead.

But now there was a new dimension to his hatred of Bob. His idiotic ex-wife had sent his daughter—against his wishes—to visit the family of that rich, effete prick of a new husband. When he found out it was Bob who delivered her, he was furious, but when his daughter told him this man had touched her and treated her badly, it made his blood boil. For this alone the man would die and Uli would watch the blood flow from the wound he would put in his head.

Uli's rage over this ate at him constantly. But this time, it would be very different. Uli would not only destroy Bob, he would take the cargo and kidnap the client. His ice-blue eyes almost sparkled as he thought about what he was going to do to Bob. The fact was, Uli liked to hurt people. And, to kill them. It made little difference so long as he got paid, even if the hurting part was especially enjoyable. The fact that he would finally get to put a bullet in Bob made it even better.

The room in Pensione Sanssouci reeked of sweat, stale tobacco and leftover food. Nobody noticed. Four of the gang played cards. Uli and Vitaly took turns watching the computer displays for the telltale ping from the RFID tag.

"What if this Bob takes the cargo and runs?"

"Not in his character. He's the consummate professional."

"I thought you hated him, wanted him dead."

"I do. But that doesn't mean I don't respect his professionalism. I do respect it. Right up until the moment I put a bullet in his brain." Uli laughed as his little joke.

"Uli, I'll say this again, this sounds personal. Are you sure you can hold your anger back enough to complete the job?"

Uli barked back, "Don't worry about me, I know my job!"

Vitaly's face darkened and he decided to change the subject. He knew better than to get Uli worked up more than he already was.

"So, why do you think everything went dark? We had them until just after Ulm."

"He's not stupid. He knew he was being tailed, so once he shook that amateur team Mr. X deployed, he stayed off the main roads." Uli stared at the screen. "Don't worry. He'll deliver. He always does."

"I hope you're right Uli."

"Have faith. You'll see."

"It is not faith I lack, Uli. It is the constancy of men that I doubt."

While Uli and his team stared into their computer displays in Potsdam, Rene was about 40 km from Potsdam. At

15:30 he received an untraceable one-way text, without the option to reply. The text displayed the delivery address and security-access code to a building. Rene immediately programmed the address into his Sat-Nav just as the message faded from his iPhone. Fortunately, he had memorized the message. He programmed the security-access code into his iPhone as well, then he called Marc.

"Here is the address for the delivery in Potsdam. Program it into your iPhone and GPS: DortuStrasse 50. How is your head for numbers?

"Depends on the numbers, why?"

"There is a security code, too. Better program that into your phone. Ready?

"Yes."

"581167-6-673382."

"581167-6-673382," Marc repeated.

"That is it."

"Anything else?"

"Yes. These are probably a sequence to access the building and a secure area where The Client is waiting."

"Got it."

"Good. Not far now. Good luck. Just keep to the plan. We should be okay."

Sweet Jesus, I hope so, thought Marc.

At 16:12, the caravan passed a sign. POTSDAM: 10 KM.

Now or never, thought Rene.

Suddenly the RFID tag appeared on the grid, entering Potsdam from the south along the E51/115 highways. Uli and Vitaly both jumped as they heard the soft ping from the PC indicating contact. The four other team members dropped their cards. Uli checked the digital read out on the PC.

"16:20, right on time. I told you Vitaly, this guy's a pro."

The courier van, Marc and Rene crossed Berliner Strasse almost as one vehicle, then Rene and Marc peeled off from the van. 50 m later, the Potsdam Parking System suddenly registered three different tags—all with the same number—all going in different directions.

"Shit, what does this mean? Which one do we follow?" Vitaly glared at his laptop.

"Not sure what to make of it," Uli replied tersely. He slammed the computer table with his fist then sat, staring into space. He looked up at his men, "That fucking Bob! New plan. Follow all of them!"

Uli located two laptops that were loaded with the tracing app while Vitaly scrounged around the room, looking for headsets. After several tense minutes, Uli handed each team of two a laptop loaded with the tracing app and a headset.

"Here's the plan. You and you are one team, you two are the other team. Go to your cars on Zeppelin Strasse and monitor the tags using your laptop loaded with the tracing app."

He pointed to the three signals driving erratically around the city.

"Wait for my signal. Vitaly and I will stay here and watch on this computer. If a signal stops for any of the three tags for more than three minutes, I'll send one of you out to intercept and move in. If a signal disappears while you're on your way, go to the last displayed location on the Potsdam grid and then use this hand-held RFID reader to reacquire the signal." He handed one man from each team a hand-held reader.

"Got it?"

Four heads nodded as the teams headed out the door to their cars. The two teams sat in their idling cars, smoking Russian cigarettes, waiting for Uli's signal to head out. He and Vitaly remained in the room watching the three red dots, representing the three RFID tags, move about on their monitors.

Part One of Rene's plan had the courier with the cloned tag arrive at its location first. When it became stationary,

Rene hoped some of the thugs would close in.

Marc, with the second cloned tag, orbited the inner city, trying to lure pursuers into following him. After driving for a few minutes, he would stop and wait briefly, then start up again before the pursuers could close in and physically identify him. Rene counted on the bad guys suspecting that whoever was driving this vehicle might be waiting for a signal to pull over so The Client could drive up alongside and quickly transfer the cargo. If his assumption was correct, they would want to identify Marc's vehicle and maintain visual contact.

Meanwhile, Rene meandered through the city center, looping back occasionally, all the while drawing increasingly close to his destination on DortuStrasse. At 16:38 he received a text that the package was delivered to the church. Part Two of the plan coming up.

Uli Petrovski noticed that the first tag stopped moving. After a few minutes, it disappeared from his display. He ordered Team One in. The last referenced location was at the corner of Kirshallee and Bornstedter Strasse. The two other tags were still moving. They would be hard to pin down until they stopped.

Team One closed in cautiously. They parked on Ribbeck Strasse, got out of their car, turned on their RFID readers and immediately acquired the tag ID. The portable reader indicated the tag was within 50 m.

"We're at a church," reported the Team One leader to Uli.

Of course. A perfect place for a rendezvous. So many ways in and out. I might have picked the same location myself, Uli thought.

"Okay. Move in. Locate the tag and the satchel. If you find anyone with it, take him alive. DO NOT KILL HIM, do you understand?"

"Find the tag. Find the package. No killing."

Uli dispatched Team Two to follow up on the second tag, which was still moving around the city center in slow circles.

"Park near Reiterwag and Allee Strasse. You're looking for one vehicle that keeps passing in that vicinity. I've seen the tag go by there three times."

After several minutes, Uli heard from one of Team Two's members.

"Traffic in this vicinity is heavy and all the cars look alike."

"*Sheiss.* Stay there. Keep looking."

The second time he passed it, Marc noticed a black Mercedes E55 AMG with tinted windows parked at a slight angle to the curb so it could instantly accelerate into traffic. A wisp of exhaust smoke showed the engine was running. He could barely make out two men sitting inside it. Turning right on Avenue Neuen Garten, Marc circled around behind them. He saw them, still waiting.

Okay, I know where they are.

He sent a text to Rene, who told him to park nearby. Marc pulled into a tiny space between Eisenhart and Behlert Strasse a short distance from the Mercedes and waited for the pursuing team to come looking for him. He knew that once he stopped, they would come looking. He kept the motor running with the car in gear, waiting. Sure enough, after a few minutes, the black Mercedes slowly turned the corner onto the short segment of the street between Eisenhart and Behlert Strasse.

Rene had encountered a problem. An empty parking lot and a large building that looked to be deserted. It did not feel right. The Sat/Nav system had brought him to DortuStrasse. He saw Number 52, but did not see 50. A very large #52 was on an enclosed walkway connecting a six-story black steel and glass building with a four-story building next to it. This entrance was set back off the street. Number 50 must be nearby. He made a slow pass, circled around and drove past in the opposite direction. He parked off the street, backing the Maserati in a parking place near an alleyway. From his position, he would have a good angle of escape and would not be as exposed as if he were on the street. Before exiting the car, Rene opened the center console and put on a pair of skin-tight silk and nylon gloves like he had given Marc earlier. He preferred not to leave any evidence that he was at the drop-off location which definitely included fingerprints. He retrieved the cargo satchel and walked up to the building.

Team One reported to Uli. "The church is locked tight, but the reader shows the tag's in there."

"This could be a diversion or they could be meeting inside. Force the door. Do it quietly and don't attract attention."

Uli glanced at his display and noticed that the second tag had stopped near the location where Team Two was parked. At that moment Team Two noticed the same thing and checked with Uli for instructions. *Coincidence? Better safe than stupid.*

"Team Two, move in carefully."

Vitaly elbowed Uli. He pointed to the screen. The third tag had stopped too, just off DortuStrasse. Uli and Vitaly looked at their watches. It was 16:50, very close to the exact delivery time.

"I know that area. Lots of high-tech office buildings. That's got to be the real delivery place," said Uli. "Come on!"

The two men jumped up and ran out of the *pensione* to their waiting Mercedes. Tires complained as Uli floored the throttle and took off for DortuStrasse.

As Rene approached DortusStrasse 52, he noticed a side entrance to the six-story building behind some tall bushes. A discrete #50 displayed on a small plaque next to the entrance. He'd found the address, with minutes to spare. At 16:52, Rene stepped into a small lobby, satchel in hand. Black and grey marble geometric designs on the floor, opaque black glass walls, and a large oval-shaped marble planter in the center of the lobby lent a somber feeling to the building that seemed appropriate to Rene's mission. He found an elevator on the opposite side of the lobby. It appeared to be the only one but when he pushed the Up button, nothing happened. He pressed it again and still nothing.

Maybe I missed something.

He circled the lobby, this time looking more intently. He noticed a glossy, black metal door incased in a very thick hardened stainless-steel frame which he had passed a few moments earlier. He walked up to it. No Up or Down arrows but there was a small, black touch screen. He pressed it and a number pad illuminated. He retrieved his iPhone. He pulled up the code he had programmed earlier and keyed in 581167, then Enter. An elevator door opened. He entered and found another touch screen. It only allowed one number. He keyed in 6. The door closed and the elevator rose. It stopped on the sixth floor but the door remained closed. He keyed in the last set of numbers: 673382. Instead of the door opening, he heard a soft chime ring.

Marc noticed two men get out of the Mercedes and start walking towards him. He gunned the motor and shot out of his spot, wheels spinning, and accelerated away heading up Eisenhart. He got a glimpse in his rear-view mirror of the two men running back to the Mercedes. Jumping inside, they immediately gave chase. Now Marc had to lose the tail and be ready to head to where Rene was in case he needed Marc's help.

"Uli, Team Two, we're chasing a black VW Golf."

"Intercept them! But I want whoever is in the car alive. Do you hear me?" He had expected one tag, not three, and one *Driver*, Bob. He was confident Bob was the one at DortuStrasse, but he could not take a chance. Better to capture whoever was in the black Golf as well as Bob.

Surprised that the elevator door did not open, Rene stood and waited. After a few seconds, he heard a male voice greet him through the speaker built into the control panel.

"Not a moment too soon. Your exact time of arrival is 16.58. Two more minutes and you'd been fined for being late."

"I had reason to time it this close."

"Really? Hmm. We'll see. When the door opens, you will exit the elevator and approach the table at the end of the room. Place the satchel on the table then return to the elevator and wait for further instructions."

"You do not understand. We do not have much time."

"We have all the time we need. I want to make sure my shipment is intact."

"That is not what I am talking about. You are in grave danger."

"Oh please. From whom?"

"I do not know, but they tracked us from the time we left Milano."

"Us? Is this some sort of ruse? Are you trying to shake me down for a larger fee? Really Bob, I didn't expect this kind of ploy from you."

"Sir, I am insulted that you would think that. This is serious. You must have some sort of external surveillance in there. If I am right, they will be arriving very soon."

"Then I shall take a look."

Marc's VW Golf had a distinct advantage over the Mercedes as the bigger car chased him. While the Mercedes had the power and ability to accelerate quickly, the Golf's size and handling made it the superior vehicle in the tight confines of Potsdam's narrow streets. Marc had a second advantage as well. While making his slow, looping patterns around the city center, he had learned the streets.

Driving north on Jaegerallee, he suddenly put the Golf into a 180º sliding turn using the handbrake. He was now going the wrong way down a one-way street, aiming directly at a white BMW Series 1 coupe headed in the right direction. The panicked driver flashed his lights and honked his horn. Marc drove up on the curb to avoid the oncoming car by scant centimeters. He heard the other driver screaming invectives at him.

The Mercedes tried the same maneuver, but its mass would not allow such a dramatic turn. Braking heavily, the Mercedes skidded sideways into a parked car. Team Two's driver stopped the Mercedes then mashed the accelerator down. The car bolted forward, leaving black tire marks on the road, somehow barely missing the outraged driver who remained in the center of the road flashing his lights and screaming obscenities. Marc continued racing down narrow streets, turning into cross streets at the last second, as the Mercedes tried to follow.

Standing in front of a control board, The Client pressed a few keys on a keyboard to switch views on the surveillance cameras outside. As he watched, a black Mercedes E55 AMG pulled up and parked. Two men got out. Zooming in on their faces, The Client touched another key and sent the video signal to a small monitor in the elevator where Rene still waited.

"Do you recognize either of these two men?"

OH SHIT! Painful scenes flooded into Rene's memory. The man Uli Petrovski could inflict pain so easily, kill so casually. And to think that he had just had a run in with his daughter. Deep in a recess of his mind, he knew it would come down to this, a confrontation with the one man he feared. Rene did not know the other man, but the scenario had changed from bad to worse in one aching, painful second.

"Please listen to me. The silver-haired man is Uli Petrovski, and he is not here to talk about the weather. Secure the building, now! If I am right, he is here to take you." *And if he can kill me in the process, so much the better for him.*

"Are you sure? That's impossible! How could they have found me?" The Client's voice cracked.

"Let us start with Horowicz. I will give you odds he is involved in this."

The Client and Rene watched Uli and his partner stop at the building entrance. Each carried two black duffel bags. Uli pulled out his cell phone, spoke briefly, and shoved it back into his pocket.

Marc knew he had to lose the Mercedes before the local *Polizei* got involved. He had increased the distance between them, but the pursuers were just in sight when Marc approached MittelStrasse. He saw an empty space on the street, so he turned abruptly right and as he approached the parking slot, he simultaneously spun the wheel to the left, tapped the brakes to shift the weight forward and pulled the E-brake up firmly. The Golf spun on its front wheels and pirouetted 180° into the empty space. As the wheel hit the curb, the car settled into the space rocking softly back and forth for a couple of seconds. Three other black cars the same size as the Golf, were parked close by. The Golf had just settled back onto its suspension as the black Mercedes came roaring past. It turned left onto Hegelalee, tires squealing and smoking.

What Marc did not know was that Team Two had just received instructions to drop the pursuit of the Golf and drive as quickly as possible to DortuStrasse 50 and rendez-vous with Uli and Vitaly. He was about to pull out and go in the opposite direction from the disappearing Mercedes when his phone announced a text message: *Get to DortuStrasse 50 fast. I need your help.* Just as he started to pull away from the curb, a pair of Potsdam *polizei* shot by, lights flashing, sirens screaming Pah-Pom, Pah-Pom. Marc knew they'd never catch the Mercedes. He headed toward DortuStrasse 50, but took a different route to avoid the *polizei*.

The door to the elevator whooshed open and Rene found himself face to face with The Client, who was standing near a splendid Louis XIV table, two chairs of the same period on either side. Everything about this man spelled wealth and power from his bespoke suit to his expensive handmade Italian loafers to his Panerai Luminor watch. Even this room, displayed The Client's obvious taste and unlimited resources.

Waiting in the elevator, Rene had decided The Client was an arrogant SOB, just from listening to the man's voice. While Rene had performed a couple of Engagements for The Client before, using an intermediary, he had never met the man.

As he walked out of the elevator, he had to hide a smile. The Client had suddenly realized that he was way out of his depth. He looked scared. He gestured to Rene to follow and walked into an adjoining room. Twelve monitors filled one wall. On two of them, Uli and his henchman were busy working the building's door locks.

"You know this man, Bob?"

"Not personally but we have crossed paths before. Both times he tried to kill me."

The Client looked sick.

"Do you have another escape route?"

"Yes, but we'd have to go down to the lobby."

"*Merde.* Okay, we need to shift to Plan B," said Rene flatly. Realizing he still held the satchel, he handed it to The Client.

"It is in there, you know."

"What? The shipment? It better be."

"No. The RFID chip. It is how they tracked us, how they got to you."

"Who is *us?*"

"My protégé, Billy, and me."

The Client looked like he was about to say something, then thought better of it. He moved into the other room and put the satchel on the elegant table. Reaching into his jacket, he took out a slender key, inserted it into the tamper-proof lock, and turned it counterclockwise. Both men heard a muffled click. With the self-destruct system deactivated, the lock opened. The Client reached into the satchel and removed one of the canisters. He opened it to reveal hundreds of diamonds. He turned the satchel inside out, but found no chip.

"Where is it? Where is the chip?"

He slid the satchel across the table to Rene who ran his fingertips along the top flap. He felt a slight rise along the fabric next to the plate where the tamper-proof lock attached. He examined the patch of cloth that was the same color and texture as the rest of the lining. Picking at it, he was able to grab the tip and pull it. Attached to it was the RFID chip.

"May I?" Rene asked.

The Client nodded. Rene dropped the patch to the marble floor then ground the chip into dust. He pulled out his iPhone and pressed a button to kill the signals of the other two chips.

Uli and Vitaly had no trouble breaching the main entrance. They swept into the lobby, pulling H&K MP5s from their duffel bags. Each fully automatic submachine gun had an extended 40-round magazine. They approached the first elevator and found it was locked down. Vitaly pulled a skeleton key from a compartment in one of his duffels. He inserted it into the top of the locked elevator, turned it and unlocked the doors. Reaching into his duffle, Uli pulled out a small bar. Uli and Vitaly pulled the doors in opposite directions until there was enough space between them to insert the bar between the doors. Uli started ratcheting the bar, slowly forcing the elevator doors apart. They pulled out a couple of high-powered LED flashlights and peered into the shaft, looking for the locked elevator cab. They saw it several floors above them. Next trick, bring it down.

On the opposite side of the outer control panel was the circuitry that called the elevator to the lobby. Reaching around, Vitaly popped the panel open with a small knife. With the flashlight clenched between his teeth, he reached inside and quickly cut four wires. Taking a box from his hip pocket, he inserted the wires into the appropriate holes, pulled the adhesive strip off the back of the box and attached it to the wall of the elevator shaft. He pulled out a small remote-control module from the opposite hip pocket. He turned it on and saw three green lights.

"We have control of the elevator," he called over his shoulder to Uli.

"Good, but come over here. I've found something interesting."

Vitaly crossed the lobby to where Uli stood, pointing to a small, dark touch screen.

"What do you make of this?" Uli asked.

"Hmmm. The door is flush against the wall. No seams,

no exposed edges, no exterior keys or access points. Notice the frame surrounding the panel? It's case-hardened carbon steel, buffed out in a stainless-like finish." Vitaly was silent as he thought through this. "Very impressive."

"But how do we get access?"

"We don't, but with some C-4, maybe we can damage it enough so it won't open."

"I don't follow you."

"I'm not familiar with this type of door, but I think it leads to a secure area. Probably secure from everywhere else in the building. If we jam it shut, our prey can't escape and we can take our time searching them out."

"Good. Keep going."

"We secure the lobby then go floor by floor until we find the secure area where they're hiding."

"How will we enter the secure area?"

"Uli. You ask Mr. C-4 such a lame question." Patting the bag holding his explosive charges. "And with this box, we control the main elevator." He said pointing to his pocket.

Both men laughed.

Outside the entrance to DortuStrasse 50, Team Two's Mercedes arrived and pulled up at an angle behind Uli's

Mercedes and a Maserati, blocking them both. They checked their laptop one more time, but didn't see a display showing the RFID chip. For a moment they were puzzled, but with Uli's Mercedes at the location, they figured they were at the right address. They exited the car and went to the trunk to retrieve their gear.

Seconds later, Marc pulled up silently, daytime running lights off, and pulled in close to a parked car a few meters away. He recognized the Mercedes. He saw the two men standing at the trunk as it slowly opened. He noticed they had blocked the Maserati. Parked nearby was a similar Mercedes, nobody inside. Marc realized that Rene and The Client were probably trapped inside the building, at least one interception team was already inside and another one was heading in. He panicked for a second, not sure what to do. But a long-buried voice spoke up and in one clarifying second, Marc realized that he had to neutralize these bad guys if Rene was going to have a chance to survive. He knew he could help, he had faced this kind of situation once before and had come out alive. Now other lives depended on what he did next.

Looking around the interior of the car for something to use, Marc reached down and pulled up the rubber floor mat and rolled it up, wedging it almost all the way around the accelerator pedal. He wedged the gun Rene gave him into the small of his back against his belt. He put his iPhone into his front pants' pocket.

Next, he put the car in gear and opened his door slightly as he coasted the car toward the Mercedes. As the Golf closed the gap to the two men standing at the rear of the Mercedes pulling out duffel bags from the trunk, Marc kicked with his foot, jamming the rolled-up mat up against the pedal, pushing it to the floor.

There was an explosion inside the building. The two men looked up, one turned around and saw the accelerating Golf rapidly closing. He raised his pistol and started firing, but Marc had already rolled out of the car and hit the ground, smacking up against the rear-quarter panel of a parked car by the time the rounds smashed into the Golf's windshield.

He heard the sickening sound of smashing metal on metal, and screams. Looking up over the parked car's rear, he half expected to hear more pistol shots. All he heard was silence.

Marc stood up and saw the smashed cars. He took the pistol from the back of his pants, raised it and pointed it towards the wrecked cars. He was not sure what to do with the pistol, but holding it somehow made him feel safer. He walked toward the cars and looked at where the Golf impacted the Mercedes. What he saw made his stomach turn. He felt bile quickly rising in his throat. He turned away, gagging, trying to swallow it back down. Taking a deep breath, he turned and looked again. One man was surely dead, his torso completely crushed between the two bumpers. The other man moaned, his upper leg completely pinned and broken. Dark spots of blood seeped through his trousers.

Marc felt another flush of nausea. He had just used the Golf as a weapon against two fellow humans, killing one, probably both. But at the back of his mind, a voice said, *If you hadn't done this, Rene and whoever The Client is would soon be taken and probably killed. You did what you had to do—now move!*

Marc tore his eyes away and tried to focus on what to do next. The past few seconds were surreal. It felt like a dream where you see yourself doing things, almost as if someone else did these acts. *This was not Marc Lange doing these things was it?*

He knew he needed to get inside, see how he could help. *Maybe Billy, the Driver, is starting to emerge*, he thought as he carefully made his way to the building's entrance.

Watching both external and internal surveillance systems, Rene and The Client saw Uli and Vitaly open and access the first elevator and then find the second. They saw the second black Mercedes arrive, blocking the Maserati. As the two men emerged from the second car and move to the trunk to access their gear, Rene and The Client watched transfixed as the VW Golf appeared out of nowhere and crashed into them right after an explosion rocked the building. Both of the thugs were down and Marc was moving towards them.

What is going through Marc's mind right now? I am sure he did not start out expecting anything like this. Very resourceful under pressure. Impressive! But Uli and his helper are still in the lobby.

Rene grabbed his phone and sent Marc a quick text: *Saw what happened. Take cover. Wait outside till I signal you again.*

Vitaly rigged a series of small C-4 charges around the perimeter of the secure elevator panel. He assumed he could not get past the strongly reinforced door, but he could bend and damage it enough so it would not open, effectively trapping whoever was above. He ran wires to the detonator, took cover behind the large central planter with Uli and set off the charges. As the dust and debris settled, Vitaly looked up and wondered whether the fire-sprinkler system would activate. Nothing happened. *Whoever controlled access to this building must be paranoid*, he thought. *No security alarms going off to reveal the precious hiding place.*

Rene turned toward The Client. "Are there any other ways to access this area?"

"No, only the secure elevator."

"So in essence, we are trapped. How many floors does this elevator service?"

"Just five and six. The elevators in #52 accesses the other floors, but is programed not to open on these two."

"What is on the fifth floor?"

"It's a storage area for rare antique business I dabble in. I keep items stored down there until I'm ready to hold an auction."

"How secure is this area from the rest of the sixth floor?"

"It's totally sealed off. Nobody knows about it. I bought this building from a former dealer in goods. He had already put in some of this secret area. I improved on it."

"What kind of *goods*?"

"I'm not sure and I didn't ask."

Rene hoped that the building's former owner had enough foresight to have a secondary escape route nearby. He began sweeping both the office and control room areas. He started in the small office then proceeded to the control center which had the console, a desk, a chair and a couple of small tables. He tapped the walls, looking for a hollow or false panel. After several tense moments, he heard a hollow sound. Near the floor, on the wall opposite the monitors, he found a panel that had been taped and filled over so no edges showed. Pulling the paratrooper knife that he had taken from the Maserati out of his pocket, he snapped it open and plunged it into the wall. He cut around the edges until an outline appeared. Using the knife as leverage, he pushed it towards the wall and the panel popped loose. He used his phone's flashlight app to look inside the hole.

Looking at Vitaly, Uli pulled out his phone. "It's time to get the others in here. We need to search this place."

Team One responded first. "We're on our way from the church, Boss. Traffic's bad."

"When will you be here?"

"Maybe five minutes, give or take."

"Hurry."

No response from Team Two. Uli didn't like it. *Where the hell are those guys? They should already be here. They were only a couple kilometers away ten minutes ago.* He went to the entrance and stepped out, expecting to see them pull up. Instead, he saw the carnage.

"*Scheiss!* What happened out there?"

Vitaly ran over to Uli's side. "*Gott.* Must have happened while the C-4 charges went off, otherwise we'd have heard the crash. Do we help them?"

"No time. They're dead or close to it. Goddammit! I needed them."

Uli called Team One again. "Be careful coming into

#50. Team Two's eliminated. If you see anybody outside the building, kill him."

"Okay Boss."

Uli and Vitaly headed to the main elevator.

Rene heard surprise in The Client's voice, "I bought this building three years ago. Nobody told me anything about a secret exit."

"It does not matter," said Rene shaking his head at the irony, then peering into the hole. "Stay here, I will check it out."

He crawled through the opening and came out in the space on the other side of the control room. The flashlight app revealed a space about three meters by six meters, not quite one and a half meters high. IPhone in one hand, he crawled east to the far corner and found a screen embedded in the wall. Shining the light through it, he saw a hidden crawlway leading to the secret elevator shaft. The odds of getting out alive just got better.

He removed the screen and crawled through. Standing up, he pointed the light toward the elevator shaft. Near the shaft, he saw a ladder attached to the wall. Going down in the secret elevator was not an option; he was sure the C-4 explosion a few minutes earlier had put the elevator out of commission. He looked up as far as the flashlight could penetrate. He had no idea what was up there, but options were limited, so up they would go. He crawled back towards The Client.

One floor below, Uli and Vitaly were making their sweep.

"I still don't get it. Why have two elevators for this building, doesn't make sense?" Vitality asked.

"Who cares? It makes our job easier. They must be up here, we just have to find them."

"Ready? Cover me."

They moved from the elevator and tried to enter the first door on the right. It was locked. Vitaly laughed. Seconds later, he opened the door. It was a huge room full of furniture. Uli spotted another door on the far right of the room. They entered this room. Rugs. Dozens of Oriental rugs, all shapes and sizes. Their value was lost on the two men. Another door led to a room full of statuary and paintings. Uli was getting frustrated. He wanted to shoot at all this junk. But another door beckoned. They went into another room. Empty. Another door. They went through an empty office to the next door and opened it. Back at the elevator's foyer.

Uli turned and shot a few rounds at the office furniture

to relieve his frustration. He and Vitaly stormed into the elevator and went up another floor to six. As the elevator door opened, there was a loud *ding*.

From his hiding place, Marc saw Team One arrive and pull up behind the crashed Golf. The two men exited their Mercedes and moved to the front of the VW. One pulled out a pistol and began looking around while the other bent over the bodies crushed between the two cars. Marc knew only one of the trapped men from Team Two was dead, but the other had passed out. The Team One thug gestured to his partner who shook his head, so the second thug turned his back on the bodies and he too pulled a pistol and began looking around, his face grim.

Marc hunkered down. Rene said to stay hidden. He thought for a brief second of using his own pistol to try and stop them, but decided against it. He saw them return to their Mercedes' trunk and take out two duffle bags and carry them toward #50's entrance. He sent Rene a text telling him another team had arrived and headed into the building. He wondered again why he was in Potsdam, but quickly pushed that thought aside. He needed to focus. Shaking his head to clear his mind, he determined to help Rene anyway he could.

Rene saw Marc's message and immediately sent him a message to stay put. The Client stood next to the control console, his face tense. He had hung the closed satchel around his left shoulder.

"I have found another way out," Rene said, watching as The Client's face displayed his relief. "We must get out of here. Crouch down and follow me, and *be quiet*!"

The Client swallowed nervously, his eyes huge. He nodded and followed Rene through the opening. Rene reached behind them and pulled the opening back in place hoping the space would go unnoticed.

Holding his iPhone flashlight in one hand, Rene moved cautiously forward toward the east end of the space, The Client close behind. They both heard the elevator ding its ominous arrival.

They moved as fast as they could without making any noise. When they reached the screen, Rene exited first and helped The Client through. He also pulled the screen back into its slot until there was a soft click. They both stood up inside the elevator shaft. Rene pointed his flashlight at the ladder.

"We go up. Quietly."

"I'm afraid of heights," whispered The Client.

Jesu, thought Rene. *What next?* "Okay. I will steady you from below. The ladder is our only chance. You want to die, stay here or, better yet, go back to the meeting room."

"Oh God," said The Client softly, but he walked to the ladder and started climbing. Rene waited until The Client was a few steps up, then he got on the ladder. They climbed very slowly, very quietly.

Uli and Vitaly arrived on the sixth floor. Covering each other, they moved away from the elevator. The elevator's interior light revealed a large room stuffed with furniture and statues.

"*Gott*, what's with the furniture anyway?"

"And all these effing statues!"

Using the LED lights mounted on their weapons, they worked their way through and clear of the clutter and headed to where the secret elevator should be located. Suddenly, a dead end. No elevator, just a wall. Uli turned to Vitaly and put a finger to his lips. Vitaly nodded. He opened his bag and removed a doctor's stethoscope and placed it against the wall, listening for voices. Moving the stethoscope around to several different places, he finally looked at Uli and shook his head. Nothing.

Uli raised his weapon and pointed it towards the wall as Vitaly quickly moved behind him. Uli fired the weapon at a slight angle to avoid bullet slugs ricocheting back in their direction. He fired a short burst of five rounds into the wall. The sound was deafening. Splinters from the wall showered the surrounding space, but when the dust settled, there were just a few indentations in the wall, but no full penetrations. Even with 9 mm 124gr +P+ high power rounds, the bullets had barely made a scratch.

Uli turned around to Vitaly.

"Have any C-4 left?"

"A few spares," grinned Vitaly. "I always come prepared! Enough to get this job done and maybe a few others too; if we need it."

Uli congratulated himself on picking Vitaly for this assignment. When it came to explosives, this guy was simply the best.

Reaching the top of the ladder, The Client and Rene found a small metal platform about two meters wide. Rene steadied The Client as there was no guardrail. Some light seeped from around the roof door.

"Put your hand on my shoulder while I open the door," Rene ordered. "Just hang tough for another few seconds."

Rene turned the handle on the unlocked door and pushed it open. There was a brilliant flash of light from the late afternoon sun, but The Client quickly stepped through the door onto the roof. Rene followed. Suddenly they heard an automatic weapon ripping off a short burst on the floor below. The Client cried out.

"Shhhh!" ordered Rene. The Client shuddered but obeyed. Rene froze and listened for a moment. He heard nothing else.

Rene surveyed the rooftop and saw several large air conditioner units. He walked toward them and after circling around two of them, he found a standalone unit with a door in it at the center of the roof. The door was locked but The Client whispered that his key card might work. Rene used the card to open the door, entered and found a steeply inclined stairwell leading down one flight of stairs.

Merde! This is the maintenance access to the roof from the sixth floor.

Rene's options for saving his client dimmed. They were trapped there. As soon as Uli and his buddy did not find their quarry in the secure area, they'd start looking around. If they found the access panel to the secret elevator, Uli would come up to the roof. Uli and the other guy had at least one machine gun, probably two. Rene had a pistol and some additional ammo. Still, they had no choice but to go down the stairs. He turned from the staircase and gestured to The Client. Deer-in-the-headlights followed.

As the dust settled from the C-4 blast, Vitaly went through the hole. The powerful LED light on his weapon cut through the haze, revealing the control room. Uli entered, weapon ready, finger on the trigger. Both men looked around the room. Vitaly spotted the uneven panel close to the floor. He moved over to it and poked it with his weapon.

The panel moved. Uli pulled the panel out and threw it on the floor. Knowing each would be an easy target if either of them tried to squeeze through, Vitaly reached into the nylon sack at his hip and took out a Flash/Bang grenade. He looked over at Uli.

Looking at the size and location of the wall hole Uli realized they had no choice. He nodded. Vitaly pulled the pin and tossed the grenade inside. Both men turned away and covered their ears as the Flash/Bang grenade exploded, showering the secure area on the other side of the wall with debris and almost taking down the structural frames. Uli crawled through, weapon first. Once inside, he rose up on one knee and played his weapon's LED light around the area. The haze and debris from the blast obscured his view; he failed to notice the screened access to the secret elevator shaft in the far corner.

Uli returned to what was left of the Control Room. All of the monitors were black. The C-4 had destroyed the surveillance system. They had no ability to scan the rest of the building. The two men swept the room, finding nothing. They charged into the other room and saw only a table and two chairs and the door to the secret elevator.

"*Gott und scheiss*. That little maggot can't have escaped again. Impossible!" raged Uli

"So now what?" asked Vitaly.

"We keep searching. They can't have escaped yet. They must be hiding on another floor."

"But how did they get to another floor?"

"How should I know? But we better find out. Now!"

"Okay. Let's go. If I have to, I'll use the rest of the C-4 to blast every hiding place in the building until we find them."

They turned and retraced their steps to the hole blasted in the wall.

Rene and The Client descended the iron steps as noiselessly as possible. At the bottom, Rene used the same key card and opened the door a crack. He saw a huge roomful of furniture and a small fire escape sign about ten meters away. He whispered to The Client, "Look out the door. Where is the main elevator from here?"

The Client peered out the door.

"It's on the other side of the furniture to the left about fifteen meters."

Rene pulled The Client back from the door and closed it. He had to think.

They heard the C-4 explosion a few meters away. Some of the dust from the wall explosion seeped beneath their door. Their timeframe for escaping the building just got smaller.

Rene dismissed the main elevator as it would take them

directly to the lobby. There were at least two team members of Uli's gang waiting down there. That left the fire escape. Getting there was the problem.

Rene opened the door again and looked toward the left and saw the breach in the secure wall and the right side of a man's body go through the hole. Rene had to assume the other man was already through the hole and in the Control Room. He decided it was now or never or he would never get The Client out alive. They would have to crouch and run through the furniture and statues towards the fire escape and hope that Uli and his henchman didn't come back out of the hole into the auditorium.

Rene opened the door and stepped out. He motioned for The Client to follow. As they started to run towards the fire escape sign, they heard the Flash/Bang grenade explode. The Client froze.

"Do not stop now!" ordered Rene in a harsh whisper. He grabbed The Client's arm. "If you stop now, they will take you and kill you."

This snapped The Client out of his trance. He crouched back down and followed behind Rene.

Suddenly, a movement to the left and behind caught Rene's eye. A figure of a man was emerging from the hole in the wall behind them.

Rene had his gun out as he pushed The Client behind some statuary.

Peering through the dust Vitaly looked up in time to see Rene leaning forward, pistol held two-handed, pointed at him. They locked eyes for a split second as Vitaly jerked his weapon up, but his shoulder strap snagged on a jagged piece of the wall from the blast. He pulled the machine gun with everything he had, but Mr. C4 could not shake his gun free. His eyes got even bigger as Rene squeezed off a triple tap, hitting Vitaly three times in the chest. Vitaly grunted sharply, the realization that he had had been shot by Bob twisted his face into an angry death mask as he pitched over and was dead as he hit the floor.

Rene heard a scream of pure rage. Motioning for The Client to stay put, Rene lowered himself into a prone position and steadied his aim. Uli came crashing through the hole in the wall and tripped over Vitaly's dead body just as Rene squeezed off another triple tap. *Merde*! The shots were high. Rene rolled behind a huge armoire as Uli came up firing.

The sound of the H&K MP5's rounds ripping into the ancient wood of the armoire was chilling, as dozens of rounds reduced one side of it to splinters. Rene rolled towards and behind a large sarcophagus sitting on a stone pedestal near the remains of the armoire. He leaned out and returned fire, squeezing the last six rounds from his magazine. He dropped the empty magazine out of his pistol, pulled a replacement from his shoulder holster, slammed it into the pistol grip and thumbed the catch to chamber a round. He looked over at The Client and saw he was still safe and focused again on Uli.

"Bob! Bob! You know I'm going to kill you this time!"

Rene did not reply.

"Bob! You shit! Did you hear me? I have a bullet with your name on it."

Crouching low, Rene said nothing, hoping this would infuriate Uli even more, maybe drive him over the edge and for a fraction of a second, make him sloppy. It was his only hope.

"You touched my daughter, my baby. Your touch defiled her. I am going to put a bullet in your head, and then another and another, DO YOU HEAR ME YOU FUCK?"

"Bob! Then I'm going to find this man, this diamond whore, they call The Client and take him to Mr. X. We'll bleed him and learn all his secrets. There's not a DAMN thing you can do about it. Do you hear me?"

Silence.

"BOB!!! YOU FUCK!!! DO YOU HEAR ME???"

Uli stood up firing and put dozens more rounds into the area where Rene had been, he then quickly moved to cover the distance so he could outflank him. Splinters and chips of stone from a nearby statue exploded all over Rene as he ducked even lower and then realizing his position was at risk, dove behind another nearby armoire. He bounced up balancing on one knee, he had to be ready to keep moving, keep outflanking Uli and more important keep him away from The Client.

The firing stopped and Rene heard the magazine hit the floor. He quickly looked around the armoire. This was his chance. The consummate killing machine got sloppy for one split second and forgot to duck and cover while exchanging magazines. Rene stood up from behind the armoire and fired two triple taps in quick succession. Consumed by his rage, his facial features shifted to shock as Uli realized his mistake, he tried to move, but too late. Three of the bullets slammed into him and the force of the impact spun him backwards as he fell to the floor. Rene rushed forward, his pistol pointed at Uli, but no need. One of the bullets caught him in the right eye, the other two in the chest and upper shoulder. Rene kicked Uli. No reaction. Uli was dead. Rene had to remind himself to inhale. That one breath tasted better than any he had ever breathed before. The air filling his lungs meant that he had survived against Uli Petrovski.

The two explosions above rocked the building slightly. The two men from Team One looked upwards and grinned. One of them started towards the elevator.

"We're supposed to stay down here," said the one closer to the entrance.

"Maybe they need our help."

"If they do, he'll call us."

Not sure what else to do, they waited. Then they heard muffled gunfire.

"That does it. I'm going up," said the first one.

He took out a remote similar to Vitaly's and pushed the Call button. The elevator started moving down from the sixth floor. When the door opened, he had his machine gun ready just in case, but the elevator was empty. He entered and yelled "Wish me luck," to his partner as the elevator door closed. The elevator began its journey back up to six.

Marc could not take it anymore. He heard two muffled explosions from his hiding place outside the building. He moved to the entrance and cracked the door open. He saw two of the thugs from Team One talking together. A few moments later when there was muffled gunfire, one of them entered the elevator, as the other stood watching. Mark crept inside the building. Forgetting about the pistol in his belt, instinct took over. Lowering his shoulder, he rushed the second thug, hitting him square in the back, Marc's momentum caused both of them to crash to the floor. Both landed hard, rolling in different directions.

The man dropped his weapon in the fall. Marc also lost his pistol. It skittered across the floor away from him.

Marc recovered first. Lurching over, he landed a round kick to the right side of the thug's face. The man fell back, very close to his machine gun. Marc saw him reaching for his weapon. Marc's pistol was a few meters away, near a marble planter in the center of the lobby. Diving, he pushed out with his hand and shoved himself and the pistol behind the planter to safety.

Firing his weapon, Uli's man from Team One put a couple dozen rounds into the top of the planter, sending marble shards flying in all directions, adding to the debris in the lobby. Marc's neck and arms took some small shards, but he reached up and over the planter and returned fire squeezing off five rounds before ducking behind the planter. Immediately Uli's thug returned fire, kicking up more marble splinters. Marc shot four more rounds at the man. Realizing he was in an exposed spot, he started crawling to the other end of the planter. Uli's thug realized Marc's vulnerability too and ran to the end of the planter firing continuously. Bullets slammed into the floor behind Marc as he scrambled faster. Fortunately for Marc, running while firing did nothing for the thug's accuracy. His ears ringing, Marc heard a click and somehow knew the machine gun was out of bullets. Marc stood up and fired the last four shots in his magazine at his attacker.

One bullet struck home hitting the attacker just below the shoulder. Even though he had just been shot, adrenaline coursing through his veins, the thug tried to take Marc down. He ran, lowering his head, aiming at Marc's belly.

Marc instinctively threw his pistol at the attacker's head, hitting the man square in the face, stunning him. Then Marc tried to turn the tables, rushed in using a Krav Mega technique, hitting the attacker's temple with the side of his fist, then throwing the other fist out caught him square in the side of the chin. Uli had chosen his team well, the man refused to go down. On his knees, grunting with pain, sweat popping out of his face, his eyes huge with fury, he thrust upwards and threw his weight into Marc. Marc took the blow to his mid-section and staggered backwards but managed to grab a hold of his attacker's shirt before he too fell to the floor. His attacker struggled against Marc's weight to get free, but Marc swung his fist, hitting first in the temple. The blow stunned the thug, allowing Marc to lash out at him again hitting him in the chin with the open palm of his hand, rocking his head back. Marc staggered up and gave the thug a swift Krav Mega smack to the chest to give himself a bit of space before he snap kicked a shot to the man's rib cage. Hearing a crack and a groan, the attacker slumped to the floor, out cold. Marc staggered backwards and sat back on the marble planter dazed and exhausted, then taking a couple of deep breaths, he stood up walked over to the unconscious man to make sure he was indeed out cold.

Rene heard the elevator motor and knew that someone from the remaining team was on the way up. Grabbing the

MP5 from Vitaly's dead hands, he rushed towards the elevator door. He saw The Client coming out from behind the statue and motioned for him to remain where he was. Rene positioned himself so he would have a good field of fire when the doors opened and waited. A few seconds later, the elevator dinged and the door opened. As the attacker emerged, Rene fired a short burst at the man. Too soon! The man jumped back and hit the button closing the elevator doors. Rene fired again, but only hit the closing door. At that moment he heard the distinct sound of machine gun fire from below.

SHIT! MARC! Rene thought in a panic. He rushed to the elevator and pressed the Down button over and over but nothing happened. It dawned on him that someone from the group figured out how to control the main elevator. He turned and ran over to Vitaly and searched his many pockets. He had almost given up when he felt a small, square-shaped box in one of the pockets on Vitaly's upper leg. Flipping up the Velcro tab, Rene reached in and took out the remote. He ran back to the elevator and pressed the Up button and heard the motor start to wind the elevator back up. He could not believe how long it took. Each second took an eternity.

As Marc stood over his unconscious adversary, he was

tackled from behind. Preoccupied, he had not heard the elevator's ding signaling its return to the ground floor. Seeing his friend down and Marc's back to him, the other thug from Team One charged. Rather than shoot him in the back, his attacker wanted to hurt Marc first, beat him bloody, then shoot him.

Marc fell to the floor, trying to turn, but was pinned, his attacker's elbow pressing into the small of his back. He felt the sharp pain as the attacker hit him twice in the back of the head near his ear. Reeling from the pain, Marc tried a Tai Chi movement. He went completely slack, relaxing his whole body, then heaved upward, unbalancing the man on top of him for a second, which allowed Marc to get to his knees. He threw himself against the attacker, knocking him off balance and managed to straddle him. But his attacker rallied quickly, hitting Marc hard on his ear again, staggering Marc, who fell backwards onto the floor. The attacker moved to jump on him, but Marc kicked out and caught him in the side of the knee, breaking it. The man screamed in pain, falling forward onto Marc who was trying to get to his feet, knocking Marc back onto the floor.

Still dizzy from the blow to his ear, Marc's head smacked into the marble floor with an audible *thwock*. He almost passed out but using every technique that Jose had drilled into him, he fought through the fog to refocus. He tried to raise himself to his knees when his attacker, fighting through his own pain, swept his other leg across Marc, knocking him back down. He lunged back on top of Marc pinning him to the floor. He put his hands around Marc's neck and started to strangle him.

Marc tried to use his knees to hit his attacker, thrusting upwards he tried to hit the man in his balls, but this man was a better fighter than the first. He blocked Marc's attempts, absorbing them with his body, he released one hand from Marc's throat and hit him again in the side of the head. He followed with an open palmed slam to Marc's chest almost knocking the breath out of him. Marc knew he was in real trouble, this was nothing like training. This was real life and death. He hit his attacker again and again. Closed fist, open fist, any fist, but this man was locked in, able to endure any pain, any attack to kill Marc. Starting to lose consciousness, Marc tried to pry the man's hands from his throat, but his strength was failing.

Marc could not breathe. He looked up into his attacker's eyes and saw nothing but hate and rage and then, blood. The attacker's grip relaxed completely as he pitched forward and landed next to Marc. Gulping down huge amounts of air, Marc turned to see the back of the attacker's head was mushy. With more oxygen in his system, Marc focused his eyes and saw Rene approach him, then reach down and offer his hand.

"Marc, are you all right? Are you OK?"

Gasping and rubbing his neck, Marc croaked, "I think I'll be okay. Thank you Rene. That bastard almost killed me. You saved my life."

"Stay here and catch your breath. I am going back up to the sixth floor to get The Client. And take this. If anyone but me gets off the elevator, shoot to kill." Rene handed Marc his pistol.

Rene returned a few minutes later with The Client in tow.

"Marc are you going to be okay? Can you make it to the car?"

Marc could only nod his head as the three men exited the building and moved toward the crashed cars. The wounded thug, still pinned by the crashed Golf, was unconscious but alive. While Marc worked to wipe down and move the Golf back from the Mercedes, Rene pulled the wounded one away from the crash, then the dead one, laying him nearby. He entered the Mercedes and saw the keys still in the ignition. Starting it, he moved it back a couple of meters, freeing the Maserati.

"Alert the Politzie?" Rene asked The Client.

He shook his head. "I have assets that are on route."

The Client was busy sending a series of texts as he and Marc got into the Maserati. Entering the car, Rene glanced at Marc and was relieved to see the color return to Marc's face. Glancing in the rearview mirror, Rene noticed the smug look of superiority had returned to The Client's face. Rene shrugged. *Same old, same old.*

Starting the Maserati, he pulled into the driveway. As the

car exited down the smaller side alley onto Yorek Strasse, Rene looked at the clock on the dashboard. 17:26. They'd only been inside the building twenty-eight minutes. It seemed like a lifetime.

Chapter 10

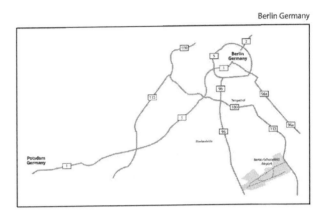

Several hours later, Rene dropped Marc off at the Berlin Schoenfeld Airport. Completely exhausted physically, in addition to a sore neck, Marc discovered it hurt to swallow. Mentally and emotionally drained as well, Marc barely managed to find the ticket counter, exchange his original full-fare ticket for a new ticket back to London Gatwick. Once past security, he stopped at a café for a triple espresso. He added a large amount of sugar and gulped the hot, sweet, caffeine-laden drink down and walked slowly to his gate. Marc was numb. His mind and body had taken a beating. He'd stared death in the face and it wasn't pretty. Nevertheless, he *was* alive. Marc walked, not seeing movement all around him, all his senses oblivious to his surroundings.

The whole world seemed to crawl past him in some haphazard pattern.

He got to his gate, found a seat and slumped down in it. As he waited for the plane to arrive, he tried to make sense of his experience with Rene, but it was like a raw sore, open and too close for comfort. He, Marc Lange, had killed a man today, quite possibly two. He had no answer for what had happened other than a thinly held belief that if he had done nothing, Rene, The Client and probably himself would all be dead. He had learned that the term "professional killers" meant just that—they had no problem killing their prey. He clung to that thought like a life raft, it was the only thing he had and he clung to it.

He pulled out his new iPhone and, after a couple of false starts, actually sent text messages to Bala, Stella and especially April letting them know he would arrive home early on Saturday morning. After he sent the messages, he sat and wondered what he would tell them, what he could tell them. And what about the money? He needed to think about how to handle that too. €500,000 was a lot of cash to materialize out of nowhere.

Where to begin? He thought. *It started off seemingly innocent enough, but the end! My God! Some bloody thug tried to kill me! Saved by Rene or Bob or whoever he is.* Remembering his close call made him shiver. *If today was Driver 101, what further hell is waiting for me down the line? Though to be fair, Rene did say this Engagement was as close to a factor ten as he could remember. Half joking, he said they might need to notch the factor scale up to eleven.*

Marc laughed silently to himself. It seemed absurd now. Factor of eleven. Like the movie gag about turning up a silly guitar amp. He let his mind drift back, recalling the events that followed the getaway from DortuStrasse 50. Driving out of Potsdam, Rene asked The Client where he wanted to be dropped.

"Any Metro that services the outlying areas of Berlin."

"I can do that. We're heading to Berlin as it is."

"Thank you for saving my life. I must admit, I got complacent and let my guard down. Strange, I had worked so frequently with Horowicz he was the last person I expected would sell me out. Pity for him." His face hardened for a second, then the look of superiority returned to his face.

"I will certainly upgrade all my security arrangements in the future, although probably not at DortuStrasse 50-52. I had to utilize some of my resources to clean up that mess at DortuStrasse. There will be nothing left to see there, even while the police conduct their investigations."

"You are welcome. I advise you to take care of Horowicz as part of your security upgrade," said Rene.

"Of course. I cannot condone a traitor."

Marc exchanged a knowing look with Rene. Neither of them had a crumb of sympathy for Horowicz. He had very nearly got all three of them killed. His skinny ass was about to be turned inside-out by his really pissed-off boss.

No one spoke for the next 20 km. On the outskirts of

Berlin, Rene found a Metro stop.

"Is this close enough for you?"

"Indeed," replied The Client. "It's also time for me to pay you." He reached into the satchel. "I was able to get to my safe and extract this while you were dealing with Billy." The Client said as he pulled out two envelopes. "Since you exposed a plot to kidnap me and also saved my life, I think you'll be satisfied with this." He handed the two envelopes to Rene.

As the very fat envelopes exchanged hands, The Client reached out and shook Rene's hand, then Marc's.

"I hope to engage your services again in the future. Oh, and make sure to count it in a quiet place."

"Only if the factor is less than three," replied Rene as The Client got out of the Maserati.

As Rene drove away, Marc saw The Client smile, the satchel slung across his shoulder, swinging gently from side to side as he walked away. Rene drove for a few minutes before pulling off the Autobahn. He found a parking space on the street near the exit ramp and pulled into it, killing the engine. He turned and looked directly at Marc.

"You have every reason to tell me to go fuck myself after what you have been through, Marc. I am sorry. I had no idea how dangerous this Engagement would eventually turn out. Usually, when a client names a factor for a job, he inflates the danger. You may have a little car chase and that is about it. But this …." The words left him and trailed off into silence.

Marc rubbed his forehead, trying to find words to say what he felt.

Rene continued. "If you want to tell me 'Rene you are a bastard, you are not my co-driver, shove your money and your Engagement, I never want to see you again,' I would understand. In any event, I want you to have this. It is half the fee."

He handed Marc one of the two envelopes.

"Take it. It is yours. You earned it."

Marc took the envelope without looking at it and put it in his jacket pocket.

"One last thing," Rene continued. "I promised you I would pay to be the co-driver for the rest of the season. No matter what you decide, I will still pay you. That was our agreement and I owe you that."

Marc took several deep breaths before he replied to Rene. "I need time to think. My system is in complete shock and I'm simply too overwhelmed to even begin to have an answer for you."

"I understand and I respect that as well."

Rene drove the Maserati back onto the Autobahn. After a few minutes, he pulled into the Galeria Kaufhof shopping mall.

"You look like hell, *mon ami*. Look in the visor mirror."

Marc pulled the passenger visor down and accessed its mirror. Yes, he did look like hell. His face had tiny cuts, bruises and layers of dried sweat and dirt. He looked down at his clothing. Splattered with blood and ripped in places. No way he would get through security looking the way he did.

Rene got out of the Maserati, went to the trunk and returned with the medical kit. "Use what is in here to clean your wounds. I will be back in a few minutes."

By the time Marc finished tending to his cuts and bruises, Rene emerged from the mall carrying several bags. He got back into the car and drove a few blocks to an anonymous and cheap motel. He went inside, returning a few minutes later. He handed Marc a room key.

"Go get yourself cleaned up and change into some clean clothes. I will wait here."

Marc took the room key. He took a long, hot shower to clean his wounds, relax his muscles, heal the pain and wash off some of the Engagement's memories. Try as he might, however, those memories did not go down the drain.

Night had fallen by the time they ate a silent dinner at a café near the airport, each man left to his own thoughts. After espressos arrived, Rene looked at his watch, "Time to go. You have a plane to catch."

Arriving at the airport, Marc opened the car door to get

out when Rene said:

"One last thing. Marc, I am really proud of you. You made decisions today that far exceeded your level of experience. It may sound *creux*, how would you say—hollow?— but you will make an extraordinary *Driver*. And I promise to teach you everything I have learned these past ten years."

"I don't think you want to hear my answer right now, Rene. It might disappoint you."

"You are wrong my friend. Whatever your answer is, whatever you decide, I will accept it. We have just been through the worst. This Engagement is off the charts. If it is any comfort, I cannot imagine one that will ever compare to it."

"I'm not sure that's much comfort, Rene."

Chuckling to himself, Rene said, "I think we need to re-write the Factor List Marc. Maybe this one, what was that phrase from that movie, 'should be turned up to eleven?'"

"You're close. The phrase is: 'These go to eleven' and the movie is *This is Spinal Tap*. I'm impressed. I thought only musicians and classic movie geeks knew that scene."

Shaking hands, Marc told Rene he'd think about everything and let him know. He got out of the Maserati and walked into the airport terminal.

"Mr. X, anything from Potsdam?"

"No Diego. Nothing. We had operatives sweep the building posing as the police. No bodies, no diamonds, no Uli, no Vitaly, his team gone, no Bob and no Client. We came up empty handed. Someone cleaned the building very thoroughly."

"The operation was a failure then?"

"Yes, a complete failure. But now I suspect we have a new enemy. Whoever The Client is has the financial means to counter our organization. We may need to change tactics and stay off the grid for a while."

"Very well, what should I do?"

"Contact my lieutenants and let them know to be cautious until we understand what we are up against and how to counteract it. Then we resume business as usual."

"Yes Mr. X." Diego ended the call and started sending out messages via Signal. It was time to lie low for a while. But for how long he wondered.

Marc's reverie was interrupted by the arrival of his plane. He sighed with relief. He was finally going home. He remembered how much he hated flying and hoped he would be able to at least close his eyes for a few moments. The next thing he knew, the plane landed hard on the runway and he was lurched awake. At last, back in England. He arrived at his apartment about 2:00 am, fell into his bed without taking his clothes off and was deeply asleep in seconds. There were no dreams, only the black sleep of his body trying to restore itself.

The next morning he called April, but she was out, so he left a message that he was home, he was exhausted but OK, and that he'd call her on Monday, that he was too tired to talk. He hoped she would accept this. He called the office and left a message for Bala and Stella saying pretty much the same thing. He spent the rest of the weekend trying to figure out what had happened. Who was he? Was it possible he and Billy could co-exist?

Introspection was new to him. He had lived his life with a constant, singular vision: to be a top notch race-car driver running a top-notch racing team. He had known he was good, very good really, driving a racing machine against all comers. And he knew he had the talent and the mettle to produce a winning team. But this past year he had run head-on into reality. Nothing happens without money. There were bills to pay, parts to buy, salaries and bonuses to pay out. He remembered the commitment he had made to himself: he would do anything—*anything*—to keep the team afloat and keep racing. Well, *anything* had reared its ugly head and it had turned out to be a flying leap off a sheer, very high cliff.

So, what was it going to be? Marc Lange and Team

Technik struggling along from race to race, season to season, the specter of closing the doors for good only one bounced check away? Or would "Billy" help make the job easier with plenty of funds to take the team to the next level?

He wrestled with his thoughts the rest of Saturday and all day Sunday. As he got ready to go to the Monday morning Physio, he was not sure who this person was who stared back at him in his bathroom mirror. Was it Marc Lange or had someone else moved in? He needed to find out.

A round of hugs and back slaps greeted Marc when he arrived at Team Fortunata's plush HQ. It felt like years since he had been with his friends.

Refreshed after a full weekend of rest and reflection, he was ready for anything Jose threw at him. After small chit chat (the more meaningful conversations always waited until after the workout), they went through a round of stretching, Tai Chi and yoga positions to limber up.

Then they really hit it hard. To a man who had been fighting for his life—and losing—less than forty-eight hours ago, Jose's new Krav Maga moves were absolutely exciting. To the uninitiated, it looked like Marc and Luis simply waved their arms and slapped each other. There's waving and slapping and then there's Krav Maga. Their hands crossed back and forth in front of each other in a circular pattern to block an opponent's blows. If an opening in Marc's blocking appeared, Luis used a two-finger knuckle blow to inflict pain or he used open hand slaps to disorient

Marc. Of course, Marc did the same to Luis. The whole point of the movements was to confuse and overwhelm the attacker while landing critical blows to stop him cold. Krav Maga isn't pretty, but it's simple, effective movements make it a favorite with personal defense coaches and Special Forces.

Some of the moves seemed awkward or jerky, but they were built around two things: protection first, then extrication. Marc had a particular reason to love Krav Maga. Those moves he had already mastered had worked in a time of extreme duress with the first thug in Potsdam. Okay, Rene had saved him from the second thug, but Marc had let his guard down. Lesson learned.

Jose was impressed. Usually Luis was his most consistent student, but today Marc had passion. He pushed through the movements as if his life depended on it. There was something new here. Jose could not quite grasp what was going on, but he saw that Marc was on fire. The depths and heights of the human spirit always surprised and delighted Jose and right now, Marc's spirit soared.

Finally, it was over. Sweating and sore, tired yet rejuvenated in spirit, the three men gathered for their familiar post-workout ritual, water and conversation. Both Luis and Jose stared at Marc, studying his face,

"So, what is it, a booger, a pimple, blood? What gives? You guys are both staring at me like there is something on my face."

"No, mate, something different about your face. Like you've been somewhere and you've seen the measure of yourself," started Jose.

Luis chimed in, "Marc, what the hell happened this week in Milano with Rene?"

Marc sat quietly for a few moments. All weekend he had rehearsed what he'd tell everyone, but now that the moment had arrived, he wasn't sure. These two men knew him so well they sensed he was somehow different. They looked at him willing him to answer. He was glad his face had healed so he did not have to explain that.

"I don't know where to begin or end, although I've learned that when you travel with Rene, you should be ready for quite literally anything." He stopped for effect before continuing. "We went on a business trip of sorts for one of his clients. You can't believe what this client put us through. I guess 'grinder' works here."

Luis and Jose both moved closer to listen as Marc continued. "First of all, the guy didn't tell us about his competitors nor about their aggressiveness. Rene did tell me there were, well, factors—what might be called degrees of difficulty—in these deals. Sometimes these factors are overstated, sometimes they aren't."

"Marc, you're kind of vague here," Luis said.

"I have to be. These are Rene's private business deals. But I can tell you ...." Luis and Jose leaned in even closer, so Marc whispered, "this particular client deals in rare and expensive gems and our job was to advise and assist in a delivery. His competitors wanted to steal his trade secrets and his sources. Rene helped his client turn the tables on them."

Marc filled them in on some selected details, leaving out the violent bits. Perhaps one day he' would tell them, but not today.

"Marc, these business dealings sound dangerous," exclaimed Jose.

"Oh, they are!"

Both men sat up and took deep breaths, looking at him seriously.

"Have you ever seen any of these business or jeweler types? They can kill you with a look. Imagine paying a shit-load of money for a gem and then you learn it's worthless. Or maybe they'll bleed you out with a stroke of their silver Mont Blanc pen on a contract. Once you do a deal with these guys, you just know that you are dealing with professionals—professional sharks."

"Marc, you're making fun of us. You had us worried for a minute. I'll remember not to deal with such a dangerous kind of guy," laughed Luis.

"Oh yeah, they're dangerous all right. They whip out that pen and everybody jumps. But seriously if you're buying a gem or signing a contract or finalizing a business deal with them, watch out."

"Rene deals with clients like that all the time?" asked Luis?

"Yeah, he advises them on security arrangements and the like. He calls them Engagements and believe it or not, these people pay him well for his services."

"OK, Marc, let me get this straight. He wants you to advise these same clients. What do you know about security arrangements?" probed Jose.

"I know nothing about security arrangements. He just wanted to show me what he does when he's not growing grapes or driving a car very fast." Marc paused to gather his thoughts. "He told me that he wanted to open a door for me to look in, to show me another side of Rene Dufour. Who knows what Rene was thinking? Maybe I'd like what I saw? And if I was interested, he'd teach me options I'd use once I retired from racing."

His friends stared at him with their mouths open for a few seconds and then suddenly they burst out laughing.

"That was a good one Marc, 'once you retire from racing.'" Luis grinned, shaking his head.

Jose pretended he could not catch his breath. "I read something about one of your American ex-presidents who celebrated his eighty-fifth birthday by parachuting out of a plane. You are like that. I can see you setting a track record in a nuclear Porsche or whatever people are racing fifty years from now. You'll stop racing cars or managing a team a few hours before they start embalming you. What is Rene thinking?" choked out Jose between fits of laughter.

Marc couldn't believe his plan worked so well. They bought it! And he did not have to tell them what really happened. He hinted here and there around the margins, put in a few grains of truth, but it was what he left unsaid, letting their imaginations run, that filled in the blanks for Jose and Luis. Of course, what happened to his integrity once he started misleading—let's face it, *lying to*—his closest friends? One part of him hated what he had just done, but the other part? *Where am I going with this?* He thought. He realized he was walking on thin ice and was not sure where to place his next step.

Marc left his friends in a jolly mood, heading to Team Technik HQ. He arrived just after 9:00 AM. Everyone was busy at work repairing the Porsche's front suspension and bodywork, installing the new updates from Porsche Motorsports and preparing the car for the next race at Paul Ricard HTTT. Trying to be nonchalant, Marc entered the team office.

"Well it's about bloody well time you showed up!" said Stella. She jumped up and hugged Marc, kissing him on the cheek. "You had us worried all week. Your communication skills outside a race environment really suck."

"Stop! I got a new phone and I did call you. I even sent

you a couple of text messages!" Marc held up his new iPhone while taking a seat behind his small desk. "I am becoming a *kommunikation-meister.*"

"Yes dear. One or two calls or text messages is not what I call communication! Let me show you. Just press those buttons on that very bright screen and you either make a call or send a text message and let your loved ones and business partners know where you are and what you are up to in real time. With you, a text message is progress of sorts, but we want to hear from you live. Some of us actually worry."

"OK Stella, I get the point."

Just then Bala charged in. "Geez, Marc Lange, you're giving me gray hair and ruining my good digestion. Trust me, everyone at home is unhappy about that!" He was so animated, his British accent slipped just a tiny bit, letting his family's Indian tongue slide in. Stopping, he sat down and gathered himself together before continuing. "Bloody hell man! You go dashing off with this new co-driver. You barely know him and you're hopping around Europe like you've got the money to spend. Marc, we have a car to fix and get ready for the next race!"

They both sat behind their desks waiting for Marc to answer. He went through the same thought process he had earlier with Jose and Luis. But this one was more difficult. So he reached into his Porsche messenger bag and pulled out a very thick envelope and tossed it to Stella. She gave him a questioning look. He nodded at her to open it. She carefully slid a perfectly painted nail along the envelope seam and pulled the flap open.

She looked inside and gasped at the sight of hundreds of Euros. She looked back at Marc, her eyes narrowing, wondering where this cash came from. Bala got up from his desk and stood beside Stella as she took the stack of bills out and thumbed through them. For several seconds they looked at the stack of bills, then at Marc, at the stack of bills and then Marc again.

"Do you want to count it?" Marc asked.

"You could save me the time," Stella said.

"€50,000"

"Marc where did you get this money?" asked Bala with a trace of worry and excitement.

"Long story. Are you sure you want to hear it?"

"YES!" they both said at the same instant.

For the most part, he told them the same story he had told Luis and Jose earlier.

Better to keep it consistent he thought.

But they questioned him on every part, every turn of events. He talked about The Client and the problems with his competitors. He left out all the dangerous bits, making it sound like he and Rene were dealing with serious people that were a bit unscrupulous and maybe sometimes unethical too. He went on to explain to them that this is what Rene does, he takes on these Engagements for clients, helping them with security arrangements and advising them on how to transport important items from one place to another.

"So he's a consultant then?" asked Stella, still trying to get her mind around Rene and the cash.

"Yeah. That's close enough. Look, this client was worried about his shipments, but they really wanted his trade secrets and sources. Rene just helped him figure out his options."

"Marc, what about the money?" implored Bala, trying to get Marc to give them the details.

"I'm getting to that." He leaned back in his chair and looked at his two partners. He hated what he was about to say. But he could not let them know what really happened; it would upset them too much. They would insist on firing Rene right away, before the next GT3 race. "He knows Rafi backed out on paying for the damages."

"How did he know?" asked Stella.

"Because I told him, of course. The Client was so happy with the results of the engagement (*and happy to be alive*, Marc thought), that he paid Rene double the agreed-on fee. Rene feels like he's made an investment in the team too, so he gave me part of the fee, since I was along for the ride, so to speak. He said it covers the cost of the repairs, plus a little extra."

"I'll say! This helps us get past the mid-season hump." Bala jumped up from his desk and bolted towards the shop, shouting for the boys to get busy, they were back in the business of winning races!

Stella sat quietly for fifteen or twenty minutes while Marc went through the invoices from Porsche Motorsport and made comments on the prices of some of the parts. He looked up at Stella from time to time and he caught her staring back with a look on her face. He had seen that look before. It said she sensed she had been given a line of bullshit and it was one she could smell more than a kilometer away.

Marc spent a good part of the afternoon talking with April, convincing her that he was okay. She was still not sure about Rene. She kept reiterating her opinion of him throughout their conversation. He did not dare tell her what actually happened. One whiff of that and she'd explode and repairing a rupture like that from another continent was almost certainly beyond his skill.

Hanging up from talking with April, he leaned back and thought about what all this meant. He wanted to marry and settle down with her. They had worked a long time towards her moving to the UK so they would be together. He'd thought about returning to the US and racing in one of the many racing series there, but the WRF GT series gave him the best opportunity to move up through the ranks and get to the Prototype LMP1 or LMP2 level he sought. Racing at venues like Le Mans was like champagne to him. As soon as April's law firm expanded into the UK, their dream of being together in London was very close.

Marc wanted to become a good husband, to do the right thing by April, to create a life they could share. He also wanted to be a success in his career and his life. This hand-to-mouth existence, trying to get Team Technik off the ground these past few years, put a lot pressure on him. He wanted to win, to attract more sponsors, and someday have a second car, maybe even race in a second series. This was how team owners built up a nice living for themselves, by expanding out of a tight fitting garage into a bigger one, with room for more race cars as well as the people that make a successful race team. For Marc, racing and building a championship team was something that he *lived* for.

The connection with the race car, feeling every element, each tire patch, suspension component, steering, accelerator and brake input up through the muscles, nerves and brain of the driver, all came together in the heat of the race to become something beyond just a car or a man. And the team was included—in fact, they were an integral component of the human/mechanical organic/inorganic entity that was Team Technik. It was just extraordinary! Skating that knife-edge between perfection and disaster, that is what drove him. There were times where he could place the car exactly where he wanted it on the track, sometimes even when physics told him otherwise. In those moments, he knew he was pursuing his life's calling.

Rene really has opened a door, and my peek at what's inside was disturbingly exciting. It's mentally and physically demanding, dangerous at times, even life threatening—like racing. If Rene teaches me everything he knows, I can take the best parts and maybe find a balance.

OK, I can balance racing and being a Driver, but what about loving, making a life with April? Well, I'll deal with that later. Just learning to keep Marc Lange and this new guy, Billy, separated and yet still the same, comes first. Somehow I'll have to integrate them ….

Suddenly he realized that Stella was shouting in his direction, dispelling his mental fog like an air-raid siren.

"Marc! Pick up the phone. It's that bastard Luca!"

"Luca? What the hell does he want?"

"I don't know. Ask him."

Reaching for the phone, he gave Stella the WTF look.

"Marc Lange."

"Allo, Marc. It's your friend, Luca."

"My friend. That's a good one. What do you want?"

"You've been busy, so it seems."

Marc froze. *What the hell did Luca know, what did he suspect? Did he know anything about Rene?* A thousand thoughts raced through his head and looking up he saw that Stella was staring right at him, right through him.

"You must be in big trouble, sneaking off to Dijon to run

in the *little* Renault Clio Cup races."

"I don't know what you are talking about."

"And fighting too. Very un-sportsman like."

"Fighting huh? Don't know about any fight, but Luca, if the situation arises, I can take care of myself."

"Ha, ha. I always knew you were a funny guy."

"Luca, I'm hanging up now unless you tell me why you called."

"OK then. You're in over your head Marc Lange and your puny little team will never amount to anything. Sure you can go begging to that effete snob DeSilva and he'd bail you out, but I doubt it. Your pride gets in the way."

"Like I said, I'm hanging up now."

"Wait! Hear me out. I know you're a good racer. I have resources and could set you up with your own team, working indirectly for me, nobody would have to know. I have things I could teach you, things I could show you, who knows, some of them might interest you. I'd even let you bring over some of your people."

"I can't think of one thing I can learn from you, besides how to cheat. And if you think I'd even consider working for you after you insult me, my team and my friends, then you're a bigger *ciglione* than I thought. I wouldn't work for you or with you, not in a million years. Not gonna happen."

"You're right. Maybe I did take things a bit too far. So if

I asked you to think about it?"

"Still the same answer—and Luca—that would be a NO."

"As you wish. Consign yourself to the bottom of the heap." The phone went dead. Marc stared at it for a second before he gently placed it back in the cradle.

"What the bloody hell was that all about Marc?"

"Stella, it's finally dawned on me. That Italian prick is afraid of us. He knows we can beat him, even beat him this year. He's trying everything he can think of to make sure that doesn't happen."

"Well love, if I was a bettin' gal, which as a matter of fact I am, I'd double-down on us."

Marc nodded, grinning. It had suddenly hit him. *We have the talent, the team, and even Luca knows it. My job now is to do whatever I have to do keep the team competitive and to keep assholes like Luca Marchesotti down. All we lack is a reliable source of funds. Becoming a Driver will fix that.*

Man, this is something else! There's danger, perhaps greater than on the track. And there's fear. NO! Conquering fear and using my brain and intellect to overcome the danger. My God! Apply that to racing, I'd be unbeatable!

I can do this, Marc thought. *But only for a while. Until I get Team Technik to where I want it to go. Until I can get April over to the UK and we can finally settle down. I'll do it until then and let Rene know he'll need to find a new protégé. Hell, maybe by then, I'll find my own protégé. I can do this. I've always been able to do whatever I put my mind to since—forever. It's just another way to get where I want to go.*

He sat and reflected on this for a while longer. He figured he had seen the absolute worst and if he could survive and learn from that, he could take the leap and become a *Driver*.

Walking outside the team HQ, he pulled out his iPhone, unlocked it and dialed Rene. On the third ring Rene answered.

"Allo Rene, it's Marc. I'm ready. When do we start?"

To be continued in The Driver Book II, Training

Appendix

Glossary

Aero package – Spoilers, fins, wings and ducts that comprise the system used by race car designers and engineers to create downforce that is used to suck the car to the track for better handling in turns.

Alcantara – Durable suede like fabric that can cover seats, steering wheels, gearshifts, and other car interior surfaces.

Armco – Metal barriers that ring a racetrack and keep a race car from flying off the track. These have been replaced in a lot of places by tire barriers, gravel or sand traps and Safer Barriers.

Apex – Mid part of the turn; taken closest to the inside part of the turn.

Apex, early – When turn is early, either on purpose on by accident. Early apex can be dangerous when the turn is fast and more than 90°. An early apex in a fast turn usually means that the car will run out of track.

Apex, late – When turn in is late, usually in fast 90° corners, this allows the car to come closest to the proper apex and track out points.

Arrondissement – Neighborhood or sections of Paris – numbered 1-18.

Backmarkers – Slower cars at the back of a grid.

Balaclava – Protective fireproof head sock that all professional race drivers wear under their helmet.

Bench racing – Talking about the race after it is over, usually accompanied by beer or other adult beverages.

Boot – British term; trunk

Bhp – Brake horsepower; a measure of engine power

Calmate – Italian slang for calm down.

Camber – Turn where the road surface turns in towards or in the direction of the turn. This allows the car to use more speed through the corner as the corner is helping the car steer into the turn.

Camber plates – Plates that allow a race team to quickly set the camber, toe and caster on a race car.

Carbon composite rotors – Brake rotors made of Carbon fibers. These are considered better than their iron counterparts as they have better stopping characteristics and dissipate heat faster. The downside, they are very expensive.

Caster – The angle to which the steering pivot axis is tilted forward or rearward from vertical, when viewed from the site

Centro Citta – *It.* City Center

Check ride – A ride with an instructor or race official that checks to make sure a student or racer uses the best race craft, shows the proper track etiquette and skill to move on to a more advanced level.

Corner Workers – Part of the team the works at a race track during events, these works use flags to alert the derivers to possible dangers on track, slower moving cars ahead, or alert a slower moving driver that a faster car is behind. These are also the first people on the scene in the case of an accident. Drivers appreciate the dedication of the corner workers to get them safely through a race weekend.

Decreasing radius corner – Corner that starts to turn in on itself, usually a corner more than 100°. This means that a car must scrub or reduce more speed as it takes the corner.

Delrin – Very hard rubber compound used in suspension components.

Double apex – Long or challenging turn that actually has two apexes that a driver must negotiate. Turn 8 at the Turkish Grand Prix at Istanbul Race circuit has 4 apexes!

Downforce – Movement of air over artificial surfaces that forces a car down onto the race track for better traction.

End plates – The part of a rear wing that helps channel the air and maintains downforce.

Eurostar Train – Bullet style train that runs in between

London Pancras Station Paris Gare du Nord.

Flags: Signals used by corner workers used to communicate to racers during the race.

> ***Black*** – pointed at a car, means that car must come into pits; general black flag, all cars must return to pits
>
> ***Blue / Yellow*** – passing flag, means that there is a faster car behind
>
> ***Checker*** – the race has been concluded
>
> ***Green*** – the track is clear, the race has started or can resume
>
> ***Red*** – bring all cars to a stop immediately, usually means there is a large crash and it is not safe to continue
>
> ***White*** – slow moving car ahead
>
> ***Yellow / Red*** – debris flag, means debris on track, could be oil or car parts, flag taken away after 3 laps
>
> ***Yellow / Double Yellow*** – single yellow means local caution, waving or double means trouble ahead

Front splitter – Lower air dam that is part of the race car aero package, the splitter sits low to the ground and creates downforce to assist keeping the front end of the race car pressed into the track for extra traction.

HANS Device – A protective device that surrounds the neck and front of the chest. Properly attached to the helmet, it restricts a driver's head movement in the case of a crash.

Heel and toe – Technique for keeping revs up when shifting from a higher gear to a lower one. The driver places the heel of his right foot on at the bottom on the accelerator pedal and while rocking the ankle back and forth can apply brakes with the ball of the foot under the big toe, while "bleeping" the throttle with the right side of the foot.

High Downforce – Race car set up optimized for maximum speed through turns. On tracks with many turns, a high downforce set up may be employed to force the car down on the track to allow it to take corners faster. Many tracks are a compromise between low and high downforce set-ups. meaning that a race team must decide what is more important, straight-line speed or faster-cornering speed. One of the many race car set-up decisions that must be made during a race weekend.

Hot hatch – Class of car in Europe that is characterized by small size (3 and 5 door) increased engine capacity, firmer suspension and interior appointments such as deep seats suitable for keeping the driver properly aligned with the steering, gear shift and pedals during spirited driving and cornering.

Increasing radius corner – A corner that starts off at a steep angle but opens up as the corner is taken. These are usually fast corners as there is not much steering effort required.

Jing Wu men – Chinese martial arts fighting style.

Kph – Kilometers per hour. 100 kilometers per hour equals approximately 60 miles per hour.

Krav Mega – Self-defense fighting style developed by the Israeli military. Uses fast short motions to incapacitate attackers. Many armed services and Special Forces use Krav Mega, sometimes in combination with other martial arts techniques.

Left foot braking – A technique where the driver of the car uses the left foot (usually the clutch foot) to stab at the brakes to settle a car. Used prior to high-speed turns where the car needs to become set before initiating a turn.

LMP1 / LMP2 – LeMans Prototypes 1 and LeMans Prototypes 2, are the fastest, most advanced, and powerful race cars competing in the FIA GT series.

Lorry – British slang for truck or semi.

Low Downforce – Race car set up optimized for maximum speed on a straight. On a race track with many or very long straights, the ideal set up allows the car to reach maximum speed. A low downforce set-up means that less air will be used to force the car onto the track, thereby increasing top speed.

Merc – Slang for Mercedes Benz

Milano Duomo – Central Cathederal in Milano City Center

Momentum Car – Slow race cars that require the driver to keep the speed up over a lap. The engine is usually not too powerful in these cars and it takes a long time to get the speed back that was lost due to braking and cornering.

Off camber – The opposite of a cambered turn where the road surface falls away from the direction of the turn. This makes it more difficult for the car as the road surface is working against it as the tendency is for the car to move towards the edge of the track. Very tricky!

Oppo – Slang for opposite lock.

Opposite lock – Using the steering wheel to steer a car's wheels in the opposite direction during a slide and when combined with the throttle allows the car to slide a path through a corner.

Oversteer – A handling characteristic where the back end of the cars wants to push out in a turn. In other words the rear wheels want to come round. This can be countered with opposite lock and can be controlled in a slide or drift until control can be regained, the steering wheel straightened and the car can now travel straight ahead. Many 911 drivers (especially early Turbos) know exactly what oversteer is. They all experienced it as they jabbed at the brakes in the middle of a fast turn and slid off going backwards!

***Panzoratti* from Luini Panzoratti in Milano** – Tiny bite sized fried pizza. Perfect, eat 5-6+

Performance Penalty – In racing sometimes one particular race car has such a performance advantage over its
competitors that the race organizers issue a Performance Penalty on the car. This is usually accomplished
via extra weight or ballast or a decrease in the throttle
body opening in the engine to allow less air to enter the
engine.

Physio – Or trainer, is a person that many racers rely on
to help them with workout routines, stretching, mas-
sage, diet, etc.

Pit speed limiter – An electronic device that limits a race
cars speed as it moves though a pit area. Usually set to
60 mph / 100 kph.

Push (understeer) – Another term for understeer; see
above.

Quali – Slang for qualifying.

Qualifying – Prior to race, all racers must drive around
the course under a time session, this helps set the grid
for the race event.

R Rated tires – Race compound tires that are very soft
(not recommended for street use). These "cycle", getting
very hot during a race stint and give excellent grip until
they go off and degrade based on using the available
rubber.

Race Car Tub – Central chassis of a race car, sometimes

unibody (in the case of race cars developed from production cars like the cars in the GT3 series), or can built up from aluminum or carbon fiber for purpose built race cars.

Race line – The fastest way around a racetrack. Frequently there is more than one race line around any given racetrack and racers will try to find the best combination for the best speed and time.

Racing ECU – Engine Control Unit, module that controls the parameters of the engine. In racing, these are frequently fixed and supplied by an outside source to insure uniformity and compliance to rules and regulations.

Renseignements Generaux, now called the DCRI – Similar to American FBI, MI5, this branch of the police focuses on internal crime investigation.

Rev limiter – Device that artificially limits the amount of revs a motor can rev to. Employed to ensure that a motor does not over rev and become damaged.

Rumble strips – The raised bumps that line a racetrack in the turn, this is a signal to the drive that this area is the furthest edge of the track. Many racers use these strips as a part of their cornering technique

SA 2010 Certification – Current helmet safety certification based on studies and testing of the Snell Foundation. Most racing drivers must use helmets that meet

Snell certification to be allowed in a race.

Sadev 6-speed sequential gearbox – Six-speed transmission popular in many sedan-based race cars. Rather than shift the gears through the normal "H" pattern, the racer simply moves the shifter back or forward to select the proper gear.

Saloon – British term; large 4-door sedan.

Sciopero –It - Strike, usually held for a one-day union protest.

Scrubbed in – Tires that have had one or more cycles on them. A properly scrubbed in tire will get up to temperature faster and maintain optimal handling characteristics until fully used, when they start to "go off".

Shift forks – Transmission components that work to shift a transmission from one gear to another.

Slip angle – Is the angle between a rolling wheels actual direction of travel and the angle to which the wheels are pointing. In other words the measured amount of slip a car exhibits as it slides through a turn.

Spetsnaz – Russian Special Forces, specially trained military

Suppressors – Silencer used on pistols and machines guns. When combined with sub-sonic rounds, greatly reduces gun noise.

Threshold Braking – Hard braking right up to the point

of locking up the front tires. Also braking into a corner while turning the steering wheel.

Toe – When viewed from above, the amount of tire or wheel angle pointing in towards the center of a car (toe-in) or pointed out from the center of a car (toe-out)

Toe Link – Component of a car suspension that controls Toe.

Track days – Popular way for drivers to get their cars (race, high performance or whatever) out on the race-tracks. Most professional race circuits host track days around the world. Check their calendars to find out how you can get your car on a track. But be forewarned – once you start.....

Track out – The part of the turn where throttle is increased as the car unwinds and heads down a straight.

Turn in – Initial part of a turn where a race drive initiates the sequence of events that will hopefully make the car go through a turn the quickest. This is where the cars start to turn in towards the apex.

Understeer – A handling characteristic where the front end of the cars wants to push. In other words when the wheels are turned the car still wants to continue straight. A lot of front wheel drive cars exhibit this tendency as the weight and drive is in the front.

Up and under – Sometimes when one racecar passes another, it may have to go way off line and be on the wrong side of the track, this can open the door for the just passed car to take the proper line and come out "under" the other car, repassing upon accelerating out of the turn.

Upper control arms – Top part of suspension component attached to wheel spindle.

Viticulturist – Specialist in the management of a vineyard.

WC - Restroom